OF SEPARATION

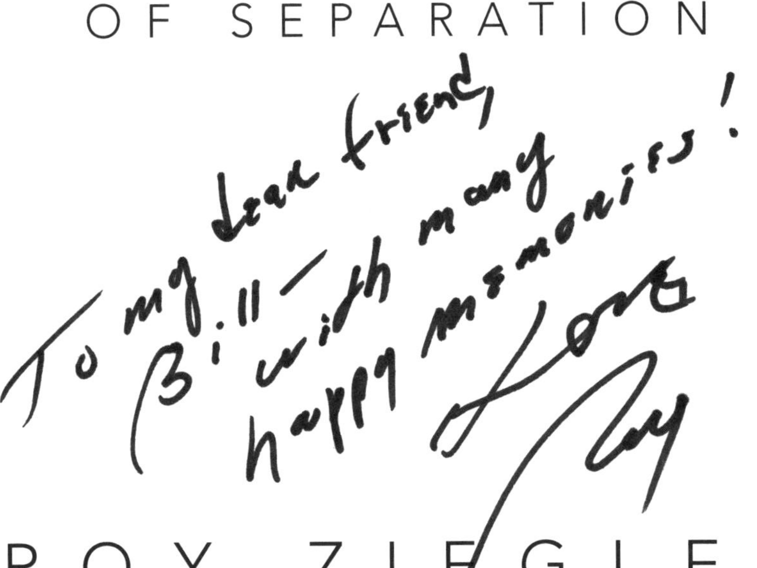

ROY ZIEGLER

Twilight of Separation

This is a work of fiction.

ISBN: 0615803504
ISBN 13: 9780615803500
Library of Congress Control Number: 2013910181
Roy Ziegler, New Hope, PA

Acknowledgements

The author wishes to acknowledge Charles F. Tarr, Stephen T. Krencicki, *The New Jersey Herald* and The Sussex County Historical Society for their assistance with the production of this book.

Special Acknowledgement

to Bernard F. Stehle for his invaluable copyediting advice.

In Loving Memory of

Anna J. Dimovitz Ziegler

Also by Roy Ziegler

New Hope, Pennsylvania: River Town Passages

The Parrys of Philadelphia and New Hope

Twilight of Separation

CHAPTER 1

For as long as he could remember, Leo Weber wanted to be a Catholic priest. As a young boy Leo admired the priests who served in his parish because they always seemed happy and content. He enjoyed going to Mass, listening to them pray and chant, often imitating them before a makeshift altar he built in his attic, his mother's old robes becoming his new church vestments. He was in awe when he saw priests taking Holy Communion to his elderly neighbors, and comforting not only the sick and dying, but also their families. When he was fourteen years old, Leo read a story in a Catholic newspaper about the growing need for priests; asking young men to consider the priesthood as a calling in life. Leo responded, requesting that a priest visit him and his family to discuss the requirements for entering the seminary. But when he told his mother about it, she became frantic, telling Leo he was far too young to go to the seminary. She insisted that he cancel the visit. Embarrassed and disheartened, Leo withdrew his request.

In high school, where priests taught English Literature, Latin and Christian Doctrine, Leo's admiration for them continued to grow as he learned more about them and their work. He watched them praying silently from the thick, black, leather-bound books they always carried with them. He knew that they also visited hospitalized parishioners, prepared new Catholics for the sacraments, and celebrated Mass. Leo was convinced more than ever that he wanted to be one of them, but he just couldn't take that first step toward pursuing his goal. After the demoralizing incident when his mother thwarted his attempt to enter the seminary, Leo was reluctant to discuss with his parents any plans for life following high school. They assumed he would graduate, get a job and become a productive member of the family. So he decided not to reveal his true feelings, avoiding any further controversy with his parents. But Leo's desire to become a priest continued to intensify, tormenting him as time was rapidly running out. He had to make a decision before his high school graduation day, only a few weeks away, or he would never realize his dream.

While shopping at Hess's Department Store a couple of weeks before graduation, Leo met Sister Mary Christina, his sixth-grade teacher. She had frequently praised him to his classmates as an example they should follow. When she asked Leo to help manage one of her emotionally troubled students in the classroom, he gladly accepted the task, intriguing Sister Mary Christina by his keen ability to help the boy. In the bustle of the Easter holiday shopping crowd, Leo and his former mentor exchanged pleasantries. When Leo mentioned that he was looking forward to graduation and a job as a bookkeeper, Sister Mary Christina paused and looked up at him. He could easily detect in the aging nun's squinting eyes her clear disappointment with his decision. She expected much more from her revered protégé and class leader. Ignoring Leo's answer, she grasped his right arm firmly, raised her head higher, and looked directly into his eyes, challenging him, as she had so often done before. "Leo, what are you going to *do* with your life?"

Leo mumbled that he had a few ideas he was thinking about and would soon have to decide what to do.

"Pray to the Blessed Mother for help, Leo. She will guide you."

Leo thanked the venerable old nun, telling her how wonderful it was to see her again.

"God bless you, Leo. I know you will make the right decision."

Leo was stunned by Sister Mary Christina's challenging question. He was not prepared for it. She seemed to have known his innermost thoughts. Her poignant question forced Leo to confront the fact that he would never realize his long-time goal of becoming a priest unless he acted soon. Her jarring words overwhelmed his thoughts during his final days in school.

Finally, on the last day before graduation, Leo made his life-altering decision. It was his last chance to pursue his dream. When class was dismissed, Leo raced through the deserted corridors of the high school anxiously seeking his favorite faculty member, Father David. Leo found the young priest packing up his black brief case at his massive oak desk in what had been Leo's old home room, preparing to leave the school for summer recess.

"Hi! Good morning, Father!"

Father David looked up from his desk, surprised to see one of his students in the doorway.

"Well, *hello*, Leo. You're still in *school*? Come on in."

Leo approached the desk nervously. The young priest was smiling as he looked up at Leo's distraught expression, trying to relax him.

"Congratulations on your graduation, Leo. You must be very excited right now."

"Yeah, I mean, *yes*, Father. Everything's moving so ... so *fast* now. I just, uh, I wanted to talk with you about my ... well, Father, I, uh, I want to be a *priest*. I've been thinking about this for such a long time, but I just, you know, I didn't know what to do."

The school year was over. Janitors had already begun waxing down the green-and-white tile floors of the wide hallway outside the room in preparation for the long summer break. The strong, pungent scent of industrial soap and wax permeated the air; the loud, steady hum of the electric waxing machines frazzled Leo's concentration.

Father David was astonished by Leo's outburst. Leo was a bright student, but his laid-back approach to his studies garnered him only mediocre grades. His records showed that he had excelled in elementary school with First Honors nearly every year, and Leo's popularity with both the nuns and the students made him the easy choice for class president every year from the fifth to the eighth grade. Leo often told Father David about the thrill of singing in his parish choir in the grand choir loft of his magnificent parish church. The boys choir sang the Requiem Mass for funerals several times each month. The priest also remembered Leo's story about his unusual experience in seventh grade. Prior to the beginning of that school year, the nun who had been scheduled for Leo's class was severely injured in an automobile accident, leaving her unable to teach. Since no substitute teachers were available at the time, the principal of the elementary school decided to place Leo in charge of the class. Under the guidance and supervision of the nun who taught the eighth-grade class, Leo instructed his fellow students for nearly three months using the assigned textbooks for English, geography, civics and math. He administered tests, all of which were graded by the supervisor. Leo was able to keep order most of the time. There were instances, though, when the class bully, Donald Hertzog, tried to disrupt the class, testing Leo's patience by shouting, "Recess!" or "School's out!" but Leo managed to restore order quickly. An incident with Donald in the previous year, when he sneaked up behind Leo and knocked his books out of his hand, may have helped. Leo had become so enraged by the bully's antics that, uncharacteristically, he shouted at the top of his voice, "Pick them *up*!"—startling Donald and everyone else in the corridor. The young bully scrambled to gather the books to avoid getting into trouble with the nuns, handing them back to Leo before scurrying away. Donald was wary of Leo after that incident, usually avoiding contact with him. And there were a few mornings when Leo had to wake up some of his classmates who had stayed up far too late watching television. When his teacher finally returned, Leo won high praise from the supervising nun for the work he had done. The unique experience in leadership engendered a feeling of self-confidence and poise within him.

Leo was a fashion plate at school. He was thin, weighing about one hundred and thirty-five pounds, and was five-feet, eight-inches tall, but his body was wiry and firm. He had developed his strength through his part-time job in the warehouse at a local restaurant supply company, and by playing baseball and basketball in the city league. Leo's short-cropped, light brown hair was always neatly groomed, parted straight as an arrow on the left side. His bright green eyes, fair complexion, quick wit and broad smile communicated an exuberance for life. The fashion rage of the late 1950s consisted of pegged pants with side stitching, pink shirts with cuff links and narrow black ties, and white buck shoes. Leo had them all.

Father David embodied all the traits Leo admired in priests. He was pleasant and always seemed to enjoy his time with the students, often telling jokes or stories in class about his years in the seminary. But he was very serious when he taught Christian Doctrine class, clearly communicating his love for the Church. Small in stature, and slim, the priest was about thirty-two years old. He wore his dark blond hair short, accentuating even more the penetrating pale blue eyes that peered out from behind his thin, gold-rimmed eyeglasses.

"Please close the door, Leo, so we can hear each other speak."

"Yes! Sure, Father." Leo quickly closed the door without turning his attention away from the young priest, eagerly awaiting a response.

Father David hesitated. He pressed his hands together, touching them to his lowered chin before looking up from his seat behind the huge oak desk. He spoke slowly.

"Leo ... I'm afraid that it's *too late* to apply for the seminary this year."

The priest's unexpected words shocked Leo.

Seeing Leo's desperate expression, the young priest sought to give him hope. "But don't give up, Leo," he counseled. "You can still prepare for the seminary … and apply next year."

Leo was encouraged when he learned that more time could be allowed to prepare for the seminary. After further discussing Leo's intentions, Father David became convinced of his sincerity and conviction.

"How do your parents feel about all of this, Leo?"

"Well, Father, I wanted to apply for the seminary when I was in the eighth grade, but my mom had a fit!"

Father David laughed heartily. "Why, I can just imagine *that* scene, Leo. That is a rather young age to want to go to the seminary." The priest admired his young student's deep sincerity. "You've obviously thought about this for a long time, and you seem to be very serious and convinced this is what you want to do. Leo, you must talk with your parents about this now, and explain how important it is to you. You'll need their support. Normally, candidates for the priesthood enter the seminary immediately after completing high school, but if it takes you a year longer to prepare, that shouldn't make any difference."

The young priest recited a list of things that had to be done, reviving Leo's hope for the future he so deeply desired to pursue. He had to contact the pastor of his church to begin the work that lay ahead of him. Father David noted that the entrance examination for the seminary was comprehensive and difficult, requiring much study and discipline. These were traits that Leo had pretty much abandoned during his high school years. He remembered how Father David sometimes chided him when Leo came unprepared for class, saying that he was "frequently lethargic," but he was determined to buckle down and do whatever his pastor would prescribe. Leo knew that he faced an even greater challenge. His powerful libido dominated him since his early teen years. Saying "no" to its frequent demands was rarely possible for him. He knew that, as a priest, he would be required not only to take the vow of chastity, but he would also have to be celibate—not ever get married. But he believed he could overcome all of that. *I'm going to go to the seminary,* he was thinking, *and I am going to become a priest.* Father David's voice startled him to attention.

"Leo, I know that it's a lot to think about, and it will take a lot of hard work. But your strong determination and faith will help you get through it. God bless you, Leo, and do *not* give up. You have received a wonderful calling. Please don't hesitate to contact me if you need any help or advice as you move forward with your plans." Father David walked Leo to the classroom door. "I'll remember you in my prayers at Mass every day, Leo," Father David promised, as they left the room. "Stay close to Jesus, Leo. He will never abandon you."

"Thank you, Father, ... for everything."

Leo scampered down the front stairway, leaving his beloved Alma Mater for the last time.

Leo enjoyed his high school years. He was unable to participate in many of the extracurricular activities because his part-time job required that he go to work directly after classes most days. As much as he loved baseball, he could not try out for the team nor attend the afternoon games. He was also an ardent basketball fan, attending all of the high school team's evening games both at home and at other schools. The wrestling coach, seeing Leo's prowess on the mat during gym classes, practically begged Leo to try out for the team, but it was not possible. He wrote stories for the high school newspaper and magazine, however, and managed to find time to be a staff photographer besides.

In his junior year Leo began dating Terry Cranston, one of the most popular and talented girls in school. They had met at his Aunt Paulette's wedding. Terry soon became his first steady girlfriend. They enjoyed being together, whether going to the movies or just sitting home on Saturday nights watching horror movies. Anything, as long as they could just be together. Leo liked visiting with her family, too. He always had fun being with them. Her mother was a music teacher, and her father was the branch manager of a local bank. Her grandmother told many fascinating stories of her childhood in Austria. Leo quickly became accepted as part of the family. They would often sing along as Terry's father strummed on his prized *Martin* guitar.

Leo had joined the glee club in his sophomore year. In his senior year he auditioned for a solo number for the high school musical, performing his best rendition of "A Foggy Day in London Town" in his favorite Sinatra style. He made the final cut, but lost the solo part when he was unable to reach the highest notes in the crooner's hit song "All the Way," which was to be featured in the show. So, he settled for a spot in the barber shop quartet singing "There's a Barber in the Harbor of Palermo." To his mother and to his aunts and uncles who attended the show, it made no difference—he was the star.

Leo loved to entertain his relatives when they gathered at his home to watch television shows on Saturday afternoons. He delighted them with his impersonations of Johnny Ray and Elvis Presley. Sometimes he performed magic tricks for them until his family couldn't take any more and shooed him off the living room stage. His mother was one of thirteen children, seven of whom, in addition to their mother, lived within a few blocks of one another in the same neighborhood of their childhood. He and his grandmother had become very close during his childhood. He loved her deeply. When he was younger, she spent Saturday evenings with him and his sister Ellen whenever their parents were out for the evening. In the old European tradition, his grandmother baked strudels and bread several times a week, and her chicken soup on Sundays was deemed "spectacular" by everyone who had the good fortune to be served it.

Leo was very much admired and appreciated by his boss, Irv Davis, for whom he had worked after school and on Saturdays during his high school years. Leo was a hard worker, honest and loyal; he enjoyed his job at the restaurant supply company. He prepared orders, maintained inventory, and loaded and unloaded delivery trucks. He could walk to his job, the company being just a mile west of his high school. Walking home each day helped to keep him lean and fit.

Irv had offered Leo a full time position as bookkeeper for the company, a job which would begin after he graduated. Prodded by his mother, Leo had accepted the offer. At the time, he could think of no alternative. He had not yet spoken with Father David about his life's dream of pursuing the priesthood, and he could think of nothing else to do. He was trapped.

As he headed out the front door of the high school toward Fourth Street, Leo knew that his life was about to change. He looked back at the yellow brick building that loomed like a fortress along the east side of the street. It was nearly a block long, four stories tall, and was attached to the Immaculate Heart Elementary School he had attended. The city's second largest hospital was located directly across the street, next to his parish church. As he proceeded up Fourth Street he passed the row houses, shops and factories of the inner city neighborhood. He paused briefly, a pang of bittersweet nostalgia hitting him as he walked by Terry's house. So many memories! All the good times with Terry's family, late-night television and cuddling with her on the living room sofa as her parents slept upstairs. On their first date, Leo's only negative reaction was to the taste of that pancake make-up and lipstick during their first kiss. He remembered telling her later that she was so beautiful she didn't need any make-up. Terry responded by never wearing it on their dates, but he noticed that she did wear it to church. He smiled as he thought about the time when he and Terry had fallen asleep in each other's arms in the back seat of his car at the drive-in movie, awaking to the alarming realization that theirs was the only car still parked on the huge lot of the outdoor theater. How embarrassed they had been to see the security guard tapping on the windshield with his key and pointing to his watch. Glancing up at the bay window of her parents' living room, he remembered trying to explain their early morning return to Terry's mother who, with her husband, had been pacing the living room floor for hours. All of that seemed so distant to Leo now. His mind was mulling over Father David's advice and the future that he was about to pursue. Leo was going to become a Catholic priest.

Now, he had to tell his mother.

Leo's mom was his soul mate. Both were silly, funny, light-hearted spirits who loved music, dining out, and good times. Anna Weber had been plagued since childhood with severe bronchial asthma; as fate would have it, laughing was one of the things that aggravated her condition. When they got silly together and laughed, his mom often experienced an asthmatic attack. The tightening of her bronchial tubes would cut off her breathing, causing her to cough uncontrollably as she gasped for air. They were very frightening episodes. Weather conditions and dietary considerations also compromised her ability to breathe. His mother had been hospitalized on a number of occasions when Leo was younger. The oxygen tent was the only effective medical remedy, but it took days for her to recover her normal breathing ability. Yet, knowing what the frightening consequences would be, nothing could keep her from freely laughing and enjoying herself—right up to the brink of the next attack. Despite this persistent and sometimes debilitating health problem, she was a very attractive woman who, at thirty-seven years old, was often told she looked exactly like the popular actress Susan Hayward.

Anna Weber was slightly taller than her husband, and noticeably so when she wore high heels. Her hair was a deep chestnut color, accentuating her bright green eyes. She often wrapped her hair in curlers during the week, especially when she attended to the housecleaning chores. When released from the binding curlers, it unfolded in long waves reaching to her shoulders. She dressed fashionably when she stepped out on weekends for dining and dancing with his father.

The Allentown area was home to some of the nation's most powerful and prosperous corporations. Mack Trucks International had long established its world headquarters there, and the mammoth Bethlehem Steel Corporation was located nearby. Their tens of thousands of employees prospered. Thursdays were paydays, when the downtown's "Miracle Mile" bustled with thousands of shoppers. Leo and his mom often went into town on those evenings, enjoying the shopping, the excitement of the crowd, and dining at their favorite restaurant, the Marble Bar, on Center Square. His mom was ecstatic that he had chosen Terry for his girlfriend. Not just a bright student, Terry was also a swimmer, ballet dancer and singer. She had starred in the latest high school musical production of *Brigadoon*. Leo had been dating her for about a year. *Mom so wants to be a grandmother*, he often thought. It was she who suggested that Leo ask Terry to dance at that wedding, and to ask her out to the movies the following weekend.

He turned the corner and walked down Green Street, approaching his home. His pace slowed down as his heart began beating faster. *What's mom going to say? Does she already suspect something?*

Opening the front door, he took a deep breath and stepped inside. Leo's father had renovated the house about ten years before, tearing down walls that had divided the living room and dining room. The open space gave their home a more expansive feeling, and it enabled those entering to see directly through to the kitchen, which was about thirty feet from the front door. Leo remembered helping his father sweep up each day after the repair work had been completed. He smiled as he saw his mom in the distance, busy at the ironing board in the kitchen, singing along with the Everly Brothers at the top of her voice.

"Dree-ee-ee-ee-*eam*, dream, dream *dree*-eam," she sang. "Whenever I want you-ou, all I have to do is dree-ee-ee-eam, *dream*."

The radio was her constant companion during the day. He remembered her listening to the *Stella Dallas* and *Lorenzo Jones and His Wife, Belle* shows when he was at home during the early afternoons. But when it came to house cleaning or laundry, the upbeat sounds of popular songs were always filling the house. On this day, his mother was wearing her favorite housedress—a dark blue-and-white-checked cotton fabric embroidered with a bright red rose (her favorite flower) on the upper-left-side pocket. Leo always loved seeing her in that dress.

God! How am I going to get through telling her this? he thought, approaching his mother to kiss her.

"What's wrong, Leo? You look so serious."

God! How does she always know what's going on? He hugged her.

"Mom, I was just talking with Father David after school."

"Father *David?*"

"Mom, I, um, I told him that I want to be a priest." Leo knew that what he had just said shocked and saddened her. They embraced, then she stepped back, still holding his arms, and spoke seriously.

"You're such a good boy, Leo. I'm so *proud* of you, but you're so *young*. You haven't yet experienced what life is all about. You're ready to begin a new job, and now—all of this is so sudden!" She paused, looking into his eyes that mirrored her tears. "Let's talk with dad when he gets home and see how he feels about all of this."

Leo loved his father and had great respect for him. He was always there for the family, and as far as Leo knew, his dad had never missed a day's work in his life. Leo Weber, Sr. worked hard as an automobile mechanic. For several years he owned his own business before selling it and going to work for a friend. His dad provided well for his family. They were the first family in the neighborhood to own a color television set. They had a comfortable three-bedroom, red brick row house with a fenced-in backyard stretching thirty feet to the back sidewalk. It was Leo's job to mow the lawn. On more than one occasion, as he daydreamed about Terry or about his future as a priest, he had mowed down the prized rose bush that his father had planted for Leo's mother.

His dad enjoyed helping to prepare Sunday dinner every week. His mom would bake the cakes or pies while his father took care of the roast beef or chicken. It was his way of contributing to the household chores, for one day at least, to relieve his wife. Leo and his two sisters wore the latest clothing styles. The family automobile, a black 1955 Buick *Century Dynaflo,* was usually spotless. Their Sunday afternoon drives created lasting memories. His dad would always joke about the poky old drivers clogging traffic lanes. His mom would randomly point to roads where she wanted his father to turn so they could explore new areas of the city. They sometimes stopped to take pictures in the sprawling Lehigh Parkway. Always, before returning home, they enjoyed ice cream sundaes at the Lehigh Valley Dairy's restaurant on Seventh Street. At home, Leo often browsed through the family photo album. Among his favorite pictures was one that his mother had taken of him and his father, near the lake in the parkway, standing beside their car. Yet, Leo and his father had never really become close. They rarely had conversations about school or Leo's plans for his future. The family would gather for dinner each night, but after that, the television schedule usually dominated any discussions until bedtime. So, it would not surprise Leo if, upon hearing of his life-changing decision, his dad's reaction would be rather nonchalant, but he feared the opposite. His father had the proverbial short fuse. He would get upset if he returned home from work and found his parking space taken; or if Leo sang along too loudly with his Sinatra records; or if Leo and his sisters expressed dislike for the dinner that their mom had prepared. And sometimes, when Leo or his sisters would misbehave during the day, his father's anger would erupt into physical punishment when he got home. But when his father was watching one of his favorite television shows—like *The Honeymooners*, *Petticoat Junction*, or *The Danny Thomas*

Show—he would roar with laughter. Leo enjoyed seeing his father relaxed during those many good times.

Although his father was often cold and aloof, Leo knew that his father loved him. He often thought about how his father had carried him around the house when, at the age of eight, a serious case of what was diagnosed as childhood rheumatism had paralyzed Leo's legs, making it impossible for him to walk for nearly a week. He fondly remembered his father carefully picking him up, holding him, gently pressing Leo against his chest as he carried him from his bedroom to their living room, or to dinner, or back to Leo's room upstairs. Leo still remembered the familiar fragrance of the *Old Spice* after-shave lotion on his father's face when he embraced him. It was the closest contact he had ever had with his father. When his condition improved, and he was able to walk again, Leo actually regretted it. He sorely missed that unprecedented closeness with his dad. He hoped that, just maybe, the rheumatism would return for at least one week each year so he could feel his dad's loving embrace once more. But his father's moments of anger and general lack of concern for his son's activities and plans had gradually taken their toll. Leo never felt truly relaxed with his dad.

His sister Ellen was three years younger than Leo. She was a skinny, awkward teenager with unruly light brown hair. Ellen was a tomboy who loved swimming and absolutely hated school. She struggled with her studies. Her rheumatic fever, in the form of Saint Vitus' Dance, went undiagnosed for years, causing her serious and extensive health problems. The fidgeting and restlessness created by the condition caused numerous problems for her in the classroom, where nuns demanded strict self-control. Adding to her burden was the fact that she had the cruel misfortune of following her brother through school. The nuns, who fondly remembered Leo as the model student for his academic achievements, self-control and leadership, continually contrasted his record with Ellen's ongoing issues. Her frequent outbursts to the nuns about her brother's misbehavior at home did not help her cause. She was, of course, telling the truth. Like any big brother, Leo knew exactly which buttons to push, and when to push them to harass his sister. He loved singing, and she hated it. So, all he had to do was break into song to push her totally to the brink. There were numerous scuffles around the Weber household. But he loved his sister and, when their parents were out for the evening, he would often read to her until she fell asleep, then tuck her in safely.

His baby sister, Donna, was the apple of his eye. She was just four years old. Donna was a lively, happy and loveable little girl. She was a late arrival in the household, eleven years separating her and Ellen. Leo loved to show her off, taking her with him to Mass on Sunday mornings, then stopping by the popular Heimbach's Bakery for some fresh-baked bread for dinner. Their mother would dress her up in the most beautiful clothing, always placing colorful ribbons in her light blond hair. He often thought about Donna gleefully banging on the keys of her tiny toy piano in the living room, her bright blue eyes sparkling.

When they had all finished dinner that evening, Leo's mom shushed his sisters upstairs to their room. Leo and his mom and dad remained at the table.

"Leo spoke with Father David today, and told him that ... he wants to go to the seminary ... to become a priest," his mother said.

His father was silent. After a long pause, he responded.

"Is that what you really want to *do?*" he asked in a low, hesitant voice, flashing a glance at Leo. "Haven't you already accepted a job at the restaurant supply company?"

His father, not being a Catholic, knew little about the Church. Belonging to no religious organization, he could be found in a church only for weddings or funerals. Yet his dad liked watching Bishop Fulton J. Sheen's weekly television show, always sitting in his recliner across from Leo, who enjoyed listening to his dad talking about the show, especially when he retold the Bishop's many jokes. Leo remembered his dad's favorite about the two nuns being hassled by a grumpy man behind them as they sat on a bus. The man was complaining that everywhere he went he ran into Catholics. Finally, one of the nuns turned around, faced the man, and said, "Why don't you go to hell, there aren't any Catholics there!" His father would laugh uproariously every time. This was not one of those times.

"Dad, I've thought about this for so long. I waited until the last minute to tell Father David about it, and he's given me some information about what to do next."

"Well, if that's what you want ... you should, uh, you should listen to what the priest told you and try to do it."

But his mom pleaded with Leo and—indirectly—with his father, to consider his age and lack of experience of the world.

"One year's not enough, Leo. You should wait a *couple* of years to see if this is truly what you want to do," she said. "You'll still have a lot of time to decide then. After all, you can't enter the seminary this year anyway. So an additional year may help you to make sure this is what you want."

"Mom, I really don't want to miss this opportunity."

"But you have a nice job waiting for you in September, Leo, and you can save some money for your education if you decide to go ahead with it later."

As usual—now in this most serious decision he ever had to make—his mother had presented the most powerful argument. He looked into her eyes, seeing her desperation, trying to convince him it was in his best interest to delay his decision.

"I love you both very much, and I understand your concern for me," he said. "And you're right about the money, mom. I'll need it for my tuition and books, if I'm accepted by the seminary."

So, it was decided. Leo would wait *two* years before pursuing his dream of the priesthood.

Leo and his family watched *I Love Lucy, To Tell the Truth* and *The $64,000 Question* after dinner. He was exhausted from all of the drama that had taken place that day. He loved his mom, and, truthfully, he would need the money for his education.

"Good night, everybody. I've got to get some extra sleep tonight."

But all the excitement of the day made sleep impossible. As he lay in his bed wide awake, Leo's head was spinning. He thought about Father David's advice to "pray often and avoid the near occasions of sin." He kept seeing that sad look in his mother's eyes when he revealed his plans for the future.

He thought about Terry. During the previous summer he placed a large photograph of her on his bedroom wall. It was taken on one of their weekend outings to the local swimming pool shortly after they had met. She looked sexy in her skimpy, black swimsuit. He pictured Terry naked under him—how she had moaned with pleasure when he softly glided his hands, then his tongue, around her firm, smooth breasts, then grasped those ample buttocks, pulling her against him, penetrating her. He could feel himself inside her ... the picture faded; his thoughts returned to his first sexual experience, a couple of weeks before his twelfth birthday. On an unusually humid July morning, Leo and his closest friend and classmate, Rob, had walked to the city park near their homes to go swimming. They were wearing only their swimming trunks. Rob was a handsome youth who was nearing his twelfth birthday. He was about the same height and weight as Leo. His straight black hair was usually combed back and groomed neatly with *Vitalis* hair lotion; his deep brown eyes always seemed playful and mischievous.

After he led Leo to a wooded area in the park, Rob sat down on a wooden bench, removed his swimsuit and began manipulating his penis, first gently, then stronger—violently until a stream of creamy white fluid erupted from it. Leo was sitting next to him, stunned by what he was seeing. Rob then reached into Leo's swim trunks, grasping Leo's already erect penis as Leo pulled off his trunks, then emulated Rob's motions until an uncontrollable release surged through Leo's body during his first orgasm. It was an ecstasy he had never before experienced. Over the next few months their youthful experimentation progressed to oral and anal sex, as they voraciously probed each other's young bodies seeking every sensual, erotic pleasure they could discover. When school reopened in September, Leo could barely wait until the last class so he could rush over to Rob's house, where they had set up a small loft in a storage closet that could be accessed only by climbing a ladder on the back porch. It afforded the young sex partners a perfect place for continuing their erotic rituals in undisturbed privacy. Their sexual relationship continued periodically over the next two years. It wasn't until catechism classes, when the nuns taught about how contrary those "despicable sins of the flesh" were to the natural law and to the will of God that Leo began to feel guilty about what had been so natural and enjoyable at the time. But it wasn't only the guilt that compelled him to get to confession as soon as possible after performing the sinful acts. He feared that if he died without absolution, he would surely suffer everlasting damnation as the nuns had warned. Six years later, the memory of those steamy orgies still aroused him. Now he was battling those erotic impulses, fighting off another passionate moment that could plunge him into yet another mortal sin.

"My God, please don't let these sins destroy my will and force me to abandon my goal," he prayed aloud, remembering Father David's parting words about staying close to Jesus, who would never abandon him. "Jesus, please stay with me. Help me overcome whatever may stand between me and your sacred priesthood." He reached behind him, pulling his black rosary beads off the bedpost. He clutched the silver crucifix in his right hand, praying ever more fervently until, at some merciful point—his prayers reduced to murmurings—he drifted off.

CHAPTER 2

The long, somber summer of 1959 finally ended. To the eternal dismay of his mother, Leo ended his relationship with Terry. As they sat in his car in front of her house following what would be their last date, Leo struggled to find the words he had rehearsed so many times.

"Terry, I, there's something I've got to tell you, but I … I don't know where to start."

"What *is* it, Leo?"

"Terry, I don't know how to say this … but after so many years thinking about it, I've finally, uh, I've just recently decided that … I want to become a priest."

Leo's announcement shocked Terry. She was confused. She was angry. They had been close and intimate over the past two years. Leo was the only one with whom she had ever had sex. After one of their passionate evenings together, she even talked about getting married right after they graduated. Terry was certain that Leo was serious about a lifetime relationship with her. She struggled to understand Leo's sudden announcement, and began crying as he told her about his plans. Leo tried to calm her, but she couldn't grasp what was happening. It made no sense to her. They had been lovers and best friends for nearly two years. She wanted to be with him.

"Leo, I love you so much. We ... I thought we were going to get married next year." Tears were streaming from her dark brown eyes. "We have so much in common—and so much fun together!"

"Terry, I can't tell you how sorry I am for all this. I didn't, you know, I just *didn't* know what to do. I've been thinking about this for so long, but just couldn't make a decision until—"

"Why didn't you talk about it with me, Leo—you know, like we always talk about everything together."

"I know, I know. I just, I was just so *damned* confused about all this. But it's what I want to do. I can't put it off any longer. I'm so terribly sorry to hurt you like this."

"What *you* want to do! What about *us*? What about me, and *my* future? I thought we were going to be together, Leo."

"I just, I don't know what else to say, Terry. I've been through this so many times in my mind over the years until I had to make a decision and—"

"Yeah, in *your* own mind, but not with *me*. You've been unfair; you've taken advantage of me, Leo. I never thought you could be so cruel."

"Terry—"

But Terry had grabbed her purse and was pushing the door open. She stepped out and slammed it shut. They both were crying, unable to look at each other. She turned around and rushed up the steps to the porch. Leo watched as she disappeared through the front door. He rested his head back against the driver's seat, closed his eyes, and sighed. The memory returned of that night when he and Terry had fallen asleep at the drive-in movie, how they giggled when they realized what had happened. They had so many great times together. But he knew he had to end their relationship now, even though his goal still seemed so very far away. He wondered if Terry would ever be able to forgive him. As he drove away, he shot one last look up the stairs to the porch that was now in darkness.

Leo reported to his new job on the Tuesday after Labor Day. As he entered the office of the restaurant supply company where he had worked part-time for the past four years, he was plagued by conflicting thoughts. Just a few days before, he was laboring in the warehouse and inventory section, dressed in his white uniform; now he was in the business office wearing a dress shirt and tie as the bookkeeper, separated from his friends and fellow employees, who over the years had become his close friends. He was no longer one of them. But that was not the worst part of it. A deeper conflict was already looming. *I could be starting my studies for the priesthood today, if only I had acted sooner.*

Irv Davis was in his late forties, about five feet, ten inches tall and slightly overweight. His short, black, thinning hair was always neatly groomed. Frequent trips to Florida assured him the constant suntan he desired. He dressed fashionably and neatly, his trousers always sharply creased. Irv was a graduate of the University of Pennsylvania. He usually had the *Wall Street Journal* and *New York Times* on his desk, and was an avid reader of the latest best sellers. He and his wife, Faith, regularly attended Broadway shows. Irv had owned and operated the Lehigh Restaurant Supply Company for about fifteen years. He was motioning to Leo as he entered the office, proudly pointing to Leo's new work station—an antique maple desk with matching swivel chair.

"Welcome, my boy!"

Leo managed his best smile, thanking Irv for the wonderful opportunity. Then he sat at the desk, pondering the ledger, the journal, and the stacks of invoices and receipts.

He imagined himself meditating on passages from the Old and New Testaments as he stared blankly at this meaningless commercial rubble on his desk.

He did not belong there.

Leo lamented his self-imposed exile. He had bravely withstood the good-natured catcalls and taunting by his friends when they saw him arriving in his business attire. As part of the old gang in the warehouse and shipping area, he had enjoyed listening to their obscene jokes and lurid tales of sexual conquests. Most of the guys were handsome young men around Leo's age and, like him, physically fit. They had formed basketball and baseball teams, which Leo had promptly joined. He loved the camaraderie and interaction with the teams as they competed in the Allentown City Leagues. His displacement from his old crew, combined with his feeling of deepening despair about a future that now seemed out of his grasp, weighed on Leo more than his new mundane responsibilities. It was a long, tedious day. About five-fifteen in the afternoon he filed the remaining paperwork neatly and emerged from his maple prison, thanking Irv for the "wonderful opportunity."

Two more years of this before I can start my education at the seminary, he anguished. He removed his tie and began walking home.

In early October, Leo received a letter from Rob. His best friend had moved to New Jersey, far from the old neighborhood. Leo had written to Rob earlier in the year that he and his friend Eddie, who worked with him at the restaurant supply company, were thinking about joining the Marines. Before Leo decided to pursue the priesthood, he and Eddie had planned to visit the Marine Corps recruiting office one Monday after they had decided to enlist during their Friday afternoon coffee break. Leo smiled widely when he remembered approaching his mother about the idea. "Are you *crazy*, Leo?" his mom had shouted. "No, there's no way that I'm going to let you enlist in the Marines. Where did you get such a ridiculous idea?"

Rob wrote that Leo would "look great in a Marine uniform." Long after their boyhood orgies had ended, Leo still thought about Rob often.

Leo was grinning again as he finished reading Rob's letter. He remembered how angry Eddie had been when having enlisted in the Marine Corps, he got back to work after lunch and learned that Leo had "chickened out." They remained friends, however, and when Eddie visited the supply company after boot camp, Leo was amazed at the change in his friend's physical appearance. When he left for military service, Eddie had been a handsome if boyish-looking lad with long blonde hair crowning his five-foot, seven-inch, 125-pound frame. In just six months he had been transformed into a seemingly taller, clearly more muscular, robust young man whose blazing blue eyes were now set in a well-tanned face topped by a military buzz cut. In his Marine uniform agleam with its decorations for marksmanship and leadership, Eddie was a totally different person.

If I don't get into the seminary, maybe I can still join the Marines, Leo mused.

As he held the letter, Leo's thoughts drifted back four years to his last sexual encounter with Rob. He paused, looked at the letter, folded it and carefully placed it back in the envelope.

The winter months dragged on, but it became increasingly more difficult for Leo to concentrate on his accounting responsibilities. His resentment for the position in which he found himself deepened each day. Only his continued participation in the league sports—and his frequent, if brief, lunch breaks—helped him to maintain the personal contact with his former crew members he so much enjoyed.

He thought about the seminary every day, and prayed for perseverance every night before he went to sleep. Leo attended Solemn High Mass on Sunday mornings. The sacred music thrilled him. His two years of Latin in high school helped him understand much of the service in the official language of the Roman Catholic Church.

His admiration for Pope John XXIII had grown since the new pontiff's open-mindedness and palpable warmth replaced the austerity and impersonal demeanor of his ultra-conservative predecessor, Pius XII. On his bedroom wall, Leo placed a color photo of the pope dressed in his gaudily elaborate papal attire, replacing the photo of the nearly-naked Terry that had been gazing upon him for the past two years.

John XXIII became the symbol of the revitalized Church Leo deeply desired to serve. It was not unusual for Leo to hear his uncles and aunts, who rarely attended Mass, expressing their fondness for the pope who wanted to "open the windows of the church." Even his father—hardly a religious man—could often be heard praising the pope. Leo's mother surprised the family when she returned home from shopping one day with a beautifully colored, laminated portrait of Pope John XXIII. It was affixed to a foot-wide, oval-shaped slice of wood cut from a tree. Everyone admired it, and nearly everybody remarked that it seemed like the beloved pontiff's eyes followed you as you walked by the portrait. It was the topic of frequent discussion in the Weber household.

Leo attended the Solemn High Mass at midnight on Christmas Eve with his mother. The joyous service, magnificent music and colorfully decorated church greatly inspired him. A brass trio proclaimed "Joy to the World" from the open windows of the elementary school across the street as Leo and his mom emerged from the packed church after Mass. There was silence in the car as they drove home. His mother, no doubt, perceived Leo's growing devotion to the Church and his strong desire to become part of its ministry.

When they arrived home, Leo hugged his mother.

"Merry Christmas, mom!"

"I love you so much, Leo."

Leo felt that his mother knew he still longed to become a priest—and that nothing she could say or do would change his mind.

When spring arrived Leo began to feel more positive about his situation.

It was the last year he'd have to endure the miserable office work before entering the seminary, he thought. Having saved some money from his new job, he decided to buy a car. His father found him a beautiful 1954 Chevrolet *Bel Air* with a cream-colored roof and light-green body. It was in great condition, so Leo bought it and immediately volunteered it to transport some of the company's baseball and basketball players to their games.

As the months passed, Irv Davis could see that something was bothering Leo. During the four years he had known him, Irv was always impressed by Leo's cheerful, energetic demeanor. Those characteristics seemed to have faded since Leo graduated from high school. It was clear, too, that Leo's disenchantment was affecting the quality of his work in the office.

"Leo, let's go to lunch today," Irv said one Monday morning. "I want to speak with you about some ideas I've been contemplating for my business."

Leo was surprised by the sudden invitation. Had he done something wrong?

The lunch meeting was odd since Irv never brought up any business. They talked about the Phillies and Irv's son's plans for college. After they had eaten, Irv drove to his home, located on a fashionable street on the west end of the city, and invited Leo inside. He soon found himself sitting opposite Irv in the spacious, modernly-decorated living room of this handsome red brick ranch house. *Wait 'til mom hears about this*, Leo thought, as Irv began speaking.

"Leo, my business is growing; we're doing very well at this time. I expect it to become even more successful. Leo, I want you to be part of my business's future. You've had some experience working with the bookkeeping aspect, and you know the warehouse, inventory and shipping routines better than anyone who's ever worked for me. I'm nearly fifty years old now. Eventually I want to have fewer responsibilities for the direct management of my business. I totally trust you, Leo, and I know your great capabilities. I want you to manage the warehouse, inventory and shipping crews for me. When my son completes his college education, he'll join us as manager of marketing, accounting and purchasing. The three of us can form a great team that will grow this business and provide wonderful opportunities for all of us. What do you think, Leo?"

Leo searched for words to deal with the impossible conundrum he now found himself in. He longed to leave the office routine and get back to his old crew. But could he really be their *supervisor*? How could he turn down Irv's offer of a promotion? Irv had no clue about Leo's plan to enter the seminary in the following year. If he revealed this plan to Irv, how would that affect his employment with the firm? As he considered this sudden predicament, he noticed that Irv was smiling widely and shaking his head back and forth.

"Leo, *Leo*, my boy! Look, I know I've broadsided you with all this information." He was laughing as he watched the perplexed expression on Leo's face. "How about talking it over with your parents?" he advised, "and we'll discuss it again next week."

Leo was relieved to be even momentarily off the hook.

"Irv, I ... I can't tell you how, um, flattered I am that you'd even consider me for this promotion. I'll speak with my mother and father about it. Thanks so much."

They headed back to the office in the middle of the afternoon. Leo worked late to catch up with his work. That evening at the dinner table, other drama preceded what Leo was about to share. His father had arrived home late from work, perturbed that his parking space had been taken by a neighbor. He was in an angry mood as he settled into his dining room chair. They all finished a very quiet dinner before his mom served the strawberry shortcake left over from Sunday. Only as Ellen began clearing the dessert dishes from the table did Leo finally begin to tell his story of the day's events.

"Irv took me out to lunch today," he beamed. His father gave him a puzzled look. "He wants to promote me to supervisor of the warehouse, inventory and shipping areas. He thinks I could play an important part in the future of the company."

"What about that office job you *just started*?" his dad asked.

"I haven't enjoyed that work at all, Dad. It's boring and I *hate* it. And I miss working with my friends in the old department."

"And now you're going to be their *supervisor*? Don't you still play on the same basketball and baseball teams with them?"

"Yeah, but that's outside the office—in the evening and on weekends."

"It's not going to be easy telling those guys what to do, giving them hell for their mistakes, then going out and playing ball with them."

"I know, dad. I thought about that, but we've worked together for years and we know one another so well. I think I can handle that aspect."

"Will you be earning more money than you're now being paid for the bookkeeping job, Leo?" his mom asked.

"Yes I will, mom. Irv hasn't yet talked about the salary, but he said that it would be higher than my present position is paying."

Satisfied with his answer, she got to the heart of the matter and raised, as usual, the critical concern.

"Leo, what about your plan to enter the seminary next year? Is Irv aware of your thoughts about the seminary? Do you think it's fair to accept the promotion just a year before you plan to leave?"

"Mom, I've never told anyone at the company that I intend to become a priest. I don't want to bring up the topic until I'm absolutely certain I'll be leaving. I'm sure I can handle the responsibility to supervise the guys that I've worked with over the years. Remember that time I took over the class when I was in seventh grade—and taught my own classmates?"

"But what about Irv and his business?" his dad pressed.

"Dad, Jonathan, Irv's son, just started college. He won't be ready to work with the company for four years. So, it's not like I'd be creating severe difficulties for the company should I have to leave next year."

Leo had grown to despise the antique maple desk and all its monotonous contents. The wide black books in which he entered endless columns of perfectly formed numbers within blue-and-red lines had become entirely loathsome to him. He missed the guys with whom he had enjoyed working over the years, longing to be with them again in the warehouse and shipping area—even in the tenuous new role of their supervisor. He would work very hard over the next year to make his parents and Irv proud of him.

"I'm going to accept the new position," he said. The broadest smile his parents had seen on Leo's face in many months soon produced their own in the silence that followed.

The next morning Irv was elated to hear Leo accept the promotion he had been offered.

"I'm so glad you've decided to join us, Leo. I know you're going to be very happy in your new role."

Leo's weak smile barely masked the turmoil spinning in his head.

"I know I will, Irv," he replied. "I know I will."

Leo felt he was betraying his good friend Irv, but his desire to enter the seminary had never waned since he had first spoken with Father David nearly a year before. He followed his mother's advice to wait, but nothing he had experienced since that time altered his determination in the least. By Thursday morning, Irv had already hired a new office assistant to assume Leo's bookkeeping responsibilities. A bright graduate from the city's public high school, Samantha caught on quickly to the office routines. Leo enjoyed working with her, and joined her for lunch on Fridays at the Greek luncheonette around the corner. Samantha was a very attractive girl; she weighed about a hundred pounds and was about five-feet, five-inches tall, with long light-brown hair, which she sometimes wore in a ponytail. Her dark brown eyes seemed flirtatious. He managed to keep their conversations focused on the duties he was transferring to her at the office, despite Samantha's continued probing about Leo—"Do you have a girlfriend?" she had asked. "Are you dating anyone?" "What do you like to do on weekends?"

One week later Leo was back with his old crew. Irv's introduction of their new supervisor was met with a good-natured, if surprisingly extended, cacophony of catcalls, whistling and groaning from the guys. In the ensuing days, calm returned to Leo's demeanor. He was settling down emotionally for the first time in nearly a year.

Leo grew keenly interested in politics during the summer of 1960. His admiration for a young and energetic senator from Massachusetts increased as he read John F. Kennedy's books, *Strategy for Peace* and *Profiles in Courage.* He was impressed and inspired with the intellect and bravery of the young senator, whom he regarded as the symbol of a new generation, just as Pope John XXIII had become the leader of a renewed Catholic Church. That Kennedy was a Roman Catholic added to Leo's enthusiasm for the presidential candidate. Later in the year, following the Democratic convention, Kennedy visited Allentown. The largest crowd ever to assemble in the city's history gathered in Center Square for his campaign speech, just thirty yards from the Marble Bar restaurant that Leo and his mother enjoyed so much. The local newspaper estimated the crowd at more than one hundred thousand people. Leo received permission to take off from work for a few hours to attend the extravaganza. He carried a three-foot-square Styrofoam board on which he had painted the phrase *Kennedy Our Remedy for Nixon Contradiction.* He drew scowls and jeers from many of the Republican folks who were attending the rally, but Leo was elated when he opened the newspaper the next day to see his sign visible in the vast crowd. Senator Kennedy seemed to Leo to be pointing directly at it. Was the Senator acknowledging Leo's support?

The legendary golfer Arnold Palmer was another of Leo's heroes. Palmer's amazing comebacks to win major tournaments thrilled Leo immensely. He bought a putter and practiced at home. Within a few months, he could sink twenty-five-foot putts from his dining room into a small tin cup in the living room. He often talked with Irv about his admiration for the golf great and his love of the game. One morning, Irv showed up at the office with a complete set of old golf clubs, the shafts made of hickory and bamboo.

"My old back won't let me play this game anymore, Leo, and Jonathan doesn't like golf. So, I thought you could use these," he said, presenting the bag of clubs to Leo.

"Irv, I, I can't thank you enough for these beautiful clubs!"

"Enjoy them, my boy."

In the fall, Leo asked his close friend Tony to accompany him to the annual open house at Saint Francis Seminary in Philadelphia, scheduled for the last Sunday in October. Tony was a Korean War veteran who had seen combat action. Leo got to know him through his work at the restaurant supply company, where Tony was a driver for one of the delivery routes. They enjoyed going to the movies and often went bowling together. Tony was a very serious person, probably because of his experiences in the war, Leo had thought. He was often the butt of jokes around the warehouse because he was slow to catch on to pranks that the guys played on him. Sometimes they would move his truck to another bay when he left to report to the office, leaving him puzzled when he'd return and couldn't find his truck; or they would playfully hide his route schedule before he left for his deliveries, delaying him. But Leo admired Tony and was intrigued by the stories of his war experiences, especially the one where he had almost been wounded by friendly fire. Tony was curious about the idea of visiting the seminary. He was raised Catholic, but was divorced from his wife. He was interested in seeing the place where so many hundreds of priests had been educated over the years. Leo explained that, although he had often read about the seminary, he had never had the opportunity to visit it. Of course, he never mentioned the true reason why he wanted to make the trip.

Tony and Leo drove to Philadelphia on a crisp fall afternoon, chatting casually over the hour-and-a-half journey. Jokes about the guys at the restaurant supply and Tony's most recent dates were the major topics of their conversation. As they turned off County Line Road onto Winthrop Road, Leo became excited by the sight of the massive, grey-granite edifice unfolding before them. The rolling green lawns surrounding the seminary were speckled with a variety of colorful leaves falling furiously in the last week of October. A young seminarian dressed in a long black cassock with a white Roman collar was beckoning to them as they drove through the front gate, directing them to the huge parking area on the lawn. Unable to wait, Leo was already opening the door before Tony brought the car to a halt.

"Hey, Leo," Tony shouted. "What the fuck's the big rush? You almost wound up under my car, for Christ's sake!"

But Leo was too excited to respond. They strolled along the driveway and entered the front door of the seminary in the center of the building that housed the classrooms and dormitories. The lobby's white-and-grey marble floors shined brightly under the vaulted ceiling's brass chandelier. A series of smaller chandeliers dangling majestically on long black iron chains added an aura of solemnity to the entrance.

Seminarians in their clerical garb were directing visitors to various rooms within the Greco-Roman style edifice. Leo easily pictured himself similarly attired.

This is where I'm supposed to be, Leo thought as he and Tony were guided into a classroom. *I'll be sitting behind one of these desks just one year from now. I know it!*

The tour continued to the second floor where what seemed like a football field-size dormitory, with an endless row of crisply made beds on either side, rolled out before them.

"This is the dormitory for our first-year seminarians," the young priest-like guide was explaining. "After the first year, each seminarian is assigned to his own private bedroom, located on the other side of this building."

Leo imagined himself asleep in one of those beds as part of a long line of a hundred other young men sharing the same goal to which he aspired. He was ready to move in *now*.

Finally, Leo and his unsuspecting companion were led to Saint Matthias's Chapel to attend vespers. Leo was thrilled by the seminary choir's rendering of the *Magnificat*. His love for liturgical services had grown over the years, but he had never heard sacred music that sounded so beautiful. After they left the seminary chapel, and had made their way down the huge marble steps to the driveway, Leo whisked up one of the large leaves that had fallen from the great elm tree towering overhead, carefully placing it in his jacket pocket. He was sure he would soon be returning to this magnificent place. The leaf would be a constant reminder of his visit and of his pledge to return.

"Hey, Leo, what's with you today? First, you almost made me run over you when we got here; then, you're way out of it as we walked around the school. And you should've seen yourself in chapel. I thought you were in some kind of a trance or something!"

They both laughed.

"Yeah, I know. It's quite a place!" Leo responded.

Their drive back to Allentown featured a recapitulation of all they had seen during the open house tour. Leo did most of the talking. Tony couldn't remember seeing his young friend so animated during the five years he had known him. He smiled as he listened to all of Leo's superlatives, never suspecting for a moment Leo's plan to return there as a seminarian. The radio was playing "Save the Last Dance for Me." They had dinner at the Queen City Diner before Tony dropped Leo off at his home.

Leo burst into the front door of his house. He had to tell his mother everything—right away—about the details of his exciting day.

The Ed Sullivan Show was dominating the household scene. "The Chipmunks" will be a tough act to interrupt, he thought, so he decided to wait for the first commercial break. His dad was seated in his recliner across from the sofa, where his mom was sound asleep. Leo was amazed at his mom's ability to sleep almost anywhere at anytime. Once, when she actually fell asleep at the dining room table during dessert, his father playfully squirted whipped cream in her mouth, startling her awake as everyone laughed heartily.

"Tony and I just got back from Saint Francis Seminary!" Leo blurted out—with great relief—over the "Plop, plop, fizz, fizz" of the *Alka Seltzer* TV commercial.

His mom awoke. His dad turned around.

"What was it like, Leo?" his mother asked.

"Mom, it was the most incredible experience I've ever had in my life. You should see the size of the entrance hall. They have a dormitory that's longer than our whole block. And the choir was beyond anything I've heard—or even imagined."

His dad had turned back to the TV, as the fizzing had stopped, ending the commercial break. Ed Sullivan was introducing his next guest. Leo's mother continued to gaze at him, pondering his new excitement. She knew that all of her efforts to persuade Leo to rethink his goal in life were failing. She was going to lose him—an unbearable thought. Leo sat down beside her and took her hand in his.

"Mom, you've got to come with me and see that place," he whispered. Leo sat with his mother and father for a while. His sisters had already gone to bed. He needed to be alone—to try to relive all he had experienced that day. After watching the local news, Leo kissed his mother and father goodnight, and headed upstairs to his bedroom.

There were no erotic temptations that evening. After sliding into bed Leo could think only of the mind-numbing experiences of the afternoon. He could still hear the seminary choir singing the *Magnificat* in four-part harmony. He recalled the wide marble corridors and vast dormitory. Thoughts of strolling along the expansive lawn as he meditated or said the rosary filled his mind as he fell asleep.

Back at the restaurant supply company the next morning, Leo once again felt estranged. After all the excitement he experienced the day before, his work at the company seemed less important than ever. When Tony returned from his deliveries that afternoon, he sought out Leo.

"How're ya feeling today, buddy?"

"Tony, I still can't believe that experience yesterday. It was mind-boggling. I think I dreamed about the place all night." Leo laughed.

"What place, Leo?" asked Irv, emerging from his office and overhearing the tail end of their conversation.

Leo was a bit rattled. A crack in his carefully constructed wall of secrecy had just appeared.

"Me and Leo drove down to Philly yesterday for the open house at the Catholic seminary down there, Irv," Tony reported.

"Now why in the world would you guys want to visit a place like that?" Irv asked, glancing back and forth at each of them.

Leo's mind was frantically devising a story to explain the trip.

"Irv, you know, uh, that I just graduated from high school a year or so ago," he began. "I remembered how the priests used to talk about the place, so when I found out they were having an open house, I was curious about it. I coaxed Tony to drive down there with me. We had a great time. It's a fascinating place."

"You know, I saw the seminary from the outside many times when I lived in Philadelphia. I was always impressed with the grand scale of the architecture," Irv responded. "Hey, Leo, next time they have one, let me know; I'd love to tour the inside of the buildings."

Leo was thinking that Irv might very well be visiting the seminary sooner than he imagined.

"Oh, uh, yeah, Irv; that'd be great," Leo said.

Both returned to work, Leo feeling he had dodged another bullet.

Election Day was at hand. Leo read the daily and Sunday newspapers, carefully analyzing the race. It looked like a dead heat with vice president Richard Nixon given the slight edge. Leo had watched the debates and was impressed by Senator Kennedy's vast knowledge and calm demeanor. Leo was one of the few Catholics working at the restaurant supply company—and the only one who thought that Kennedy had won the debates. Most of the news media sided with him. Then it was election night. When the long wait for the counting of votes was over, Leo was exuberant at Kennedy's victory. His mood soared higher than it had been in months.

Thanksgiving Day brought the usual feast to which Leo had become accustomed over the years. His mother and father had gone all out to make the meal spectacular. The turkey, a gift from his dad's boss, was large enough for two families. As was traditional, Leo's mom baked three pies: mince, pumpkin and apple. The chestnut stuffing was a family creation that had been handed down through the years. Turkey soup with its deep-flavored stock was the opening course. His father carved the perfectly roasted turkey. Five vegetables—corn, peas, carrots, mashed potatoes and red beets—completed the dinner. Leo's mother asked him to say the prayer before dinner.

"Bless us, O Lord, and these Thy gifts which we are about to receive from Thy bounty through Christ our Lord, Amen. And bless us all in the coming year," he added, suddenly realizing it could be his last Thanksgiving Day with his family before entering the seminary.

Following the Christmas Eve Midnight Mass with all of its glowing pageantry, the Weber family exchanged gifts by the Christmas tree in the living room. The severe asthma attack that his mother had suffered an hour earlier had finally subsided. Such episodes were frequently induced by the excitement of the holidays. Leo was stunned when he opened his mother's gift to him: a *Saint Joseph's Missal* in Latin and English, with beautiful color pictures of Christ, the Blessed Mother and the saints. It was a black, leather-bound book of prayer. The edges of the pages were gold-leafed. His mom had finally acknowledged her support of Leo's goal.

Donna was playing away on the new miniature piano she received from Santa Claus. It replaced the one that had mysteriously been broken. Ellen was admiring the purse and shoes she had just unwrapped. Leo gave his mom a bright red sweater and to his dad a handsome pair of wool-lined brown slippers. After singing a few carols Leo's favorites being "Silent Night" and "Hark, the Herald Angels Sing", led energetically by Leo, the family retired for the evening. Leo took the missal with him to his room. He opened the middle drawer of his desk and pulled out the leaf that he put in a plastic envelope after his visit to the seminary in October. He put the leaf inside the *Saint Joseph's Missal*, closed its black leather cover, and pressed the book to his lips, kissing it fervently. *Next year, I'll be using this missal in the seminary, and I'll never forget this night as long as I live.*

After returning home from work one evening during the week after New Year's, Leo telephoned his favorite parish priest, requesting to speak with him "about something very important."

"Of course," Father Joe responded. "Come on over so we can talk." Father Joe always seemed to be smiling when he spoke—even on the telephone.

Leo changed into his grey slacks and a long-sleeve white shirt, pulled on his blue woolen jacket, and headed over to the rectory. As he walked down Fourth Street he passed the old familiar landmarks: the school where he had attended first grade; Terry's house, just across the street, and the produce market on the corner. Soon he was making his way up the hill to the rectory. His heart was pounding as never before.

He ascended the eight steps to the front door of the rectory and softly pressed the bell. Leo waited. The passing seconds were unbearable. He turned to face his old elementary school across the street. He could see directly into the second-floor classroom where Sister Mary Christina had taught him in sixth grade. He thought about the words of encouragement his favorite nun had whispered in his ear on the main floor of Hess's Department store during their brief but providential encounter. *It's because of her inspiration that I'm standing here now at the rectory door, finally ready to take the most important step in my*—the sound of the door opening disbursed his reverie. Mrs. Finn, the housekeeper, greeted him: "Good evening, young man." Leo said nothing as she escorted him down the hallway to a small conference room.

Five minutes later, Father Joe burst into the room. He was, as usual, cheerful and energetic. Leo smiled when he saw his favorite priest.

"Well, Leo, what a nice surprise this is! I noticed you at Midnight Mass with your mom. How is she?"

"Uh, good evening, Father. She's coming along pretty well. She gets those asthma attacks, but she seems okay right now."

"So, what's this important thing you want to discuss, Leo? You're not getting married already, are you?"

Leo laughed nervously. "No, uh, no, Father. I, uh, well, I've been thinking about it for a long time and ... I've decided that I want to become a priest."

"Leo, what wonderful news!" The priest's tone quickly turned serious. "Have you spoken about this with your parents?"

Leo told the priest about his desire to apply for the seminary; how his mother had asked him to wait for a couple of years to make sure that it was really what he wanted. But he was more certain than ever that he wanted to be a priest just like him.

As Leo sat across table from him, the priest gave his blessing: "May almighty God bless you, the Father, the Son and the Holy Ghost."

"Amen."

"We've got a lot of work ahead of us, Leo," said Father Joe, his voice now briskly practical in tone. This is one of those wonderful years! God has especially blessed our parish. Two other young men who have just graduated from high school have also decided they want to go to the seminary. So, you'll have two good study companions for the tasks that lie ahead. We'll schedule a few briefing sessions for you and the other fellas to help you all get acquainted with the application process and prepare for the seminary examinations. Your study of previous examination topics will give you a good idea about the areas of study you'll need to pursue over the next few months."

Applications had to be completed and submitted to the seminary by April 15, two months before the day the oral and written exams would be given.

As he listened to Father Joe, Leo felt emotionally relieved for the first time in two years. The tension that had been building inside him was gone. All the delays and uncertainty disappeared. He had taken a major step in the journey toward his dream. Leo Weber was going to be a priest.

Around mid-morning at the restaurant supply company the next day, Irv appeared at Leo's workstation.

"Listen, my boy," Irv started, looking around and assuming an air of confidentiality. "I know that you and, uh, Samantha have had lunch together a few times since she started working here," he whispered. "You know, Samantha is *very* fond of you, Leo, and she'd love to have you ask her out on a date sometime." He undoubtedly detected the concerned look on Leo's face.

The same kind of determination that Leo experienced on that last day of high school, when he decided to tell Father David about his desire to become a priest, now pushed him another step forward.

"Irv, may I speak with you privately?"

"Sure, Leo, let's go into my office. Samantha is off today, so we can talk."

They sat at the maple desk that not long ago had imprisoned Leo. "Irv, I have something very important to tell you. I know I should've spoken with you about this a long time ago, but events in my life are now moving more quickly than ever."

Irv's demeanor turned somber.

"Leo, you're, uh, not going to tell me that you're leaving us, are you? I noticed you've seemed somewhat, oh … I don't know, *distant* over the past few months, but I just assumed your new responsibilities were affecting you."

"No, Irv, it's not my new job that's creating this strange feeling. I've been working with my parish priest to prepare for the next entrance examination for admission to Saint Francis Seminary, in Philadelphia. I want to become a Catholic priest." Leo enunciated those last seven words like a declaration of independence. "You've been so kind and generous to me over the past six years. When you offered me the bookkeeping position when I was still in high school, I had not yet taken any steps toward my goal. Then, it all happened rather suddenly. My mom asked me to wait a couple of years, and right after that, you offered me the supervisor position. I just couldn't say 'no' to you, since nothing had yet been set in motion."

"You never cease to amaze me, my boy! This is the last thing I could have ever imagined you telling me!"

"Irv, I'm just beginning my studies to prepare for the entrance examination," Leo continued, encouraged by the change in Irv's tone. "My application will be submitted in April, and the tests will be administered in June. If I pass the tests and the bishop accepts my application, I will enter the seminary in September—the day after Labor Day. I know you're counting on me to become part of your growing business, and I'm so sorry to have put you in this situation. I had no intention to deceive you. I just kind of got caught up in all the events unfolding at the same time."

"No, *no*, Leo! Look, don't even *think* about that. I've always admired your character and forthright behavior. I think I can understand what you've been going through over the past couple of years. It all kind of makes sense to me now. And my admiration for you is greater now than it's ever been. I can't tell you how thrilled I am for you. What a wonderful life you have chosen."

Irv went on to explain how deeply interested he was in religion, and that he frequently attended lectures at his synagogue. "Leo, I'd love to have you accompany me sometime to those great discussions about the Old Testament."

"I'd really like to do that, Irv."

They looked at each other for a moment, then laughed. Part of it was relief; another was sheer bewilderment at the sudden twist of fate for both of them.

"I haven't told anyone here about my plans, Irv. I think it would be a bit difficult to handle at this point."

"Your secret is safe. Tell them when you're ready. In the meantime, I know you'll continue to do an excellent job here, and I'll be very busy at the impossible task of trying to find a replacement for you."

As Leo was thanking him for being so understanding, Irv grabbed him by the shoulders. "I can't tell you what you've meant to me and to this place. I'll miss you a lot, but I know you're doing what you must do."

On the following Monday evening, Leo rushed through dinner and joined his fellow aspiring seminarians, Patrick and Thomas, at the rectory to begin poring over examination topics. English and history were easy for Leo. Algebra, geography and biology would most certainly present serious challenges. Leo had always done well in Christian Doctrine classes, so those questions would present no problems.

A recent high school graduate who smoked cigarettes with abandon, Patrick was liberal and irreverent. He was about six feet tall; his slightly overweight body was topped off by a thick shock of long, straight black hair that partially covered his left eye. His father had been killed in action during World War II. Having no siblings, Patrick bragged that he was "the quintessential spoiled brat." He could barely wait until the break in their study sessions to light up another cigarette. He treated somewhat whimsically the whole exercise they were about to launch. Patrick's mother was a devout Catholic who attended Mass regularly. She had raised Patrick by herself after the death of her husband, working full time as an office supervisor to support herself and Patrick.

Thomas had a directly opposite personality. Conservative in dress, he took as gospel everything the parish priest advised. His father was a sales supervisor for the Fuller Brush Company; his mother taught kindergarten at a local public school. Being the youngest of three brothers may have accounted for Thomas's quiet demeanor and docile attitude. He was slightly taller and heavier than Patrick. His short, dark brown hair, combed straight back was held firmly in place with what looked like *Wildroot Cream Oil* hair tonic. His gold wire-rimmed glasses highlighted his large brown eyes. Thomas seemed to have difficulty concentrating on the task at hand. He was totally devoted to Saint Jude, the patron saint of hopeless causes, praying often for the saint's assistance.

The study session lasted about two hours. By the time Leo got back home, around 9:30, he was exhausted. He figured the exercises had probably been a lot easier for Patrick and Thomas, since they had just finished school and had no full-time jobs during the day.

A severe snowstorm on January 20 forced the closing of all area schools. Leo received a call from Irv that the restaurant supply company would be closed. It was a blessing for Leo because his hero, John Fitzgerald Kennedy, was to be sworn in as President of the United States that day. Leo would be able to watch the entire inauguration on television.

The following weeks seemed to melt away as quickly as the late winter snow. Leo was surprised at how much his study habits were improving. He delved into the topics with discipline and fervor. By the end of March, Leo was able to answer correctly nearly all of the mock-examination questions. He felt confident that he would be ready by the June deadline. Over the weeks following the study group's formation, Leo developed a friendship with his two would-be classmates. Patrick continued to complain about the rigorous study routine the parish priest had established, while Thomas never ceased emphasizing the seriousness of their work. Leo was frequently amused by the way their temperaments clashed. The drama added entertainment to the serious work in which they were all engrossed.

Leo was upbeat about his future. His work on the preparation for the examinations was successful; he enjoyed the company of his new friends, and he was confident that he was finally on his way toward his goal. He began attending Mass every morning before work, praying earnestly for strength and guidance. The April 15 deadline for submitting the application had arrived. Mandatory documents included his Baptismal and Confirmation certificates, and his parents' Marriage certificate. Also required were letters of commendation from his pastor, Monsignor Gregory, and from the school principal, along with a transcript of Leo's grades—all to be sent directly to the rector of the seminary. The application form itself was to be completed in pen and ink by the applicant. All of the documents were assembled under the meticulous supervision of Father Joe, who mailed them to the seminary at the end of the first week of April.

Within two weeks Leo received a form letter from seminary officials notifying him that, should he be selected for the entrance examination, he would be screened for proficiency in oral English by a board of priest professors, then be interviewed by the rector of the seminary. A complete physical examination would also be required. The long wait followed. Every day when he got home from work, Leo rushed to the kitchen table to look through the mail. Nothing! April was soon over, and now May was already two weeks old, but still no response to his application.

By Memorial Day weekend, Leo had been losing sleep night after night worrying about his status. When he arrived home from work on Wednesday, May 31, his mom was sitting at the kitchen table. Dinner was on the stove; the aroma of one of his favorite meals, meatloaf topped with bacon, wafted through the house. His mom was resting her head in her hands as she sat there waiting for Leo. He didn't have to ask for the mail. He knew from the look in his mother's eyes as she turned toward him that the long-awaited letter had arrived.

"Mom, ... "

She handed him the envelope.

Leo stared at the envelope in his hands, dreading to open it. Finally, no longer able to bear the uncertainty, he picked up a dinner knife from the table, slit open the envelope, and began reading aloud:

> *Dear Mr. Weber,*
>
> *Your application for admission to the Seminary of Saint Francis and other documents have been received and approved. You are hereby granted permission to take the entrance examination, which will be held at the seminary on Saturday, June 24, 1961, beginning at—*

Leo's mom had gotten up from the table. He took her in his arms. Thoughts of separation from her and his dad and sisters swirled in his mind. The long-anticipated response now gave way to its ultimate, bittersweet meaning: He was on the path to another life, a world apart from the family he loved so much.

As they stood in the middle of the kitchen trying to deal with the drama of the moment, Leo saw his dad entering the house. He walked toward his father, announcing the news as he approached him. For the first time he could remember, Leo saw tears in his dad's eyes. He felt warmth from his father that he hadn't experienced since his dad had cared for him so tenderly during the horrible paralysis Leo had suffered nearly ten years before.

His dad grabbed Leo's hand and shook it firmly. "Congratulations, son. You deserve this. You've worked so hard this year with your job and all those long study evenings at the rectory. I'm very happy for you."

Ellen had just gotten home from visiting with Rena, her best friend, and next door neighbor.

"What's going on?"

Her mom broke the good news.

"So you're really gonna *do* this, Leo?"

"Ellen, you know how long I've wanted this to happen. Now I'm ready."

Ellen had not yet completed high school, but she had already become involved in a serious relationship. Despite the reluctance and concern of her parents, she was planning an August wedding. Always a loner, Ellen had found someone whom she really enjoyed being with and who seemed to be very fond of her. Although she and Leo had been somewhat distant over the past couple of years, he often thought about the times when they and several cousins who lived nearby would go to the movies, have picnics, and put on shows for the neighbors. He remembered the time when Ellen found a wounded sparrow, put it in a box with a screen on top, then charged the neighborhood kids a nickel apiece to see it. Leo treasured those nights when he would tell her stories about when she was a little girl, or read books to her—her favorite being *The Blue Streak and Dr. Medusa*—then tucking her in whenever their parents were out for an evening. Ellen would not bring herself to say it, but Leo knew she would miss him terribly. Ellen paused a moment:

"Great, Leo! Hope you make it."

"Thanks, Ellen." His sister's eyes darted to the dinner table, then back to Leo.

"I *know* you will."

"Okay fellas, now we really have to get to work," sang Father Joe, as Leo, Patrick and Thomas entered the rectory the following evening. Leo's new friends had also received good news the previous day. "We've got to move on to some specific examination questions that have been used in previous years. We need to go through them several times so you can get well acquainted with the answers."

Patrick, of course, balked at the thought of poring over the old questions. "Is all of this truly necessary, Father? I mean, honestly, we all just graduated from high school. A lot of this stuff seems so repetitious."

He settled down a bit when Father Joe explained how the exercises had benefited previous candidates for the seminary. Patrick had generally been rebellious and suspicious of authority during most of his young life. Enjoying his sense of independence, he frequently got into trouble in elementary school for ignoring the safety patrol on his way home. In high school, he was a regular in the detention group after school hours—punishment for one or another of his indiscretions or for insubordination in the classroom. His doting mother had little control over his actions. Having been accepted to take the seminary examination, he had more clout with her than ever.

Thomas scolded Patrick for his cavalier attitude. "Look, Patrick, we need to get down to *work*. If we're gonna get into the seminary, we just have to get this done." Thomas's parents were strict, and he had learned early on to be obedient.

Leo just smiled and watched, silently amused to see his buddies sparring once again. They were soon sorting through the stack of documents that Father Joe had retrieved for their study, spending the next two hours engrossed in silent reading.

Leo needed all the discipline he could muster to keep his happy secret from his co-workers in the morning. He spoke briefly with Irv as he arrived at the office, notifying him of the good news. Irv was, of course, delighted. Leo's friends knew something was up. He was in a particularly good mood when they all went to their favorite Greek luncheonette around the corner and slid into a large booth.

"Hey, Leo, so who's the new chick?" Mickey asked. "She must be pretty good, 'cause you're walking on air today, buddy." The other guys joined in the joking. As a young waitress took their orders for hamburger barbecues with french fries, Mickey continued, "Dawn, baby, get a load of our Leo, doesn't he look great!"

Leo was blushing. "C'mon, guys, what's this all about? You've been on my case all morning now."

"Look, Leo, we know when a guy's getting it, and you sure as hell look like you're scoring," said Billy. "So who is it? Samantha? You've looked tired these last couple of mornings, but goddamned happy, too. That means only one thing to me."

"You guys all have a one-track mind," Leo objected. "Your imaginations are running away with you."

But the more Leo protested, the more convinced his buddies were that he was having sex with Samantha. They knew she and Leo had gone to lunch a few times, and they saw the warm look in her eyes whenever Leo was around.

The next morning Leo awoke from a frequently interrupted sleep, deeply troubled. All the work he had done over the past five months—strengthening his study habits, going to Mass every day, getting accepted by the seminary—now seemed to have been for naught. Before going to sleep, his old erotic impulses had stormed back. Lying awake, his thoughts had drifted back to Terry, then Rob, and finally, Samantha.

He had managed with great difficulty over the past year to avoid placing himself in situations that would lead to sin, but this time he failed. The memories of his erotic experiences had overpowered him. No longer able to resist the surge he had been suppressing for so long, he surrendered to its demands, then slumped back in his bed. The fleeting pleasure of his orgasm had just as quickly been displaced by nagging remorse, guilt, despair. He had failed. How could he go on to the seminary if he could not avoid committing mortal sins of the flesh, sins that would not only destroy his goal of the priesthood but condemn him to hell?

He had to confess his sin before taking Holy Communion at Mass, so he skipped services that morning, telling his mom that he had to get to work early. On Saturday he went to confession and vowed to avoid sin. He had frequently read about the lives of some of the saints. He remembered being disturbed when he learned how monks had whipped themselves until their bodies would bleed, the pain helping them to avoid falling into the grip of sexual self-abuse and mortal sin. But as bizarre as those tales once appeared to him, Leo now thought they might well be the only way to save himself from abandoning his life goal. He was determined to overcome the next temptation when it would present itself. That evening, Leo removed a long, sharp needle from his mother's sewing box and put it in the nightstand drawer next to his bed. *I won't let this sin ruin my dream of the priesthood.* He went to sleep feeling newfound stress over this latest failure to defeat his erotic passions.

The scheduled entrance examination date was drawing near. All the tension it created seemed to quell his carnal drives. Saturday, June 24, was just a week away. He and his two buddies had completed their last cram session with Father Joe in the quiet, peaceful confines of the rectory.

"Relax, now, fellas," Father Joe counseled. "Take a little time off to enjoy the new summer days. And pray for God's guidance. May almighty God bless you, the Father, the Son and the Holy Ghost."

"Amen!" Patrick shouted above the others, pulling a half-empty pack of *Marlboro*s from his shirt pocket.

Father Joe laughed. "Patrick, I'm so glad you're relieved. I know this has been tough for you, but I think you'll eventually see that it was well worth your long-suffering struggle."

"Well, Father, I sure do hope you're right," Patrick chuckled, lighting a cigarette.

Leo awoke at five o'clock to prepare for the ninety-minute drive to the seminary. His mom prepared a stack of pancakes swimming in *Log Cabin* syrup, topped with bacon, which he wolfed down before shaving and showering. Then, a few minutes before it was time to leave, Leo emerged from his room dressed nattily in a light blue serge suit that he hadn't worn since the day of his graduation from high school. The narrow, navy blue, knitted necktie was new. He was wearing a crisp white shirt his mom had starched and ironed the day before. His dad had already left for work, and his two sisters were upstairs, asleep.

"I'll be praying for you today," his mom assured him.

"I love you, mom." As he glanced behind her, his eyes focused on the wall next to the front door; seeing the smiling visage of the pope added a further note of assurance. Thomas's father was tooting the horn of his 1960 Chevy. Leo bolted out of the house.

Mr. Richardson had volunteered to drive them to Philadelphia, accompanied by his wife. Her sister lived in the Spring Garden section of the city, so the trip offered her an opportunity to visit while the boys were taking their examinations. All were invited for dinner afterwards. As they approached the seminary, the enormous, grey-granite structures stretched out before them. The carload of five solemn, nervous passengers entered the driveway.

"There it is," said Thomas's father, pointing toward the Center Hall entrance. "That's where you're supposed to meet for a briefing before the examinations." He pulled up to the entrance. He and his wife got out of the car and hugged their "three future priests."

"God bless you, fellas," Thomas's father said.

His wife kissed each of the boys. "I'll be praying for all of you this morning, and so will Aunt Elsie."

Leo, Patrick and Thomas bounded up the stairs to the Center Hall. When they stepped inside, a seminarian greeted them, checked off their names and directed them toward the small auditorium down the hall. They were astonished as they took their seats.

Patrick whispered to Leo, "There must be more than a hundred and fifty guys in this room."

"This is amazing. I can't believe we're finally here!"

"Believe it, my friend," Patrick scolded in his characteristically nonchalant manner. "We worked our *rumps* off for this, Leo, and I really, *really* need a cigarette right now." Thomas didn't say a word as he sat up stiffly in the uncomfortable auditorium seat. He glared at Patrick, disappointed once again by his friend's lack of seriousness.

None of the three had noticed that a tall, bald, overweight priest at the podium was about to speak.

"Haaarrrummpphh," Father Brad began. "Good morning, gentlemen. And all Saint Francis men *are* gentlemen. A schedule is being circulated to all of you. It includes the rooms to which you've been assigned for the various segments of the entrance examination process. Please observe the times for your respective sessions, and don't be late. And now, gentlemen, it's my privilege to introduce the rector of Saint Francis Seminary, Monsignor Connors."

Everybody seemed to straighten up in their seats as the rector began speaking. Even Patrick seemed impressed. The rector was a short, thin, stark figure with snow-white hair and piercing, dark brown eyes peering out from beneath thick, black eyebrows.

"Gentlemen, welcome to Saint Francis Seminary. You have been given the wonderful privilege of taking the entrance examination for this venerable institution. Congratulations! Now it's time to prove that you are worthy. Good luck with your tests, and may God bless you in the name of the Father, the Son and the Holy Ghost." The sign of the cross that he had formed over the entire room with his right hand was reciprocated immediately by each nervous candidate in the room.

Seminarians guided the young men to the various rooms and halls where the examinations were being held. Now it was time to put all of their preparation into action.

Finally, after two years, I'm here. I've got to do this right. This is my last chance. He had learned from Father Joe that only rarely did the seminary allow a second chance to apply, if one should fail.

Leo was surprised that the three-hour long written examination seemed to be so easy. He was one of the first applicants in the room to turn in his paper and leave. His next challenge was the interview with two Saint Francis seminary faculty members. He was anticipating a rough session, but to his surprise, the priest examiners were rather pleasant. They asked him a number of questions about Christian Doctrine and world history, then quizzed him on his knowledge of grammatical constructions.

"What is a split infinitive?" asked Father James, a pudgy, bald-headed priest who appeared to be about sixty years old. "Please give us an example of the subjunctive mood," asked Father Stephen. "Explain the difference between a relative pronoun and a demonstrative pronoun," Father James asked. Leo was ready with a quick, correct answer for each of their questions. At the end of the session, his examiners seemed pleased.

"Now, Leo, please go to the room next door and write a five-hundred-word composition about a modern day event, showing how it relates to our Christian faith," directed Father Stephen, the younger, taller priest. "When you are finished, please leave it with the seminarian who has been assigned there. Good luck, son."

Leo reported next door, where he was given a small booklet with a light-blue cover.

"Please use this book for your composition, and return it to me when you have completed it," the friendly seminarian directed.

It took Leo about an hour to finish his work. He was required to write with pen and ink, so he had to be careful to avoid errors. He wrote about the new NASA space program that was stunning the world, comparing the enormous power of those jet-propelled engines to the omnipotence of Jesus Christ so vividly demonstrated on the day of his Ascension into heaven.

Following a full morning of written and oral examinations, all the applicants returned to the auditorium as they had been directed.

"Well, boys, how did it go?" Patrick seemed confident that he had done well.

"Okay, I think." Thomas seemed a bit uncertain.

"And you, Leo?"

"Well, you know, Patrick, I really thought it was going to be a rough morning. But I have to say, I think it went quite well. The faculty members were pleasant and they seemed to be content with my responses; and I think, thanks to Father Joe, we were all well prepared for the written tests. Don't you agree?" he asked, looking at Patrick.

"*Honestly*, Leo, you keep bringing up those *damned* cram sessions," complained Patrick. He continued to be annoyed by the thought of all the time that Father Joe had taken out of his personal schedule.

"Look, Patrick, Leo is *right,*" said Thomas. "What would we have done without Father Joe's guidance?" Thomas was ready to debate the work sessions yet again.

"Okay, all right, it's all over now," Patrick conceded. "All we have to do now is worry about our final scores and see if we get in."

While they were reviewing the events of the morning, Father Brad had returned to the podium. "Gentlemen, I trust that you have all done well this morning. I'm happy to announce that we have prepared lunch in our refectory for you. A seminarian will escort you there now. I hope you enjoy your lunch, and above all, I hope to see you all back here in September."

They all walked down the hallway that stretched along the entire length of the fortress-like front wall of the main building. The large white terrazzo floor with its marble base was shining in the glare of the sunlight streaming through the arch-shaped windows. The refectory, as the seminarian guide called it, was located about a hundred yards from the auditorium. The aroma from the kitchen greeted them long before they reached the dining hall's huge wooden doors with their stained-glass windows. As they entered the room Leo saw what he estimated to be about twenty rows of tables arranged on each side of the room, each table set for twelve people. It reminded him of his high school cafeteria, except that all of the tables here were covered with white linen and, in the middle of the dining room, a large, intricately carved wooden pulpit gave a chapel-like effect to the room.

A seminarian in his final year of study for the priesthood led the prayer before meals: "Bless us, Father, and this food which we are about to receive from Thy bounty, through Christ our Lord. Amen."

One hundred and fifty or so nervous, hungry young men, all fervently hoping this would soon be their new home, echoed the deacon's "Amen." After the older seminarian completed a reading at the pulpit from the *Lives of the Saints*, a bell indicating the end of their silence was rung, followed by an eruption of excited conversations throughout the room.

Their day at the seminary ended with a visit to Saint Matthias's Chapel. Leo and the other seminarians were seated in the pews at the back of the chapel, where he and Tony had sat during their visit at the open house. As the memory of that day returned, Leo was thinking about all the progress he made over the past year that led him so close to his goal. His long wait was nearly over. Only one more step remained.

After giving his benediction, Monsignor Connors bid farewell to the anxious crowd of young men who had completed a full day at the seminary trying to prove that they were worthy of pursuing their dreams. As he left the chapel, Leo studied the faces of his fellow applicants. He could see the same kind of anticipation he was experiencing. He knew he would return.

Thomas's parents were waiting in the car in the front driveway for them as they exited the chapel. They piled into the back seat and were off to Thomas's Aunt Elsie's home in the Spring Garden neighborhood of Philadelphia. A devout Catholic, Aunt Elsie attended Mass nearly every day. She considered it a rare blessing to have the presence of three young men in her home who were about to begin their studies for the priesthood. Aunt Elsie cooked a delicious roast beef dinner. They delighted her with their accounts of the examinations by the professors, their lunch in the refectory, and the benediction service by Monsignor Connors.

Thomas's father lit up a cigar as he sat back listening to their animated discussions. "You fellas have had quite a day!"

"I think we should start back home," Thomas's mother began. "You fellas look exhausted!"

They all thanked Aunt Elsie for the enjoyable dinner.

"I know you boys will soon be back here. You know you're always welcome here. So, if you get some time off after you begin your studies for the priesthood, remember, I will always love to have you over."

Thomas kissed his aunt. "Aunt Elsie, you've been so generous to us. I hope we can indeed get together again soon."

When Leo returned home that evening he was trying to deal with all that had happened. As he opened the front door he could see his dad seated in his recliner watching a professional wrestling match as he waited for his wife to come downstairs. They were going out for their usual Saturday night of dinner and dancing.

"Hey there, how did it go?"

As far back as Leo could remember, his dad had never in his life called Leo by his first name. It was especially odd, Leo often thought, because he was "Leo, Jr." But the closest his father ever got was "son" or "boy." And those words on only a few occasions, like the time when Leo was paralyzed, and when he was accepted for the seminary exam. There was some kind of indefinable barrier that existed, preventing him from calling Leo by his name. Leo could never understand it, nor did he feel comfortable enough to ask him why. It contributed significantly to his feeling of separation from his father.

"I thought I did well on the examinations, dad. I mean, most of the questions were familiar, so I was able to answer them." His mom was coming down the steps as he spoke. She walked over to Leo.

"How was everything, Leo? Did you have any problems with the exams or interviews? You look so *tired*, Leo. Did you have anything to eat? You must be hungry."

"Mom, mom, they had lunch for us at the seminary, and Thomas's aunt had us over for an early dinner in Philadelphia before we left for home."

"I'm so glad everything worked out all right for you today. Try to get a good night's sleep." She was studying his face carefully. "You look so happy. I'm so proud of you, Leo."

His mom and dad left for their weekly evening of dining and dancing. Leo smiled as he watched them drive away. Then he checked in on little Donna, before going to his room. He changed into his light blue chinos and white T- shirt. Seated at his desk he opened the center drawer and removed the *Saint Joseph's Missal*. He lifted out the dry leaf from between the pages and kissed it.

"I know I'll make it," he whispered.

This time Leo did not have long to wait. When he got home from work on the Monday after the Fourth of July weekend, his mother was waiting for him in the kitchen with a letter in her hand.

"This is from the Bishop of Allentown!" she said, handing it to him.

The letter was dated July 1, 1961, exactly one week after he had completed the entrance examination. He began reading:

> *Dear Mr. Weber:*
>
> *I am pleased to inform you that you have been accepted as a student for the priesthood in the Diocese of Allentown and that you will begin your studies at the Seminary of Saint Francis in September. Please report to the seminary on Wednesday, September 6, 1961, no later than 4:00 P.M., D.S.T. With sincere—*

Leo raised his eyes from the letter, dropping it as he turned toward his mother. No words were needed. Two years had passed since both had stood in that same room together following Leo's surprise announcement about his future plans. With all that had happened since that time—all the delays and setbacks—he had finally succeeded. His mother was by his side, but now, instead of asking him to wait, she was praying for his dream to come true. She wiped tears from her eyes, stepped back and looked at Leo.

"I'm so happy for you, Leo. You worked so hard for this, and now you are ready to begin your new life."

"I'll always love you, mom."

News of Leo's acceptance by the seminary quickly spread throughout the family and neighborhood. His grandmother walked across the street from her home as soon as his mom telephoned her, barely able to contain her joy. Entering the house she embraced Leo. He had enjoyed so many wonderful times with his grandmother over the years. Whenever he was ill as a child and couldn't go to school, she would take care of him so his mom, who was working part-time at a local clothing manufacturing plant, wouldn't miss any days. He liked to watch his grandmother bake strudels and pies, and was delighted when she let him help her roll out the dough. He remembered that the dough was so thin he could see through it. He enjoyed playing in her backyard near a giant peach tree and being asked to help pick the softball-size fruit for use in her popular pies. Later, his grandmother would spend Saturday evenings with him and his sisters so his parents could go out for the night. When he was in high school he spent many a Sunday afternoon at his grandmother's house playing pinochle with her and several of his aunts and uncles.

Leo had no sooner kissed his grandmother when a loud knock on the door interrupted his reminiscence. It was Nick, the owner of the grocery store halfway down the street. He was a part-time barber, as well, and he enjoyed betting on the horses, but his real dream in life was to become a judge. He and Leo had become good friends over the years. Leo loved hearing his stories about the race track. Nick had told Leo the story of the day he won the daily double so many times that Leo could recite it word for word. But he never tired of hearing it.

"Leo, congratulations, son," he shouted as he rushed into the living room. "Look, I've only got one thing to ask of you—I want to be an altar boy for your first Mass. What do you think, Leo?"

"You know, Nick, that's ten years away! But I'll make a note of it and call you ten years from now."

By the time Leo's dad got home, a small, excited crowd had gathered in the living room. His father knew immediately what the news was.

"So, you got *in*, son!"

"Yeah, dad, here's the letter from the Bishop of Allentown. I've been accepted to study for the priesthood."

His father held the letter in his hand, studying it, then looked up at Leo. "You've been waiting a long time for this. I know how hard you've worked all year to earn this," he said, placing his left arm on Leo's shoulder as he handed the letter back to him. "I'm sure you'll—"

"Congratulations, Mr. Weber," Nick interrupted. "You've got quite a son here! You know I'm going to be an altar boy for his first Mass."

"Nick, I'm sure you'll do a great job, too." Mr. Weber said, smiling at Nick's enthusiasm.

As Leo's mother made her way from the kitchen through the crowd of friends and neighbors, bearing bowls of potato chips and pretzels, she saw his dad. Their eyes met, realizing this was the beginning of a new kind of life for their family.

After the living room and dining room had emptied and the final excited good-byes had been exchanged, Leo sat down with his mother and father. They were still trying to absorb the news. Their lives would soon change.

"It's so hard to believe this is really happening," Leo said. "You know, I've been thinking about this and planning for more than two years. Now, it's all going to happen. It just seems—"

"Leo, you're going to have a wonderful life," his mother said. "We're all so proud of you." Sitting next to him on the sofa, across from his father, she placed her hand on Leo's.

"Yeah, before you know it, you'll be giving us your blessing!" his dad quipped.

"You've both been so good to me. I've been so lucky."

The following morning, Leo went to the office to tell Irv the good news.

His good friend shook his hand. "God bless you, Leo. I know you're going to be very successful. You're such a hard worker, and I know how much you have wanted to do this. If there's ever anything I can do as you work toward your goal, make sure you let me know, my boy."

"Thanks, Irv."

Later, at lunch, Leo and four of his co-workers from the stock room had just finished their hamburger barbecues and french fries at the Greek luncheonette, and were ordering their black-and-white milkshakes. The usual chatter about their hard jobs, the hot dates they had over the Fourth of July holiday, and their plans for new conquests during the coming weekend filled the lunch hour. Still a popular hit, Paul Anka's "Put Your Head on My Shoulder" was playing on the jukebox in the background. When Leo sensed an opening in his buddies' banter, he jumped in.

"Hey fellas, I've, uh, got something I want to tell you."

"Ooohhhhh, here it *comes*," crowed Billy. "You and Samantha, huh? You're finally going together, right?"

"Nah, c'mon, Billy." Leo said. "Look, I want to tell you all that I've been working hard over the past year to get ready for an examination for admission into the seminary. I'm going to be leaving the restaurant supply company in September to begin studying to become a Catholic priest."

Their booth suddenly grew totally silent. All around it diners were engaged in lively conversations, and waitresses floated about, joking with their customers. But the group could not process what they had just heard. They sat staring at Leo, trying to come to grips with the startling announcement.

At that moment, Alex, the luncheonette owner's son, was passing by the booth. "Hey, guys, what's going on? Who *died*?"

Mickey broke the ice. "You're not gonna believe *this* one, Alex," he said, grabbing Alex by the arm. " Leo's gonna be a *priest*."

"Does *Samantha* know about this, buddy?" Alex asked, poking Leo's arm. "You know, I've seen you two in here for lunch a few times—she sure looked starry-eyed to me, buddy."

"We've only had lunch a few times when I was training her," Leo said. "It's not like we're close or anything."

"My uncle's been a priest for almost twenty-five years," Alex volunteered. "And he's married! You should be a Greek Orthodox priest, Leo, then you could get married, too. You could have it *all*. You know what I mean?" His laughter only emphasized Leo's stone silence. "Well, good luck, Leo, I'm gonna miss you and Samantha around here." Laughing even harder now, he sauntered back to the kitchen.

The other guys—George, Ron and Billy—started punching Leo's arms.

"Yeah!" they exclaimed.

George was an avowed atheist who used every opportunity to proclaim his lack of faith publicly. He and Leo had engaged in many heated debates about religion during the past two years. When John Kennedy announced his plans to run for president, George was convinced that the young senator's campaign was being financed by the Vatican as part of the Roman Catholic Church's massive conspiracy to take over the government of the United States. But with all of their deep disagreements, Leo and George continued to be good friends. They went to the movies and often went to the local minor league baseball games together. George had an extensive stamp collection. He proudly showed Leo hundreds of the first-day-covers that he had carefully placed in dark blue leather binders. He was especially proud of his new acquisitions, the Naval Aviation 50th Anniversary and the Liberty Bell Air Mail stamps. He also made his own wine. Leo's favorite was strawberry. They had many good times sharing a bottle of George's homemade vintage while looking through his stamp collection or sometimes playing blackjack. Leo was alarmed, however, when George showed him the pipe bombs he had made and kept hidden in his basement. George tried to reassure Leo that the bombs would only be used to defend himself "from the communists" or—he half-joked—"from the pope, himself."

George gave Leo an old crystal radio set he was no longer using. It consisted of a wire about four feet long with a tiny metal box on one end and a small earpiece on the other. Leo tied the wire around the metal frame of his bed, as George had instructed, where it made reception of radio waves possible. Although it could pick up only one local radio station, Leo thoroughly enjoyed it. His parents never knew he had it. It made no noise, so it did not disturb his family. Many evenings after he got into bed, he would insert the earpiece into his right ear and tune in to his favorite disc jockey, Darryl James. On many a night the DJ's light banter preceding and following each popular song he played entertained Leo into the early morning hours. Leo would often wake up in the morning with the earpiece still in place, the daily greeting of the Reverend Herb Millbrook, pastor of the local Gospel Revival Church, arousing him to consciousness: "Good morning! I have good news for you today—Jesus loves you!" Leo often playfully exacerbated George by quoting the Reverend's Good news: "Good morning, George, I have good news for you today ...," but deep inside, Leo hoped that one day he would be able to change George's thinking about God. When the restaurant supply company's basketball team began their previous season, Leo was astonished when he saw that the schedule included a game with the Gospel Revival Church.

"George, you're not going to believe this—we're going head-to-head this season with our friend, Reverend Millbrook."

"Whoa!" said George, getting a sudden burst of energy sparked by Leo's announcement. "I can't wait to go one-on-one with that guy!"

Leo assumed the preacher would coach the Revival Church's team. So he was amazed on the night of the game when he learned that Reverend Millbrook would not only coach the team, but also would start in one of the forward positions. The Reverend was five-feet, five-inches tall and weighed about 185 pounds. Shortly after their opening prayer, and the tip-off, the "Revival" guys turned ugly. The Reverend and his followers used typical football moves on the basketball court, throwing body blocks at Leo and his teammates—and hacking them as they tried to score. Leo thought there were more personal fouls called on the Reverend Millbrook's Revival team, than on any other team since they began playing in the league. George and Leo laughed hysterically after the game. The Revival team lost by one point, mainly because George had "accidentally" body-checked the Reverend late in the fourth quarter, putting him out of the game. Leo never listened to the Good News on his crystal radio set again without some laughter about his encounter with the "other side" of the good Reverend.

The group finished their black-and-whites at the luncheonette, then rushed for the door since they were well over their lunch hour. It was a jostling group that headed back to the supply company two blocks away. Leo held his own with all their antics, because deep down he knew his friends were rooting for him. Within minutes of their returning to work, everyone in the company knew about Leo's plans. He had a difficult time getting back to his work because of the continual interruptions over the afternoon from his friends and well-wishers, Samantha among them.

"Leo," she whispered, appearing in front of his workstation. "I just heard the news about your plans to leave here and study for the priesthood. I'm, uh, I am really *surprised.* I just, um, I guess I've never thought about you in that kind of life, Leo. You've been such a terrific friend over the past year, so helpful to me when I started working here. I hope everything works out okay for you, Leo—with your studies, and … I hope you'll be happy." Despite her efforts to appear polite, Leo could see that she was fighting back tears.

Leo leaned on the edge of the workstation that separated them, moving closer to her. Looking into her eyes, he told Samantha how much he enjoyed their times together at lunch when she first began there; how quickly she had learned the office duties he had taught her, and how glad he always was to help her when questions arose about any of her responsibilities. Samantha's eyes were glistening. Her emotional response surprised Leo, then he remembered how Irv tried to get him to ask her out. He never intended to lead her on. He just thought they were good friends.

Leo watched Samantha as she walked away, her head bowed slightly. He was thinking about Terry. How difficult it was when they broke up the year before. How angry Terry had been.

As the drivers returned from their deliveries, Leo was greeted with all kinds of reactions to the news. Some of the guys just could not understand it. One of them, Ernie, his golfing buddy, actually tried to talk Leo out of his "crazy" idea. Leo laughed them all off, waiting for his friend Tony to return. He wanted Tony to hear about the news directly from him. When Tony backed his truck into the warehouse garage Leo left his workstation and walked across the floor to meet him, stepping into the truck before Tony had a chance to get out.

"Hi, Tony, how did it go out there today?"

"Hot as hell, and the asshole drivers on Route 22 just keep getting worse all the time. I swear to Christ that one of these days they're gonna run me right off the fuckin' road at dead man's curve, near Easton!"

Leo was trying to find the right words to tell his good friend the news. They had so many fun times together, but now he had to be serious.

"What's wrong Leo? You're not gonna *quit* are you?" He twisted around in the driver's seat to face Leo directly.

Leo began, awkwardly revealing what he had been pursuing over the past year and how, finally, he had been accepted for admission to Saint Francis Seminary.

The widest smile Leo had ever seen on him seemed to divide his friend's normally serious face in two distinct parts. The lower part began speaking: "Leo ... you're a sly fox. Yeah ... a real *fox*. So *that's* why you wanted, uh, why we went to that open house last fall. This explains your excitement as we walked around the seminary halls and rooms, and that look on your face in the chapel that day. You were checking it all out to make sure that's where you wanted to be. I always *thought* you were a smart kid, now I know for sure. This really floors me, buddy."

Leo tried to explain that he had no intention of deceiving his friend; that he just didn't know what was going to happen, asking Tony to imagine how embarrassing it would have been if he had announced his goal—and then not been accepted by the seminary.

"Okay, Yeah, I get it. Well, look, let me get my shit together here, and we can go over to my place and celebrate with a couple of brews."

Leo called his mom, telling her he would be getting home late. He finished the delivery schedules for the following day, placing them on the counter of his workstation. Then he walked past the many rows of shelves that housed the chef hats, uniforms, linens, glasses, cookware, dishes and kitchen accessories. Thoughts about his time there, and all the good friends he had made raced through his mind. He truly loved the place and all of the characters he had grown up with over the past six years. He left the office and walked down the block to his car. Climbing inside he sat there resting his head far back on the seat. After two years of keeping his important secret from his best friends, he could finally relax. Relief streamed through his body as he started the car. Leo drove up to the bake shop that he and his buddies had subsidized at their many hundreds of coffee breaks over the years; he turned right and headed for Tony's house

Tony lived in a mobile home just outside the city. He and his wife had been divorced shortly after he returned home from the service. He had lived alone ever since. Leo had barely settled into a chrome-lined kitchen chair when Tony whisked two *Neuweiler* beers out of the refrigerator and popped them open.

"Good luck, Leo. You really got me *this* time, buddy!"

"Cheers!"

Tony plopped several *Oscar Mayer* hot dogs into a pot of boiling water, and heated up a can of baked beans as the two chatted about their visit to the seminary.

"So, when will you be able to hear my confession?"

"*Whoa, Tony!* That'll take someone far more experienced than me to deal with," Leo laughed. "And besides, it's going to take ten years to complete the seminary program."

"I hope I'm still around to see you get ordained," he deadpanned.

As they finished eating and were working on their second beer, Tony talked about his ex-wife. He was glad they had no kids, especially with the way their marriage had fallen apart. They talked about George and all of his antics at the restaurant supply company, the pranks that he would pull on Tony with the other guys. They had a lot of fun reminiscing. Tony would miss seeing his good friend around, but wished him luck with his career.

The familiar sight of his dad in the recliner watching television, and his mom asleep on the sofa greeted him once again upon his arriving home a little past eight o'clock. When he closed the door behind him, his mom awoke.

"Leo, how did everything go at work today?"

"Mom, the guys were just wonderful. You know, they had a good time kidding around and all, but they were all supportive, and—"

"Are you hungry, Leo? Grammy made some apple strudel today. There's a full pan of it in the kitchen."

After gobbling down two pieces of his grandmother's delicious apple strudel, he went upstairs to his room. Each night all summer he had been lighting candles next to the pictures of the Blessed Mother and Pope John XXIII while listening to his new record album, *Hymns of Heaven on Earth*, featuring one of Leo's favorites, the *Pange Lingua*, performed by the Sistine Choir. This night he was more moved by the sacred music than he ever had been in the past. "Maybe it's the *Neuweiler*," he mused aloud, thinking of Tony. But certainly the relief he felt from breaking his long silence about his future plans had lifted his spirits dramatically. He slept more soundly that evening than he had in many months.

When he got back to the restaurant supply company the next morning, things were noticeably different. The guys, usually quite vocal and animated, seemed subdued. They greeted him courteously, but without their usual funny remarks, or the profanity that normally punctuated every other sentence they uttered.

During the coffee break at the bakeshop, Leo finally had his say. "Look, guys, you've all been acting kind of strange today. It's as if I told you I was gonna die or something yesterday. Going to the seminary is almost like attending college, except that you have to pray before and after every class and meal, and spend practically all day in the chapel on Sunday. But we are allowed home for the holidays, spring break and summer recess. So I'll be seeing you guys around."

"You mean they let you go home?" said Billy, faking disbelief.

"Wait," Mickey interrupted. "I thought you never get out of there until you're a priest. Don't they shave the hair off the top of your head and dress you in a brown cloak?"

"You know, like Friar Tuck," George added. He folded his hands in mock prayer, blessing everyone.

"Amen," said Leo. "Now let's all get back to work—we're running late again."

After that bull session, things were back to normal around the supply company.

Preparations were underway for Ellen's August wedding. Leo had already been fitted for his rental tuxedo. *My last night out before the strict seminary routine*, he thought, looking in the mirror at his formally-clad body. He knew the seminary rules prohibited drinking alcoholic beverages of any kind under threat of immediate expulsion, and, of course, there would be no more nights out dancing. Leo's mom was beside herself with the details of the ceremony and reception. Leo was able to get a good deal on all of the floral arrangements from his fellow employee, Billy, whose cousin owned a flower shop in the city. So that took some of the pressure off his mom's overburdened shoulders. Ellen's fiancé was not affiliated with any religion, and was outspokenly hostile to most of them. So, Leo took on the role of mediator: trying to bridge the gap between having no religious service whatsoever, and having a service in the Catholic Church without a Mass. Father Joe offered valuable assistance, and a deal was struck—the service would be held in church, but, the prospective groom insisted he would not kneel during the Mass, whether padded kneelers were provided or not. The reception was planned with the help of his Uncle Stan, a member of the Austrian-Hungarian social club in town.

Events were moving quickly in the Weber household. In the span of just a year, Leo had been accepted by the seminary, and Ellen had set a date for her wedding. In one of those ironic twists of fate they would both be leaving home and moving to Philadelphia in the same month. Ellen's fiancé was a contractor whose work took him mostly to the city, so they had decided to relocate there for his convenience. On Sunday afternoon Leo and Ellen sat on the living room floor with a street map of Philadelphia spread out in front of them, each searching to identify the locations of the new residences where they would be moving. Ellen would be relocating to the West Oak Lane section of the city, and Leo, near the Main Line. Leo glanced at his mother as she sat watching their enthusiastic reactions to the map—how close they were going to be to each other, and how far away from her. Their mom was fighting back tears. She was about to lose two of her children at the same time. It was a heart-wrenching moment for her—one of those passages in life that, although inevitable, creates feelings of irrevocable loss.

On the following Saturday, Leo, Patrick and Thomas drove to Philadelphia to purchase black cassocks and Roman collars—the required garb for all seminarians. Thomas drove his father's car, fighting off constant interruptions from Patrick over which turn to make on what street and when.

"Wait a minute, *Thomas*, we're going the wrong way. You should've made a turn back there," Patrick scolded.

"Now just a *minute*," Thomas would object, "I've been visiting my aunt down here for years and I know which way to go!"

Leo sat in the back seat amused by the act with which he had become so familiar over the past year. They found the store with no wrong turns. A few minutes later Leo stood on the fitting block before the tailor's mirror. Two weeks earlier, he had been greeted from just such a tailor's mirror by a young man in a formal tuxedo. Now he was looking at a priestly young figure wearing a black cassock and Roman collar, about to enter a different kind of world. Leo's mom had already bought him the black suit, black ties and white shirts that he would have to wear for all public functions outside the seminary, and during his first month in the seminary. They all stopped by Thomas's aunt's house in the Spring Garden neighborhood for lunch before returning home.

The ceremony in the church went well, except for a couple of glitches. The bridegroom, who had refused to kneel when the service was rehearsed, inexplicably did so during the ceremony, even though no kneeling benches had been set up. His unexpected move caused a bit of a stir as Ellen, startled, tried to kneel on the floor while adjusting her wedding gown. Leo, for his part, had rolled the white carpet down the aisle the wrong way. Instead of beginning at the altar railing, where the bride and groom would meet before stepping up into the sanctuary, Leo started in the rear of the church, leaving a large heap of carpet at the step in front of the sanctuary, creating a barrier that the bride and groom would have to step over.

Billy's cousin had created glorious white and silver floral arrangements that included Ellen's favorite—white lilies. The wedding reception included about one hundred guests. Polkas and rock 'n' roll kept them entertained all night. Leo enjoyed the wine and savored the last vintage that he would taste for a long time to come. He danced with all of his aunts; and when he and his mom were dancing she shared her mixed feelings of joy and anguish at the thought of the abrupt changes about to transform their lives.

"Leo, I still can't believe you're both going to leave at the same time. I just don't know what I'm going to do without you around the house."

The reality that he was about to leave home tugged at his heart. He had yearned for this to happen for so long. Now, it was time to change his life, to pursue his dream, to leave those he loved more than anything in the world.

"I love you, Leo. I want you to be happy, that's all."

They embraced when the music stopped and then returned to the table to join their family. The evening was winding down. Leo's mother admitted that the planning for the wedding left her totally exhausted. His dad joked that it left him totally broke. Leo's godmother kidded him about his mishandling the white carpet at the service. His Uncle Evan, an excellent dancer, was just completing his last circuit of the dance floor after Leo's father had paid the band to play an extra half-hour. Ellen and Alan had left for their honeymoon. A new kind of life was beginning for all of them.

After all the hyper-activity surrounding the preparations for the wedding, calm settled over the Weber household as the week began.

"Hello, *Leo*? This is Ronald Grim," an unfamiliar voice intoned after Leo picked up the phone on the Tuesday night following the wedding. "Leo, I'm the Grand Knight of the Knights of Columbus here in town. I want to congratulate you for your decision to become a priest and for your success in gaining admission to Saint Francis Seminary next month."

"Hi, uh, Mr. Grim. Thanks so much. That's very thoughtful of you," said Leo, intimidated somewhat by the "Grand Knight" part.

"Please, please call me Ronald," the excited voice continued. "Look, I want to take you, and your friends Patrick and Thomas, out for a night on the town before all of you begin the, uh, rigors of the seminary. Are you free on Saturday night?"

"Yes! Sure, Mr., uh, I mean, Ronald."

"Okay, how about I stop by your home on Saturday evening around six-thirty on my way to pick up the other two fellows?"

"That'll be fine, Ronald. Thanks. Do you know how to get here?"

"Yes, yes. I've already worked that all out, son."

Leo was elated as he hung up the telephone. Turning to his mom and dad, he said, "You're not going to believe this, but the Grand Knight of the Knights of Columbus is taking me and the guys out for dinner on Saturday night." He remembered the Knights of Columbus from the Kennedy Inaugural ceremonies and parade, and was now dazzled at the thought of being taken to dinner by one of them.

"Do you think he'll be dressed in his plumes and carrying a sword?" his dad asked, laughing.

"I don't think so. They only wear them for ceremonies."

They all laughed and went back to watching the *Milton Berle Show.*

At 6:25 on the following steamy August Saturday evening, a long, shiny black Cadillac *Fleetwood* convertible appeared in front of Leo's house to the astonishment of about a dozen of his relatives and neighbors sitting on their front porches trying to keep cool.

After Ronald tooted the horn, Leo parted one of the venetian blinds and peeked out.

"Oh my God, mom. Look at *this*."

His mom and dad looked out the window to see the Grand Knight in all of his glory—even without the ceremonial garb—seated behind the wheel of the long black vehicle with its glistening chrome. The fins on the back of the car seemed to stretch out to the house next door.

Leo slipped into his black suit-jacket and began to leave.

"Have a good time, Leo!" his mom said.

In an instant Leo was inside the exotic automobile, extending his hand to Ronald.

"It's a real pleasure to meet you in person, Ronald. Thanks so much for stopping by for me." As Leo nestled back into the cushy black leather seat, he waved to his grandmother and aunts gawking at the spectacle from their front porches across the street.

"The pleasure is certainly mine," Ronald said. "God bless you. I'm so thrilled to meet you at last. We've been talking about the three of you all summer at our meetings. What a blessing for us to have three young men committing themselves to serve the Church. Leo, you boys are certainly blessed. What a wonderful life to have been chosen to follow Christ. We are all so proud of you fellas."

"Well, um, thank you. Thanks, Ronald."

Ronald drove up to Fifth Street and turned right toward Patrick's house. Patrick, waiting out front when the car pulled up, virtually leaped into the back seat of the convertible as it pulled over to the curb.

"Hi there, I'm Patrick. You must be Sir Ronald." Patrick's eyes roamed the magnificent dashboard with all of its chrome dials and fluorescent gauges.

"Yes, I'm Ronald. It's great to meet you at last, Patrick."

Thomas lived just three blocks south. He, too, was anxiously awaiting the Grand Knight's arrival. He trotted down the front steps of his home and greeted his host.

"Hello, Mr. Grim. It's an honor to be with you. What a beautiful car!"

"The honor is truly mine," Ronald responded.

Ronald drove them to the Village Inn, one of the city's most popular restaurants. It had been a fixture in Allentown for decades. They each ordered the house specialty, King-cut Prime Rib, with luscious pop-overs. Ronald selected a bottle of St. Estephe to complement the beef. He monopolized the conversation during most of the evening, asking them questions about how they had decided to become priests. After dinner, Ronald reached inside his coat pocket and handed each of them a Cuban cigar. Thomas, an avid cigar-smoker, was the first to light up, and was already puffing away before Patrick and Leo managed to remove the tips of the *Corona*s. Ronald paid the bill, and all three exited the restaurant in an upbeat, giddy mood.

Next, Ronald drove them through nearby Dorney Park, which, as usual on Saturday evenings, was mobbed with young people enjoying the carnival atmosphere. As the shiny black convertible moved through the crowded amusement park, the sight of three young men wearing identical black suits, white shirts and thin black ties seated in the back seat of a Cadillac convertible with its top down, smoking big cigars, created a furor. Most of the crowd thought the guys were the singing group that was playing at the park's Castle Garden Theater that evening, and thus were screaming and shouting at them. Before the situation got out of control, the traffic speed picked up, and they were exiting the park.

"Whoa! That was exciting," Patrick said. "Let's go around again!"

Ronald laughed. "I knew you boys would get a kick out of that!"

Leo's parents had already gotten home from their evening out, and were sitting at the kitchen table enjoying a late-night snack as Leo, feeling a bit tipsy, burst through the door. He was thinking that the second bottle of wine had really not been necessary.

"It looks like someone's had a good time tonight," his mom said, noticing Leo's uncertain gait as he entered the kitchen.

"Mom, it was one of the most unbelievable nights. Wait 'til I tell you what Ronald did."

Leo proceeded to recount the whole story about their evening at the best restaurant in the city—the prime rib, the French wine, the Cuban cigars, followed by their parade through the crowded park as would-be rock stars. His parents laughed along as Leo joined them at the table, dreamily recounting the tale of his last night out on the town. He kissed them goodnight.

Slightly intoxicated by the fascinating evening and the red wine, Leo tossed and turned as his familiar, haunting, erotic nemesis returned. He was sexually aroused, unable to control the passionate surge that suddenly overwhelmed him. In two weeks he would be entering the seminary. Chastity was essential. Surrendering to this latest temptation would destroy the future he had dreamed about for so long. He thought about the monks who had flagellated themselves in order to thwart the temptations of the flesh. Saint Peter Damian, for one, often whipped himself until he bled.

Leo remembered the sewing needle he had placed in his night stand a few months before. The room was dark. He reached over to the nightstand, fumbling around for the four-inch needle and removed it. He pointed it just above the middle of his stiffened shaft. The first jab hurt, but failed to diminish his sexual arousal. He jabbed again, harder. Then again. "Oh, *God!*" The stinging pain rid him at last of his passion. Falling back on the pillow, he felt blood running from his penis and frantically yanked a handful of Kleenex from the box on his nightstand to help stanch the flow. He lay awake worrying whether he had caused irreparable damage to himself. But even greater was his relief that he had overcome the one last obstacle threatening his goal.

Leo awoke groggily the next morning. Getting out of bed, he pushed the sheets forward. He was shocked by the sight of the bloody tissues and the red stains blotching the clean white sheets—sanguine testimony to the success of his nocturnal cleansing ritual. Then he panicked. *What's mom going to think when she sees this?*

Leo turned the sheets forward completely and gathered the bloodied Kleenex into a ball. He couldn't find the needle at first, but there it was: on the floor a bit under the bed. He went into the bathroom and carefully examined himself. He felt some pain, but except for the clotted dots that remained where he had pierced it, his penis appeared to be uninjured. He washed off the needle before returning it to the drawer. After showering, he dressed and went down to the kitchen for breakfast. It was a typical Sunday morning at the Weber home. While his dad was getting the beef roast ready for the oven, his mother was mixing a confetti-cake recipe for the early dinner that they enjoyed every Sunday after the High Mass at noon. When his dad left the room, Leo whispered to his mother.

"Mom, I had a bad nosebleed during the night. Sorry, but I really messed up the sheets."

"Are you all right, Leo? You know you had quite an evening and you're not used to that kind of night out."

"Yeah, I think you're right, mom, but I'm okay."

Only two weeks remained before Leo would leave his home and those he loved most. His new residence would be the spectacular fortress rising majestically in the middle of 140 acres of green fields and trees. His new family would be several hundred young men who shared his noble vision.

On Monday, Irv asked Leo what he and the employees of the restaurant supply company could do to help him with the items he would need to begin his studies. They were planning a farewell party for him. The Friday afternoon coffee break was relocated from the tiny bake shop to the supply company's large stockroom. Leo found himself wiping away tears more than once as he chatted for the last time with his fellow employees. Then, with an air of triumph, he cut the cake—a beautifully decorated dark chocolate confection topped with a large white cross made of vanilla icing.

He addressed the dozen or so of his fellow employees remaining at the end of the party. "All of you guys have been such great friends to me over the past six years. I started working here when I was only fourteen years old. It was my first real job—not counting my newspaper route."

"Well, you must have learned something with that," Irv interjected, "because you sure as hell have done a great job for us here."

Catcalls and whistles followed.

"Hey, guys," Irv continued, "you know we're all going to miss Leo around here, and we hope he'll come back to visit us when he gets the time."

They all cheered in agreement, applauding their departing friend. Billy and Mickey then appeared, struggling noticeably under the weight of the main farewell gift.

"Jesus Christ! This fucker's almost big enough to get buried in!" Billy exclaimed as they lowered the unwrapped gift to the floor. "Uh ... sorry, Leo," he then added, suddenly aware how loudly he had spoken.

Leo had told Irv days earlier that he would need to buy a locker for storage of his personal items at the seminary. The footlocker was the perfect present for him.

Leo reminisced about the interesting times they had together, telling all of them how much he would miss them and how much he valued the support they had given him during the past year.

Irv shook Leo's hand and patted him on the back as the guys from the stock room and warehouse crowded around, wishing him success. The delivery drivers were returning, so it was time to get back to work after what undoubtedly had been the longest coffee break in the history of the Lehigh Restaurant Supply Company. After the party, Irv took Leo aside and handed him three one-hundred-dollar bills.

"Leo, keep this for the many expenses I know you'll have to face. Jonathan is in college, and I know how costs can increase during the school year."

"You've always been so generous to me, Irv. I truly appreciate it."

The end of his last day at the restaurant supply company had arrived. Leo was struggling with conflicting feelings of separation from his old friends and enthusiasm for the new life that he was about to begin. After loading the footlocker into Leo's car, all of the guys stopped by his workstation to say their good-byes. He told them how much he looked forward to seeing them at his Christmas break. Alone now, he looked around the old warehouse, walking through the long aisles where scores of old, grey storage bins, each twelve feet high, contained the familiar restaurant and kitchen supplies. He thought about all the great times he had there and the friends he would miss so much as he walked out the door and headed home.

Leo helped his mother sew laundry labels on every item of his clothing as the seminary guidelines called for. He had to go shopping for several white, collarless shirts that would accommodate the Roman collars, part of the required attire at the seminary. It was Thursday evening. His mom accompanied him to Hess's Department store, where they found the shirts he needed. At the Mohican Bakery, they ordered the cake for his farewell party. After stopping by Fanny Farmer's for a box of chocolate-covered mixed nuts to take home for his dad and sisters, they stopped at Adams Clothing Store to buy several pairs of black chino trousers Leo would need to wear under his long black cassock. Then they walked around the northwest corner of Center Square past Whelan's Drug Store and headed for their favorite dining venue—the Marble Bar—as they had done so many times over the years. They sat in the cavernous restaurant located in what had once been the lobby of the old Dime Bank building, under the crystal chandeliers. The shiny white marble floor reflected the lights from above. Enjoying their menu favorite, fried chicken-in-the-basket, their eyes were fixed on each other.

"I can't believe there are only a few days left before the seminary year starts. It's all going so fast, mom."

"We're going to have a big crowd for Saturday afternoon," his mother said, shifting the topic. "Both of your grandmothers will be there and nearly all your aunts and uncles, too. I also invited all of the neighbors. The house will be packed. So you'll have quite a send off, Leo."

"Wow, what a farewell party, mom! I may not want to leave."

His mother winced.

After dinner they caught the 10th Street Loop bus for their journey home.

His dad and sister were waiting for the expected chocolate treats their mother never failed to bring home from her shopping trips.

"Dad, I think I'm ready. We got it all done tonight!" Leo said, as his dad opened the bag containing the chocolate.

Leo was up early on Saturday morning. Immediately after breakfast he began cleaning the living room and dining room. His mother was busy scrubbing down the kitchen. Half an hour later as his dad waxed the floors, Leo left to pick up his farewell cake. The ride through the city in his '54 Chevy evoked many memories. As he drove by Hess's Department Store, he thought about the time he had been stopped by a police officer for driving through a caution light in front of store, when his dad had taken him out for a driving lesson. *This may be the last time I take this old baby out around town*, he mused. His father had arranged to sell the automobile for Leo. Seminary rules prohibited students from keeping cars at the school, so it made no sense to leave it parked on the street for months at a time. The sale of the car helped with Leo's tuition and book expenses. When Leo returned home with the cake, the house was already buzzing with the dozen or so guests who had arrived early. He placed the cake on the kitchen table and helped his mother serve drinks to the early birds.

"Here ya go, Nick," he said.

"*Saluta,* Leo! God bless you, son."

"*Saluta*, Nick, my future altar boy!"

By three o'clock in the afternoon the Weber house was filled to capacity. Some of the neighbors sought out the back yard to relieve the overcrowding. His aunts brought some food for the feast. The guests were happily chomping on meatballs, cold cuts, macaroni salad, beef barbecues, deviled eggs, potato salad and homemade coleslaw.

Leo's paternal grandmother lived out of town, so he saw her rather infrequently, mostly on holidays. Although she was not a Catholic, she was thrilled by his decision to pursue the priesthood. Her husband, who had died shortly before Leo was born, had been a Lutheran minister, and she saw this occasion as one to celebrate his career in the ministry in conjunction with Leo's wonderful goal. Leo told her how much he appreciated her encouragement, noting that his grandfather's work would surely continue to inspire him.

The party reached full steam. As the afternoon wore on and the food began to disappear, Leo's mom emerged from the kitchen with the beautiful cake created by the Mohican Bakery. Everybody cheered as the cake came into view. Deep purple icing covered the chocolate cake. Its several layers were filled with strawberry cream filling. A miniature red-candied Bible lay atop the cake. Leo helped his mom clear a space for it in the center of the table.

"*Ser*-mon, *ser*-mon, *ser*-mon," his Uncle Evan began chanting.

Everybody joined in the chant.

Leo took no time obliging them. Remaining in front of the table next to the cake, he began speaking.

"Thanks so much for coming over today. You know, I love you all so much, and I'm really, *really* going to miss you. You've been my life for twenty years. This neighborhood is so warm. I've always loved listening to that mandolin on summer evenings, John. And the aromas of the food you all cook up every day is surely like nowhere else in he world. I've been so lucky to have grown up here with all of you." He wiped tears from his eyes and pushed on. "You've all been such good friends to me, even when I was a crazy kid riding that noisy orange crate contraption up and down the street in front of your houses." Leo had no doubt that the grinding roar of roller skates at both ends of a yard-long 2-by-4 reverberated even now in the nodding heads of just about everyone in the room. And smiles turned to laughter as Leo recalled how he and his cousins used to set up stunts to catapult his red *Radio Flyer* wagon two or three feet into the air off makeshift wooden ramps.

"Wednesday will be a big day for me. It's gonna be a whole new life. I know it's not going to be easy. Leaving all of you is really tough. And leaving this wonderful neighborhood will be painful. I'm going to miss all my aunts and uncles. You're so much fun all the time, especially when playing pinochle on Sunday afternoons. So, thanks again for coming. Thanks so much for your generous gifts. My mom and dad have been amazingly understanding through all this. They've always been there for me when I needed advice and help. Yes, I'll be praying for all of you, and your prayers will be essential for me to make it. I love you all so much."

His mom, also in tears, embraced him as cheers and shouts from the well-wishers filled the house. After dessert, as his friends and family were leaving, Leo embraced each and every one of them.

The next morning Leo went golfing with Ernie, one of his friends from the restaurant supply company. Ernie was the co-worker who had tried to talk Leo out of his "crazy idea" of becoming a priest. They had fun reminiscing about the old company as they played eighteen holes of golf.

"Well, good luck, kid. You know I've been kind of bitchy about your idea to become a priest. I only hope you'll be happy and that you're making the right decision for yourself. Let's get together for a round next time you're home. Take it easy, kid."

"Let's do that, Ernie. Thanks!"

When Leo returned home he showered and dressed for church. He took Donna with him to the Solemn High Mass at noon. Then they made their traditional visit to Heimbach's Bakery on their way home. It would be three months before he would again be having Sunday dinner at home with his entire family.

Leo spent most of Monday and Tuesday cleaning up his room and preparing his clothing for packing. As he opened the drawer of the nightstand he saw the sewing needle. He removed it. Twirling it slowly with his fingers, he gazed upon it as he might upon something sacred. *This saved me from destroying my dream.* He hesitated before returning it to his mother's sewing box. *From now on the seminary will provide all of the spiritual power that I need.*

Tuesday evening Leo visited his grandmother. Hugging her, he whispered his good-bye. Then it was on to see his aunts and uncles.

Each of them slipped him cash as they bid him farewell. Before heading home, he visited the grocery store to bid farewell to Nick.

"Don't forget," Nick said as Leo left the store, "I want to be an altar boy at your first Mass!"

Leo looked back. "I can hardly wait!"

CHAPTER 3

On Wednesday morning Leo awoke earlier than usual. He showered and dressed, then left for the seven o'clock Mass at his parish church.

"God, thank you for guiding me to this day," he prayed as he consumed the sacred host at communion.

Back at home everyone was caught up in a heightened state of activity. Leo's mother was folding the last part of the laundry she had done for him. She had his light blue serge suit dyed black at the neighborhood dry cleaning shop. He thought it looked terrific. His father dragged out the large footlocker the guys at the supply company had bought for him. Leo changed into his light blue chino trousers and white T-shirt. After devouring a bowl of shredded wheat with bananas, drenched in *Freeman's* milk, he went up to his bedroom to arrange the multitude of items to be jammed into the trunk. His mother prepared a variety of snacks, including her homemade chocolate chip cookies, his grandmother's apple strudel, Miller's pretzels, and a 24-count box of *Hershey's* milk chocolate candy bars. She placed the items in a huge pretzel can to help keep everything fresh. Leo told her earlier that he had learned on the day of the entrance examination that pretzel cans were the traditional method used by Saint Francis seminarians for storing snacks. By ten o'clock in the morning everything was assembled, ready to be loaded into his father's 1955 black Buick *Dynaflo*. His father took a day off from work so he could drive Leo to the seminary.

At eleven o'clock Leo, with his mom and dad and Donna, began the long-anticipated journey. It was a familiar route. They drove south on Route 309 and stopped for lunch at the old R & S Diner south of Quakertown around noon. Leo had accompanied his mother and father along that route to Germantown on several occasions when his mom had appointments with a prominent allergy specialist whose office was located on Green Lane, about ten miles north of the seminary. The specialist had virtually cured his mother of her asthma attacks with a prescription that had been produced specifically for her type of the illness.

The Buick entered the rambling grounds of Saint Francis Seminary at one-thirty in the afternoon. The frenetic scene that greeted them was almost comical. Cars lined the driveway along the back of the seminary property. Under the direction of older seminarians, who seemed simultaneously amused and annoyed, hundreds of young men with their families were unloading trunks, suitcases and... large pretzel cans. They were busily dragging these essential items up the courtyard to a vast porch lined with grey granite columns. Leo and his family were directed to the cavernous open dorm on the second floor of the main building, where he was shown his assigned bed, closet and sink, all of which looked exactly like the scores of other beds, closets and sinks lining the dormitory hall. Leo and his mom stared out the window next to his bed. A long rolling green lawn descended from the courtyard below them, ending at a tree-lined fence along the Old Limekiln Pike. Across the highway, the modern, pink-brick-and-glass building that housed a nationally prominent cardiac care hospital hovered majestically atop a steep hill.

Leo's father and sister were fascinated by the long line of narrow beds arranged on either side of the oversized room. Donna jumped onto the edge of the bed and sat there with her legs kicking. Her mother quickly lifted her off.

"Don't mess up that clean white bedspread," she said.

After looking around Leo's new sleeping quarters, they all went back downstairs and walked through the courtyard to the driveway where the Buick had been parked. The next move would be incredibly difficult. No one could speak. They all glanced around the grounds, then back at each other. Leo's mother broke the silence. She reached out and hugged him, fighting back her tears.

"We'll all be praying for you, Leo. This is a beautiful place. I know you'll be very happy here."

"Thanks, mom. I'll be praying for all of you, too. I'm going to miss you all so much."

"When are you coming *home?*" asked Donna.

"Not for a few months, hon. I'll be home for Thanksgiving, but you'll be able to come to see me here at the end of next month."

"Mommy, Leo's coming home for Thanksgiving!" Donna shouted.

Leo reached out, lifted up his baby sister, and kissed her.

"I love you, hon! Be a good girl for mommy and daddy on the way home."

His dad grabbed Leo's hand and shook it firmly. "Well, good luck, son," he said in a low, halting voice," I hope everything goes well for you here." His dad's eyes were tearing.

"I love you, Leo," his mom whispered.

They all packed into the car, waving through the open windows as they headed around the building to the main gate.

Leo turned toward the seminary, lowered his head, and closed his eyes, forcing back tears. He looked up, facing the back of his massive new residence and began walking toward the entrance, catching a last glimpse of his departing family out of the corner of his eye.

Chapel was scheduled for six o'clock. The 110 aspiring priests joined about 500 older colleagues for the *Angelus*. Leo and his fellow "new men" sat in the back of the chapel. Not until "Cassock Day" would they be authorized to sit in the sanctuary or wear the black cassock and Roman Collar. They watched with curiosity as their fellow seminarians filed into the chapel, clad in black clerical garb. The dark figures seemed to glide into genuflection just before making it to their assigned pews in the sanctuary. The new men were in awe of the magnificent Saint Matthias's Chapel. The richly-colored stained glass windows, set among the huge travertine marble stones, were lit by brass chandeliers.

"Thank you, Jesus, for helping me through my long journey," he prayed. "Keep me in your care and do not let me waiver." *Finally, I'm here, where I belong!*

Dinner was served after the benediction services. Leo was so hungry that any thought of criticizing the quality of the food was impossible. A visit to the chapel after dinner prepared them for the religious retreat that would begin on the following afternoon after the annual unpacking and storage rituals. Five days of "grand silence" were about to start. Leo was ready. Soon it was "lights out" at nine o'clock. Leo fell asleep faster than in recent memory.

At five-thirty the next morning, the clanging of the loudest bell that Leo had ever heard in his life jolted him awake. He would soon learn it was no ordinary bell. It was, indeed, *Vox Dei*, the Voice of God. The ear-splitting ring would soon command his every waking hour, announcing the beginning and end of all the various activities and classes each day. Until this morning Leo had awakened in his quiet, cozy, ten-by-twelve-foot bedroom. There, a window at the right side of his bed faced the side of the brick row house next door. The other window, at the foot of the bed, faced the long backyard. In the distance he could see the Tilghman Street Bridge leading to the east side of town. Today, however, as he opened his eyes, he was looking around a dormitory where scores of young men in various stages of undress were scampering toward their assigned sinks in the center of the hall. The metal-and-porcelain wash basins seemed to sprout like metallic plants from the dark brown linoleum of the dormitory floor. Leo sat up, groggily surveying the strange scene surrounding him. Some of the students, like Leo, sat motionless, hesitating to take the first step out of what seemed to be a time machine that had just landed from another world. Then Leo remembered he had only thirty minutes to wash, shave, dress and be ready for the six o'clock morning prayer. This would prove to be a difficult test for Leo. His heavy beard made shaving a tough task—shaving quickly would mean more razor cuts than usual. But he finished without any bloodletting, splashed on the strong green *Mennen* after shave tonic that his mother had packed for him, and was kneeling at the foot of his bed as the bell for the *Angelus* rang. "*Angelus Domini nuntiavit Mariae*," intoned the seminarian assigned to lead the prayer that morning. Leo's first day at the seminary had begun.

After morning meditation and Mass, breakfast ended the grand silence that had begun at nine o'clock the evening before. Afterward, everyone rushed down to the back porch to retrieve their trunks and luggage and stow their personal items away in the tiny closet behind each bed. Leo noticed the fellow seminarian whose bed was located about five feet from his. Jeff was a tall, athletic young man with a shock of black hair partially covering his deep brown eyes. He appeared to be much younger than Leo.

"Hi, I'm Leo."

"Jeff! Nice to meet ya, Leo. Guess we'll be kind of bunk mates!"

"Sounds great! Some strange kind of bedroom, huh?"

"Yeah! Haven't seen anything like this since my cousin's barracks at Fort Dix."

"What high school did you graduate from, Jeff?"

"None. I didn't graduate. I came here to the seminary after my sophomore year. I'll be getting my diploma after our two years of college prep here, I guess."

Leo was astounded. The kid next to him in the dormitory was only sixteen years old. Leo was already twenty. How could Jeff have gotten through to his mother and father and made it to the seminary at such a young age? His thoughts were interrupted by the young voice.

"Do ya play *basketball*, Leo?"

"Yes. Yeah! I played in the city leagues in Allentown for a couple of years."

"Wow! That's neat. Maybe, uh, we can shoot some hoops after the retreat's over?"

"That sounds terrific." Leo was already feeling less alone.

The beds were arranged in the same order as the desks in the study hall on the first floor, an order determined by the scores the seminary applicants had achieved on their entrance examinations. Leo had ranked fifth, Jeff sixth, on the list of those who had been accepted. So, Jeff and Leo sat next to each other not only in study hall, but also during each and every class throughout the day.

Leo brought some stationery and other school supplies, a few books—among them Bishop Fulton J. Sheen's *Life Is Worth Living* and John F. Kennedy's *Strategy for Peace* and *Profiles in Courage*—and a box of *Fanny Farmer* chocolates that he and his mother bought the week before.

At noon the loud bell summoned everyone to chapel for the beginning of the religious retreat.

"My dear seminarians, you will have the next five days to get closer to Jesus," the spiritual director, Father Solliday, said solemnly as the 600 students settled into the pews. "Take this time of silence to let Him speak to you. Shut out the outside world and listen. For some of you it will be the first time you've ever tried to meditate on the words of Christ. Treasure these moments; let them lead you closer to Him than you have ever been."

Leo never tried to meditate before this day. *Five days of total silence—even during meals; this is going to be totally different.*

So, the grand retreat began. Prayer sessions and spiritual talks were scheduled for the greater part of each day. Listening to the word of God would be followed by hours of contemplating its meaning and application to each individual. It involved long walks over the same back road where Leo's parents and sister had said their good-byes. Leo walked along the familiar road, exchanging fleeting and awkward glances with the other young men. How odd he thought it was to be walking silently by so many strangers who had entered the seminary for the same reasons that brought him to this sacred place, not to be able to speak with any of them about their feelings and thoughts regarding their decisions to come here.

As the retreat advanced into its second day, the routine had set in. Leo was trying to realize the objective. He listened for the inspiration of Christ, but all he could think about was his family back home and the guys at the restaurant supply company. It's almost noon; the guys would be heading over to the luncheonette for their hamburger barbecues. It's Thursday, so mom would be cleaning the upstairs bedrooms today. His mind wandered. *This isn't what I'm supposed to be thinking about.*

Finally, on Monday evening, after the benediction service, the retreat ended. Five days had gone by, but still there was no message from Jesus. Leo felt he might not have applied himself diligently enough to probe the meaning of the words of Christ. After all that time in silence, listening to spiritual talks, his greatest inspiration still came from Bishop Sheen's book.

Leo received a letter from his mother the next morning. Perhaps not understanding the regimen of a religious retreat, she wondered why he had not yet written to her. Everybody missed him so much, she reported. Donna had started first grade. His Aunt Paulette asked for his new address so she could ask him to be godfather for her new baby girl. Seminary rules prohibited students from leaving the grounds during the school year, so Leo would be unable to attend the baptism of his goddaughter. It was strange, he thought, that now, as an aspiring priest, he could not be there for such a fundamentally important religious service. Two days later his mother responded to the first letter he had written her after leaving home, saying how wonderful it was to hear from him and how she couldn't imagine him not speaking a word for five days. She heard on the grapevine that his former boss was really missing Leo and having a hard time keeping his old crew in check. Leo laughed as he pictured the guys taking their old shortcuts and skipping whatever they could to make things easier for themselves. He felt sorry for Irv—and guilt for having abandoned him. A few days later a package arrived from home containing a new pair of pajamas and a dark blue pea jacket for the upcoming winter months. Several packages of *Hershey* bars were included and a copy of the *Morning Call* reporting a minor earthquake in the Allentown area. His mother described the near panic that erupted as the neighbors dashed from their homes fearing the worst. Apparently, a 3.0 quake seemed as catastrophic to those in Allentown as a 7.0 quake would be to San Franciscans.

Classes had begun on Tuesday morning. Leo's courses included Latin, Ancient Roman and Greek History, Ascetic Theology, Public Speaking, College Algebra and English Grammar. The first class, English Grammar, began at eight o'clock in the morning. Leo was assigned a seat in the first row. It was an odd feeling to be sitting at a school desk again. All the classes interested him, except for College Algebra. Mathematics always presented a formidable challenge to him. Later that day Leo completed his first oral reading for the public speaking instructor, who told Leo that he sounded like John F. Kennedy.

Nothing could have thrilled Leo more than hearing this. He rushed a letter off to his mother that afternoon telling her about his teacher's comment.

Time moved swiftly. Class work and research activities were quite demanding. Strangely, with all of the work and the meager seminary menu, Leo had gained nearly five pounds in less than two months. He was no longer arriving at the supply company every morning, loading orders and stocking inventory. Instead, he was sitting in classrooms most of the day. It was a sea change in his daily activities. *No wonder I'm getting fat. I've got to get more exercise.* Leo began playing basketball with his "bunk mate," Jeff, whose family lived in Olde City, the most historic part of downtown Philadelphia. Leo felt like a big brother to Jeff, and it was clear that Jeff, whose only sibling was an older sister, enjoyed being with him. They were both keenly interested in American History, especially the Revolutionary War era.

Leo looked forward anxiously to the open house that was scheduled for the last Sunday in October. His mother wrote to him several times a week, keeping him up to date with the happenings at home, but Leo soon discovered there is no antidote for nostalgia. It seizes one's senses like an emotional fever growing insidiously in the soul. The only cure is reunion with those whose absence creates the painful void. And soon they would all be together again.

The day for the open house finally arrived. A half-hour before the doors opened, Leo was pacing the sidewalk in front of the seminary building, anticipating the first sight of his dad's car. Not a minute after the noon hour he spotted it—a familiar black Buick moving along Winthrop Road toward the seminary gates. As the *Dynaflo* drew near the sidewalk along the main building, Leo was already rushing up to it. He could see through the side windows that his grandmother and godmother were accompanying his parents and Donna, who was yelling his name out the window.

Leo guided them to the temporary parking spaces that had been set up on the front lawn. It had been only two months since he had seen his family, but it seemed much longer. He had never been separated from them except for a one-week vacation with Ellen, when their parents arranged for them to spend a week with a family friend whose home was across the street from a dairy farm in Breinigsville, about twelve miles west of Allentown. He and Ellen had a great time helping to make delicious homemade ice cream—with raspberries they themselves had picked alongside the barn where the cows were being milked.

"It reminds me of Austria," his grandmother said of the seminary buildings and grounds.

"Can we see your big bedroom again?" asked Donna.

"Sure, but let me first show you the classrooms along the front hall, then we'll explore the game rooms downstairs."

Leo's study hall had desks for more than one hundred students. It was the huge room where he and his fellow classmates spent many hours each day before and after classes. He proudly showed them his desk.

"I see you brought your Bishop Sheen book with you," his dad said.

"Yeah, dad. I wouldn't leave *him* behind," he laughed, thinking of his father's fondness for the bishop's television show. "And look, Donna, here are the *Hershey* bars you sent me." Leo removed some books from the small top shelf on the left-hand side of the desk, revealing the candy.

"They don't give you much space for things," his mom said, looking at the bookshelves. There were only two shelves and a top drawer to store his books, snacks and other items.

"Well, you know mom, there are an awful lot of us to squeeze into this place, and as huge as these buildings may seem, there are more than six hundred seminarians studying here now," Leo explained.

He guided them down the long front hallway to the center of the house—his new house—walking through the sprawling lobby, over the freshly waxed white marble floor that led to the library. Thousands of beautifully bound volumes—all shelved neatly in handsome mahogany bookcases—enhanced the magnificently appointed room with its blue Persian rugs and long mahogany tables and matching chairs. Then they headed downstairs. He showed them the barber shop, the music room, the reading room. Leo was watching his mom closely. He could see from her reactions to each part of the seminary that she was pleased.

"Oh-kay," Leo sang out, "let's go up to Donna's favorite place—my big bedroom." His grandmother and godmother had not seen the dormitory before.

"Such a huge room! How can you sleep with all these people in here so close together?" his godmother asked.

"It's really not so bad, Aunt Sheryl," Leo replied. "No one around me snores!"

Donna ran up and down the aisles, scurrying around and between the vast array of porcelain sinks. His mother flagged her down, bringing her back to Leo's bed.

"Here's my closet, Donna. See, it's no longer empty like it was the last time you were here."

His grandmother seemed tired from the long trek they had made during the afternoon. "Everything okay, Grammy?" Leo asked.

"Oh, I'm all right, Leo. My legs get tired all the time. It's okay."

"Well, look everybody, it's getting close to the end of our open house, so how about we all go downstairs to the chapel, and I'll show you around." It was going to be another long walk for his grandmother, but Leo knew she could sit down and relax in the chapel.

As they passed through the doors to the chapel, his family sighed when they saw the beautiful scene before them.

Leo led them up the twelve-foot-wide, grey-and-white marble aisle through the sanctuary. The main white marble altar was ablaze in candlelight. Fresh, bright yellow mums, white lilies and red carnations decorated the space around the golden tabernacle. The brass candelabra glistened in the glorious light. They paused to say a brief prayer. Leo escorted them to the sacristy, where the red and gold priestly vestments worn at High Mass were on display. The floor was covered with a massive, bright red intricately embroidered Persian rug surrounded by numerous mahogany closets. Seven small altars lined the circular wall in the hallway that ran behind the main altar. Leo explained that priests from the seminary faculty said their Masses on those altars each morning. His mom's face glowed with pride as she listened to Leo speak. The day ended far too quickly. Leo wanted to share so much more, but time had run out. He led his family back down the chapel aisle to the large vestibule, then out the front door.

"Leo, we'll all be praying for you," his grandmother promised.

"Thanks, grammy. I need it! I'm so glad you were able to come down here. I hope you're not too tired."

They all said their good-byes. Leo checked with his dad to make sure he knew the way home. They all piled into the Buick. As his dad backed out of the parking space, Donna's head emerged from the back window.

"Good-bye, Leo!"

Leo watched the car move through the seminary gates, back to Winthrop Road. He waved one last hardy good-bye before walking back to the chapel for evening prayers and benediction.

CHAPTER 4

"I couldn't get to sleep last night," his mother's letter began. "After walking through the seminary with you and getting a glimpse of your new life—I was excited. I realized that there is nothing for me to worry about after all. Seeing how beautiful everything is there, I don't think you could ask for more. I am so glad you like the seminary life. It made me feel a lot better when I saw you. You look just wonderful! I am glad that you are happy. That's all I ever wanted for you."

After reading it twice, Leo lifted the letter to his lips and kissed it softly. His mother had come to realize he had chosen a life that would truly satisfy him. It may not have been the kind of life she had envisioned for him, but she was resigned to it. The way he looked when she visited him convinced her that he had made the right decision.

The following week was momentous. All the new seminarians would be authorized to wear the Roman collar and long black cassock. Cassock Day was filled with all kinds of intrigue. Rumors abounded that after the "new men" attended chapel wearing their cassocks for the first time, they would be facing a kind of hazing when they returned to their dormitory that evening. So there was much trepidation and anxiety among them when, after the vesting ceremony, they approached the dormitory wearing the traditional clerical garb. To their great relief, however, they were surprised only by the hundreds of "holy cards" strewn across each of their beds. Bearing pictures of the saints on one side, and on the other the welcoming words of fellow seminarians to their new classmates, the cards created a virtual showroom of colorful collages on the snow-white bedspreads.

Six weeks later, examinations had begun; Leo was working extra hard. His mother had written several letters that he found no time to answer. She was worried. It was clear from her correspondence that she continued to miss him very much. She repeatedly mentioned how wonderful it would be when he would be back home again on Thanksgiving Day. She noted painfully that she would be traveling to Germantown with his dad for her annual appointment with the allergy specialist. His office was located only ten miles from the seminary, but she would not be able to visit him. She wrote him a note on that day as she waited in the doctor's office for her examination: "Well, we will be seeing you at home soon—can't wait to see you again."

On Thanksgiving Day, Leo, Patrick and Thomas were driven home from the seminary by Thomas's father. When Leo got out of the car in front of his house, he felt an eerie sensation. He had returned from a totally different milieu. The expansive lawns and huge granite structures that had been his home for the past three months made his old neighborhood appear infinitesimally smaller than he remembered it. When he entered the house he was greeted by the familiar, smiling portrait of Pope John from the left side of the entrance—and by Donna bolting toward him before he could even close the door.

She grabbed him around both his legs, screaming, "Leo's home!"

His home looked tiny now. The long halls and cavernous ceilings of the seminary buildings seemed to have shrunk his memories of the house where he was born and raised. Leo's mom was in the kitchen, working on the huge Thanksgiving banquet she had been planning for weeks. When she heard Donna's peals of joy, she rushed to the living room and kissed Leo, exclaiming through tears how wonderful it was to have him home.

Leo was grappling with the intriguing feeling of coming home after the longest period of time he had ever been away. It was a blend of happiness and loss. Life moves along in separate dimensions. All the love that Leo had shared for twenty years in his home with his family seemed to linger there in suspension. He had been gone for three months, but life continued to go on there without him. He missed those mornings with his mom and sisters at breakfast; he missed his returning home at the end of the workday to hear about their day. He knew it was a lost part of his life—a part he could never retrieve. Separation. It begins at birth when you are separated from your mother's body, and ends when death separates you from your own body.

His mom had gone all out for the dinner. She prodded him to eat more, even though he was soon stuffed with all the turkey and trimmings he could eat. His day at home moved far too quickly, and he was a bit late getting started back to the seminary. In the back seat of the car that evening, Leo was thinking how all of the excitement and hard work of preparing for the Thanksgiving Day event had taken its toll on his mother. She had begun experiencing severe asthmatic attacks again.

"I believe your mother has skipped her injections now and then," Leo's father had told him after dinner. "She has been a bit lax, and I'm afraid it's begun affecting her condition."

The revelation from his father increased Leo's worries about his mother's health.

For the first time in his life Leo was absent from home on his mother's birthday, November 29. At the seminary store, he bought a beautiful card with red roses on a sky-blue background, sending it early enough that she would receive it on the very morning of her birthday. In a letter she wrote that night, she said how delighted she was to receive it, and how his sisters and neighbors had sung "Happy Birthday" to her after joining her for some homemade chocolate cake.

But Leo was depressed. He had missed another important event. Several days later his mother announced that he had become an uncle. Ellen had given birth to a baby boy. Leo would not be there for the christening, but he was going to be the godfather. Again *in absentia.*

His mother described the baptismal ceremony. Leo's Uncle Phil stood in for him at the christening. His mom prepared a roast chicken dinner for the family and godparents. They all wished that Leo could have been part of the big day. Nobody's wish was more deeply felt than his own. Leo was having difficulty reconciling the Church's teaching about the necessity of strong family life, even while the seminary was, at the same time, depriving its future ministers of taking part in the very fabric of their own family's most sacred events.

Leo's mom had taken on a whole new line of duties. She was giving her new grandson, Alan, Jr., baths, making his formulas, and washing diapers for the first time in years. She apologized for not writing more frequently. But she never failed to send him newspaper clippings describing in detail his high school's basketball games. Several days before Leo would return home for the Christmas holidays, his mother wrote that she and his father and his sisters were baking cookies. "But I'm leaving the house-decorating duties for you, Leo, because I know how much you enjoy it." Leo loved the Christmas season. This year would have more meaning than ever. He would be home for nearly two weeks after his first extended absence—and completing his first semester in the seminary.

The schedule at the seminary was winding down for the holiday break. A committee of his fellow students several years ahead of him had begun to decorate the student lounge for Christmas. It was an annual event that was fiercely competitive. Each year the students responsible for the décor labored to outdo the work of the previous class. With the supply of film and flash bulbs his mother had sent him, Leo was busy photographing everything so he could show his family how beautiful the seminary looked for the holidays. His dad was scheduled to take him, Thomas and Patrick home on December 21. He would have plenty of time to prepare the Weber home for Christmas.

On Christmas Eve, Leo was thrilled to participate in the Midnight Mass, serving at the altar with Thomas and Patrick. For the first time in their parish church, they were all dressed in their black cassocks and wearing their Roman collars. Leo's duties included lighting the incense and swinging the thurible containing the burning, fragrant incense toward those attending Mass as the priest blessed them. Leo could see his mother seated in the third pew. He thought of Donna asleep at home while his father watched the Midnight Mass broadcast from Vatican City on TV. The memories of the previous Christmas flooded back. All the tension he experienced that evening about his future had long since passed. The wide sanctuary was bedecked with bright red poinsettias; the colorful Nativity scene highlighted the right side. Leo glanced again at his mom as he turned toward the altar, presenting the thurible to the Deacon.

A couple of days later Leo had a lively reunion with Irv and his former co-workers at the Lehigh Restaurant Supply Company. Leo called his former boss to make sure he would be available that day. When Leo walked into his old office, Irv greeted him with a bear hug.

"Look, Leo, things just haven't been the same around here since you left. You know, these kids just don't want to listen, and they don't want to work! You were so reliable and did such a great job for me here. I really miss you."

"How are things going for Jonathan in school, Irv?"

"Oh, I didn't tell you in my letter that Jonathan is experiencing some health problems right now. There's something wrong with his stomach; he's missed a lot of days at school. I'm really *concerned* about him, Leo."

"Irv, I'm so sorry to hear that. I know how much Jonathan was looking forward to starting school. I laughed when he told me he selected his fraternity house when he heard the sound of Sinatra's 'The Lady is a Tramp' coming from one of the windows of the building. Remember me selling him my bongo drums before he left? That was the night you got a flat tire on the way to my house to pick them up."

"Yeah, that was some night. Well, I'm sure that Jonathan will be all right. You know he's always been very tenacious," Irv said. "Well, look, Leo, I *know* you want to say hello to the old gang, and I know they'll be happy to take another break."

"Thanks, Irv. I'll stop by on my way out."

Leo opened the office door that led to the warehouse and garage. As he closed the door behind him, the first voice he heard was the loudest of the old crew, Billy's.

"Hey, everybody, c'mon over. Father Leo is here to bless us!" he said, his voice deeper—and louder— than ever.

Welcoming an excuse to stop working, Mickey, the oldest member of the crew, dropped his packages and walked toward Leo.

"Hey, Leo, if you've been praying for me, it sure as hell ain't workin'— I'm still here in this old rat hole," Mickey said, his voice low enough that Irv couldn't hear him.

"Still the same old Mickey, I see," Leo grunted. "Hi, Ron, Billy, George. How's it going, guys?"

"They're working us to death around here since you left, Leo," Billy complained. "You know, you just *understood* us better."

"Irv's a slave master, and it sure as hell ain't no fun anymore," Ron chimed in. "We miss those basketball games we used to sneak in over in the garage when Irv was out to one of his long, fancy lunches."

"Yeah, they were a lot of fun," said Leo. "Remember how we used the stacks of crates of new kitchen towels as the backboard and stuff a hoop between the crates for the basket. It was a ring from a remnant of an old metal rack that pots and pans once hung from in a restaurant kitchen."

"Hey, Leo," George broke in, "how about the time when we were playing catch in the garage and you missed one. Remember old Irv running out of his office—a baseball glove on his hand—and fielding the ball?"

"Yeah, that was some grab he made, and it ended that game in a hurry. But, somehow we always got all our work done on time."

"So, what's it like in there, Leo?" Mickey asked. "How are they treating you? You look like you got a little heavier, kid."

"Mickey, I just love it. I know George won't believe it, but it's where I belong. I know I made the right move."

"That's great kid," Mickey replied, his tone now serious. "So glad to hear it. You gotta go after what you want. You only get one chance."

"Well, I know you have a lot of work to do, because the trucks will be arriving any minute."

"Listen to this guy! He still remembers our schedules! After being out of here for almost a half year," Billy exclaimed, sparking a boisterous reaction that Leo was sure Irv must have heard behind the closed door of his office.

"Hey, look guys, I'm sorry I couldn't spend more time with all of you. How about we get together at the old luncheonette when I get home for the Easter break? I'll have a lot more time then—we can catch up."

"You got a date, buddy," Billy promised.

Leo returned to the office. "I know how busy you are, Irv, so I'll say good-bye. Thanks for letting me stop in."

"Not at all, Leo. Look, please stay in touch. With Jonathan's condition, I'm not sure if he'll be able to work his normal summer schedule here. If you are available, maybe we can discuss it."

"Irv, I hope he is okay, but if you need some help around here, I think I'll be able to work it out."

"Great! Good-bye, Leo. I'll be praying for you." They shook hands.

"Thanks so much, Irv. I'll keep you and Jonathan in my prayers, too."

As his holiday vacation was coming to an end, Leo's concern about his mother and Ellen continued to grow. They had been suffering from severe colds. He knew that colds would dangerously exacerbate his mother's bronchial asthma, so he was preoccupied about her condition as he began his trip back to school. Shortly after Leo returned to the seminary, his mother wrote to tell him that she had met Terry, at the Sears, Roebuck store on Seventh Street. His mom mentioned that his former girlfriend had shown her the beautiful diamond ring she recently received for her engagement. Leo tried to imagine what had gone through his mother's mind as she stared at the dazzling ring. Fortunately, his mother now seemed completely comfortable with the decision he had made.

His mother continued to write to him every other day. In her first letter after the holiday break, his mom complained that Donna, who was always creating some kind of mischief or another, had been rummaging through Leo's room after he went back to the seminary after Christmas. In the drawer of his nightstand, she found the stack of holy cards. While, of course, Donna was severely reprimanded for this violation of Leo's privacy, his mother confessed to being moved by the messages on the cards. "I couldn't put them down, the thoughts were so beautiful." As he read his mother's letter, Leo's thoughts drifted back to the nightstand and the episode with his mother's sewing needle. He remembered how close he had come to derailing the course he had set for himself. The seminary routine was so structured and so terribly busy that he had not once thought about the temptations that had come so close to destroying his plans. The nearly total lack of privacy precluded such temptations. There were common bathrooms and shower areas. From the time he woke up in the morning surrounded by nearly a hundred classmates, through the many hours he spent in the presence of his fellow seminarians in the study hall, classrooms, refectory, and at recreation, and in numerous visits to the chapel for prayer, there was absolutely no time nor place for personal privacy. So Leo remained free from sins of the flesh.

Studies were going well. He enjoyed studying Ancient Roman and Greek History, but the public speaking classes were his favorite. English grammar was very easy for him, but he continued to struggle with College Algebra. He seemed to catch on quickly to Latin. The two years of foreign language in high school under the strict supervision of the Sisters of Mercy had prepared him well for the course. He was thrilled with the camaraderie he was developing with his fellow seminarians. After classes on most days, Leo played baseball or basketball with his classmates, then ran a few laps around the mile-long perimeter of the campus, sometimes alone, but usually with a few other stalwarts. He sometimes played golf as well. After gaining weight initially, he managed to work himself into the best physical condition he had ever enjoyed.

The February mid-term examinations loomed, but Leo was confident he would do well. And he did, excelling in all his courses—even earning a "B" in College Algebra. It was a brutally cold winter in Philadelphia. As the Easter season approached there seemed to be no relief in the below-freezing temperatures. Leo was thrilled to learn that the seminarians would be transported by bus to the Cathedral of Saints Peter and Paul, in Philadelphia, for the Holy Week services there. He remembered when he practically forced his father to drive into the city from Germantown after one of his mother's appointments with her allergy specialist. His father nearly had a stroke negotiating his way into and out of the five lanes of frantic traffic surrounding city hall. Horns were blowing all over the place, but his dad thought all of the mindless honking was being directed at him. Never again would his dad be persuaded to drive into center city Philadelphia.

On Palm Sunday the cathedral was magnificent. It's ornate décor and towering marble columns resembled the Basilica of Saints Peter and Paul in Vatican City. The altar was bedecked with dozens of palms and brilliantly lighted by three six-foot-tall white candles on each side. The seminarians, dressed in black suits, white shirts and black ties, were seated in the front pews reserved for them. As the Cardinal walked in procession down the main aisle, dressed in bright red vestments with gold trim and carrying a huge braided palm in one hand, and his crozier in the other, Leo stretched to see his face. It was a grand ceremony. The seminary choir sang in perfect voice. Leo remembered hearing the choir in 1951 at the televised funeral of Dennis Cardinal Dougherty, the archbishop of Philadelphia. He often dreamed about hearing the choir singing live, and perhaps even being part of the seminary that trained them. His dream had come true.

After the Mass, the seminarians were free for the day. Since Leo was unable to travel home to Allentown and be back at the seminary in time, Thomas's aunt invited him to join them for dinner. Leo had visited her when he, Thomas and Patrick had taken their entrance examinations and when they had gone to the city to purchase their cassocks before entering the seminary. Although the Spring Garden area had numerous dilapidated, unmaintained structures, many homes were being restored by young professionals who were moving into the city. Leo was impressed with the beauty of the neighborhood with its billowy trees along the streets and the small, handsome gardens lining the front of some of the stately red-brick townhouses that were being restored.

All the seminarians returned to the cathedral for Shrove Tuesday services. The stark, dimly-lit church was a sharp contrast to the bright spectacle that had been presented there on Sunday. Leo was inspired and thrilled by the beauty of the sacred music performed by his fellow seminarians. He had never attended Tenebrae services before. The serene sound of the polyphonic music of Palestrina and Perosi was beyond anything he could have imagined. Two Masses were scheduled for Holy Thursday. After the morning Mass of the Holy Oils, the seminarians were free to go to lunch in the city. Leo, Thomas and Patrick walked about three blocks from the cathedral to have lunch at Stouffer's in the new Penn Center complex. Leo's eyes roamed around the popular, crowded restaurant: Women with their fashionable dress hats sipping martinis, well-dressed businessmen smoking cigars after steak for lunch, waiters scrambling to their beck and call. The scene was not so very different from the sacred liturgy he had just experienced—the sparkling mitre on the Cardinal's head, the elaborately designed vestments, the altar boys scurrying to assist the Cardinal and priests. As Leo stared at the large, fancy menu with ornate print describing numerous choices for lunch, he thought about his mother—all the good times they had enjoyed at the Marble Bar where the laminated menus offered a very limited variety of dishes. *Wait 'til I tell her about this place!*

After their enjoyable lunch, the trio strolled around the City Hall courtyard and back up to the Logan Circle to the cathedral for the Mass of the Last Supper. As magical as the ceremonies had been during Holy Week, nothing could compare with the profound liturgy that evening. The splendid, angelic-sounding Gregorian chant combined with the strength of the polyphonic sounds of the choir singing the *Vinea Mea* motet transported Leo to a spiritual realm he had never before achieved. Returning to the seminary that evening he was convinced more than ever that his life had been blessed—he was on the path that God had selected for him. As he lay in his narrow bed with its thin straw mattress in the middle of the crowded dormitory, his thoughts turned to his family who had helped make it possible for him to be there, to whom he owed his love and undying gratitude, and for whom he was praying as he drifted off to sleep.

Easter Sunday arrived with all of the new life that the holy day celebrates. The cathedral was glorious with hundreds of white lilies filling the sanctuary. Joyful chords from the massive pipe organ filled the air. The Cardinal, dressed in stunning white and gold vestments, spoke about the new beginning made possible for all by the Resurrection of Jesus Christ. Leo understood that message more than ever.

It was an odd trip home in Mr. Richardson's car. Although it was Easter Sunday, the closer they got to their homes, the more snow they saw on the ground. As he entered the front door, the intoxicating aroma of homemade chocolate filled the air. His mom had prepared a basket of sweets for him. Then Leo found out that that Nick's wife had made three pounds of homemade Easter eggs for him to take back to the seminary. *Nick is really serious about being an altar boy at my first Mass!* he laughed to himself. It took Leo a couple of hours to come down from the inspiring experiences of Holy Week capped by the Solemn High Mass he had attended at the cathedral, receiving Holy Communion from the hands of the Cardinal himself. Leo had a couple of term papers to complete during his week at home, but he still had a lot of time to visit his family and neighbors. Nick at the Italian grocery store continued to remind Leo to make sure that he would be selected to serve at Leo's first mass. Leo, once again, assured him he would not forget, and thanked his wife for the chocolates. On Wednesday, Leo visited the guys at the Lehigh Restaurant Supply Company for a reunion at their favorite luncheonette. This time, "Sherry Baby," The Four Seasons' big hit, was playing on the juke box as they consumed their traditional hamburger barbecues, french fries and black-and-white milkshakes. When Leo stopped by to see Irv Davis, he found his good friend very busy—and troubled.

"Jonathan is not well, Leo. I was hoping that he would be feeling a lot better by now and able to resume his full class schedule, but he just can't do it. I hope you'll keep praying for him."

Leo was deeply concerned about his good friend Jonathan. He was saddened by Irv's sullen, depressed appearance. On his way back home Leo thought about the plans he and Irv and Jonathan had been making before Leo decided to enter the seminary. They would have been working closely together every day. And now, plagued by the constant worry about his son's illness, Irv had to face the grim likelihood of operating his growing business without either of them.

Leo and his mom went into town on Thursday evening as they had done so many times over the years. At the Marble Bar, Leo recounted his experience at Stouffer's in Philadelphia; his mom's laughter turned heads when Leo described the sophisticated ladies sipping martinis at lunch in their fancy hats.

"I guess I'll have to buy a new hat before you come home for the summer," his mom joked.

"No, you stay the way you are, mom. I love you *exactly* the way you are." A roving photographer in the restaurant captured the moment Leo put his arm around his mom as they both continued laughing. Leo purchased the Polaroid shot as soon as he saw it. "That's how I always want you to remember me, Leo," his mother said.

It had been an exhilarating week for Leo, his head spinning from the highs and lows of it. A day of grand silence before classes commenced would do him good, he thought. Final examinations loomed on the horizon, so Leo buckled down to prepare. His English Literature professor assigned him the task of reading all the works of Mark Twain—and to find at least one fact about the irreverent author's life that the professor did not know. He had just two books to go to complete the onerous assignment. While at home over the Easter break, Leo discovered in a local magazine that Mark Twain once held stock in the Lehigh Valley

Railroad. Fortunately, Leo's professor had never heard about the investment. The information was a God-send. When the exams ended and the final grades were distributed, Leo was awarded the highest grade in English Literature.

In the first week of May, Irv Davis wrote to inform Leo that Jonathan had not yet recovered. He offered Leo a summer position with the company. As required by seminary rules, Leo cleared it with the seminary officials, and with his pastor at home, before accepting the new summer job. He would be driving a delivery truck every day to northern New Jersey restaurants, hotels and summer camps. He had never driven a truck, but was eagerly anticipating the new experience it would bring. Being outdoors everyday would be a wonderful change of pace from the daily schedule of classes at the seminary. Summer break was near—he would have three full months at home with his family, neighbors and friends.

Leo, Thomas and Patrick loaded up the station wagon that Leo's father had borrowed to drive them home for the summer. Seminary rules required that all personal property be removed from the seminary at the end of the school year.

One week later, Leo reported to work for his new job as a driver salesman. Accompanied by Rick, the foreman, he anxiously inspected the walk-in truck. There was a large sliding door on the driver's side and an identical one on the passenger side. The double doors on the back of the vehicle opened out, allowing ample room to remove packages for deliveries. Inside, shelves to hold the supplies were installed in the back of the vehicle. The truck was similar to those used by bakeries to deliver *Tastykakes* and *Twinkies* to grocery stores. Leo had often seen one parked in front of Nick's place. On Leo's first day on the job, the foreman provided driving lessons in the company's parking lot and gave tips on caring for the vehicle. It had a four-on-the-floor manual transmission that was manipulated by using a three-foot-long gear shift. It took Leo a couple of hours to get used to the new contraption—so different from his old '54 Chevy. Each day for the rest of Leo's first week, the foreman accompanied Leo on a delivery route.

Rick regaled Leo with stories about his experience over many years as a driver for the Greyhound Bus Lines, including driving passengers home from New York City in near-blinding snowstorms. He described how, on one such occasion, he narrowly avoided a tragedy when his bus skidded out of control on the steep, icy Ferry Street hill in downtown Easton, Pennsylvania. The bus caromed down the hill until it was slowed by a steep snowdrift, which nearly tipped it over. Only a telephone pole had stopped the bus from capsizing and possibly killing many of the passengers.

Had he not decided to go to the seminary, Leo confided, he would seriously have considered a career as an innkeeper.

"Why would you think of that alternative?" asked his perplexed foreman.

"You know, Rick, all of the hotels I've visited with you on your sales trips over the past few years really intrigued me. There's something that amazes me about the hotel industry. I mean, a hotel is a home away from home, and if it's managed properly, it can be a wonderful place to spend time relaxing."

"Yeah, kid, you know I kind of like the business myself. If I had it to do over again, I might be doing just that! Listen, Leo, just let me know if you ever, um, change your mind about being a priest. I've got a very good friend who runs a Holiday Inn. I'm sure he can get you an assistant manager job at one of their places."

Leo was silent as he wistfully watched the winding road ahead.

"Thanks, Rick."

After a week of Rick's expert guidance on the delivery route—and exposure to his mentor's endless tales of heroic driving exploits and descriptions of the magnificent hotels in New York that he had visited—Leo was ready to begin the delivery route on his own. He could still get to the seven o'clock Mass every morning before going to work; and he soon found he had time to pray the rosary as he speeded along U.S. Route 22 East on his way to New Jersey. As the summer months progressed Leo made new friends along the established route. He thought about the words of the seminary's Spiritual Director: "Remember, boys, this summer when you are away from the seminary you will be able to take Jesus to places that he would never have been able to go without you." Leo was determined to carry out that mission.

When Leo approached the northernmost stop on his delivery route at Culver Lake for the first time, he thought there was something magical about the place. After an hour and a half of driving along the busy, crowded, noisy highways, he was suddenly struck by the phenomenon before him: multiple shades of green foliage stretching out as far as he could see were reflected in the sparkling blue waters of the glassy lake. He drove to a small gas station and got out of his truck. As the attendant pumped the gasoline, Leo strolled over toward the lake. There was something unexplainable about the place. He was captivated by its natural beauty. A cool breeze drifted across the water bringing with it the sharp, sweet fragrance from the countless green pine trees surrounding the lake.

At the hotel near Culver Lake he met June, a woman who appeared to be about twenty or so years old. Her parents owned and operated the grand old hotel for decades. She helped them with the various activities during the summer months when she was home from college. She was a perky, attractive girl. Her short blond hair and deep blue eyes captivated Leo. She wore a white shirt with its collar flipped up in the back, and tight denim jeans with frayed cuffs (proudly calling it "reverse sophistication"). June's whimsical style appealed to Leo. He found her sexy. She was also boldly flirtatious, informing him early on that if he ever wanted to "fool around," the hotel had a spare room they could use for privacy. But Leo reminded her he was going to be a priest.

On his next trip to the hotel, two weeks later on a sweltering July afternoon, June was standing outside the hotel's storage room in a white bikini, beckoning to him.

"Hey, Leo, the Pope is *busy* right now. He's not gonna care if you skinny dip in the pool with me, or have a couple of puffs of my Colombia Gold—it's great stuff!"

Leo laughed it off. He assembled the order in his delivery truck and brought it to the room where June was standing in her sexiest pose. They both laughed this time. June hugged Leo after he placed the packages on the shelves. She liked him, and he felt tempted by her but pulled himself away.

"June, you're a really beautiful girl. But I, uh, you're just *too much*. I, um, I just can't, you know, the seminary has strict rules that I've got to follow, or … "

"Sorry, Leo," she giggled. "You're just so *goddamned* cute!" She poked the dimple on his chin with her right index finger.

Leo completed the order, gave June the receipt, and drove off without a word. June watched as he drove away from the hotel.

When he returned on August 5, June was sitting on the front steps of the hotel with her arms propped on her knees and her face pressed into her hands. She was weeping. He parked the truck and rushed over to her.

"June, honey, what's the matter?

"*Marilyn's* dead! She's *dead*! I just can't believe it."

"Marilyn?"

"Marilyn Monroe is dead, Leo. It just seems so unreal!"

"Oh my God, June! What happened?"

"They said on the radio they think she died of an overdose of sleeping pills. She was only thirty-six years old!"

"This is awful, June. We need to pray for her."

June's hands dropped from her face, her reddened eyes glaring up at Leo.

"Oh, *yeah?*" she screamed. "And what's *that* gonna do? Is that gonna bring her *back? You* pray for her, Leo. See what the fuck *you* can do about it!" She jumped to her feet and ran into the hotel.

Leo slumped onto the steps of the hotel, feeling at once helpless and useless. *What comfort or hope did I offer her?* he thought, the words of his spiritual director resounding in his mind. *I've failed her.*

The incident with June replayed in his mind all the way back to the restaurant supply company. How could he explain death to someone? He couldn't understand it himself. What do you say? How do you comfort one who's lost a dear friend or someone they truly love? Leo had no answers. His only other encounter with death was when his Uncle Wayne died—he too was just thirty-six years old. The family was in total shock. Leo's mother had been inconsolable. Her brother had survived the Korean War without any injuries, only to be stricken by an acute form of bronchial asthma, succumbing to an overwhelming attack of the disease. The horrible memories flooded back. He had no comfort for her then, either.

When he arrived home that night, Leo's mother was upset, too. She had been listening to the story about Marilyn Monroe on the radio all day. Instead of the lively popular music she normally loved to sing to, she was silenced by the grim reports coming out of Hollywood. Leo walked into the kitchen and hugged her.

"It's just like Wayne, Leo. He was so young, too. Why does this happen?"

"Mom, I was thinking about him, too. I wish I had an answer."

Leo washed up and changed his clothing. His mother was finishing dinner. Arriving home from work unaware of the day's events, his father was taken aback by the news. A somber mood persisted throughout the evening. It was like a death in the family.

As a dry August heat continued to worsen and pollen filled the air, Leo's mother began experiencing asthmatic attacks that were worse than they had been in years. The ragweed and golden rod combined with the dry air to clog her bronchial tubes severely. Medication was proving ineffective. Leo and his father stayed up with her every night, keeping a watchful eye on her. One evening her attacks were so frightening they had to call the family doctor, who immediately ordered that oxygen be sent to their home. Within an hour, a technician arrived with an oxygen tank. A short, thin, almost bald young man, he struggled with the large, heavy tank as he tried to wheel it into the living room. Leo and his mother looked at each other and, despite the serious nature of the situation, laughed out loud in the silly way they had done so many times before. This, of course, aggravated her condition. They stayed up the entire night helping her with the oxygen mask and medication.

By the last week in the month, when there was no appreciable improvement in his mother's condition, her physician recommended that she be hospitalized so she could receive proper health care twenty-four hours a day. She was not willing to go, but Leo and his father convinced her she had to do it. His father drove her to the hospital on Labor Day. The doctor ordered that she be placed in an oxygen tent. A clear plastic canopy was suspended over her head and tucked in securely under the mattress to maintain the high level of oxygen supply she needed. Zippers were located on each side so his mother could be given medication and food. As Leo sat by her bedside, he recalled the previous time she had been in the same situation. It was different then—he could stay with her. But he was going to return to the seminary in the morning, so he would not be with his mother when she was suffering this latest battle for her health. All of the excitement over the past few weeks about going back to the seminary to begin his second year of studies, and having his own private room, vanished. He wanted to stay home with his mother. She needed him. Leo's mom assured him she was feeling better and would soon be going home.

"Leo, don't worry about me. You *know* I've been through these attacks before. They always clear up. Why don't you go home and get your things together so you'll be ready when Thomas's father stops by for you tomorrow morning."

Her confinement made it impossible for him to kiss her good-bye, so he kissed his fingers and placed them against the oxygen tent that separated them. "Goodnight, mom," he whispered.

The gruesome incidents of the past few months deeply depressed him. Adding to it all, he had not seen June again during the remainder of the summer. Leo thought she was deliberately avoiding him because of the incident about Marilyn Monroe. He missed seeing her. She had been so vivacious, so entertaining—until the sad tragedy that parted them. Maybe she was feeling guilty about her outburst, or maybe she just didn't want to hear Leo's noble pleas for prayer. Either way he felt he had lost a good friend. Leo was about to begin his second year of study for the priesthood, but with little of the excitement and enthusiasm he had experienced the year before.

CHAPTER 5

Leo's closest boyhood friend, Rob, and his family moved out of their old neighborhood in the previous year. Leo remembered how much Rob's parents enjoyed vacationing in Havana in the 1950s. They often told vivid stories about the enchanting hotels, marvelous beaches and crisp Cuban cuisine. Although they had traveled to Europe and South America, the little island off the coast of Florida was their favorite destination. They even enjoyed a couple of New Year's Eve celebrations there. Rob's father owned and operated a large, successful dry cleaning firm in Allentown; his family was more financially well-off than Leo's. Rob's mother enjoyed having elegant clothing and wearing the latest styles. She kept her house furnished with modern designer fixtures. She upgraded her kitchen regularly, insisting on having the latest gadgets and color schemes. She had Rob's father install a shower in their basement so they could shower after completing the lawn chores. Leo and Rob enjoyed using it frequently—together.

Cuba had recently been taken over by Fidel Castro. After Leo began following John F. Kennedy's political career, he grew increasingly interested in politics and international affairs, reading newspapers and magazines regularly to keep up with world events. Castro was an enigma. Leo sympathized with the Cubans' desire to overthrow a greedy, ruthless dictator. But, even worse, Castro had declared himself a communist and an atheist. He shut down the Catholic churches and silenced the Catholic Bishop. Pope John XXIII quickly excommunicated Castro. In an effort to weaken Castro's oppressive regime, President Kennedy ordered an embargo against Cuba, blocking all exports from and imports to the island. Leo followed the story over the summer, voraciously reading the *New York Times* and *U.S. News and World Report.* He brought back several of the most recent issues with him to study during the new school year.

When he returned to the seminary, Leo was assigned his own private room. His first year in the open dormitory, in close proximity to scores of his classmates, had ended. His new private space was about seven feet wide and ten feet long—just a bit bigger than his parents' bedroom closet. It was furnished with a small single bed that looked more like a cot. The sound of the thin straw mattress crunching beneath him reminded Leo of the bales of hay at the farm where he and Ellen had once stayed. A tiny wooden desk, an old and worn, small gooseneck reading lamp, and a plain wooden chair were the only other furnishings. There was a small closet in the far right-hand corner of the room. Directly opposite the entrance door, a large window, three feet wide by eight feet in length, afforded a view of Winthrop Road, which ran in front of the main building. Leo's sink was located in the hallway, one of a dozen porcelain lavatories outside his room. The bathroom facilities were located a short walk down the hall. Class-order protocol assigned his friend Jeff to the room located directly to the right of Leo's.

Since seminary rules prohibited making or receiving any telephone calls, there were no public telephones in any of the buildings. Leo had to wait for the mail to find out about his mother's condition. He was growing increasingly bitter about the rule, lying awake for hours worrying about his mother and praying for her recovery; during the morning meditation, and throughout the day, it wasn't Jesus he thought about, but the uncertainties about his mother's fragile condition. Even though she had been hospitalized for a full week, Leo's mother wrote him a letter as soon as the oxygen tent was removed. She tried to comfort him, telling him she was feeling much better, but she had to remain there for nearly another full week. Two days after her discharge from the hospital, she was required to return to her allergy specialist in Germantown.

Leo's concerns intensified when she told him she had lost fourteen pounds during her latest asthmatic attacks and was having difficulty gaining weight. In her usual way she made it sound fine, claiming to feel a lot better "without the extra pounds." So he waded into his new courses: New Testament Latin, Classical Greek, Church History, Chemistry, Spanish, Ascetic Theology, Trigonometry, English Literature and Public Speaking. His Spanish teacher, Father McMurty, while not the only eccentric professor on the faculty, was certainly the most comical—indeed strangest—person he could remember meeting. Leo and his classmates vied to imitate the professor's odd mannerisms and gestures, their antics driving them to laughter as they tried to outperform one another. All of the professors seemed more like academicians than ministers of the Gospel. Only the Spiritual Director, Father Solliday, was truly inspiring. Leo was enthralled by him. His tall, thin figure was topped by a shock of straight white hair over his high, pale forehead. From behind wire-rimmed glasses, his piercing grey eyes seemed to probe deeply into one's soul whenever he spoke. It was rumored that the fervent priest had once been an exorcist. When Leo served Father Solliday's Mass in the morning, he would closely watch every move the venerable cleric made during the service. At the elevation of the host following the Consecration, Father Solliday would hold the sacred bread high over his head for nearly thirty seconds after pronouncing the words that transformed it—according to Catholic theology—into the body of Jesus Christ. The solemn way the aging priest genuflected afterwards communicated that, indeed, he truly believed he was kneeling before his Lord and Savior, Jesus Christ himself. Leo had read Thomas Merton's *The Living Bread* several times during the most recent retreat. Whenever he served one of Father Solliday's Masses, he recalled the contemplative monk's haunting words: "When you are assisting at Mass, you are present at Calvary." That was the feeling Father Solliday's Mass created. At other times around the seminary grounds, the unflappable priest seemed totally in control of his emotions. He always had kind words and blessings for Leo whenever he would see him about the campus. Leo found hope and true inspiration in the character of the devoted priest.

The annual open house at the seminary was scheduled for Sunday, October 28. Leo's mother had already written about it to him several times. His favorite uncle, Evan, would be accompanying his parents and sisters this year. Leo could hardly wait to see his mother, especially since he was eager to assess her condition. Of course, she continued to assure him that all was well, but he knew how she always tried to shield him from any worry.

One week before the open house, serious international problems began to develop. On Sunday, October 21, the *Philadelphia Inquirer* reported that President Kennedy would address the nation in a televised speech from the Oval Office on matters of national security. Saint Francis Seminary was one of the most conservative seminaries in the United States. Their rules prohibited contact between seminarians and their families during the school year except for written communication. Incoming and outgoing correspondence was monitored by seminary officials. So, it was not possible to communicate privately with one's friends or relatives. Only one copy of the newspaper was provided for the entire student body; so every morning after breakfast, hundreds of seminarians would dash to the recreation room where it was delivered, trying to glean the latest news stories as they crowded around the Ping-Pong table on which the pages were spread out. No televisions or radios were allowed. The only radio that could be heard in the entire seminary was the small portable Motorola that belonged to Pete, the barber. It was always tuned to WIBG, playing the top tunes of the day. Consequently, most seminarians were always well-groomed, rarely missing an appointment for a haircut.

The students were astounded when, on Monday evening, October 22, 1962, a television was wheeled into the dining room. It was the first time in the seminary's history that a television was allowed in the student section of the campus. Clearly, there was some shocking news to be announced by the young president. The students finished dinner and anxiously awaited the address from the White House. In deliberate, clipped phrases, the young president informed the nation that U-2 spy planes had taken photographs of nuclear missile installations on the island of Cuba, just ninety miles off the coast of Florida. The missiles had been installed by the Soviet Union. President Kennedy announced that a naval blockade of Cuba was underway and that B-52 bombers had been deployed, many of which were already airborne. The president demanded that the Soviet premier, Nikita Khrushchev, dismantle and remove them immediately.

Like the rest of the world, the crowd of more than three hundred seminarians was stunned. All that had been written about nuclear warheads, and the long-range missiles that are used to propel them, was frightening, but it never seemed possible they would actually be launched. Now, the chilling reality of the potential consequences of the nuclear arms race was staring them maddeningly in the face. The world was on the brink of an unimaginable catastrophe. After the president ended his remarks, the seminarians were directed to go to Saint Matthias's chapel, where a rosary for peace was recited—in unison—with more fervor than Leo had experienced since his arrival at the seminary.

Not since the Soviet Union launched the first satellite into space had the world experienced such frenzied hysteria. Sputnik soared into orbit around the Earth in October 1957, when Leo was sixteen years old. He remembered being bed-ridden because of a serious case of the Asian flu. Lying in bed with a high fever, he could hear the sharp beeping sound of the Soviet satellite as his radio eerily broadcasted its orbit around the Earth every ninety minutes—and he was terrified. The Soviet Union had surpassed the United States in the quest for outer space; the country was staggered by the scientific achievement of the Soviets, and no less so by the potential threat it held for the future.

Leo was shaken by President Kennedy's address. The cold reality that nuclear war could begin at any moment and destroy most of the earth was beginning to solidify in his mind. It was impossible to comprehend fully the tragic consequences that lay ahead. Khrushchev was defiant, announcing that the missiles had been installed at Cuba's request to defend the island from aggression by the United States. The raging dictator of the communist bloc reminded the world of the failed attempt of the Bay of Pigs invasion, which Kennedy had ordered to overthrow the Cuban government. Khrushchev countered that he had ordered twenty Russian ships to Cuba to provide further defense, then accused the United States of acts of piracy. The already heightened tension that existed was further exacerbated by the appearance of the first Russian ships entering the area of the blockade that the United States had established.

Studies at the seminary seemed irrelevant. It was impossible to concentrate on anything but the threat of global nuclear war. Discussions in the classrooms turned to the news, as various scenarios were explored by the students and professors. Would Kennedy order the destruction of Soviet ships as they entered the blockade? How would Khrushchev respond? Would he order the invasion of Berlin in retaliation? Would the United States launch a nuclear attack on the Soviet Union? Four days after President Kennedy announced the discovery of the Russian nuclear missiles and ordered Premier Khrushchev to dismantle them, it was learned that the construction of missile bases continued without interruption. On the following day, when a United States U-2 plane had been shot down over Cuba, global nuclear war seemed not only inevitable, but imminent. Leo was numb. Would he ever see his family again? All hope seemed lost. Even the normally calm Father Solliday appeared grim and preoccupied. Prayers for peace were held in the chapel several times each day, and Masses for peace were celebrated every morning.

God had not prevented World War I or World War II, nor had he seen any wisdom in stopping the Korean War. Countless numbers of people had been slain and massacred throughout history in wars that God allowed to happen, Leo thought. Why should the world in 1962 be spared? What had his generation done to merit being saved from total annihilation in a nuclear holocaust?

Two days before Leo was scheduled to see his family during the long-anticipated open house, he worried that he would never be with them again. The world was about to end.

On the morning of October 28, after six of the most terrifying days the world had ever experienced, the White House announced that Premier Khrushchev had agreed to dismantle the nuclear missile bases in Cuba if President Kennedy, in exchange, would end the blockade and agree not to undertake a military invasion of the communist-led island. The crisis was averted. But after teetering on the brink of annihilation, the world would never be quite the same. The open house went on as scheduled. A celebration—of any kind whatsoever—was needed. Leo and his family would be reunited again. Things would get back to normal— that's all that mattered now. But a *new* kind of normal had been established. The naïve feeling of complacency and safety would be gone forever.

Leo watched his mother emerge from the Buick on open house day. She had gained weight. Her color had returned. She looked happy. His Uncle Evan was beaming as he climbed out of the back seat.

"Leo, this is such a magnificent place. Congratulations," he bellowed. Before Leo entered the first grade, his uncle had taught him spelling, and throughout the rest of grammar school had continually hounded him to become a lawyer. When Leo was about twelve years old, his Uncle Evan took him to the fairgrounds to see the Ringling Brothers and Barnum and Bailey Circus. On Friday night he sometimes took Leo to the high school football games. Leo was recalling how much he owed this man emerging excitedly from the car.

"Hi, Uncle Ev! I'm so glad you could come." They embraced.

The ritual tour of the seminary buildings and grounds commenced. This year Leo had his own room to show off. Donna was thrilled.

"This is smaller than my room, Leo," she joked as she dangled her legs from the straw mattress.

"Well this is all that's allowed in here, honey. Everybody has the same size room. Only so many of us can squeeze into this building."

Leo's mother looked well. She seemed to have gotten her energy back. He was relieved to see her recovery going so well. All the conversations that day turned to the macabre events of the past week. It was difficult to imagine how the world had come so close to destroying itself.

Time was fleeting; once again it was time for Leo and his family to part. Thanksgiving Day was just a few weeks away. So, even with the anxiety of the past week not entirely dissipated, the thought of all of them being together at home made this latest separation a bit easier to reconcile.

They were all packed into the car, ready to start the long trip back home. His mother told him she was feeling so much better that she was planning to make a special Thanksgiving dinner in gratitude for all that God had given them this year. "For one thing," she pointed out, "we're all still here!" Leo cautioned her to take it easy, knowing that indeed she would probably go all out for the holiday.

Leo closed his eyes momentarily, thanking God for his mother's good health. The horrific days before the open house continued to dominate his thoughts. Now, it was back to the chapel for more prayers of thanksgiving.

Leo was settling into his second year in the seminary, but the aura of the initial exuberance he experienced was waning. He began to question both the wisdom and the intelligence of some of the rules. Why would a Church that had established a fundamental objective to strengthen the family decide to separate family members at crucially important times, such as the baptisms of his two godchildren? Why would he not be allowed to attend the weddings of two beloved aunts, or the funerals of two of his dearest friends; and be prohibited from telephoning his mother when she was so seriously ill? It all seemed absurd. Studying to become a priest, he found himself excluded from some of life's most sacred and solemn occasions. Life, baptism, illness, death—all were sacramental realities he would be called upon to preside over as a priest. Shouldn't the preparation for those important moments start now?

During the evening prayers Leo sought the strength to continue on the course he had been determined to follow for so long. *Jesus, please do not let me stray from your sacred calling.*

Thanksgiving Day arrived; this time it was Thomas's father who drove all of them home. Leo entered the house to find his mother busily preparing the dining room. The mouth-watering aroma of roast turkey filled the house. As soon as he removed his coat, he helped her set the table.

"Now you sit down, Leo. You're home to relax."

"No, mom! It's now time for *you* to relax. You've been cooking all day, and probably part of yesterday, too." His mother had baked apple, pumpkin and mince pies on the day before he got home.

When he finished setting the table, Leo crept into the kitchen and grabbed his mother, turning her around. He looked into her eyes and smiled.

"Mom, this is the best Thanksgiving Day ever! You look so well, and we've all survived one of the most terrifying years in the history of the world. We're all so very lucky, mom!"

Donna had run down from her bedroom and was pulling at his leg, begging for a hug. Leo picked her up and held her close to him, then whispered: "You're the best little sister in the world!"

She jumped down and ran into the living room to announce what Leo had said. The room erupted in applause from all who were gathered there: his father; his sister and brother-in-law; his godson, Alan, Jr.; and his neighbors who lived next door, Jim and Rena, who had been so very helpful to his mother while his dad was at work. His mother had often written about them in her letters. It was a great feast, but once again, Leo had to leave his family and go back to school. Christmas holidays were approaching. Soon they would be having another full week together. On the ride back to the seminary Leo, Thomas and Patrick, having feasted on home cooking most of the day, were uncharacteristically quiet. Leo broke the ice.

"How do you fellas feel about all these separations from our families? I mean, look, I've missed weddings, baptisms, and funerals. I couldn't even speak with my mom over the telephone when she was so ill a few months ago. Does it make sense to you that this is the way we should be preparing for our future role as ministers of the Church to its people?"

"Oh, Leo. You mustn't think like that. You're going to get yourself into trouble," cautioned Thomas.

"No. *Wait* a minute," Patrick said. "He's right. This seems crazy to me, too. We're so separated from everything. All the guys I know who are in college can communicate with their friends and families anytime they want, and they're still able to complete their education.

They still have successful careers. And we're supposed to be ready to offer counseling and guidance to people in just about every one of life's most significant events."

"Look, boys," Thomas's father interjected. "You know the church makes these rules for a good reason. You can't question them. After all, look at the priests you have known. Weren't they good role models for you? Haven't they been there when the people needed them? Isn't that one of the reasons you boys are in the seminary now?"

"I don't know; maybe you're right, Mr. Richardson," Leo said softly, trying to end the conversation.

"Uggh!" grumbled Patrick. "*Honestly*, they're stuck in the Middle Ages here!"

"Patrick!" Thomas nearly shouted. "That doesn't make any *sense*. We need to follow the rules. They've been made for our own good."

"Well, they're sure not doing *me* any good," Patrick retorted. "And look at poor Leo. He couldn't even talk with his mother when she was so ill recently."

They got back a half hour early, so they strolled around the old enclosed stone courtyard along the back of the seminary, chatting about their day at home until the bell for evening prayers sounded.

The Christmas holiday vacation that followed gave Leo a chance to be closer to his family than he had since leaving for the seminary at the end of the previous summer. He and his mother went shopping, and he spent many hours with Donna, listening to her stories about the "crabby" nuns in school. He visited with his grandmother and spent some time with a few of his aunts and uncles who lived nearby. Leo returned to the seminary feeling more relaxed, knowing that his mother's health had improved.

In her first letter following Leo's Christmas vacation, his mother expressed how much their separation continued to sadden her: "I miss seeing you reading the newspaper, sitting in your favorite chair in the living room; or playing with Donna and making her laugh the way you do, Leo. I miss our shopping trips to the A & P and watching you choose those big T-bone steaks you like so much. I'm just so glad you are happy. Maybe you don't think I pray often, but I do. I always pray for you and wish all the best for you. I don't see you enough to tell you, but I think of you often. I am very proud of you. I always was and always will be."

The relatively mild January weather provided some precious relief. Leo was able to get outdoors to play basketball with Jeff, and they played a few rounds of golf each week, usually on Thursday afternoons and Saturday mornings when the schedule allowed for additional recreation time. He enjoyed Jeff's youthful, uncaring manner. It was a joy being with a young man who was just nearing his eighteenth birthday, yet had so much poise. Leo admired Jeff's intelligence as well. He seemed so much more mature for his age than might be expected. Jeff enjoyed reading about American History. It was Leo's favorite course in high school. So they had long debates about the Founding Fathers. Leo thought Alexander Hamilton was the most brilliant, while Jeff argued for the prominence of Thomas Jefferson and his role in forming the new nation. They were seated next to each other in every class, as required by seminary rules regarding class order. They would often look at each other and giggle at the antics of the more eccentric professors—especially Father Joseph, who could be regularly seen walking down the center of the long seminary corridors reading the *Wall Street Journal* and his daily prayer book at the same time—all the while praying the rosary out loud.

As she had always done since Leo entered the seminary, his mother included newspaper clippings of stories about his high school's basketball games. She knew how much Leo enjoyed them. His mother told him she agreed to be a bridesmaid in his Aunt Megan's wedding but was having second thoughts, wondering whether she was, perhaps, too old to be in a wedding party. Leo, knowing she looked far younger than her forty-two years, wrote to reassure her that she would be marvelous in the wedding party. She told him how disappointed everyone was that he would be unable to attend.

Leo knew how excited his mother was feeling about the big event. He realized how much she wanted him to see her in the pink satin gown she would be wearing that day. His heart sank when he imagined how deeply disappointed she would be without him there.

A few days later, on March 15, Leo was called to the central mail room, where he was handed a Western Union Telegram. He paused and looked at the pale yellow envelope that had already been opened. Nervously, he pulled out the Telegram and read it:

GRANDMOTHER PASSED AWAY TODAY FUNERAL ON MONDAY 8 30 A M SORRY YOU ARE NOT HERE= LOVE=MOM=

To learn of his beloved grandmother's death by way of a stark, impersonal message—the words typed on two narrow strips of paper, each pasted onto a pale yellow base of similarly cheap pulp—was the cruelest shock of Leo's young life.

He immediately requested approval to telephone his mother, knowing how totally devastated she would be. He would have to console her via a long-distance telephone call as she suffered the worst tragedy of her life.

Leo's grandfather had died twenty years earlier of jaundice, which he developed through injuries suffered in an automobile accident; he was just forty-four years old. Leo's mother was the middle child of thirteen, so she assumed the major role of helping her mother care for the six younger children. His mother's older siblings had to go to work to help support the family. Fortunately, there were five or six huge factories nearby, all of them located along one bank of the Jordan Creek. Their products ranged from cigars to shirts and hosiery. At the north end of the neighborhood the nationally renowned Bonney Forge and Tool Company produced massive numbers of a variety of industrial tools. Jobs were regularly available. Two of his mother's older brothers, who dropped out of school to help with the family finances, were still working there after all these years.

When Leo's mother and father got married, they bought a house directly across the street from his grandmother. Before leaving home for his seminary studies, Leo had seen his grandmother nearly every day of his life. Seminary officials told him that he would be allowed to call home when he learned of her death, but that the rules prohibited attending the funeral of a relative unless—to cite exactly the prescribing phrase from the rulebook —that relative "lived under the same roof" as the seminarian. He would have to tell his mother that he could not be with her on the saddest day of her life.

His mother answered the phone weeping. She told Leo that his grandmother was found unconscious in her backyard; she had suffered a heart attack while sweeping the patio next to the old peach tree—the broom was still in her hands.

Leo then told her the unbelievable news—he would not be allowed to go home for the funeral. He tried to explain the seminary rules.

"But Leo, Grammy lived just across the street. We were always like one family."

"I know, mom, but their rules here are very strict and they don't make any exceptions. I'm so sorry, mom, so *very* sorry. There's no place in the world I want to be but home. I want to be with *you*."

"We were just laughing together yesterday afternoon. She was so happy to receive your letter when she was sick last month. It really cheered her up. And now ... she's ... Oh, God, Leo, I wish you could be here now."

"I know, mom. I can't believe they won't let me go home. But my thoughts will not be here."

"It's not your fault. I know you would be here if you could. Please pray for me. I feel so weak. I just don't know what to do. Good-bye, Leo."

Leo dropped the phone onto the receiver and slammed his hands down on the desk, pushing the telephone away; the bell tone sounded as it crashed to the floor. Once again, he was separated from his family when they needed him most. He went back to his room and tried to pray. But prayer was not possible. His anger prevented it. As he sat on his bed looking up at the ceiling, he could imagine the scene at home: phone calls coming in, relatives and neighbors stopping by to offer comfort and sympathy, flowers being delivered. But Leo was fifty miles away, isolated from those he loved so deeply, unable to give them any form of relief and comfort. This was not the kind of life he wanted.

On the day following his grandmother's funeral, his mother wrote to him about her feelings. It was clear to Leo that a large part of his mom's life had died with her mother. She told him about the Solemn Requiem High Mass that was celebrated for her. The pastor, Monsignor Gregory, was the main celebrant. It was attended by many of his family, friends and neighbors who nearly filled the large church. Leo thought about how he had often sung the *Dies Irae* there for persons whom he had never known. *Yet my voice was silent at my own grandmother's Requiem Mass.*

His mother's letter continued: "At Mass this morning, I was thinking only of you, Leo. I knew in my heart that you were thinking of me. I could feel it, Leo. I could hear you talking to me, comforting me."

Over the next few weeks Leo's mother would write that she continually looked out the front window of their home, gazing across the street at her mother's empty house, unable to accept the fact that she was gone. And she admitted that her appetite had vastly decreased, causing her to lose weight again. The abject pain of losing forever someone whom she had loved so deeply was causing her life's meaning to unravel. Food seemed unimportant. It could not possibly provide the nourishment that her mother's love had given so bountifully all her life.

On top of all this, a few days after the funeral, Donna contracted chicken pox. Because of the illness, family and friends had to stay away to avoid exposure to the contagious disease. For nearly two weeks, his mother was isolated during the day when her husband was at work, at a time when she really needed to have someone with her.

Examinations were over. Leo had not done well, barely mustering even passing grades in most of his courses. He was looking forward to the Easter break, when he could finally help his family through the bitter sorrow that continued to grip them. His mother had written that she was keeping busy tending to the rose bushes in the back yard.

On Holy Thursday, Leo received a beautiful Easter card from his mom and dad. As always, she signed the card for herself and his father. He knew his mother had taken extra care to find a card with just the right message: "May the peace of Easter bring you happiness today, and God's love be always with you as you follow in His way." He was struck by his mom's resolve to encourage his life's ambition.

The joy of Easter Sunday at the Cathedral was quickly stifled by the emptiness that befell Leo when he arrived home. Mr. Richardson parked the car directly across the street from his grandmother's vacant house—a dark, silent remnant of what once had been a warm, cheerful, welcoming place. After Mass on most Sundays, many members of his large family gathered there to visit his grandmother and enjoy her delicious chicken soup. And every Easter Sunday until now, the large window in her living room would be packed with a dozen flower pots overflowing with bright white lilies, colorful hyacinths and stately tulips sent by her children in celebration of life. Today the window was dark and empty, its shade drawn.

Donna was already dancing at the curb at the door of the car as Leo was getting out.

"Leo, Leo! Look, my chicken pox is all gone—I'm all *better* now! Look!" She was displaying both arms to her distraught brother.

"Honey, you look so pretty in your new Easter outfit!" Leo hoisted her into his arms and carried her into the house. She was wearing a beautiful white dress with pink ribbons, and her matching white shoes shined brilliantly. Leo felt a twinge of pain as he glanced at the colorful portrait of the Pope, remembering how much his grandmother loved speaking of it.

Leo was shocked when he saw his mother. She looked sad, weak, thin and depressed. Her instant smile at seeing him could not hide the fact that her heart had been broken.

"I thought about Grammy today when we attended the Solemn High Mass at the Cathedral this morning," Leo said. "The Cardinal spoke about death as the beginning of a new life. Christians, he said, should celebrate death and look forward to meeting Christ at last. But all I could think about was you—how sad and alone you must be feeling."

Leo's dad had come down from upstairs to help prepare dinner.

"Hello, there. How was your drive home from Philly? Did you hit much traffic on the turnpike?"

"No much, dad."

"Let me help you set the table."

"No, just relax," his father objected. "We'll take care of everything."

Leo sat down in his favorite grey chair in the corner by the window, picked up *The Sunday Morning Call*, and was about to read the local news. But Donna was soon sitting on his lap, showing him all the candy the Easter bunny brought for her. Then, she ran into the kitchen and returned with two baby chicks. One was bright green, the other neon pink. The dyed birds chirped with alarm as Donna swung them back and forth in the basket, chortling about her colorful new pets. When Ellen arrived with his godson, Alan, Jr., Leo jumped up.

"Well, look who's here! Hi, Alan; how ya *doin'*, buddy?"

Sickly during his infancy, Alan, Jr. was now a year and a half old and looking perfectly healthy. Leo kissed his sister. "Hi, El. It's been a long time. It's great to see you." Ellen appeared unhappy and preoccupied. Leo's mom had told him that Ellen was having problems adjusting to life in Philadelphia. She and her husband were planning to move back to their old neighborhood in Allentown. Ellen asked about Leo's life in the seminary; he told her about the classes, the meditation, the other seminarians—everything was going well so far.

Ellen had dropped out of high school in her senior year. She never liked going to school, especially because of her health problems. Living up to her brother's sterling reputation with the nuns was impossible, adding to her ordeal in the classroom. Leo always felt guilty about that, realizing how unfair it was.

"Okay, kids, dinner is ready!"

As he sat down for dinner Leo looked directly at his mom. All his life he had sat across the table from her during meals. Her happy smile provided so much comfort to him over the years. Today, it was his mother who clearly needed to be comforted. Leo led the prayer.

"Almighty God, please remember those who are not with us today. May you keep them in your constant love and glory. Bless us with the courage to continue without them until the day we all meet again in heaven."

Leo's mother was weeping quietly as they began dinner. Leo tried to cheer her up. "Mom, where did those colorful chicks come from?"

"The Easter Bunny brought them last night, Leo. But I think he may have gotten the wrong address, because he must know I have asthma and I'm not supposed to have feathers around the house."

"No, mommy. They are for *me*. I will take care of them. You won't have to worry about them," Donna promised. Everyone chuckled, knowing how tenuous that promise would be.

Leo had a couple of term papers to complete, so he was busy at the typewriter for a few hours during each of the next couple of days. He walked over to the Lehigh Restaurant Supply Company to visit Irv and to find out how many of his buddies were still employed there.

"Well, hello, Leo. So glad you could stop by. Listen, Leo, I wanted to write to you. Because of a number of changes here, we won't be running that summer camp route you handled so well for us last summer. I'm really sorry, but we've had to shift that work to one of our regular drivers to make up some of the slack in our revenue that we've experienced this year."

"Hey, Irv, that's not a problem. I'm sure I can find something to do this summer. I'm just sorry you're having problems here."

"Leo, we've had a lot of turnover. Most of the fellas you worked with here are gone. Ron is the only one left."

Leo knew how difficult it was breaking in new employees. He realized how tough it must be for his friend, especially with his son being ill and needing a lot of attention.

"Well, if I can be of any help at all over the summer, be sure to let me know."

"You bet, Leo. Thanks so much for stopping by, my boy." Irv looked very tired and sad as he said good-bye. His son's severe illness had taken its toll on him, changing his normally outgoing attitude. He was aging prematurely.

When Leo stopped by the warehouse to see Ron, he could see how his buddy's attitude had changed from a rather carefree demeanor to one that seemed stressed. The old gang had disbursed. All of the laughs were gone. It was another separation in Leo's young life.

When he got home Leo told his mother the bad news.

"I'm sorry it didn't work out for you, Leo. But don't worry," she said. "I've talked with Uncle Stan about a summer job at the General Electric plant. You know, he had spoken to you about it last year, but you decided to take the delivery job. Well, it looks like they'll be hiring new summer employees this year, too. I'll ask Uncle Stan to get an application for you."

Leo told his mother he didn't know what he would ever do without her. She promised to send him the application.

It would not have been a real vacation at home without a trip to the downtown shopping area and dinner at the Marble Bar. As they sat in the familiar booth, surrounded by the clamor of festive shopping and dining patrons, they looked at each other in silence. How life had changed since the last time they had been there! There was a deep emptiness in his mother's eyes that Leo had not seen before. She appeared lost. Then she spoke.

"Leo, ... promise me ... you'll never forget me," she whispered.

"Mom—"

"No, listen Leo, please. I hope you'll never forget me."

"Mom, how would that be possible? You're the most wonderful, thoughtful, loving person in my life. I think about you every day. I could *never* forget you for even one minute, if I live to be a hundred years old." He was stammering.

"I know you're so happy where you are, and that you'll be all right no matter what happens to me," she said. It was obvious that the thought of her mother's death continued to haunt her constantly.

"Mom, let's try to have a good time tonight. I love being here with you. It's one of the fondest memories that keeps coming back to me."

"Okay, Leo. But remember what I said."

His mother's mysterious words tormented Leo for the rest of the week. On Sunday, as he was packing to leave, Leo had to laugh as he heard the little chicks chirping loudly in Donna's bedroom. She was obviously rousing them up.

He walked down the hallway and looked into her room.

"Donna, what are you *doing* to those poor little creatures?"

"I'm just petting them, Leo. They *like* that!"

My poor mother, he thought. *Now she has live chickens to deal with!*

Leo packed his suitcase and briefcase and set them in the living room. His mom looked terribly sad as he approached her to say good-bye once again. He told her to take care of herself, especially being sure to take the new medicine the doctor in Germantown had prescribed—she had to keep up her strength. His dad mentioned that she had again been lax taking her medication. He kissed his mom and headed out the door.

The week at home had not been enough time with his family, certainly not nearly enough to try to console his distraught mother. Leo's father helped him pack his things into the car and they left to pick up Thomas and Patrick. Leo cast a final glance at his mother in the doorway as he left. In just five weeks he would be back home for the summer.

On the morning after his return to the seminary, Leo awoke as usual to the clanging Voice of God, rushed to the sink outside his room, and began to wash up, preparing for the *Angelus.* But something was different. He glanced over at Jeff's sink and saw that all of Jeff's toiletries were missing. And the door to Jeff's room was closed. There was no sign of him in the dormitory. After breakfast Leo learned that Jeff had not returned to the seminary after the Easter break. His best friend had given up his quest for the priesthood. He was gone.

Seminary officials continually warned the young students to avoid so-called "particular friendships," involvements that could lead to temptation. So, Leo and Jeff had rarely talked about personal matters. Their discussions were usually limited to sports, American History and light banter over life in the seminary. But Leo was distraught that Jeff never gave any inkling that he was thinking of leaving the seminary.

In early May, Leo's mother wrote to tell him she had been invited to the first Mass of one of the priests in the parish who had just been ordained.

"I'll bet his mother is really proud," she wrote, "Because I know how proud I am of you. I only hope I live to see you say your first Mass. Time flies. It will be here before you know it."

While he was home on Easter break, Leo pre-ordered a dozen long-stem American Beauty Roses in a beautiful glass vase from Sears, Roebuck on Seventh Street to be sent to his mom for Mother's Day. The flowers were delivered the day before. She excitedly placed the bright red roses on the center of the table in front of the windows facing directly across the street to her mother's empty house. Then she proudly called the family and neighbors over to see them. The specter of her mother's death continued to plague her. The family had not yet decided on what action to take regarding their family home, so they agreed to put it up for sale to test the market until they had made a final decision. His mother wrote to tell Leo how terribly upset she had been when she saw the "For Sale" sign placed on the front porch of the house. "The sight of that sign just sends daggers through my heart, Leo. I know she's gone, but I still can't accept it. I miss her so much."

Her mother's home was the fourth house from the end of a row of eighteen. Attached to each house was a front porch accessed by a staircase rising ten feet from the sidewalk. A grocer's alley led from the sidewalk to the backyard. It had been a favorite play area for Leo and Ellen and their friends when they were growing up. When weather would permit, most of the neighbors sat on the front porches telling stories, exchanging the latest gossip and enjoying snacks or pastries that they had baked. Neighbors and friends walking by would stop and chat. It had always been a festive time out there. But his mom's favorite house, the one that she was born in, was now dark and vacant—the porch was empty.

"I don't know how to tell you about the pretty bouquet of red roses you sent to me for Mother's Day," she wrote to Leo. "You never *do* forget me, do you? I was so surprised that you bought them for me that I could not help but cry. I was so very happy for them, so I say thanks a million for the pretty red roses."

She included the employment application form with her letter. He filled it out and mailed it immediately. Within two weeks he received a notice of his being hired for the second shift at the General Electric plant. He would begin his employment on June 17. Leo was relieved. His mom had done it again! On May 28, his mother wrote to tell him that the roses, more than two weeks after he sent them, had finally withered and had to be discarded. She had hoped to keep them until he came home.

"I will keep that vase, Leo, and use it again and again. I will think about you every time I put flowers in it."

CHAPTER 6

"U*hhh, uh! God, I can't … breathe!"* Leo pushed himself up from his bed and slid to the floor. It was around 4:30 in the morning of June 3, 1963. The room was almost completely dark, lit only dimly from a distant street light.

He grasped his throat with his left hand and stumbled toward the window, throwing it open with his right hand as far as it would go. The trees outside were gently swaying in the early June breeze, but Leo couldn't get any air. He was suffocating—suffering all the symptoms of bronchial asthma. He continued gasping, trying desperately to catch his breath. *I'm going to pass out!* He had barely fallen asleep when the clanging Voice of God startled him awake. Sweat was pouring from his naked body. Leo pressed his hands against the window sill, forcing himself up from his kneeling position where he had drifted off less than an hour before. He turned around, walked a few steps to the closet, grabbed a towel to dry himself off. Then he sat on the edge of his bed—dazed, confused, frightened. He slipped on his Jockey shorts, then headed to the sink outside his room.

When the seminarians entered Saint Matthias's Chapel that morning, they were surprised to see the rector of the seminary standing at the center of the chapel in front of the altar. The dour priest announced that Pope John had become gravely ill during the night; this morning's Mass would be offered for the health and speedy recovery of His Holiness. Concern and disoriented mumbling from more than three hundred seminarians broke the early silence in the chapel.

Leo was struggling to come to grips with the events unfolding on this strange Monday morning. He had been awakened by an unprecedented, alarming asthma attack, the kind that plagued his mother during most of her life. Now he was saddened by the heart-wrenching news about his beloved pope's illness. Leo buried his face in his hands, leaning his elbows on the pew in front of him. He tried to maintain his composure as the Mass began, praying fervently at Holy Communion for the pope who had so deeply inspired him

After the service, Leo sauntered out of the chapel with his fellow seminarians in two uninterrupted single-file lines along the walls of the corridor leading to the lobby. They had been told when they began their studies at the seminary that walking along the walls, as opposed to down the center of the corridor, demonstrated humility. As Leo reached the center hall, where the lines of seminarians dispersed, he noticed that Father Harvey, the dean, was beckoning to him. The priest appeared more preoccupied and uncomfortable than usual as Leo approached and stood before him. Several seconds of strained silence ensued, broken only by the weak rattle of throat-clearing as Father Harvey shifted his posture, his upper torso bending back as if swerving to at once avoid and summon the words he was about to speak. A sudden fever rushed through Leo's entire body. The words seemed to be arriving from a distant place as, one by one, they finally completed their halting, emotionless journey:

"Leo, … was your … mother … *sick?*"

No further words from the priest were necessary.

Leo's mother had died.

Had his asthma attack earlier that morning united him one final time with her? Had the person he loved more than anyone else in the world communicated with him directly as she was leaving it? The shock of his mother's sudden death removed all feeling from Leo's legs. Father Harvey grasped him by his left arm, leading him into a nearby office. Leo collapsed onto a straight-back wooden chair, his arms slumping forward on his knees, his mind frozen in the helpless stupor that only the sudden death of someone who is truly loved inflicts.

Leo's mind began drifting. While at Mass with three hundred classmates praying for the recovery of the pope he loved so dearly, Leo's mother, after suffering severe asthmatic attacks during the early morning hours, lay dying on her bedroom floor fifty miles away. The tragedy was intensified by the fact that he had already packed and was ready to go home on this last day of the school year.

A few more hours—he would have been there with her.

After regaining some of his strength, Leo was told he could telephone home. He barely understood the sobbing voice of his neighbor Doris, who was trying to communicate the chaos that had overtaken his home. Someone was on the way to the seminary to bring him home. He wasn't sure who. The dean suggested that Leo go to the infirmary where the nurse could look after him until his transportation arrived. As he walked along the familiar halls, the haunting sounds of his mother and family echoing through those corridors as they cheerfully had walked with him on open house days tore at his soul. Sounds of his classmates preparing for their journey home heightened his sudden realization that the happy times he spent with them might now be over.

What will happen to Donna? Who would take care of her? His mom raised her so beautifully. Donna's hair was always carefully combed and styled—her clothing immaculate. His mother never left her out of her sight. How would his dad be able to deal with this? How would he suddenly be able to be both mother and father to a seven-year-old girl? The nurse gave Leo a couple of sedatives. When he awoke, his father and one of his father's best friends, Ralph, had already arrived. The ride home in the black Buick was a long-distance funeral procession. Little was said by anyone for the next hour and a half as their shared grief and shock eliminated any ability to communicate verbally. Arriving home was terribly painful. Leo opened the front door. Glancing at the pope's portrait, he broke down sobbing. When his eyes cleared, he stared toward the kitchen, noticing the obscure image of a figure ironing clothes. He was confused.

"But mom is dead," he mumbled, approaching the kitchen.

His Aunt Martha had come over in the morning to help. She had been trying to put things in order around the house after the medics left, taking his mom to the hospital. His dad's sister was now completing the ironing his mom had begun the previous day, no doubt with the indispensable musical help of the Everly Brothers—or Elvis, maybe—in the background.

His mother, dead before she was forty-three years old, was gone forever. Leo rushed up to the bedroom where his mother had died. He kissed the floor, weeping and calling out to her frantically, hopelessly. He picked up her hair brush, holding it close to his face, gazing at the scant, remaining traces of her.

The next morning Leo and his father and sisters visited the funeral parlor. He could not accept the fact that his mother was lying before him in that billowy white coffin. He approached the casket, leaned forward and kissed his mother's forehead. The cold feeling of death against his lips startled him. As he stood up, he noticed the arrangement of her hair.

"Her hair is not right," he complained. "It's too flat. She never wears her hair that way."

The funeral director promised to have it corrected. Even though the director had been given two photographs of his mother, Leo remained unsatisfied—even with the final result. Over the next couple of days Leo was numb. He tried to console Ellen, and struggled to explain to Donna that her mommy wasn't coming back. It just made him sadder and increasingly morose. He turned to the Bible seeking comfort. Leo had recently bought a compact Bible with a red leather cover and pages with gold leaf on the edges. It resembled the one that the Reverend Billy Graham used in his sermons. A great admirer of Billy Graham, Leo watched most of his crusades on television. He often wondered why priests in the Catholic Church rarely preached with the same kind of dynamism and conviction that Reverend Graham always exhibited. Reading the verse "Sorrow rules the night, but joy cometh in the morning," hardly consoled him. As the family later sat together in the backyard, it seemed to Leo that his mom was looking on helplessly from another sphere, unable for the first time to communicate the joy and love she had always given them.

Leo's grief was compounded when he learned that evening about the death of the beloved Pope John XXIII, who had lost his battle with stomach cancer.

On the day of the funeral, Father Harvey visited Leo at his home to express his sorrow and promise of prayers. As the priest stood in the doorway of Leo's home, he glanced at the colorful portrait of the smiling pontiff, saying how beautiful it was. Leo, fighting back tears, explained how his mother had bought it for their home before he entered the seminary.

More than two hundred friends and family members formed an overflow crowd at the funeral parlor for his mother's wake, a vast outpouring of support. Leo's neighbors, his good friend Tony, and the former crew from the Lehigh Restaurant Supply Company were among them. The funeral director transported the family to the church Leo had come to love so much over the years. This was the first time Leo ever felt unhappy going there. Seated in the first row, he gazed tearfully at the familiar beauty of the sanctuary with its perfect balance: the colorful murals of three angels on each side of the white marble altar bedecked with brass candelabra and the gaze of the crucified figure in the center—the blurred collage of a past now evaporating before him.

As Leo sat motionless, the choir intoned the opening words of the Requiem Mass. "*Requiem aeternam dona eis, Domine.*" (Eternal rest grant unto them, O Lord.) After ten years during which Leo had sung the Requiem so many times in all his innocence and naiveté, he finally understood the harsh and bitter reality of its meaning. Nothing seemed to matter now. He stared at the casket. His quest for the priesthood that his mother shared with him over the past few years seemed insignificant now.

The funeral procession turned out to be one of the largest corteges the city of Allentown had ever experienced. A police escort was needed to guide the throng of mourners across town. Nearly all of the one hundred and ten seminarians in Leo's class attended. Leo was only a few years out of high school, so many of his former classmates were there as well. A hundred cars moved along the road for the two-mile stretch from the funeral parlor to the church and, finally, to the cemetery.

Leo pressed the last red rose against the cold grey casket, pausing as he noticed his anguished face mirrored in its metallic surface. Several hundred mourners began their measured departure. Leo and his family were driven back home by the funeral director. The gruesome day was finally coming to an end. His home was eerily empty, devoid of life as he had come to know it. Until the day before she died, his mother had continued to replace with identical fresh flowers from her garden, the red roses he had sent for Mother's Day. Slumped in his favorite grey sedan chair in the living room, he glanced at the table where she had placed the roses he sent. He was certain now he would never again experience the kind of love and joy his mother had given him.

It was time for dinner, but no one had an appetite. Their good friend and neighbor Doris was knocking on the back door. She had come across the backyard with a tray of sandwiches and Italian cannoli.

Leo thanked her for being so helpful over the past few days, and for being there for the family when he called from the seminary that awful day.

Doris kissed Leo on the cheek as Leo recalled her trembling voice on the telephone a few days earlier when he had called home. "Take care, honey. Let us know if you need anything here."

"Thank you, Doris."

Leo awoke on the following Monday morning, exhausted from his grief and irreparable loss. He cleaned up the house and helped his Aunt Sheryl get his sister ready for the day. The job his uncle had gotten for him was scheduled for the second shift, from three-thirty in the afternoon to midnight. He was about to face a whole new kind of day.

Arriving at the GE plant about fifteen minutes early, he reported to the shift supervisor's office. His boss, Al, was about forty years old, with thinning hair and a stocky build. He was wearing a crisp, white, short-sleeved shirt, a brown and white striped tie, and khaki trousers; his brown shoes were buffed and shiny.

"Leo, Al Buckman! Your Uncle Stan has told me a lot about you." He grabbed Leo's hand, wringing it vigorously.

"Now let's have a little tour of the plant."

In terms of size and scope, the assembly plant resembled the architectural drawings of an enclosed baseball field proposed for the Houston Astros that Leo had recently seen in the newspaper. Massive walls supported a domed ceiling soaring five stories above numerous clusters of whirring machinery separated by aisles about twenty feet wide. The expanse of this automated equipment saturated his view in every direction. Gargantuan spools of copper wire were being fed into huge receptors that magically begat grates for toasters. The toaster shells themselves dangled overhead, streaming their way to the foundry for final polish. Al Buckman laughed.

"I know it's a lot to absorb, Leo. Toasters are our biggest seller today. Everyone buys them for weddings, Christmas, anniversaries—and whatever else. We sell hundreds of thousands of them every year. Toasters keep this plant in the black."

Leo was still recovering from the scale of things around him as his new boss began instructing him about his work routine.

"We need to keep the aisles clean. All the areas under the assembly line have to be swept thoroughly each night. Replace all cardboard bins of toasted bread scraps with empty ones for the next shift."

There were a half dozen workers whose only job all day was to toast bread at various incrementally precise temperatures to assure the quality of the light-to-dark toasting mechanism of each appliance coming off the production line.

"Okay, Leo? I think that's it. Do you have any questions?"

"Uh, yes, Mr. Buckman. Is that *all* I will have to do for eight hours every night?"

"That's it, son. You know where my office is, so if you have any problems or questions, just come on over. Good luck, Leo. Nice to have you on board." Al's meaty hand crushed Leo's thin fingers again.

"Thanks, Mr. Buckman."

Leo was left standing in the middle of the main aisle of the arena-sized building, mesmerized still by the intricately busy electronic proceedings above and about him. Most of the workers from the first shift had left. There were only a few employees in the sub-assembly line for the second shift, creating a strange emptiness in the huge space. Leo was alone. Isolated. Estranged. He might just as well be standing on the surface of the moon as on the smooth, concrete floor of this sub-lunar workscape. It would make little difference. Just a week or so ago he was at the happiest place in his life. His mom was alive and he was looking forward to being with her and the family for the summer.

He grabbed the long wooden handle of the industrial-size broom, about three feet wide at its bristled base, and started to walk down the aisle, pushing the broom before him. An unearthly shriek abruptly ended his isolation, the broom falling to the floor with a loud bang.

"What's the *matter*, honey?" he heard someone ask.

"Oh, hi. Um, I'm Leo. I, uh, just started here tonight for the summer."

"Yeah, I *know*. The shop steward told me about ya, and the girls are already looking ya over. I'm Shirley. But what's wrong, hon? You look so sad walkin' 'round here."

"Hi, Shirley. I'm, uh, glad to meet you. Well, this place is ... well, my mom died last week, and I'm just trying to deal with it right now."

"Leo, you just lost the best friend you'll ever have in your whole life. I'm so sad for ya, honey."

"Thanks, Shirley. Thank you."

Leo picked up the broom and started to walk down the aisle as Shirley slipped back into the confines of the sub-assembly line. In about three hours he completed all the work Al had explained everything that needed to be done. But there were nearly four hours left on his shift. He didn't know what to do, so he started the chores all over again, fearing he might have missed some part or other of the routine.

"Hey, kid, whaddaya doin'? Yuh buckin' for foreman or somethin'?" The shop steward, Brad, introduced himself.

"Huh? What? I'm, uh, just doing what Mr. Buckman told me to do. This is my first night here."

"Oh, uh-huh. Ya know, ya don't have to work so *fast*, kid. You've got seven and a half *hours* to do this job right, so what's the fuckin' rush?"

"Well, I, uh, I didn't think I was hurrying or anything," Leo said.

"Hey, kid, listen. No one walks that fast 'round here. Just take it easy. Hey, look, I'll talk to you at dinner and introduce you to a few of the guys that work here. Take it easy now, kid!"

"Yeah, well, okay. Thanks, Brad."

Leo felt he would rather be doing anything anywhere in the world, or on the moon, than sweeping under toaster assembly lines at a General Electric plant. He stood at the end of the aisle, looking up again at the spinning appliances, feeling totally lost. He began sweeping the floor again, trying to slow down his pace as the shop steward had urged. About an hour later, he left the floor for dinner. The employee cafeteria was smaller than Leo had imagined it. Fifty or so wooden picnic-type tables with wooden benches were spread around a red-and-white tile floor surrounded by vending machines and a sandwich counter. Leo ordered a chicken salad sandwich and a Coke, and sat at an empty table.

"Hey, kid, I see you survived your first shift," Brad laughed, inviting himself to join Leo. Out of nowhere appeared five other guys from the sub-assembly line, joining them without a sound except for the scraping of the wooden benches against the tile floor.

"Oh, hi Brad," Leo said, a bit nervous as his coworkers descended on him. "Yeah, it's taking a bit to get used to all of the nooks and crannies around this place, but I *did* manage to find the cafeteria." But Brad was already introducing his pals.

"Leo, this is Art, Lou, Carl, Jack and Bud."

"Welcome, Leo," they said in spontaneous unison.

"Hi, guys. It's really good to meet you."

"Look, Leo, we've been talking about you, trying to decide if you should be required to join the union here," Brad said. "Since you're just a part-timer for the summer, and we heard you're in the seminary and all, we decided you don't have to join."

"Thank you all for your, uh, consideration, Brad. I'll be working here until the last week in August, just about two and a half months. I'm saving for my tuition and books and stuff, so I appreciate your decision."

Brad mentioned that he had worked with Leo's Uncle Stan. They had been friends for many years, so he was happy to be working with Leo.

The ear-splitting factory whistle, General Electric's Voice of God, as it were, declared the half-hour dinner break over. Leo headed back to sweep, once again, the floors of the entire plant. The midnight quitting time seemed to take about three days to arrive. As he was finally grabbing his jacket to leave, he noticed that Mr. Buckman was still in his office.

"So, Leo, how did it go for you on your first night?" he shouted through his opened door.

"It went okay, Mr. Buckman, plus I had a chance to meet Brad and some of the guys who work here."

"Watch out for those guys!" he laughed.

When he got back home, Leo's sister and dad had already gone to bed. Leo looked into Donna's room and smiled as he saw his little sister sound asleep. He washed up, recited a rosary and quickly dozed off.

Leo managed to get though the first week on the job without offending the shop steward, and absent any complaints from Mr. Buckman. On Friday afternoon after the break, he knocked on the half-open door of the boss's office door.

"Hi, Mr. Buckman. May I speak with you for a minute?"

"Sure, Leo—c'mon in. What's *going on* out there?"

"Well, uh, I, it's been a real crazy week for me around here, getting used to the plant layout and all, but I just need, um, a little more work to do. The evenings are tediously long because the job you gave me just doesn't take very much time to complete." Leo had unwittingly just broken a cardinal rule in the union code.

Mr. Buckman was stunned, and thoroughly amused by Leo's honest, naïve observation.

"Leo, son, listen. Don't *ever* let any of the guys out there *ever* hear you say that!" he said, regaining his composure. "Look, kid, I've been watching you; I understand what you're saying. I was just trying to give you something that would make it easy for you to adjust, after what your uncle told me about you. But, that's okay. I do have something that may be more interesting for you. There's a vacancy in our sub-assembly line, and I think you might like the job."

So, on Monday afternoon, Leo punched in and reported to the sub-assembly line where he was instructed by Shirley in the use of the electric screwdriver that hung from a long cord from the ceiling. All he had to do was use the tool to affix each shiny toaster shell to each toaster base that was deposited in his bin, using four aluminum screws. Leo was more relaxed than he had been all week.

"Yo, kid!" Shirley shouted over from her station about an hour into the shift. "Are you tryin' to set a *record* or somethin'?" She was holding her hands out, palms down, raising and lowering them. "Take it easy, Leo!"

This was a work ethic he had never before experienced. During all the years he worked for Irv Davis, Leo had given his all, working hard every day. This new, slowed-down approach to productivity made no sense to him.

"Hey, Leo, congratulations on your promotion!" Brad laughed as he sat down next to Leo for dinner. "You sure do move up quickly, kid! That uncle of yours must have a helluva lot of pull around here."

"No, uh, well, uh, I just didn't like the old job, so I asked Mr. Buckman if there was anything else available. I got lucky, I guess."

"So now you're screwin' around with old Shirley all night. That's a helluva a lot better than dancin' around with a fuckin' broom 'til midnight!"

Leo blushed, managing a quick chuckle.

After dinner Leo settled down. He continued his work with the electric screwdriver. Now that he was fully occupied for the entire shift, the evening seemed to fly by, as the number of toasters seemed endless. By the time he punched out from his last shift of the summer, at the end of August, Leo figured he had attached the shells to forty thousand pop-up toasters. He marveled at the thought of those toasters being shipped all over the country—with his fingerprints on every one of them.

The summer had indeed gone by quickly, much faster than he desired. He would soon have to leave his family in the most difficult time they ever experienced. On Labor Day, Leo packed up his foot-locker with the books and clothing he would need for the next school year. It was a sad task. All he could think about was his mom. How she joked with him as they sewed his laundry numbers into his clothing the summer before his first year at the seminary. The thought of her laughing and kidding around tore at his soul. In the morning, he sat down next to Donna at the kitchen table.

"I'm going to have to go back to the seminary today, Donna, so I won't see you when you get home from school. I'm gonna miss you, honey, but I'll be seeing you at our open house at the end of next month, and I'll show you my new room that we've been talking about. So you be a good girl for daddy and Aunt Sheryl, okay?"

Leo was holding back his tears as he kissed her before she left for school. He told his father he was sorry he had to be leaving home now with all that had happened.

"Don't worry, son. Go back to the seminary and keep working hard. You know your mother would certainly have wanted you to do that."

"I know dad, but you have so much to do around here; Donna is so young. How are you ever going to manage?"

"Your aunts and cousin have promised to help out with Donna, and you surely know I can cook. So, don't get yourself upset. We'll be all right."

Thomas and his father had arrived to pick up Leo for the trip back to the seminary. Leo and his dad stuffed the footlocker into the trunk of the car, then Leo slid into the back seat. The car pulled away. Standing where his mom had always joined them to wave good-bye, Donna and his dad were soon out of sight.

CHAPTER 7

In the 1960s, candidates for the priesthood in the Diocese of Allentown were generally required to complete ten years of education and training in the seminary. The third year had traditionally been considered the most difficult and challenging. It had historically been known as the "make or break" year, in which an unusually large number of students would be unable to meet the academic standards. Or, after three years of contemplation about their decision to enter the seminary, others would decide it was not the lifestyle they wished to pursue. Many would resign, concluding they would not be able to take the vow of celibacy and, as it demanded, remain unmarried for the rest of their lives. In still other cases, faculty members would designate students as unsuitable for the priesthood based on their observations of the students' behavior over the first three years. Of those seminarians who successfully completed the third year of studies, the vast majority generally continued on to become ordained priests.

Greek, Latin, Rhetoric, Logic, Rational Psychology and Statistics were courses that required intense study and concentration. Classes in Logic and Rational Psychology were taught in Latin. Professors lectured in Latin; students were required to respond in Latin to questions posed in the class. Textbooks were printed in Latin, and all exam questions were written in Latin, the students being required to answer them in that language as well.

While students studied Latin during the first two years of seminary training, Ancient Greek was a new language in the third-year curriculum that presented many challenges. Successfully completing the crucially important third year would require more focus and energy than in previous years. Leo began the critical bellwether year in a fragile emotional state. The traumatic events of the summer left him reeling. He constantly worried about Donna. Leaving home at such a critically important time in her young life seemed terribly wrong. Leo's guilt hounded him during the weeks before the seminary year began. Doubts about the ability of his father to care for her plagued him. What would happen to her? His mother had taken such wonderful care of Donna. How would his dad, who, in all fairness, had never before been required to take care of Donna, cope with this new responsibility?

During the five-day religious retreat before the school year began, Leo prayed for strength. His attempts at meditation turned into reveries about his family at home, especially about the difficult adjustments they would all be going through at this time—without him. When classes began, he tried to concentrate on his studies, but with little success. The lectures were hard to follow. He couldn't deal with the Latin being used in the classroom. He was singled out by several of his professors for his listlessness and "lack of preparation." Leo's life was in free fall, and he knew it. The professor-priests seemed totally unaware of the tumultuous summer Leo had endured. If aware, they were—at best—indifferent to his plight. None of them ever reached out to him to comfort him. They seemed unapproachable, so, in turn, Leo never sought out their support. The spiritual director, Father Solliday, had been assigned to other duties in the diocese, and was now pastor of a large parish church in northeast Philadelphia. The only priest he could have consulted was gone.

His mind kept going back to the morning when his mother died. He could not explain the sudden, severe asthma attack that had awakened him. Could it have been a sign from his mom that she was leaving them? Was she trying to contact him to say "good-bye"? He had read about Extra Sensory Perception and how it had been documented so many times. Was his mother reaching out to him as a prolonged, final asthma attack was about to end her life? And what about her recent plea that he never forget her? Had she known her life was about to end? Thoughts about his mom and things he could have done for her while she was alive gnawed at him. Guilt for leaving his sister behind to be taken care of by one relative or another depending on what day of the week they were available, tore him apart. His feeling of helplessness was exacerbated by the thought of his dad, with his volatile temperament, having to raise a rambunctious, energetic little girl. During one of his numerous evenings lying awake, unable to sleep, Leo resorted to writing down his feelings.

All is still—
And as I lie here in sleep's quiet prelude
Witnessing before me the day's events again
Wish I could change the course of them
But never the chance will come again.

Words I said—
Would that their uttering could be recalled
Replaced by kinder, sympathetic tones
Restoring broken bonds of confidence and trust
But never the chance will come again.

Deeds I did—
Damage done by actions now abhorred
Could I but reform them doing all things well
Clearing this nocturnal day's regret
But never the chance will come again.

Prayers not said—
Precious aids to virtue cast aside
Turning I instead to self-made panaceas
Trying, then, proud litanies to recant
But never the chance will come again.

I shall die—
Infinite nights like this I shall possess
Reliving actions past incessantly
Resolving greater love to next time show
But never the chance will come again.

Would he be able to continue on his road to the priesthood? Even the kind, compassionate letter from Sister Mary Christina expressing her sorrow at his mom's death, and discussing the "unknowable plan of God," failed to inspire him. His father's first letter arrived a few days after Leo had left home. He tried to reassure Leo that everything was going smoothly. He had Donna transferred to the parish school so she could be closer to her home. He recounted how Donna had just finished a steak dinner he had prepared, and was now working on her homework assignments with his help. "We're fine here," he wrote. "Don't worry about us."

A letter from his father arrived about every twelve days or so. Although Leo's mother had written every other day, he knew his father was extremely busy with his new responsibilities. He treasured those letters.

In one of them he stated, "Yesterday I bought a new school uniform and two new blouses for Donna. Today I'm going to take her to the Allentown Fair." As the letters arrived, Leo was beginning to feel more confident that his father was coping with his new dual role as father and mother. He seemed to be taking well to his new tasks. "Today I baked a chocolate cake, and Donna said, 'It's just like mommy used to make!' " A bittersweet feeling of pain and relief pierced Leo's heart as he read those words.

The annual open house day at the seminary, which formerly Leo had so happily anticipated, took on a different meaning this time. In the past, Leo missed his family and looked forward to being reunited with them. This time, the day would provide an opportunity for Leo to evaluate how his father was coping with his loss and new responsibilities. It was so very critical for Leo to assess how Donna was faring after these first months—four of them already—without her mother. He would have to decide whether he could possibly continue with his studies if there were problems at home. Leo's father and sister were accompanied by his Aunt Megan and Uncle Tim. As the day progressed, Leo became increasingly convinced that Donna was adjusting to her mom's death far better than he had expected. His father appeared to have taken on his new role very successfully. As he watched them leave the seminary grounds at the end of the day, Leo was relieved. Donna was still a happy little girl.

"Donna got the measles!" his father announced in his first letter after the open house. "I'm busy being a nurse, now! I learned a lot when she had the chicken pox last year." About a week later his dad reported, "Donna's measles are finally gone, and she can go back to school on Monday. Fortunately, there were no complications. Oh, and that pink, neon peep that survived Donna's care since Easter—it's now a fully grown rooster, crowing every morning, annoying all the neighbors. I had to give it to the farm where you and Ellen spent that wonderful vacation one summer. Donna was very upset, but I promised her that you would take her there to visit it."

On Friday, November 22, about six weeks after returning to the seminary from the summer break, Leo's Public Speaking class had just ended. He stayed behind to discuss some of the points of the session with the professor. His classmates had already gone to get a quick smoke on the back porch before the daily visit to the chapel. As Leo left the classroom, just after one-thirty in the afternoon, he walked down the front corridor toward the center of the building; passing by the receptionist's office, he noticed she was hunched over, her head propped up in her hands and leaning against the switchboard, close to the small radio on her desk. She was crying. Leo stopped. The somber, hesitant voice on the radio became clearer ... and increasingly more distraught with every phrase:

> *From Dallas, Texas: We repeat, President Kennedy has been shot as his motorcade passed through Dealey Plaza in downtown Dallas. One moment, ladies and gentlemen; we have just learned that John F. Kennedy, the thirty-fourth president of the United States of America, is dead. He was shot by an assassin as his motorcade passed the Texas School Book Depository building in Dallas. The President was pronounced dead at Parkland Hospital in Dallas, Texas.*

Leo stood there in disbelief. All the horrific events of the year—his mother, his grandmother, his beloved Pope, and now his president—all gone in just nine months. He ran through the lobby and down the stairs to the back porch. He approached a klatch of his closest friends who were just nearing the end of their smoke break.

"President Kennedy is dead!" he said, half crying. "He was shot—and killed—in Dallas."

"Hey, cut it out, Leo. *Honestly*, that's nothing to joke about," Patrick said.

"No, look, I'm *serious*. I just heard—"

His words were interrupted by the Voice of God calling everyone to chapel.

"Five minutes too early," groaned Patrick. "I haven't even finished my cigarette!"

The seminarians quickly made their way to chapel for the daily visit to the Blessed Sacrament and prayer of forgiveness. But this day, the prayer session would be completely different. As they assembled in the pews, the rector of the seminary was standing in front of the altar. Monsignor Connors began speaking. "My dear seminarians, we have just learned that President John F. Kennedy has been shot in Dallas, Texas. The president is dead. We have no other information at this time."

Sighs and gasps emanated from the pews on either side of the aisle. A number of seminarians began weeping at the shocking, unimaginable news.

"Please join me in prayer," the Monsignor said.

Requiem aeternam dona eis, Domine.
(Eternal rest grant on to them, O Lord.)
Et lux perpetua luceat eis.
(And let perpetual light shine upon them.)
Cum sanctis tuis in aeternum.
(With your saints forever.)
Quia pius es.
(For you are merciful.)
Kyrie, eleison.
(Lord, have mercy.)
Christe, eleison.
(Christ, have mercy.)
Kyrie, eleison.
(Christ, have mercy.)
Amen.

The cold, hushed chapel was suddenly transformed into a virtual mortuary. It was later announced that on Tuesday evening a Solemn High Requiem Mass would be celebrated by the Cardinal at the Cathedral of Saints Peter and Paul.

That evening, the cathedral and adjacent chapel were already overflowing with mourners as the buses with more than six hundred seminarians arrived among the crowd jamming 18th Street in front of the cathedral's main entrance. The small park across from the cathedral overflowed with people, filling Logan Circle and the Benjamin Franklin Parkway. The Choir of Saint Francis Seminary sang Perosi's Requiem, one of the most beautiful, ethereal Masses ever written.

Back at the seminary, evening prayers were completed and silence prevailed until the nine o'clock lights-out bell rang. Leo lay awake unable to think about anything clearly. Just as he was attempting to reorder his life after his mother's sudden passing, the shock from this latest tragedy tore open his emotional wounds. He gazed up at the ceiling of his tiny room, then jumped out of bed. Sitting at his desk he began recording his thoughts about President Kennedy. In the morning after breakfast he returned to his room to compose an ode to the man who so greatly inspired him. It was the most inspiring meditation he had yet experienced since entering the seminary.

A young man in a world grown old
From hatred, greed and strife
Set out restoring its youth again
For this he gave his life.

John Kennedy loved his land so well
He planned a New Frontier
To bring a better life to man—
A modern pioneer.
He held on high the torch bequeathed
And ne'er its light grew dim
To all the nations of the world
That flame represented him.

In states abroad that flame did glow
Fired by youthful zeal
Peasants, presidents and kings
Their hearts it would anneal.

He journeyed through his cherished land
With vigor he'd proclaim
To better learn his people's needs
And their president to remain.

John Fitzgerald with Jacqueline
Through Dallas journeyed one day
And in the shadows of the sun
A killer stalked his prey.

Awful sound that warns of death
Was never heard by him
And his glowing smile disappeared
As the flame of life grew dim.

JFK, though you are dead
Your memory lives on
A world that you made younger
Is older since you've gone.

Leo's visit with his family on Thanksgiving Day a few days later, reassured him they were coping well with the loss of his mother. After nearly seven months of shock, loss and grief, Leo began to see hopeful signs for them. The anxiety he experienced since the beginning of the school year began to ease. When his professor of Rhetoric assigned a term paper, Leo wrote a satire on his experiences the previous summer at the General Electric plant. The paper won him the highest grade in the class, and praise from the normally hypercritical professor. His confidence began to return. Leo's grades in Greek and Latin rose. And, even more importantly, he was feeling more positive about his future in the seminary.

The Christmas holidays were the saddest ever for Leo. He remembered his mother's pleas to "never forget me." During the summer break Leo had taken to a photographer in town the photo of his mother as a bridesmaid in his aunt's wedding, just three months before she died. He had the photo enlarged into an 11" x 17" color portrait, and mounted in a four-inch-wide, white wooden frame with gold leaf highlights. It was the last photograph ever taken of his mother. He gave it to his father and Donna for Christmas. It was just one way of keeping his promise to his mom that he would always remember her. Seeing the portrait for the first time was a difficult moment for his dad, but Leo told him about that strange evening with his mother at the restaurant, so his father understood Leo's reason for the gift. After the holidays, his dad hung the portrait over the living room sofa, directly across the room from the portrait of Pope John. Leo was proud and happy that his dad was pleased with the gift. Donna, too, loved the portrait of her mother. She always pointed it out when family and guests visited.

The spring semester was nearly over. The courses continued to be challenging, requiring long hours of study. Leo was happy he was finally able to concentrate on the work. It was an escape from the grief that continued to hound him. He was exhausted as the break approached. He looked forward to helping his dad with work around the house and backyard and taking Donna to the movies on Saturday and to church on Sundays—just spending time at home with them.

When Leo visited Irv Davis during the break, he learned that Jonathan's illness had worsened, preventing him from working or returning to college. Irv offered Leo his old summer job. Leo looked forward to returning to the delivery job he had so much enjoyed before. It would be refreshing to be outdoors every day, on the road.

Leo returned to the seminary with a renewed outlook. Seeing his father and Donna adjusting so well truly comforted him. He knew there were some difficult days for them, but his father and sister had become much closer, sharing the cooking chores, and enjoying their time together in the evenings and on weekends. Dramatically raising his spirits was the prospect of returning to the summer job he had so much enjoyed two years earlier. He began to apply himself more vigorously to his studies, focusing more clearly on his long-term goals. As the benchmark third year in the seminary ended, Leo felt he had at last turned the corner on what had been the most horrendous and challenging year of his life.

CHAPTER 8

Leo had done well in all his examinations, surviving the reputed worst year of the long seminary regimen. He looked forward with grateful relief to the summer break and returning to his old job at the restaurant supply company. Irv Davis had written to Leo in April, confirming his offer of employment for Leo in his old delivery route to northern New Jersey. On the following Monday, Leo checked in early with Irv, who introduced him to the new guys in the stock room as they loaded up his truck for the deliveries that day. He found his new fellow-employees aloof and uninteresting. They lacked the spark he so much enjoyed with the guys with whom he had worked for so many years. His good friend Tony was no longer employed there. As he checked his schedule, Leo noticed he would be traveling to northwestern New Jersey that day. He was going back to Culver Lake, to the old hotel where that unnerving incident with his friend June, about Marilyn Monroe's tragic death, had occurred. Driving into the old familiar parking lot, he noticed a fresh coat of grey paint on the façade of the hotel. After he backed the truck up to the storage room, he exited with enthusiasm, hoping to see June and, maybe, reestablish the friendship they once enjoyed. Leo looked across the lot to the swimming pool, where June usually awaited his arrival, but he noticed instead a young man reclining on a chaise lounge next to the pool. He was wearing red-and-dark blue madras shorts and a thin, powder-blue jersey.

His bright-blue sunglasses reflected the mid-day light; he seemed focused on the book in his hands. Leo noticed a clipboard and keys on the table next to the nonchalant figure lounging there, so he walked over to him, assuming he was in charge that day.

"Excuse me. Uh, hi, I'm Leo. I have the, uh, restaurant supply order for the hotel. I'm looking for June. Do you know if she's here today?"

The young man was silent as he continued reading. Then, finally, he raised his head, closed the book, looked up at Leo from his comfortable perch at the pool, and stared at him through blue-tinted lenses for what seemed like an hour.

"Hullo! Matt here." The young man raised his right hand, finally acknowledging Leo's presence. "I'm afraid, um, you're going to have to deal with me instead, man." As Matt spoke, Leo paused as he saw his own reflection in Matt's metallic blue sunglasses.

"Fine, uh, *Matt*? Thanks. Okay, I'll go back to my truck and unload your order for today." But Leo didn't move.

As he slid off the lounge, Matt grabbed the set of keys from the table, whisking up the clipboard and the folded *New York Times* beneath it. Barefoot, he sashayed over toward Leo, removed his sunglasses, and offered his hand.

"Pleasure to meet you, *Leo*?" Matt's thick, straight, light-blond hair was neatly groomed, falling just above his bright green eyes. He was looking directly at Leo. His firm, slender body, bronzed by an early deep suntan, indicated he spent a lot of time at the swimming pool. He was a good two inches taller than Leo.

"Hi! Yes. Uh, same here, Matt." Leo shook his hand.

"I'll open up the room for you, Leo."

Leo opened the rear doors of the truck, climbed in, and began pulling packages off the shelves. He brought the first couple of items into the storage room, where Matt by then was waiting. As Leo placed the packages on the floor for inventory, Matt stopped him.

"Leo, you, uh, you asked for *June* when you arrived." Matt's expression had turned grim—and he was looking carefully at Leo as he spoke.

"Yeah. She and I used to have a lot of fun. I really missed seeing her last year when I was unable to return to this job. I often think about her when—"

"Umm, Leo. *Wow*! I, I'm, uh, how do I … ? God, I'm so sorry to have to tell you this but, June is, is … June's *dead*, Leo."

"Matt! What are you *talking* about? She's only twenty-two years old! How could—"

"Leo, look, I'm *sorry*, man. If you knew June, you probably realize she was kind of wild. One night last summer after she left a party with some of her friends, she was flying down Route 517 in her yellow *T-Bird* convertible. She slammed into the stone wall of the bridge down there. She was thrown out of her car and broke her neck and spine when she hit a tree on the other side of the road. They found a few rolled joints in the back seat."

Leo couldn't speak. He could not deal with the shocking story about this latest unthinkable tragedy—another sudden death. It was far more than he could handle. He slumped against the wooden shelves behind him, buried his face in his hands and began weeping uncontrollably. Matt put his arms around him, embracing him.

"Leo, God, I'm so, so damned sorry I had to be the one to tell you this horrible news," Matt whispered. "We all miss June so much. She was such fun, and a terrific person."

Leo was sobbing, trying desperately to compose himself. He was embarrassed by his show of emotion. Leo was staring up at Matt's glistening green eyes that were, themselves, rapidly filling with tears. Matt looked sad, yet he had a confident and calming smile on his face.

"We were all lucky to have known her, Leo."

"You're right, Matt, but I, I just can't believe it. God, I wish my last visit with her had been more pleasant. It was on that horrible day that Marilyn Monroe died; June was so very upset. I just couldn't seem to help her." Tears were streaming down Leo's cheeks.

"She never got over that, either, man."

Matt was caressing Leo now. Leo, still crying, felt warmly comforted. He and Matt had become sexually aroused, but Leo couldn't move. He didn't want to. For a moment he didn't care. It all felt so natural, so good, so welcomed. They pushed their throbbing bodies against each other more forcefully, softly swaying. Leo was holding on to Matt—he didn't *want* to let go. Suddenly, they heard footsteps approaching the room from the steps outside. They quickly broke apart.

"Was that *you*, Leo?" a gruff voice yelled from outside the door.

Leo grabbed one of the packages from the floor, holding it in front of him. Matt turned toward the stockroom shelves and began aimlessly counting the *packages. "Mmmm, let's see, chef hats, tablecloths, cocktail glasses, ..."*

Leo recognized the voice of June's father. Mr. Freeling looked in the door and nodded.

"It's great to see you again, Leo. How've you been, son?"

"Well, uh, Mr. Freeling, uh, my God! Matt just told me the horrible news about June. I'm just so very *sorry*. She was such a, uh, such a wonderful person. I'm truly sorry for your loss, Mr. Freeling."

"Leo, I think about her every day. What a waste of a human life. You know she always loved to go out and have a good time, but she was a good girl. That goddamned *pot*; if only she could have stayed away from it."

Mr. Freeling dropped his head low for a moment, then looked straight up at Leo.

"Glad to see you back, kid. June used to talk about you a lot, how she enjoyed kidding around with you, getting you all worked up and all," he chuckled. "She really liked you, kid. Well, ... look, Matt, here, will take good care of you. I look forward to seeing you around again this summer. Good luck with your job, Leo."

"Take it easy, Mr. Freeling." Leo followed him out to the stairs and watched him amble down the sidewalk to the hotel lobby.

"Whew, that was close!" Matt sighed. "I'm sorry for, uh, for what happened back there, Leo. I guess I just got a bit carried away with the mood of the moment."

"Matt, *I'm* not sorry. That was beautiful, Matt—I loved it. Thank you for being so warm and comforting. Sorry I got so worked up and all, but, I, I just can't believe that June is ... "

Leo completed the delivery, gave the receipt to Matt, and walked toward the truck.

"Hey, Leo, you know, uh, you really look kind of groovy in that white uniform you're wearing. I'll see you in a couple of weeks, man. Be careful out there." Matt winked at Leo.

Leo turned around, and shook his head in amusement.

"You, too, Matt. See you next time." He climbed back into the truck, started it up and drove down the driveway, watching Matt in the side mirror.

Leo headed south on Route 206. As he stopped for the traffic light at the intersection of Route 517, he turned his head to the right, looking down the road he had so often traveled on his way to make his deliveries in Warren County. He knew that section where the bridge was located. He was familiar with the huge stone wall near its entrance.

How absolutely tragic this all is. Poor June—she had just begun to live her life, now she's gone. He remembered Mr. Freeling's words, trying to find some consolation in knowing that June, despite their run-in last year, had continued to like him and had spoken fondly of him to her father.

Leo was now plagued by more mixed emotions than he experienced since he entered the seminary three years before. Driving back to the restaurant supply company, he was trying to sort out what happened that afternoon. Was it wrong to embrace Matt the way he had? He was sexually aroused by this handsome guy who sought to comfort him.

Did he commit a mortal sin? There was no sexual contact between them, but would the incident have gone further had Mr. Freeling not appeared on the scene? All that Leo knew was that, for the first time in more than a year and a half, he felt close to someone who expressed real feelings and emotions for him. It was refreshing and exhilarating. His Church taught that the purpose of sexual relations is for the procreation of children. Any sex outside of marriage is forbidden and mortally sinful. Sex is intended by God to bring children into the world. But Leo's first year studying Logic began to raise serious questions in his mind about a number of the Church's teachings. He hoped to resolve them as he continued his studies for the priesthood. In Logic class he was taught that *A* is *A*. It was pure, simple logic. It was indisputable. So, what about men and women who get married knowing they are incapable of producing children? What about men and women who are elderly and thus beyond their childbearing years who get married and have sexual relations? Are they all living in sin? *A* is *A*. Can two persons who truly love each other possibly have sexual relations without committing a mortal sin, damning them to everlasting hell? None of it made any sense to Leo now. If he finally found some long-sought comfort for his sorrow in the arms of a new friend, could that really, *really* be sinful? He simply could not believe it.

The next day in confession, Leo told the priest about the incident with Matt.

"My son, you are placing yourself in a near occasion of sin that could lead you into serious sin."

"But Father, we didn't have sex. Was it sinful to embrace the way we did? Yes, we were sexually aroused, Father, but we went no further."

"You are placing yourself and your future in serious jeopardy, my son. Think of the life that you have chosen to lead. Do you want that to happen, or are you willing to give in to the temptations of the flesh, losing your vocation—maybe even your soul? You must distance yourself from the man you have met. Avoid any personal contact with him beyond your business duties."

"I, I guess I hadn't thought about it that way, Father."

"For your penance, I want you to make the Stations of the Cross, thinking about the suffering Jesus had to endure in order to achieve his grand goal of salvation for mankind. Place yourself in those Stations; apply that strength to your current struggle. May almighty God bless you, the Father, the Son and the Holy Ghost. Go in peace, your sins are forgiven."

"Amen."

Leo left the confessional, and walked upstairs to the main church to meditate on the Stations of the Cross. The church was empty and dark, except for the glow of the stained glass windows. A few candles flickered in their red and blue votive lights burning next to the altar of the Blessed Mother. Leo walked down the center aisle to where his mother's casket had been placed during her funeral Mass. Would she understand what he was experiencing? Would she be upset with him? Would she be ashamed of him? Would she still *love* him?

He knelt down, beginning the Stations of the Cross—*Jesus is condemned to death*. Had the priest in the confessional already passed sentence on Leo? Would any future contact with Matt lead to his condemnation by God and His holy Church?

He got to the third Station—*Jesus falls the first time*. This was not the first time for Leo. He had fallen many times when he was younger. Was he unable to follow in the footsteps of Jesus? Had this latest incident shown him who he truly was? Would it be possible to go through life without the love and physical passion shared with someone he really loved? Leo could not continue. He needed to get fresh air, take a long walk. He had to think about recent events. Maybe it was time for him to change his life again. Contrary to the priest's directive, he left the church without completing the Stations of the Cross.

When he went to Mass the next morning, Leo prayed for guidance. *Jesus, have I come so far only to learn that I'm on the wrong path? Please help me understand what I'm supposed to do.*

Back at the restaurant supply company that day, Leo learned that Irv's son had taken a turn for the worse and had been admitted to a hospital in Philadelphia. Irv would not be in the office that day. Leo was saddened to hear about Jonathan's deteriorating condition—the latest tragic development.

Two weeks later, as he prepared for his delivery route on a hot and humid Friday morning back to Culver Lake, Leo's mind was spinning. What was he going to do when he saw Matt again? Should he try to avoid him, just go about his business without speaking with him personally? It just didn't seem right to ignore Matt. He had been so kind to Leo on his last trip up there. Leo was haunted by the priest's admonition during his confession. Was he once again about to place himself in a near occasion of sin? As he entered the driveway of the hotel, Leo saw no sign of Matt. *This is a blessing. I can finish my delivery and avoid contact with him this week.* He backed the truck up to the storage room. He knew that a key was available at the front desk of the hotel. But when Leo stepped down from the truck and turned toward the hotel, Matt was waiting for him, two opened bottles of ice-cold Coca-Cola in his hands. He gave one to Leo, clinking his green bottle against Leo's.

"Cheers, Leo. It's terrific seeing you again, man!"

"Oh, Matt, I, uh, well, I have to … , yeah, *cheers*!" Leo's mind was reeling. *How am I going to avoid any personal contact now?*

"Leo, Mr. Freeling's not in today. I'm in charge of this great old place once again. Let's go over to the pool and get better acquainted. I'll get some sandwiches from the kitchen and—"

"Wai—, wait a minute, Matt. I have a few more stops to make before I head back to Pennsylvania and—"

"Now, hold *on*, Leo. You gotta eat lunch, man! I mean, what's a half hour or so going to do—wreck your schedule?"

"Well, yeah, okay, Matt. That sounds fine, I guess. Thanks."

"Great! I'll run into the kitchen and grab a couple of subs."

As Matt dashed off, Leo's heart was pounding. He had placed himself in a personal situation he had been warned to avoid.

Matt was animated as he returned with the sandwiches. "Here ya go, Leo. Hope you like it." Matt placed the plate in front of Leo.

"Thanks, Matt. This is terrific." He looked at the sandwich, trying to avoid Matt's probing stare.

"So, Leo, I heard from Mr. Freeling that you're in college in Philadelphia—that you're studying to be a, uh, priest. Is that *right?*" Matt was chomping on the sandwich as he spoke.

Leo was embarrassed; he knew he was blushing. He tried to respond, but searching for the right words failed.

"Hey, don't worry about it, man! I have some good friends who've done just what you're trying to do. I know what you're going through, buddy."

"Matt, I just didn't want to give you the wrong impression. I know we had become somewhat, uh, intimate last time I was here, and I hope you, uh, don't think I am some kind of hypocrite or something."

"Never crossed my mind, man! You're a human being with all the emotions that come with your mind and body. You and I were living in the moment. You know, Leo, I really *like* you. You're not like most guys I meet. You're sincere, innocent and well-meaning. I can tell you are truly concerned about other people, too. I mean, the way you broke down when I told you the tragic news about June; you were so genuinely hurt by all that—and you had known her for just a short time. I have to tell you, Leo, I don't regret our intimate contact. I surely hope it wasn't the last time that happens."

"Well, uh, thanks Matt. That's very nice of you to say. But, uh, see, the Catholic Church views things quite differently. They forbid sexual activity of any kind between unmarried people, and—"

"Is that absolutely *crazy* or what? What the hell do they think people are—*robots*? How are you supposed to live in this world as a flesh-and-blood human being with feelings and emotions, without interacting with your fellow human beings? It makes no sense at all. Are you really going to be able to do that for the rest of your life, Leo?"

"You know, Matt, that's exactly what's troubling me right now. When I confessed my, uh, transgression to a priest a couple of weeks ago, he reminded me about the consequences I'd face if I continued such contacts. It just threw me into a tailspin. I have to come to grips with it soon if I want to continue with my studies."

"Wow, Leo. You are in one *hell* of a predicament, man! You should—"

"But we've only been talking about *me* for the past fifteen minutes. What have *you* been up to? I mean, what are your plans for the future, Matt? We're about the same age, I think."

"Well, um, I'm twenty-two years old, Leo. I'm about to start my final year of studies at Muhlenberg College, in Allentown. Temple University is offering courses in psychology there now, so I thought it would be easier than studying in Philadelphia. I'll move on to Temple for my graduate work in psychology next year."

"What a coincidence, Matt. I live in Allentown, so I'm very familiar with the Muhlenberg campus. We used to go to high-school basketball playoff games there. And Temple has a beautiful campus, Matt. Last year I visited an old high school friend there. He had a small room in Johnson Hall. I had a chance to walk around the campus with him; I was really impressed with the new architecture. It's an unusual mix of college buildings, row houses, bars and shops. Oh, and, yes, we *are* about the same age. I'll be twenty-three next month."

"Well, I don't like the idea of living on campus, so during the school year I rent an apartment on Glendale Street with one of my classmates, Dave Hunsicker. He's a nice guy, funny as hell, and 'simpatico'—if you know what I mean. We get along very well and he swings the way I do." Matt laughed. "So, we're gonna have to get together some time down there when you're home. Do they let you out of that old monastery during the year?"

"It's not really a monastery. The seminary is more like a college campus. We have breaks over Christmas and Easter holidays, when we are allowed to go home. And, of course, we're off all summer." Leo finished his sandwich and washed it down with the remaining Coke. "I think I'd better get your order together before it gets too late. Thanks a lot for the lunch. I've enjoyed getting better acquainted with you, Matt."

"Right, Leo. Same here, buddy. Let's get over to the old storage room and stow those packages away." Matt grabbed his keys and made his way casually across the parking lot to unlock the room.

As Leo brought in the first few packages, Matt helped lift them onto the shelves. When Leo finished the rest of the order, he turned to Matt to give him the receipt. With no warning—no possible way to know what was about to happen next—Leo felt Matt's arms around his back drawing Leo closer to him. In an instant, he was kissing Leo firmly on his lips. Leo's mind was exploding. He wanted to push Matt away, but it wasn't possible. He was enjoying the intimate contact more than anything he experienced since his late evening trysts with Terry on her living room sofa. They were both aroused, barely able to control their mounting emotions. Leo pressed his lips against Matt's mouth, then forced himself away, looking into Matt's bright green eyes. Leo was smiling, but he felt terrified.

"God, Matt! I can't tell you how wonderful that was and how totally perplexed I am right now. You have no idea what confusion you've just created within me."

"Leo, I'm afraid you've really *gotten* to me, man. I know it sounds crazy; we've only spent a few of hours or so together, but the last time you left here, I just couldn't stop thinking about you. I hope we can continue to be friends and get to know each other better this summer."

Leo's hands were shaking as he gave Matt the crumpled receipt for the day's supplies. He looked at Matt and smiled.

"I'll look forward to seeing you next time, Matt."

"Same here, buddy. I hope you're not too late, and that I haven't gotten you into any trouble, Leo. That's the last thing I'd want to do."

"Thanks, Matt. Don't worry; everything is *fine*."

But it wasn't.

Back on Route 206 Leo's mind was running at a thousand times its normal pace. His contact with Matt was emotionally rewarding. It was the first time in years he had related to someone on such a personal level. He thought about Jeff at the seminary, and all the good times they enjoyed together playing sports. Yet they never had become close enough to share any personal thoughts. Certainly, they never experienced any sexual feelings toward each other; at least, that's what Leo thought. Now, he wasn't so sure. Had he been suppressing his feelings for Jeff? Had Jeff, too, been confused about his feelings toward Leo? Could that be the reason why Jeff disappeared from the seminary so suddenly and quietly? He would probably never know.

Leo finished his final delivery of the day, to the Boy Scout Camp in Stokes State Forest. All the way home Leo thought about the confession he would have to make the next morning. What was the priest going to say now? Had he not warned Leo about the consequences of further contact with Matt? Was the priest right in his conclusion? Was Leo now lost? He got very little sleep that evening.

On Saturday morning Leo played a few games of "Uncle Wiggly" with Donna before taking care of some housecleaning to help his father. Saturdays used to be so much fun in the Weber home—when his aunts and uncles would come over to watch television shows with him and his mother. Leo remembered how he would entertain them with his impressions of Hollywood stars. But that was all over now. He vacuumed the living room carpet and dusted off the portrait of Pope John, then looked at the picture of his mother. *Where am I going, mom?* Could she hear him? Did she still care about him? He decided to take a walk into town to enjoy the beautiful summer day. But all the while, thoughts of his impending afternoon confession taunted him. Finally, it was time to face his confessor.

"Bless me, Father, for I have sinned. It has been two weeks since my last confession. I tried to avoid it, Father, but I just couldn't. I kissed another man passionately, and, in my heart, I did not want it to end."

"My son, I warned you about the consequences of placing yourself in this near occasion of sin. You have failed, and so you are now suffering the guilt that comes with it. You are a young man with a very powerful sex drive. That is normal, but having sexual desires for another man is unnatural, and contrary to the will of God. You must abandon these thoughts and avoid that person who causes them, or you will be lost."

"Father, how can I avoid him? I have a job that requires me to see him every two weeks. I can't quit my job."

"Son, you must avoid any personal contact with that person. When you see him, do not allow yourself to be pulled into a personal conversation. Explain that your situation demands chastity and abstinence. Just complete your business with him and politely leave the place. You have practiced such strong discipline over the past few years to get to the point where you are. Don't give all that up for the lurid temptation that your infatuation has created. Remember Jesus and his temptations. Pray for strength, my son. For your penance I want you to say the rosary, contemplating on each prayer the sufferings of Jesus, and all that he has sacrificed for you. May almighty God bless you, the Father, the Son and the Holy Ghost."

"Amen."

Leo left the confessional, walked upstairs, down the center aisle to the first pew on the right, where he had sat during his mother's funeral. Cupping his face in his hands, he prayed.

"Mom, please help me through this. You've always been there when I needed you," he whispered. "Please help me now."

He began praying the rosary, determined to follow the old priest's advice.

Over the next few days Leo thought about ways to address the problem concerning Matt. He decided he would complete a few deliveries before going to the hotel—deliveries he would normally complete only after leaving Culver Lake—then double back to the hotel. That schedule would have him arriving later at the hotel, giving him an excuse to rush through his delivery there and thus avoid any prolonged personal contact with Matt. So when he set out on his regular route in the following week, he followed the plan, arriving at Culver Lake much later than usual. As he steered the truck into the driveway of the hotel on that very hot, mid-July afternoon, Leo could see that the swimming pool was bustling. There were about fifty guests around the pool that day. On previous trips, when Leo arrived at the hotel earlier in the day, few if any folks would be using the pool. He drove into the parking lot looking at the beautiful summer scene around the pool through the large front windshield of his truck. Then, suddenly, he noticed Matt sitting high above the pool in the lifeguard chair, wearing tight red swim briefs. His bright blonde hair was wet, hanging helter-skelter over his forehead. His blue reflecting sunglasses were firmly fixed over his eyes. A silver whistle dangled from a red cord around Matt's neck, nestling into the center of his bare, muscular chest. His folded arms emphasized Matt's well-developed biceps.

Leo parked the van in the usual space for deliveries. Having to make this a very quick stop, Leo hurried over to the pool to get Matt to unlock the storage room. As Leo entered the swimming pool area, Matt got out of the chair and stood up on the top step of the ladder. His slender five-foot, eleven-inch frame glistened with perspiration in the hot sun. Leo was dazzled as he shielded his eyes from the glaring sun, looking straight up at Matt, who was standing about eight feet above his head like a Greek sculpture that had suddenly come to life wearing a red swimsuit.

"Hi Matt, so ... you're the *lifeguard* today, huh?"

"Hey, Leo, whatever they want me to do, I'll do it, man. Yesterday I was the waiter. Sometimes I'm in the kitchen. Whatever! You know me, I'm always very *accommodating*." He lifted his sun glasses and gave Leo a smart wink.

"Say, uh, Matt, I'm *really* in a hurry today. You can see that I'm more than an hour late. They gave me a couple of new stops to service."

"I sure hope they're giving you a few more bucks for all of your work, buddy."

"No. I'm afraid I'm on a fixed pay scale for the summer, so that won't happen."

"They're fucking slave drivers, man. You ought to complain to the union."

Matt turned around and began to climb down from the lifeguard station. Each slow, deliberate step he took on his way down highlighted his firm buttocks trapped in the swimsuit. Leo noticed that just about everybody else around the pool was gazing at Matt, too. Just as before, Matt grabbed his keys, clipboard, the *New York Times*, and a book from the table, then walked toward Leo.

"Okay, man. I don't want to keep you from your appointed rounds," he announced, standing close to Leo and looking directly at him, his eyes dancing.

"Matt, I can't believe you're reading *The Conscience of a Conservative*?" Leo said as they ambled over to the storage room.

"Hey, Goldwater's not *all* bad. You know, man, we've talked about politics before. I'm a Democrat like you, but I can't take much more of that LBJ character! Yeah, he got Kennedy's Civil Rights Act passed, and that's great, but this Vietnam crap is getting totally out of control."

"Matt, I've been thinking the same thing. Johnson is just such a radical change from Kennedy. Those wonderful Camelot years have been replaced by Texas barbeques and dog-ear-pulling stunts. It's just too much!"

"Yeah! That, too!"

Leo hurried to get the hotel's order from the truck, bringing the packages to the storage room in record time.

"Whoa, buddy! You sure as hell *are* in a rush today, aren't you?"

"Sorry to hurry you along, Matt, but, if I get back to the warehouse late, I'll have about four guys ready to jump me."

"Hey, what's wrong with *that*, man?"

Leo laughed—too hastily, he thought.

"I got ya on that one, buddy!" Matt poked him in the chest.

"Matt, you are absolutely out of this world," Leo said, again letting his guard down. He handed Matt the receipt, shook his hand, and quickly turned away.

"Take care, Matt. See you next time."

"Yeah, *next* time, Leo! Be careful, and don't rush too much to get home to those warehouse guys." Matt was smiling again as Leo turned away.

Leo laughed. "Take it easy, Matt."

He drove through the parking lot, looking for one final glimpse of Matt in the side mirror before turning the corner to Route 206. Matt was standing with both arms raised high above his head, his nearly naked body stretched in a grand gesture of good-bye. Leo shook his head and smiled. As he drove down the familiar highway, Leo was elated. He had done it! He avoided the occasion of sin as his confessor had pleaded with him to do. He figured out a way to visit his friend without getting stuck in a situation that could destroy his chosen path in life.

When Leo returned to Culver Lake two weeks later, he had barely backed up the truck and turned off the ignition when the hotel owner stepped into the van. Mr. Freeling was a stocky, two-hundred and twenty-five-pound middle-aged man, about six-foot, three-inches tall. His tousled light-brown hair was streaked throughout with gray. His ruddy face seemed to have been etched with a perpetual half-smile, probably the result of too many years of experience accommodating the demanding public. But a closer look at him revealed genuinely deep sadness. As the stocky innkeeper sat down on the front deck of the truck, Leo could feel the vehicle sink slightly from the added weight.

"Hi, Mr. Freeling. How are you today?"

"Well, hello, Leo. Okay, I guess."

"So where's Matt today, Mr. Freeling?" Leo asked, puzzled but not wanting to appear upset.

"Matt *quit*, Leo," Mr. Freeling announced, throwing up his arms in a gesture of resignation.

The unexpected news shook Leo.

Mr. Freeling continued.

"You know, Matt's a free spirit, Leo. He lives down there in Newton with his father and stepmother. His mom died from a sudden heart attack just before he graduated from high school. He's been a bit wild since then, as you may have noticed over the past couple of months. He just can't seem to get along with his father's new wife, you know. Well, last week he came into my office telling me he wanted to go down to Fort Lauderdale for the last couple of weeks of summer and chill out. And that was *that*!"

"That's really a shock, Mr. Freeling. We were just starting to get acquainted."

"Well, that's Matt for ya!" Mr. Freeling laughed, shaking his head. "Say, uh, Leo, I, uh, there was something I wanted to talk with you about when I saw you that first week you were here, but it just didn't, um, you know, seem like the right time. I, uh, mentioned that my daughter, June, thought very highly of you. A few months before she, uh, before the accident, we were talking about Marilyn Monroe. June told me how terribly bad she felt about the way she had spoken to you on the day Marilyn died. She said she avoided you all summer because she was too embarrassed to face you after that incident. But she told me she thought about what you said, and realized it was the right thing to do to pray for Marilyn. So she did. She said she was so surprised at how really good it made her feel. I just wanted to share that conversation with you, son, because I think you should know how June felt about you. Look, I'd better let you into the storage room so you can go about your business. I'm sorry if I've delayed you."

"No, not at all, Mr. Freeling. You have no idea how much what you've said means to me. I can't thank you enough for taking the time to speak with me about it."

Mr. Freeling stepped out of the vehicle. He started toward the storage room, but stopped, turning around toward Leo.

"Oh, uh, Leo, I almost forgot." Mr. Freeling reached into his shirt pocket. "Matt asked me to give this to you before he left." He handed Leo a small, pale-blue envelope.

"Thanks so much, Mr. Freeling." Leo tried to look calm as he took the envelope and placed it carefully in the right front pocket of his trousers.

"I'll see you back at the office when you've finished, Leo. Thanks, kid." Mr. Freeling walked away from the truck haltingly, as if the hot, humid summer weather was finally taking its toll on him.

Leo pushed open the storage room door, and turned on the light. The room was lifeless, silent and vacant. He leaned back upon the wooden shelves where he and Matt had first embraced, his hands grabbing on to them. He was dreaming that, somehow, some way, Matt would magically appear before him. But Matt was gone. Leo was alone once again. He was heartbroken. He had pushed Matt out of his life. Matt was gone because of the cold way Leo had acted toward him the last time he saw him. Leo stocked the shelves and fled the storage room, heading to the front desk to drop off the receipt.

"Here you go, Mr. Freeling. Thank you. I'll see you in a couple of weeks—on my last run of the summer."

"Okay, son. Can't believe how fast it's going! Be careful."

Leo could hardly wait to read the contents of the envelope. Was Matt saying good-bye for the last time? As soon as he got back into the truck, he opened the envelope with his pencil, finding one pale-blue piece of stationery with a golden "S" embossed at the top, center of the page. He unfolded it and began reading:

August 5. 1964

Dear Leo,

I can't tell you how much I enjoyed our times together this summer.
I just had to get away for a little while. I'll tell you all about it sometime.
Sure wish you could be going down to Fort Lauderdale with me, man.
Why don't you come up and see me sometime?!
Matt Stephenson
268 N. Glendale St., 2nd Floor
Allentown, Penna.
HE-8-7736

Your friend,
Matt

Leo's spirit was instantly revived. He had not alienated Matt by his abrupt and somewhat harsh manner the last time he saw him. They were still friends. He carefully placed the letter back in the envelope, smiled broadly, and drove back to the restaurant supply company.

On his last trip of the summer to Culver Lake two weeks later, Leo learned that Mr. Freeling had been hospitalized as a result of congestive heart failure. Mr. Feeling's niece, Lillian, was a waitress in the dining room during the summer months. After Matt quit, she was given additional responsibilities, including the task of handling the deliveries. Leo thought she was a very conscientious kid. She was about to begin her senior year in high school. They discussed Mr. Freeling's condition. Lillian told Leo that her uncle had been making progress, but it would be a while before he could go home. He was still a patient at Newton Memorial Hospital.

The summer ended on this sad note, but, overall, Leo had enjoyed his summer vacation. Most of all, though, he knew that Matt Stephenson truly cared about him—and that mattered more than anything else.

CHAPTER 9

Leo's fourth year in the seminary began without the tension and anxiety of the previous "weeding out" year. He would be studying Rational Psychology, Thomistic Philosophy, History of Philosophy, Logic, Greek, English Literature, Gregorian Chant, and Holy Scripture. He was ready for the challenge. Believing he had overcome the greatest obstacle to his calling in life he had ever faced, he felt confident he would succeed. Everything back home was going well, too. That reassurance helped resolve a lot of the emotional trauma he had suffered in the past. As the school year moved along, Leo began to write for the seminary newsletter. He also joined his class chorale, and continued to play basketball and baseball. Thomas and Patrick rarely participated in sports, which accounted for them drifting apart over the three years since beginning their studies together. Now they had started enjoying long walks along the back road of the seminary after dinner several evenings each week, chatting about the happenings in Allentown from their correspondence.

Leo was applying himself to his studies more vigorously than in any previous year. Chorale practice, writing for the newsletter and frequent basketball games filled most of the other hours each day. Convinced that he had settled in for the long haul, the rapid approach of the Christmas vacation had took him by surprise.

When he arrived home for the holiday break, Leo found a Christmas card from his old friend Tony, whom he had not seen since Tony had attended his mother's funeral more than a year and a half earlier. A note was enclosed.

> *Dear Leo,*
>
> *Merry Christmas! I apologize for not writing or calling you for such a long time. I really do miss you and hope you're doing well with your studies at the seminary. You see, Leo, I've fallen totally in love with a nineteen-year-old girl, Barbara, who works at the laundry where I'm now driving delivery runs. She is the most beautiful and loving person I've ever met, and I really love her. Barbara moved in with me this year and I've never been happier in every way, if you know what I mean, in my life. I want you to meet her sometime, and I'll get hold of you maybe in the spring when you're home so we can all get together. I think about you often, Leo, and I hope you are happy.*
>
> *Your friend,*
> *Tony*

Leo was glad that his good friend Tony had found someone, after living alone for so many years following a bitter divorce. He hoped that Tony's being seventeen years older than Barbara would not jeopardize their relationship.

Later in the week, shopping at Hess's department store, Leo decided to treat himself to a gigantic slice of the famous strawberry pie in their world-famous Patio Restaurant. Half way through it, a soft hand gently touched his shoulder.

"Leo, honey! How *are* you? Merry Christmas!"

Leo looked up, then jumped to his feet.

"Samantha! It's, uh, so great to see you! Please, uh, please sit down, Sam. Would you like a cup of coffee or something?"

Samantha eased into the chair across from Leo in the bustling restaurant. She looked over at him, smiling brightly. Memories of their lunches together when they had worked for the restaurant supply company tugged at him. She had matured beautifully over the past few years. She was elegant.

"Oh, uh, no, thanks, Leo. I just finished lunch. Are you still in the seminary?"

"Yes, yeah, Samantha."

"So everything's going *well* for you, I hope."

"Everything looks good so far. So, how are *you*, Sam? Where are you working now? I missed you when I went back to see Irv last summer. I was so surprised to hear that you had resigned."

"I got a terrific job at GMAC—you know, that large brownstone building right across the street from our old restaurant hang-out! And guess what, Leo, ... " Samantha held up her left hand, displaying a diamond ring that sparkled brightly under the restaurant lights. "I got engaged for Christmas. I'm going to be married in June." She was blushing.

"Sam, that's fantastic! I'm so very happy for you! So, who's the lucky guy?"

"I don't think you know him. Jack Tatum is a student at Lehigh University. I met him at Dorney Park last spring. He lives over in Whitehall."

"Well, congratulations, Sam. I hope you both have a great life together. God bless you!"

"Thanks so much, Leo. I'm so glad I ran into you. I've got to get back to work, now. Are you still living at the same address?'

"Yes. Sure, Sam."

"I'll make certain to send you a wedding invitation, Leo. We'd love it if you could be there."

"Great, Samantha. I surely hope I'll be able to make it. Great seeing you!"

Leo's thoughts drifted back to the day when Samantha learned about his plan to become a priest. She looked sad when she found out he was going to leave. He was happy to see her so cheerful now.

Leo savored the last crumbs of the pie and hurried back up the escalator to complete his Christmas shopping. Hundreds of shoppers crowded the main floor of the renowned department store. Shiny red, green and silver holiday ornaments dangled from scores of Christmas trees mounted behind display cases. Automated mannequins depicting scenes from Charles Dickens' stories entertained the shoppers. Crystal chandeliers bedecked with bright red poinsettias surrounding tiers of electric candles were glowing brightly overhead. "The King" was crooning "Blue Christmas" over the store's sound system. Leo gathered his packages, shooting another look at the magnificent Christmas displays on his way out of the store. He walked down Hamilton Street to Center Square. Looking in the windows of the Marble Bar, he saw the crowd enjoying afternoon cocktails. Pausing, he thought about the wonderful times there with his mother. He grasped his shopping bags, headed up Seventh Street toward home. His father had bought him a '57 Plymouth to use while he was home, but he felt like taking a walk into town that day. It had been another painful Christmas season without his mother. Leo was relieved to see that his father and Donna were continuing to adjust so well. His letters from Ellen indicated that she, too, had moved on. But Leo himself was unable to come to grips with losing her. He thought about her frequently every day; and each night before he went to sleep, he shared with her the happenings of the day. On the Friday evening following New Year's Day, Donna had gone to her Aunt Sheryl's house for a sleep-over. Donna loved their aunt's homemade chicken soup with dumplings, so Sheryl often had Donna over for dinner and an overnight stay. That gave their father a break and allowed his aunt to stay close to Donna. It also allowed Leo some time for himself. His father had gone out for dinner and bowling with his friends. He would be out for most of the evening. After finishing a Swanson's roast chicken TV dinner, Leo was sitting in his favorite chair in the corner of the living room. He thought about Tony's letter—how happy his good friend seemed to be. Then about Samantha—how wonderful that she'd met someone to spend her life with.

Leo was totally alone. The living room was lighted only by the lamp on the table by the front window. He looked over at the wall to his right, fixing his gaze on the portrait of his mother, remembering her worried response to him when he told her he wanted to be a priest. "Leo, what are you going to do when you're all alone at night, staring up at the ceiling, but no one is *there* for you?"

Now those loving, cautioning words came back to him with greater clarity and meaning than he could ever have understood back then. He eased himself out of the chair, started across the room, and bolted up the stairs to his bedroom. He pulled out the pale-blue envelope from his desk drawer, then hurried back downstairs to the telephone. He opened the envelope, pulled out Matt's letter, found the phone number and dialed it.

Five, six, seven rings—finally, an answer.

"Uh, ... *hullo*, Matt here. The familiar laid-back voice dissipated Leo's loneliness.

"Hey, Matt. It's, uh, it's me—*Leo*!"

"Jesus *Christ*! I don't *believe* it! *Leo*, how the ... where *are* you, man?"

"Matt, I'm at home in Allentown for the Christmas break, so I thought I'd give you a buzz to see how things are going and all. I'll be going back to school on Monday morning." He got the words out of his mouth as clearly as he could, self-conscious of his own nervousness and excitement. "I just want to, uh, thank you, Matt, for sending the note to me through Mr. Freeling so I could, um, so I would be able to, uh, keep up to date with your movements."

"Well, um, sure. Hey, *look*, Leo, why don't you come over right now so we can catch up? My roommate, Dave, isn't back from his New Year vacation in New York yet, so we'll have some private time to get reacquainted."

Leo was not sure if, in his feeling of utter loneliness, he had called Matt just to talk, or if he really, deep inside, wanted to be with his new friend after nearly six months had passed. He thought about his Plymouth parked outside. How easy it would be to drive over to Matt's apartment on the west end of town! He hesitated, realizing how successfully he had avoided Matt last summer, but Matt was his closest personal friend. And he missed him.

"You know what, Matt, … I'm not, uh, well, I *just* can't, uh … *yeah*, yes! That would be terrific!"

"Groovy! You know where I am, right Leo?—268 Glendale. It's a small red-brick house in the west end of town. It has two white columns at the entrance to the porch. I'll turn the overhead light on. See ya in about a half hour?"

"Yeah, Matt. I have the address. That sounds great. See you in a bit."

Leo hung up the phone, slid Matt's note back into the envelope and went back upstairs. He quickly got dressed and placed Matt's note in his coat pocket. Looking in the mirror as he buttoned his favorite dark green shirt, he paused. *What am I doing? How is this going to turn out? Am I placing myself in an occasion of sin?*

Tonight, it didn't matter. He was lonely. He just wanted to see Matt again after such a long time. He missed Matt's cheerfulness, carefree attitude and warm personality. Leo turned out all the lights in the house except the night light on the column at the foot of the staircase. In his excitement, he fumbled with the key as he locked the front door, then turned and walked briskly to his car. The Plymouth had a push-button transmission. The eight-cylinder vehicle took on speed rapidly. Leo turned left onto Green Street, then left on Fourth Street to Chew Street. Then he drove west to Twenty-Fourth Street and turned left on Turner. A couple of blocks east, he arrived at Glendale Street, where he soon spotted the porch light and white columns, the one on the right bearing the worn but stylish brass numerals 2-6-8. Twenty-two degrees was colder than his dark blue pea jacket was made for. His mother had bought it for him for the much higher temperatures in Philadelphia. As he got out of the car he tucked his green shirt neatly into his black chino slacks, and buttoned up his coat. He walked up the steps. After a nervous pause, he pressed his right index finger firmly on the doorbell for the second floor. He heard the Beatles on the other side of the door: "I wanna hold your haaaaaand. I wanna hold your hand."

Leo smiled. It had to be coming from Matt's apartment. He heard the inside door to the foyer open, followed by a rush of footsteps. The outside door swung open, and there was Matt. He was wearing baggy Bermuda shorts and a tye-dye T-shirt. Wire-rimmed, John Lennon glasses magnified his green eyes. His hair was much longer, Leo thought, longer by maybe two or three missed appointments with his barber. He was barefoot. Matt reached out and pulled Leo through the doorway and into his arms.

"Leo, *Jesus*! I can't tell you how great it feels to be with you at long last. I've really missed seeing you, man!"

"Matt, that's exactly how I feel. I've thought about you so often. I so missed seeing you at the end of last summer. I was shocked when I heard you had run off to Fort Lauderdale."

"Oh, that! I just had to get the hell out of Newton, away from my dad and his old bitch, Mildred. I just can't stand their goddamned arguing and fighting all the time. It was getting too aggravating for me there. Then, I came back here to unwind. Oh, sorry. Come on up, Leo; you'll catch pneumonia down here."

The door at the top of the stairs was half-way open. "And if you touch me I'll be happy, inside. It's ... " The music, indeed, was coming from Matt's apartment.

Matt led Leo up the stairs to a small landing, then pushed the door completely open.

"Ta *da*! Here it is—my humble abode!"

Stepping into a large living room, Leo saw a brick fireplace located in the exact center of the wall facing the door. A large, light-green armchair stood on each side; a long beige-colored sofa, covered with sheet music, occupied a large portion of the center of the room, facing the fireplace. A guitar was propped up on an arm of the sofa. A four-foot-square oak coffee table separated the armchairs from the sofa. The apartment had probably come furnished, Leo thought. He could not imagine Matt decorating the room in such a drab fashion.

"Oh, uh, *sorry*, Leo," Matt said. "Let me get rid of some of this crap." He gathered up all the sheet music, tossed it onto the coffee table, then disappeared into the kitchen. Leo heard the refrigerator door open, glasses clinking, and the sound of bottle caps bouncing on the kitchen counter. Matt returned in seconds with two bottles of *Rolling Rock* beer. He handed one bottle to Leo, joining him on the sofa.

"Cheers, Leo! *Happy 1965*!"

Leo hadn't tasted any alcoholic beverage since just before entering the seminary more than three and a half years before, remembering that drinking was punished by expulsion from the seminary. Leo was flustered for a moment. *Will the seminary refuse to let me become a priest for drinking a beer? They require priests to drink wine every time they say Mass, and there's no restriction on them regarding the consumption of alcohol at any other time. Is this just another one of those rules that makes no sense?*

"Cheers, Matt! Happy New Year!"

They each took deep gulps of the cold brew—Leo gagging slightly. Matt was holding the green bottle in his right hand, looking at Leo. He stepped closer to Leo, placed his left hand around Leo's neck, and kissed him passionately on the lips. Leo tried, but couldn't pull away. He was frozen in time and space, far away from the seminary in a totally different world.

"My God, Leo, I really *have* missed you!"

Leo was unable to speak. He tried to catch his breath, but he didn't get the chance. Matt had plunked his beer down on the coffee table and similarly dispatched Leo's. In a sudden burst of passion he pressed Leo against him, just as in the old storage room on the first day they met.

"Christ, Leo! Sorry. I got carried away. Let's just relax and catch up."

"Matt," Leo said, glancing around the room for his lost composure, "when did you start playing the guitar?"

"My father bought me this beauty last summer for my maintaining a 4.0 grade point last year. So I've been practicing since then. These magnifying lenses help me read the sheet music." He cocked his John Lennon spectacles at a jaunty angle. "Yeah, he also bought me that red V-8 *Mustang* you may have seen out front when you came in. Anyway, I've been alone in this apartment just about every night since the day after Christmas. I went home to Newton, but I just couldn't stay there— it was the same old crap. I'll tell you about it sometime, Leo."

"That was really generous of your dad to buy you such beautiful things, Matt."

"Yeah, he can afford it. He's a big-shot lawyer up there; he used to be a Republican politician, too. So he's got lots of big-money clients."

"He must've been very pleased when you voted for Goldwater last year."

"Nah, he didn't know anything about it. I never really talk politics with him. He's a great guy, but I'm so *pissed* that he got hooked up with that old bitch!"

Leo didn't let on that he had heard from Mr. Freeling about Matt's mother having died. He wanted it to be an enjoyable evening for both of them. Matt went over to the record player, shutting it off so they could talk.

"So, Leo, our big buddy LBJ got back in anyway! We're *screwed*, man!" Matt simmered down once he was back on the sofa. He placed his arms behind his neck, stretching his legs as far as he could until his feet were touching Leo's thigh.

"Yeah, Matt, I didn't get a chance to tell you, but I actually joined a Barry Goldwater group here in Allentown late last summer after you, uh, after you left."

"I can't believe how much we have in common, Leo." Matt said, nodding in firm agreement.

Matt picked up his guitar, cradled it in his arms, and sat up against the arm of the sofa, facing Leo, his bare feet now under himself in yoga fashion. He began playing, singing softly: "Mi-chelle, my belle … "

Leo listened as Matt's lips carefully formed each syllable—his soft, deep voice breathing life into every word of the tenderly passionate love song. Tears. ran down Leo's cheeks and onto his shirt. He couldn't stop crying. Matt looked up from his guitar. Seeing Leo crying, he stopped playing instantly. He set his guitar on the table and sat down next to Leo on the sofa.

"What's wrong, man? Are you *okay*, Leo?"

"Matt, I haven't felt like this since my mom was alive. You're so warm and gentle. You bring an unbelievably calm, comforting feeling to me. I've never felt so close to anyone since she … You know, I think about her every day. And every night before I go to sleep, I always tell her what I've been doing. I've never spoken with anybody about this.

I know it sounds crazy, Matt, but I feel connected to her somehow. There've been times when I faced serious situations; but when I've told her about them, the problems just seem to get resolved. I have this feeling that my talks with her keep us connected somehow—like she actually hears what I'm saying. You know, it's, uh ... " He stopped, convinced that Matt, whom he had not looked at even once during this rambling monologue, was already turned off by what he had said.

"Leo! Far *out*! That is seriously *powerful* stuff. Unbelievable! You are something else, man."

"You've brought those warm feelings back to me, Matt. I know you care about me. Your loving embraces—as brief as they've been—have changed me. They've renewed my feelings of love and passion. I ... I *love* you, Matt. I've loved you ever since the first time I looked into your incredible green eyes—even more so when your shocking kiss opened my heart. When I saw you standing on top of that lifeguard ladder last July, in those damned tight trunks, I was totally gone! That image has taunted me day and night since!"

This time it was Leo who stretched his arm out, pulling Matt toward him, kissing him with the greatest passion he had ever known.

"I love you, too, Leo," Matt said. "When I saw how gentle and innocent and vulnerable you were last summer; when I realized what a considerate, compassionate person you are, I was hooked. You looked so goddamned sexy in that white uniform—I just couldn't *stand* it! Stay right there."

Matt went to the kitchen and popped open a couple more *Rolling Rocks*. Leo heard the bottle caps drop to the floor and roll around. Then Matt was groaning.

"Oh, *fuck*! It's starting to snow out there, Leo."

Matt returned with the drinks.

"Matt, I, I um, I don't think I can stay much longer. Not only is it snowing, but I just noticed that it's almost nine-thirty. My dad has probably gotten home by now, and I—"

"Leo, look, man, I don't want you to *leave* me tonight," Matt pleaded. "I don't want to be waving good-bye to you in your rear view mirror like every other time we've parted. I want you to stay with me, Leo."

"Matt, so do I, but—"

"Look, *God,* Leo! I want to be with you tonight. Why not call your dad? Tell him you're visiting some friends from the seminary or something and, uh, that, uh, they invited you to stay over because the snow's heavy here, you know, something like that." Matt was caressing Leo's right arm as he kissed his shoulder.

"I've never done anything like that before, Matt, but I really don't want to leave you tonight."

"The phone's over there on the table, next to the armchair."

Leo put his hands on Matt's, squeezing them as he got up from the sofa and headed toward the phone. He started dialing, then waited to hear his father's voice, wondering how he would react.

"Uh, hi, dad. How was your bowling night?"

"Oh, hello there. It was okay. I didn't win, but we all had fun. I was surprised when I got home half an hour ago and you weren't here. Where *are* you?"

"Dad, remember that note I got from Tony with his Christmas card? Well, just after you, uh, left tonight, Tony called to invite me over to meet his new girlfriend, Barbara, at their place near Topton to catch up on old times. Well, the evening has flown by. Now it's starting to snow pretty heavy here. They're concerned about me driving home in this weather, so they've, uh, invited me to say over. I'll be getting back home early tomorrow morning, dad."

"That's a good idea. Better to stay there than battle the snow. See you in the morning."

"Great, dad. Good night."

Matt was giving both thumbs up as Leo hung up the phone. "Leo, my man, you have my vote for this year's Academy Award. That was magnificent, buddy!"

"Thanks, Matt. I feel a bit odd about lying to him, but I really want to stay with you."

"I'll get you one of my robes so you can get comfortable, Leo."

Matt went into his bedroom, emerging with a pale-blue bathrobe with white trim around the lapels.

"Here, Leo, try this on; you can leave your things in my room on the chair."

Leo put his beer down on the coffee table, took the robe and went into Matt's bedroom. He removed all his clothing and slipped into the robe. In about a minute he was back in the living room. Matt looked over at him from the side of the sofa, whistling his approval.

"You look *hot* in that, Leo!"

Matt jumped up from the sofa and hugged him again. As he pulled Leo against himself he could feel that Leo was already aroused.

"What's *this*, man?" He reached under the robe, placing his right hand around Leo's erect penis, stroking it gently. "Mmmm!" Matt began kissing Leo passionately. "Let's get into bed. I just want to be as close to you as I can get."

They walked into Matt's bedroom with their arms around each other. Matt pulled off his T-shirt and unbuttoned his Bermuda shorts, dropping them to reveal his splendid physique. He was wearing no underwear—and was fully aroused. Gazing at Matt's incredible body, Leo untied his pale blue robe and let it fall to the floor, leaving the two of them naked together, face-to-face, for the first time. Staring at each other, they pressed their hot, longing bodies together. They lay down on the bed, caressing, sweating, longing. Matt turned slightly so he was facing Leo from above. He lowered himself on to Leo's thin, firm body, kissing him gently on the lips. Matt's tongue slid from Leo's lips to his neck, down to his chest. He kissed Leo's left nipple, then the right, gliding his tongue down the center of Leo's chest until his lips surrounded Leo's moist, hot shaft, tasting it, swallowing it. Matt rose and turned, looking down at Leo. He gently spread Leo's legs, lowering himself, penetrating Leo. Their bodies became one. They moaned and writhed in unison as Matt climaxed, remaining locked together, moving and squirming to derive every bit of pleasure from their union. They lay motionless for nearly ten minutes until Leo turned around, lifted himself up over Matt, facing his back and began softly massaging Matt's shoulders, his hands moving smoothly down Matt's muscular back. Grabbing and spreading the firm cheeks of his round butt, Leo entered Matt gently, steadily; thrusting harder—faster—until his finally unbridled passion exploded deep inside Matt. The new lovers turned toward each other, kissing, embracing—dreaming it would last forever.

When Leo awoke the next morning, he knew that everything had changed in one evening. For the first time in his life he felt personally fulfilled. His love for Matt was real, and he was certain that Matt loved *him*. He reached over to caress Matt, but he was gone. Leo could hear noises coming from the kitchen. Matt was already preparing breakfast. Leo got out of bed and picked up his robe, casually slipping it on as he walked to the kitchen.

"Matt, I didn't even hear you get up. Good morning!"

The kitchen was probably a converted bedroom. The wide, double-size window looked out upon a several poplar trees sparkling with the overnight snow. A small wooden table in the middle of the room was set neatly for breakfast. Bright red napkins were set next to two white coffee cups on the oak table. The natural oak floor accented the all-white kitchen.

"Hey, man, I just couldn't wake you up. You looked so damned angelic." Matt went over to Leo, who was still gawking at him and kissed him. "Leo, that was the most sensational evening I've ever experienced in my life. I'm so, *so* glad you stayed over."

"I can't describe the way I feel," Leo said. "I've never felt more fulfilled and whole. I love you, babe."

"I love you, man." Matt kissed Leo's neck. They sat down for breakfast. "I've made a pot of coffee, Leo. We have some *Wheaties* with sliced bananas, and here's some nice cold cranberry juice." Matt playfully placed the glass up to Leo's lips. Then he grabbed a couple of slices of *Pullman* bread—from Heimbach's Bakery—and popped them in the toaster.

"Matt, that's a *GE* toaster! I've got to tell you about my experience at their Allentown plant sometime. You won't believe it. You know, my fingerprints may already be on that thing." Leo laughed as he thought about that weird summer with Shirley and the guys at the sub-assembly line.

"Leo, what the fuck *haven't* you done!" Matt just shook his head and smiled. "Oh, we got lucky. We only got about an inch of snow last night, so it will be easy for us to clean off your car."

"So, Matt, you said last night you've been alone here nearly every night for the past two weeks. That must've been really hard for you. What did you do?"

"You know, since I got that freakin' guitar, I've been absorbed by it. I mean, learning those chords is a real bitch, but I'm starting to get the hang of it."

"There's no doubt about *that*. Look what you did to me when you played 'Michelle' last night. You really set me off."

"That was the best compliment of my work I've yet received! I've gone out for dinner a couple of times. Have you ever been to the Village Inn? It's my favorite place in town."

"Matt, you're not going to believe this, but …"

Leo proceeded to tell Matt the whole story about his magnificent night out with the Grand Knight of the Knights of Columbus and his fellow seminarians; the king-cut prime rib, the wine—the Dorney Park scene.

"You gotta be fuckin' kidding me, Leo—the Grand Knight! My old man hangs around with those guys sometimes—the Knights have terrific connections, you know."

"No, Matt, honest to God! He even handed us Cuban cigars after dinner."

"You've been holding out on me, buddy!" Matt was looking at Leo. He was smiling, shaking his head from side to side. "And Dorney Park? C'mon, Leo, you're pulling my leg!"

"Matt, there's nothing else I'd rather do right now! But, no, it's true. Hundreds of kids who were hanging out near Castle Garden Theater that night thought we were a singing group—and engulfed the car."

"I'll bet they wanted to get a good piece of *you*. I can just imagine you in that black-and-white outfit. *Hot!*"

"Well, we got away."

"What a story, Leo. Hey, listen, next time you come over, let's go to the Village Inn for dinner, and pig out."

"You've got a deal, Matt."

It was getting late. Leo felt a painful tug in his stomach at the thought of leaving Matt. He started gathering the dishes to bring them over to the sink.

"Hey, don't worry about that stuff, Leo. Remember, I'm an experienced waiter and busboy. I put a fresh towel out for you in the bathroom, and you can use my razor if you'd like."

"Thanks, Matt. I guess I'd better get myself together."

The shower was exhilarating. Leo cupped his hands over his face, letting the water stream over him. He took a deep breath. *I can't believe this is happening.*

When Leo returned to the bedroom to get dressed, he paused before the bed, staring at it. He dreaded removing that pale-blue robe. It made him feel so close to Matt. He carefully placed it on the bed, then got dressed and returned to the kitchen. Matt had already washed the dishes and cleaned up.

"I really don't want to leave, Matt. I can't believe I have to be back in Philadelphia on Monday. How will I ever be able to stand being without you *now*?"

Matt held Leo in his arms, as they swayed, kissing passionately, not wanting to part.

Then Matt whispered, "Leo, I didn't mention it last night, but I'll be in Fort Lauderdale for spring break this year. I'm so sorry about this. I promised my roommate, Dave, that I'd go down there with him this year to kinda show him around. He's never been there. I feel really bad about this, man. So, I guess I won't see you until sometime after I get back. I'm planning to be back in Culver Lake again this coming summer to work at the old hotel. I sure hope we can connect again up there."

Matt's announcement destroyed Leo's visions of being together with Matt when he got back home for the short Easter break, even if only for a few brief visits. Now, his hopes for that reunion were dashed.

"Matt, I'm sorry we won't be together at Easter, but I understand. You gave your word to Dave; you should go with him. It looks very promising that I'll have the summer delivery route again to North Jersey. But Matt, that's more than five months away."

"Let's plan to stay in touch before then, Leo. I don't want to lose you!"

Matt slipped into a pair of denims and started putting on his bright-blue ski jacket with white stripes along the sleeves.

"Okay. Leo, I'll help you get you car cleaned off so you can get back home."

They started for Matt's apartment door. Leo stopped and turned to Matt.

"Thanks, Matt! That was an incredible evening. I love you so much." Tears were forming in Leo's eyes.

"And you know I worship you, Leo."

A bitter-cold January morning greeted them as they exited the building. The overnight snow covered the street and Leo's car. Matt's red *Mustang* appeared pink beneath the thin coating.

"That's a beautiful car, Matt. You're so lucky to have it."

"I earned it, Leo," Matt laughed. He started brushing the snow off Leo's car. Two minutes later, the '57 Plymouth was ready to go.

"Okay, buddy, this has been fantastic. Let's do it again soon, Leo."

"As soon as I possibly can," said Leo, forcing a "good-bye," and a reluctant, half salute to his lover, unwilling to witness Matt's farewell in the rear-view mirror.

All Leo could think about on the way home was how much Matt's singing "Michele" had opened up his heart to him. Their time together changed him. Nothing else seemed important to him now. When he got home, even that seemed different. He walked in without returning the pontiff's gaze. His dad was in the kitchen getting lunch together. Donna had not yet gotten back from her sleepover.

"Hi, dad, it's good we didn't get too much snow last night."

"Yep, we were lucky this time. How was your visit with Tony?"

"Oh, uh, we had a terrific time, dad. It was so good to get together at last."

His father turned away from the stove, and looked at him.

"You okay? Your eyes look kind of funny."

"Wow, I hope I'm not catching a cold. My throat's been feeling kind of dry the last couple of days. I think I'll go upstairs and take a couple of aspirins."

"Yeah, you know you'll be back in school on Monday."

"It's hard to believe, dad. This vacation has gone by too fast."

His father was busy at the stove. "I made some hot chili for you and Donna. I thought this would be a good day for it."

"Thanks, dad. That sounds perfect! I'll be heading over to church this afternoon. Then I'll be right back to start packing."

After lunch Leo was trying to prepare himself mentally for confession as he started driving to his parish church. *How am I going to tell this story after all the warnings that Father has given me?* At the first intersection, he changed direction and headed to the cathedral, where none of the priests would know him; he could escape any serious confrontation with his usual confessor.

He arrived rattled and nervous. Not since he was seventeen years old and playing around with Terry on that living room sofa on Saturday evenings had he confessed a sin so mortal. He would always lose control of his raging sex drive.

There were five people in line in front of him for confession. Leo switched his stance occasionally. He kept rehearsing, then changing and re-rehearsing what he would say to the priest—even worse, what the priest was going to say to him. After twenty minutes waiting to free his mind and receive forgiveness, Leo entered the dark confessional booth.

"Bless me Father, for I have sinned. I, uh, uh, ..."

"What is it, my son?" a friendly voice intoned.

"Father, I, well, it's hard for me to explain, but I've had sexual intercourse with another man. I—"

"Son, do you *love* this man?"

Leo was astounded by the totally unexpected question from the other side of the screen. Not: "How many times?" Not: "Was it the first time?"—He was completely perplexed.

"Father, I love him *very* much. I can't bear to be without him."

"Have you had sexual encounters with any other men?"

"No, Father, not since I was a young boy, and my friend Rob and I—"

"All right, my son. Is there anything else you want to tell me?"

"Yes, Father. I'm a seminarian studying for the priesthood."

There was a long pause in the darkness. The priest cleared his throat, then began speaking very seriously.

"My son, you know that the Catholic Church forbids sexual relations of any kind between people who are not married to each other. This is a grave mortal sin. Seminarians must prepare for a life of chastity. They are prohibited from having any sexual relationships with anyone. You must devote yourself now to finding out who you are. If you love this man, as you say you do, then you will be drawn to him; but you cannot become a priest while holding on to such a relationship."

"What am I going to *do*, Father?"

"Only you can decide, my son. Meditate and pray for God's guidance to lead you to the place in life where you can best serve Him. It will be a difficult time for you for a while, but God's grace will show you the way. For your penance I want you to be honest with yourself. Think about the person whom you say you love, but give careful thought to that which led you to seek the priesthood in the beginning. Are you being tempted to end your vocation by an infatuation? You must be careful to examine your conscience and learn what it was that made you stray from your sacred goal. With God's help you will find the answer. *Ego te absolvo, in nomine patris, et filii, et Spiritus Sancti*. Go in peace, my son."

"Amen."

He left the cathedral immediately. As he walked to his car, he was tormented by the realization that Matt's apartment was only half a mile away. His body and soul were being pulled in opposite directions. He longed to see Matt again, but he knew there wasn't enough time to go back there. He was mystified by the priest's words. Why would the priest ask him if he loved the man with whom he had sex? Was the priest trying to send a message that, perhaps, if you really love someone, then a sexual act is a natural expression of your feelings for that person? The statement seemed to be so drastically contradictory to the Church's strict teaching and official mandates. Leo was confused.

Saturday evening was painfully lonely. In contrast to the evening before, when his life had taken on new meaning, Leo was alone, brooding over his separation from the one he loved. His father, at Leo's suggestion that he take a breather, had gone out for the evening with some friends. Donna was playing upstairs. After he tucked Donna in for the evening, Leo sat in the corner chair once again. The living room was silent and nearly dark. He thought about all the events that had taken place in that room over the years—his First Communion party; the Saturday mornings when he entertained his mom and aunts and uncles; the day his mom bought the portrait of Pope John and placed it on the wall; his high school graduation party; the day he told his mother he was leaving home to become a priest; that grand going-away send-off his family and neighbors had given him before he left for the seminary; that horrible night when he had to call for emergency oxygen for his mother; that heart-wrenching day when he arrived home after his mother's death, the priest from the seminary stopping by to offer condolences; hearing Matt's voice over the phone for the first time—a lifetime of happenings flashed through his mind.

Leo went to bed around ten o'clock, emotionally exhausted from the painful helplessness only separation can inflict.

On Sunday morning he took Donna to the Solemn High Mass. Their Aunt Sheryl had come over to get his little sister all dressed up and to fix her hair. After Mass, they stopped by Heimbach's Bakery for some delicious rye bread. It was still warm when they picked it up. Unlike their previous stops at the bakery, this one was bitterly painful. All he could think about was the Heimbach bread wrapper in Matt's hands at breakfast on the previous morning. He picked up the package, turned away, and led Donna home. By eight o'clock that night Leo had completed packing his clothing and books.

Mr. Richardson would soon be arriving to take Leo back to the seminary. Leo had shaken his dad's hand before he left for work earlier that morning.

"Good-bye, dad. I'll see you on April 18 for Easter vacation."

"Good luck with your exams. Take it easy."

When Donna was ready for school, he picked her up and held her in his arms.

"Bye-bye, Donna. See you at Easter."

"Bye, Leo. I'm gonna miss you. I'll tell the Easter Bunny to leave some candy for you again!"

"Thanks, honey!" Leo kissed her.

Aunt Sheryl arrived for Donna, whisking her off to school. Forty-five minutes later, Mr. Richardson pulled his car up to the house. Leo struggled out the door with his luggage. By late afternoon, he was back in the seminary. The retreat had begun; throughout the next day and a half the grand silence would be in effect. He lay in bed that night thinking about Matt—that magnificent evening they spent together just two nights before. He was only fifty miles away at Muhlenberg College, but it may as well have been ten thousand miles. Then it struck him. In all of the excitement and passion of that evening and morning with Matt, he had forgotten to give Matt his telephone number and home address. Matt would be unable to contact him. He didn't even remember telling Matt his last name. He was murmuring to himself, agonizing and panicking over such inconceivable stupidity.

There was no way for Leo to go to Matt now without ending his seminary career, abandoning his lifelong goal abruptly—only a year and a half away from graduation and a degree in psychology. The only way he could see Matt again was to wait for summer vacation—an eternity of five months. The retreat was a time for meditation, but Leo could contemplate only his utter loneliness and separation from Matt in silence. There was no one to speak to except Jesus, but Jesus wasn't listening. Why should he? Leo had been deemed a mortal sinner by the Church that claims to have been founded at the Last Supper of Christ—and Leo was unrepentant. How could he possibly rescind the deep love he felt for Matt? He was the only person on earth who truly shared Leo's life. *Jesus left but one commandment: that all persons should love one another,* Leo reflected, *but Churches had taken that singular commandment and sliced, diced, teased and parsed it into thousands of coda, regulations and precepts prohibiting love for millions of people for centuries.*

All weekend, Leo caught glimpses of his fellow seminarians smiling at him as he walked along the roads circling the seminary. *I probably look like I'm really far out to these guys. I'm walking around here in a daze; I'm sure they've noticed.*

On Wednesday morning after the retreat ended, Leo wrote a letter to Matt. Seminary officials monitored all correspondence, so Leo had to choose his words carefully.

January 14, 1965

Dear Matt,

I am writing to thank you for your wonderful hospitality over the holidays. I had a great time. I hope we can visit again soon. I realize I had forgotten to leave my family's phone number, so I am including it in this letter.

Thanks, again, for the enjoyable time we spent with you.

Sincerely,

Leo Weber

PS: Our telephone number is 49-5-2005.

The seminary introduced a field-service training program for the new semester, designed to acquaint students with the social and medical institutions of Philadelphia and prepare them for their future ministry. It was called the "Thursday Apostolate." Leo chose the program at the Philadelphia Psychiatric Hospital because it would enable him to observe psychiatrists interacting with their patients. Eventually he was able to visit with some of the patients. Every Thursday, seminarians were allowed to leave the grounds for their respective program locations using public transportation to travel into the city. It was a newfound freedom that all of the seminarians welcomed immensely.

It gave Leo the opportunity to try to contact Matt. Unfortunately, the times did not coincide with Matt's academic schedule. So Leo heard only ring tones. With what joy he would have welcomed even a busy signal! He was frustrated and angry. He wanted to tell Matt all about his experiences at the psychiatric hospital. Since Matt, too, was majoring in psychology, Leo frequently imagined the discussions they could have about his visits with the patients and doctors at the hospital. But it was not going to happen. Thoughts of Matt plagued him during the day—in class, on the basketball court, in study hall—tormenting memories of their fleeting, passionate evening together. Countless sleepless nights ensued, and his appetite decreased, causing him to lose five pounds during the first two months following his return to the seminary. Then he contracted a serious strain of the Asian flu, which put him in the infirmary for a week. He struggled through his classes, barely able to concentrate on the lectures. In his letters he continued to ask his father if he had received any telephone calls. There were none.

As soon as he got home for the Easter break, he tried to call Matt, but no one answered. He had already left for Fort Lauderdale with his friend Dave.

Leo's father was concerned about the change in Leo's appearance. He had grown pale and thin; he ate only a fraction of what he normally consumed at Sunday dinner. During vacation breaks over the past four years, Leo had always been energetic, but this year he had little desire to go into town or visit his aunts and uncles. He spent most of his days at home in his favorite chair in the living room, reading the local paper, or attempting, with little success, to review his textbooks—waiting for a phone call from Matt.

Dave Hunsicker was a campus jester whose endless supply of jokes kept his fellow students—and even some professors—laughing. His underdeveloped five-foot, four-inch body weighed in at 200 pounds. His athletic activity was limited to watching his favorite team, the Boston Celtics, on television. His long, curly, pitch-black hair accentuated his round, abnormally bright red face, that seemed to glow whenever he delivered punch lines. His dark brown eyes were mostly expressionless when he wasn't entertaining. Dave was a below-average student who barely achieved passing grades. Without Matt Stephenson's help preparing for examinations, Dave would never have made it beyond his first year at Muhlenberg. He and Matt had become close friends because Matt was thoroughly entertained by Dave's funny routines and carefree manner. Matt had readily agreed when Dave asked him to share an apartment off campus. There were a few nights during their first year living together when they would be sitting around drinking beer all night, listening to their Beatles albums. On a few of those occasions Matt had given in to Dave after he practically begged Matt to let him perform oral sex on him. Matt never reciprocated, and abruptly ended the sexual contacts. But Dave had fallen in love with a guy who was his exact opposite. He still enjoyed making Matt laugh; he felt it brought them closer together. Living with Matt for more than two years was a dream come true for Dave. When he returned from his holiday several days after the

New Year celebration, however, all Dave heard about was Leo: "Leo's so bright." "Leo's so compassionate." Leo's just the greatest ..." "Leo, this, Leo, that." Dave had grown sick of it. On the following Monday afternoon, when he got home from class, he saw a letter in the mailbox with Leo's name and return address on it. Overcome by jealousy and sudden anger, he snatched the letter and took it to his room. He had no desire to read it, not even open it. He tore it into small pieces, threw them into the toilet—and flushed.

Before Leo returned to the seminary for the final semester, his dad was so concerned about the sudden change in Leo's behavior, and his lack of appetite, that he encouraged Leo to see their family doctor. But Leo shrugged it off. It was only the unusually cold, miserable spring weather that was getting him down, he said. Summer would bring the relief he needed. His normal zest for life would surely return then. As he thought about being with Matt Stephenson, he *knew* it would.

CHAPTER 10

Somehow, Leo managed to gather enough concentration and determination to pass his final examinations, with the lowest grades he had ever received. His lackluster work had drawn curious, concerned looks from his professors throughout the final semester. But Leo was finally home for the summer. His energy had returned. He hadn't been so enthusiastic about being home since his mom was alive. He looked forward to many wonderful times with his new friend, his new love. Leo checked in with the Lehigh Restaurant Supply Company on the second Monday in June. He removed the summer account book from the shelf outside the office to review his delivery routes for the summer. Flipping through the client account records in the large two-ring binder, he found his North Jersey route. On the page for the hotel at Culver Lake, he saw a large red X covering the entire page, the symbol generally used for accounts that had been permanently closed. He dashed to Irv's office. "Irv, I was just reviewing my delivery routes for the summer … Why is the page for the hotel at Culver Lake crossed out? What in the world's happening with that?"

Leo's excitement surprised Irv. He explained that, over the winter, Mr. Freeling suffered a stroke that left him incapacitated. The hotel was closed and would probably be up for sale soon. Leo would no longer need to stop at Culver Lake. Irv appeared puzzled by Leo's sudden distance—and by the tears now filling his eyes.

"Leo, what's wrong? I didn't think you knew Mr. Freeling that well. I'm sorry to be the one to have to break the bad news to you."

"What? *Oh*, thanks, Irv for filling me in. He's a great guy. I feel so sorry for him and his family."

"Leo, you just never cease to amaze me, my boy."

But Leo's reaction to the sudden news was hardly focused on Mr. Freeling. How would he ever contact Matt *now*? He didn't know where he lived. All he had was Matt's old phone number in Allentown, but the phone had been disconnected. Matt wasn't there. He had moved back home for the summer following the end of the academic year.

Leo couldn't get started on any work. He stood outside the office looking through blurred eyes at the crossed out page in his delivery route book. Was Matt being crossed out of his life? He had to get out of the warehouse. He told the shipping clerk he was going out for coffee, and fled. As he walked along Linden Street, he tried to figure out a plan.

How could he find Matt? Where could he be living? There *has* to be a way to find him! He would have to go back to Culver Lake.

On his delivery route that day Leo stopped by a telephone booth outside the Springdale Diner, in Sussex County, grabbed the phone book, and leafed through its sun-bleached pages for "Stephenson." Yes! He ripped the page out of the phone book. There were fourteen names and phone numbers on it. There was no "Stephenson, Matthew" listed, but Leo was determined to call each number until he found Matt. Maybe one was a relative; maybe his father was one of them. Matt had never mentioned his father's first name. Leo continued to insert dimes into the telephone, asking, with each answer, "Hello, I'm trying to reach Matthew Stephenson. Could you tell me if this is the correct number for him?"

As the number of calls decreased, each yielding no success, Leo despaired. He was reaching a dead end in his quest to find Matt, his last hope reduced to the one number that rang and rang, unanswered. As he jotted down the number, he remembered that Matt had told him his father was a 'big-shot attorney.' *The Yellow Pages*! He grabbed the phone book again and quickly searched through the classified section for 'Attorneys.' *Damn!* Now he was referred to 'Lawyers.' *Finally!* There was only one law firm listed with the name "Stephenson." He knew from the address that the office was located just off Route 206 on his way back to the supply company. He finished his deliveries, then drove to the firm—on Main Street in Newton. By the time he arrived, it was late afternoon. Excited and perspiring heavily, he walked into the receptionist area.

"May I help you, sir?" a young, well-dressed secretary with a page boy hairdo asked. She seemed to be studying him.

"Yes, uh, well, I hope so, Miss. Can you tell me if Attorney Stephenson is related to *Matthew* Stephenson?" I, um, we met up here last summer, but I forgot to ask him for his phone number."

The receptionist appeared skeptical.

"I'm, uh, sorry, sir, but I cannot give any personal information about anybody employed here. It's contrary to company policy."

"Well, could you at least ring Mr. Stephenson so I can ask him myself, on the telephone?"

"No, sir. I'm sorry. That would not be appropriate. Anyway, Mr. Stephenson is not here. He's, um, on an extended leave. I'm not quite sure when he'll be back. Is there anything *else*, sir?" she asked—directing the question as much to the typewriter, to which her fingers had already returned, as to Leo.

Leo's shoulders slumped forward. "No. No, thank you."

Leo went to Mass every morning, but he could no longer derive any spiritual strength from his prayers and Holy Communion. Mass was held in the lower church where, as a young boy, he had sung in the parish choir for so many funerals. Now those days seemed far away. He couldn't concentrate on the Mass at all. He had no purpose there any longer. Everything was uncertain—useless—without Matt. Where was he going *now*?

Every time Leo drove by the road leading to the old hotel at Culver Lake, his stomach trembled, but he couldn't avoid looking up the road to catch a glimpse of the huge grey structure. On his final delivery run to North Jersey on the last Friday in August, he was determined to drive back to the hotel. He simply could not end his summer without being at that magical place. As he entered the driveway, he saw the large red, black-and-white "For Sale" sign jutting out from the portico at the front entrance. He steered the truck around to the vacant pool area, past the entrance, then back to the old storage room where Matt had caressed him that first time. Leo was writhing in pain, sickened at Matt's absence. He parked the truck, got out quickly and ran to the side of the building, where he emptied his roiling stomach in the bushes. He had to leave. Matt was gone.

Mentally exhausted and still queasy, he drove the several miles to the Boy Scout camp, his final stop of the day. The only way to and from the camp was by way of a very steep dirt road leading to the main building. He negotiated his way uneventfully down the rocky terrain and completed his deliveries. Driving back up the rough road proved more difficult. He drove his walk-in delivery truck back up the rough road. He was not used to the extra gear on the five-on-the-floor manual transmission and clutch system of the substitute truck temporarily assigned to him, he had been uncomfortable driving it all day. As he reached the crest of the hill, Leo lost control of the truck. It stalled, then began moving backwards. Leo repeatedly pumped the clutch pedal, trying desperately to shift the gears that had locked, but he was unable to bring the vehicle back under his control. Terrified, he leaped out of the truck an instant before it careened out of control down the hill. He saw in absolute horror the run-away vehicle speed down the hill toward the dining hall of the summer camp—even as he himself was hurtling through the air toward the woods next to the road.

He felt a sharp pain in his wrist and a hard blow to his head. Then, a blazing light blinded him. When he regained his vision, albeit blurred, he noticed that the rear bumper of his run-away truck had jammed between two tree trunks, remnants of two tall maple trees that had been cut down earlier at the bottom of the hill. Leo trudged through the brush toward the truck. He felt unharmed. Astonishingly, he felt no pain. After seeing the condition of the vehicle, he was stunned. There was no damage to the body of the truck except for a few scratches along the left side near the company's logo. Two Boy Scouts with hatchets emerged from the center building and began chopping away at the base of the tree stumps. Half an hour later, the truck was free. *Rick will never believe this in a million years.* Leo laughed to himself. He was feeling light-headed, giddy, enveloped by an odd sense of relief as his truck zoomed up the hill—almost as if someone else was driving—out of the campgrounds, leaving a long trail of dust behind.

CHAPTER 11

The curriculum for the fifth year of studies at the seminary had been established decades ago. It concentrated on the study of philosophy. Leo had been intrigued by the subject since reading some of the philosophers during his first year at the seminary. He often thought about Plato, who believed we are all born as half persons who search—sometimes our entire lives—for the other half that complements our being. Leo could well relate to that theory. He was only half a person since Matt's disappearance. Leo was also fascinated by Baruch Spinoza, whose observation that perhaps we are all living in some kind of heaven or hell right now, appealed to Leo.

Indeed, the more he thought about God—the more he rejected the idea of a Father in heaven who watches over us. If God watches over us, why is there so much suffering in the world among innocent people? Why are there so many tragic deaths, wars, famines, diseases? Whenever he and his classmates would raise such questions over the years, they would always be met with scorn by their professor-priests.

"Hah!" they would scold. "The problem of evil! Do you think you can know the mind of God, what his divine plan is all about?" Yet the Church seemed to have no problem knowing the "mind of God" when they established rules, precepts and edicts that harmed so many people over the centuries.

In the previous year Leo sought out the brightest priest on the faculty, Father Lenahan.

"Where are we going, Father? What's at the end of life? What is our purpose, our destiny?"

But even the most educated professor could only respond, half-heartedly, "The Light of Glory is our end. That is our destiny."

That answer raised more questions that were unanswerable—by anyone. Leo became fascinated by the profound depth of Charles Ives's symphony *The Unanswered Question*. He finally began to realize what the great composer was trying to say: The universe responds to human beings seeking an answer to the ultimate question about their reason for existence! The very notion of our bold probing elicits only silence from the indescribably vast universe, no less than from his learned professor. Leo shared the composer's frustration.

Leo was drifting with no direction. His previously strong beliefs and convictions had been shattered. Each day became more meaningless. If he could manage to get through the first part of the upcoming academic year, maybe he could somehow, some way, find Matt again over the holidays. When Leo stopped by the restaurant supply company during the Christmas holidays, Irv noticed his changed appearance and demeanor. Leo looked sad and depressed. His signature cheery smile was missing.

"Leo, what's wrong, my boy?"

"Wha ... What do you mean, Irv?"

"C'mon, Leo. I've known you for a long time now. You're not yourself. Look at you. You look sad, distant. Your bright smile is gone. You've lost weight. What's wrong? Are you having problems at school? Is your family all right? Can I help you with anything?"

"No, uh, no, Irv, I've had a difficult year, but I'm sure it will all work out okay. Thanks for your concern." He looked at Irv, puzzled. *Why is he wearing that bright white shirt with no tie? How unlike him.* "No, I just, uh, ... thought I'd stop by to see if you've made any decisions about the summer delivery routes to North Jersey yet." He was still glancing at Irv's white shirt.

"Yes, Leo, as a matter of fact we'll be adding the route again. We'd love to have you back in harness with us."

"That's great, Irv," Leo responded, his emotions subdued. "I'm, uh, looking forward to being here." Yes, he needed the job, but how could he go back up there to Culver Lake without knowing where Matt was, or how to find him? He started to leave.

"Oh, by the way, Leo, a few months ago we received this in the mail," Irv said, pushing the swivel chair back from his old maple desk. He reached inside the middle drawer and pulled out a legal-size, yellow envelope. "After Samantha left, I had a temp working here for a while. She had no idea who 'Leo' was—and, didn't bother to ask anyone, so she put this in my 'miscellaneous' file. It kind of got misplaced. When I started closing out the books for the end of the year, I found it. It was addressed to our company, with 'Attention: Leo.' I would have mailed it to you, but I figured I'd be seeing you, so I held it here for you."

"Thank so much, Irv."

"You can see it just says 'Leo' on the envelope, no last name or anything."

"Yes! Yeah! That's fine, Irv. Thanks, uh, thanks again. Leo accepted the envelope from Irv's hand like he had just been given a million dollars. "Well, I'd better get back home, Irv. I'll see you when I'm back in April. Take it easy. Thanks for the envelope, and, oh, also for the job offer."

"Don't mention it, my boy. I surely hope everything will be better for you this year. I hate to see you looking so down."

"Thanks, Irv. I'm sure it will. Please say 'hello' to Jonathan. How is he feeling?"

"Sorry to tell you, Leo, but there's been no improvement in his condition."

"I'm so sorry, Irv. Please tell him I'm praying for him."

Leo left the office and hurried down the street to the park at the corner. He sat down on an old green bench and began opening the thick restaurant supply company envelope. When he looked inside, his heart beat faster: the large yellow envelope contained a smaller, pale-blue one.

"This just *has* to be Matt's stationery!" He fumbled with the edges, opened it as carefully as his nervous hands could manage, and pulled out the letter. He unfolded the pages, revealing a gold "S" at the top. He pressed the letter to his lips and kissed it, then began reading the first of its handwritten pages.

August 28, 1965

Dear Leo,

I can't tell you how much I miss you and need you. I've gone over our times together a thousand times in my mind. When I got back to my apartment after you had gone, I took off my jacket, hung it in the closet, turned around and saw that blue robe on my bed. I sat next to it, grabbed it and pulled it to my face, caressing it, trying to find some way to be with you, realizing that we would not be together again until June. Then, it dawned on me. Christ, we didn't even exchange our home phone numbers! I don't even know your last name or the name of the seminary where you're studying. We just got so carried away that night we weren't thinking straight. When I found out about Mr. Freeling and that the old hotel was closed, I was out of my mind! How would I ever find you? I remembered you said the seminary where you were studying was located in the Philadelphia area, so I wrote letters to five seminaries around there, addressing them to 'Leo.' Three of the letters were returned as undeliverable. I never heard from the other two places. I thought I was lost, and that I'd never see you again. Then it occurred to me that you had been working for the restaurant supply company for a number of years and that, if I wrote a letter to you and mailed it to the supply company, someone would get it to you. I searched the Allentown City Directory, found the address, and sent this letter. I hope with all my heart that you will receive it and contact me. I'll be moving to Philadelphia next fall to begin graduate school at Temple University.

Man, it's been nearly a year since I've seen you and I can't tell you what a miserably painful, empty year it has been. I miss you terribly, Leo. I need your warmth and comfort.

My father has been arguing constantly with that old bag, and I don't know how much longer they can continue like this. Leo, I want to give you my telephone number so you can call me. I know that we live about an hour and a half away, but I will get in my goddamned Mustang and speed down there as soon as you say the word. My dear Leo, please call me at TR-5-1304.

I'm dying without you, man! By all that is merciful, I hope you receive this letter and that we'll be together again soon.

All my love,
Matt

Leo was mortified. They had been cursed again by the worst timing imaginable. He clutched the letter in his hands, holding it close to his chest.

At least I know that Matt is all right and that he still loves me.

He walked home from the supply company. As soon as he got back in the house, he removed the letter from the envelope, turning to the page with Matt's phone number on it. He picked up the phone and started dialing. *Wait a minute, how am I going to explain to my father this long-distance call?* It didn't matter. He had to hear Matt's voice. He dialed Matt's home phone number in New Jersey. The phone began ringing on the other end, but was abruptly interrupted by three beeps followed by a recorded message: "We're sorry, the number that you have dialed, TR-5-1304, has been disconnected. Please try again, or dial the operator for assistance."

It was Leo's last chance to reach Matt before having to return to the seminary. After that, he would have to wait until the Easter break. He went up to his bedroom and sat on the bed. Tears rolled down his cheeks. He feared he would never see Matt again. The deep, personal, sensual love he experienced for the first time in his life was being smothered by one accident after another. *If only I had received that letter sooner, we would have been together for Christmas!*

What lay ahead for him? He had to get through the final semester of the year at the seminary; then he would have only one year to go to earn his bachelor's degree in psychology. After that he would have choices to make with regard to a career. The priesthood was now a distant, forsaken goal. So much had happened to him over the past two summers. His glorious evening with Matt changed Leo's life forever. Religious ceremonies no longer inspired him. They had been reduced to empty, meaningless rituals needing to be performed only in order to move forward with his education. He tried to concentrate on his studies, but with only marginal success, his obsession with Matt overwhelming him. He needed to be with him again. Leo decided to resign from the seminary at the end of the school year.

CHAPTER 12

Leo had some savings from his summer employment, so he planned to enroll at Temple University to work toward a bachelor's degree in clinical psychology. He had learned a lot about the field from his Apostolate training at the Philadelphia Psychiatric Hospital. His father promised to give him the remainder of what he needed to take two summer courses and pay for housing there. Classes were scheduled during June and July; after completing them, he would enter the full-time program in the fall and find a job in the city, working evenings to pay for his educational expenses.

His formerly strong beliefs in the Catholic religion and its doctrine had vanished. He had no interest in any organized religions or their stifling commandments. He knew from his experiences with many people over the years how important religion was to them, how it gave them strength to carry on when life presented so much pain and suffering. But religion was no comfort at all to Leo. He was hurting. He could find no solace in any religious sacraments or prayers to alleviate his pain and loss.

Time doesn't heal emotional wounds; it compounds them. Only Matt could save him.

Leo drove to Philadelphia and checked into Johnson Hall dormitory, where he was assigned a room on the 9th floor, just two floors from the top. It was three times the size of his room at the seminary. From his window he could see several miles west to the Germantown section of the city. He thought about his mother—all those trips to her allergy specialist, in vain. He continued to stare out the window, imagining his dad in his old *Dynaflo*, transporting his mom to the doctor's office. He turned back to his room, unpacked, and surveyed the building that would be his new home for the summer. A recreation center with pool tables, Ping-Pong tables and several pinball machines was located on the first floor, behind the mail center and reception area in the front of the lobby. A row of four vending machines provided students with nourishment in the form of Cokes, potato chips, and pretzels. Surprisingly, it hadn't changed a bit since he visited his former high school classmate there six years before. He left the building, turned left and walked down Broad Street to Mifflin Hall, where he picked up his textbooks for the summer courses, and headed back to the dorm to review his class schedule. Then Leo decided to enjoy the mild June afternoon, taking a walk before dinner. He left Johnson Hall around five o'clock, and strolled up Broad Street. He hadn't gone two blocks when a sandwich board sign, propped on the sidewalk in front of the *Night Owl Pub*, froze him:

TONIGHT
MATTHEW STEPHENSON
PRESENTS SONGS BY THE BEATLES
7:00 PM

Leo kept looking at the words as if they were written in a foreign language.

He waited for more than an hour, and by the time the doors opened, at 6:30, he was the first of about thirty students in line at the pub. When he got inside he ordered a bottle of *Rolling Rock* as he looked around the room for a table. Some twenty-five small, round wooden cabaret tables, each with a candle in the center, were scattered around the room at the left side of the bar, which faced the 8-by-10-foot stage. Leo took a seat in the back and to the right of the stage, where he could see the door that led backstage. He would see the performer as soon as he entered through that door, so if Leo's hopes were once again dashed—he could leave immediately. A few minutes after seven o'clock, when most of the tables had been occupied, the manager announced the program.

"Good evening, guys and gals. The *Night Owl* is proud to present your fellow student Matthew Stephenson, performing songs by the Beatles. Let's hear it for Matt!"

The crowd was generous with its applause for one of their own. Leo sat up in his chair like he was about to witness the Second Coming of Christ. The small spotlight shifted to the left side of the stage. In an instant, after more than a year of anguish, Leo's life was restored. Matt jumped onto the platform, holding on high his *Martin* guitar. Leo leaned so far forward in his seat he nearly knocked over the table. Matt's blonde hair was a bit longer than it had been back on that cold January morning. He was wearing his John Lennon glasses. A crisp, bright white Nehru shirt, opened halfway down his chest, was tucked neatly into his white hip-hugger slacks. Leo was in a trance. Matt began the program with "Good Day Sunshine." The crowd loved him. In about forty-five minutes the performance ended with "Yesterday"—the sustained applause bringing Matt back on stage for an encore.

"Thanks a lot guys, you've been a great audience; I really enjoyed playing for you tonight. I'm going to close the show with my favorite Beatles' song of all. I want to dedicate it to the one person I truly love in this world. I only wish he could hear it … "

Michelle, ma belle Sont des mots qui vont très bien ensemble Ma Michelle. Michelle, ma belle Sont des mots qui vont très bien ensemble….

I want you, I want you, I want you.
I think you know by now
I'll get to you somehow.
Until I do I'm telling you so
You'll understand ....

Matt's voice was drying up. His eyes were tearing as he finished the song. The audience went wild.

They have no idea what just happened, Leo mused. *This is a miracle!*

Leo anxiously made his way through the maze of tables and chairs scattered around the cabaret floor as the crowd headed for the bar. He rushed toward the door through which Matt had exited upon leaving the stage. It led to a dark, narrow hallway. Leo could see light streaming from a room at the end of the hall on the right side. His heart was pumping wildly. As he reached the doorway, he heard Matt's voice still humming, "Mi-chelle."

Matt was sitting on a large grey metal desk in the sparsely furnished office that served as the dressing room, his back to the door. His guitar was propped up on the side of the desk. The overhead fluorescent highlighted his bright blonde hair and unforgettable physique. He was looking straight down, his hands cradling his neck. He looked exhausted.

"Matt," Leo uttered as he stepped into the small office.

Matt spun around. He had barely gotten to his feet when he was smothered by Leo's embrace. They kissed.

Matt caught his breath. "Leo, Christ ... I, I can't believe this! How, uh, what are you doing down here, man? I—"

"Matt, I've left the seminary. I've given up my studies for the priesthood. It's no longer the life I want to live. I have so much to tell you about my experiences over the past couple of years, and—"

"Hey, let's get a table out front and talk."

As they sat down, Leo began writing on one of the square *Rolling Rock* coasters on the table. He finished, looked up at Matt, and handed him the coaster.

"Before we do or say anything else, Matt, here is my full name, home telephone number and address."

They giggled like kids.

"At long last," said Matt, "after nearly losing each other forever, we're finally using our heads."

Together now in a quiet corner of the pub, they stared into each other's eyes.

"Leo, I just can't tell you how awfully sad and depressed I've been. When I found out that Mr. Freeling closed the old hotel, and I couldn't reach you, I panicked. Finally, I figured that I might have a chance to contact you through the supply company. So I sent the letter with my phone number and address. When I got no response, I just didn't know what to think. I called the restaurant supply company, but the chick who answered said you didn't work there. I thought maybe you decided to ignore me so you could continue to pursue your career as a priest. Or maybe the letter never got to you. I just didn't know what the fuck to think or do."

Leo told him all about his futile search when he had returned to Culver Lake that summer, calling every Stephenson in the book. "The supply company got your letter that summer, but they never found it until the end of December. I got it when I stopped by to visit during my Christmas vacation."

"This is crazy, man. Just a couple of weeks after I sent that letter, my father found out his wife was running around with another guy. One of my dad's clients had seen her at breakfast at a ski lodge over in Pennsylvania with some guy he knew. He told my father. The old hag denied it at first, but when my dad told her the name of the guy and the ski resort, she admitted it, blaming my dad because he worked too hard, ignored her, and she was lonely and … blah, blah, blah. It turns out that she had been screwing around for more than a year, always using the excuse she was going to visit her elderly mother in the Poconos. My father filed for divorce. Of course, with the adultery claim and all, he won. It was a bitter time for him. But he got rid of the old hag. She didn't get a cent from him! He sold the house and bought a really groovy place out in Swartswood Lake to get away from the whole mess. It's taken a serious toll on him, Leo. He took a few weeks off in August to get some R & R. He's aged dramatically through all of the crap he's gone through."

"I can't imagine what a tough time it's been for him and you. That explains why his receptionist told me he was out of the office for an indefinite period of time."

"You went to his office? How did you—"

"It was one of those names in the book!"

"Whew! Man! Look, I know there's no snow in the forecast, but will you stay with me tonight, Leo?"

"Matt, I don't care if there's going to be a freakin' blizzard, I'm staying with you!"

Matt told Leo that he rented an apartment down in Spring Garden—just ten minutes away by subway. They took the subway to Spring Garden, got out and walked over to 16th Street. "I haven't been down this way in a couple of years," Leo said. "I love all these new trees!" Leo thought about Thomas's aunt—how distant all that seemed to him now.

"Yeah, it's nice. There are a lot of rough edges here and there, but it's a great place to stay—so close to the campus."

They arrived at a handsome if somewhat deteriorated four-story, red-brick townhouse with a gorgeous white marble doorway and staircase.

"I'm on the third floor, Leo. It gives me a lot of exercise!"

Matt set his guitar down on the hallway floor, fished his key from his right side pocket and opened the door. "Welcome to my humble abode, Leo!"

Stepping inside was like traveling back in time to that life-altering evening two years earlier. All the countless times Leo had relived that night—lamenting the loss of the one he truly loved—had come to an end.

"Leo, come over here, man! We have so much to make up for." Matt plopped down onto the large, dark grey sofa. Leo quickly joined him. They lay there stretched out and facing each other. Matt was looking into Leo's eyes. "I can't tell you how much I love you, babe, how many times I dreamed about this happening—the two of us together again. He squeezed Leo. They kissed passionately, neither willing to break their unity. Matt had already removed his white shirt and was undoing his white trousers as they entered the bedroom. Leo was undressed before Matt had taken off his shoes. He looked at Matt's tanned bare chest golden in the last of the evening sunlight pouring through the window. They stood facing each other, totally naked, embracing, yearning to be one again at last. Leo guided himself over Matt as they slumped onto the bed. In seconds their craving bodies were united again.

"I don't want this to ever end," Leo moaned. "Nothing can separate us again, Matt." All the excruciating tension of the prolonged separation that plagued them over the past two years was released.

The next morning Leo awoke feeling Matt's warm, smooth chest pressed against his back. Was it true? Had everything really happened yesterday? Was he dreaming? Leo backed into Matt's body, arousing him.

"You really know how to wake a guy up!"

"Mmmmm! Good morning, Matt."

They lay there silent and motionless. Matt turned Leo toward him. "Leo, I don't want you to leave. I want to wake up like this every day.

This is a large apartment; we can both be comfortable here. Whaddaya say, buddy?"

"Matt, I've paid for the dorm room at Johnson Hall for the summer, but I don't see why I have to stay there. I, uh, you know, there's only one telephone on each floor out in the hallway; it sure makes communication difficult. I don't ever want to risk losing touch with you again. Not only that, but seeing you the first thing in the morning—every day—would be heaven for me. Hey, we could sleep over there once in a while for a change of scenery, you know?"

"Leo, that's fantastic! I'll go over there with you today. We'll move some of your stuff down here."

"I'll feel a lot better having my car here, Matt. There've been a few incidents of vandalism and car thefts over there; this area is much safer."

"Hey, Leo, do you remember my red *Mustang*?"

"How can I forget? It was the last thing I saw when I was driving away and you were standing there in the snow on that frigid January morning."

"Well, I don't have it anymore, Leo. My father bought me a red Porsche. He was really pleased when I graduated summa cum laude from Muhlenberg. I have it stored in a garage I've rented over on 17th Street. Do you wanna go for a spin around Fairmount Park today?"

"Are you kidding, Matt! What an amazing gift!"

"Yeah, you know, dad has mellowed a lot since he got rid of that old bitch. She was making his life so *goddamned* miserable. You wouldn't believe the crap that went on in that house. I don't know how he could have remained so deceived. After my mom died he just got so lonely and withdrawn. He worked long hours at the law firm every day just to keep his mind off her. I have no brothers and sisters, so I was the only one there for him until Miss Hot Panties came along. She made his life miserable for more than five years. I think he's starting to get over all the embarrassment and shame about the whole thing. He looked a lot better after he took that month off back then. Now he has that great house on Swartswood Lake. Leo, I gotta take you up there for a week-end. You'll love it!"

"How does he feel about you not having any girlfriends around? I mean, a hot guy like you—with no bimbos around? What does he say?"

"Leo, he knows all about me and my lifestyle. One day when I had an argument with Mildred, I shouted at the old whore, telling her how lucky I was that I didn't need to have any bitches like her around me. My dad walked in on my outburst. Later we talked about it. I told him I'm gay—and goddamned happy about it. He told me he didn't care what I did—he would always love me more than anything in the world. That's the kind of guy he is. That's one reason why I feel so lucky. You're the other reason!"

"Matt, I'd love to meet him."

"Done! We'll drive up there on that five-day break we have coming up later this month. I can't wait to introduce you to him."

They got out of bed grudgingly.

"I'll make you one of my famous breakfasts, man," Matt quipped, heading toward the kitchen.

Leo slipped into his underwear and walked to the bathroom. Matt was humming "Michelle" as he prepared breakfast. Leo was looking at himself in the mirror. *Can this really be happening? Something just doesn't seem right.* He hesitated before joining Matt in the kitchen.

The magnificent four-story townhouses in Spring Garden had been built in the middle of the nineteenth century as a refuge for people who wanted to leave the congestion of the "Olde City" area as the population of Philadelphia was growing rapidly. The neighborhood had deteriorated badly over the past few decades, but new families were beginning to move in, and there were signs of revitalization.

The apartment was large and spacious. The kitchen, painted all white, had old but shiny hardwood floors. Matt was wearing only a bright white T-shirt and Jockey shorts. He was busily getting the coffee ready as Leo came into the kitchen and grabbed him around his waist, playfully pushing against Matt's back.

"That coffee smells great, Matt."

"It's brewed specially for you, babe!"

After breakfast they headed for Broad Street, caught the subway and walked over to Leo's dorm. They took the elevator to the ninth floor and walked down the hallway toward the front of the building. Leo unlocked the door revealing a sparsely furnished room with a single bed and built-in closets. He had a few books to pack, and about a half-dozen shirts and slacks, plus some underwear, socks and three pairs of shoes.

Matt looked around the room. "Hey, buddy," he laughed. "I can sure tell you were in a monastery. I mean, look at his place. It's like a monk's cell, for Chrissake!"

"I never was one for having a lot of stuff around," Leo laughed. "I feel comfortable this way. You know, it wasn't really a *monastery*; it was more like a college campus. The rooms were only about seven by ten, but they weren't cells."

"Whatever you say, buddy! As long as you're happy."

They loaded the clothing and books into Leo's car, parked along Montgomery Avenue, near the dorm. Matt shook his head as Leo slid behind the steering wheel.

"Man, a fucking '57 Plymouth with a *push button* transmission! I just *love* it!" He patted the dashboard.

"I know it's not what you're accustomed to, honey, but it's all I got."

They drove down Broad to Spring Garden Street and turned right onto 16th. Leo squeezed the Plymouth into a space about a half-block from Matt's apartment. They got all of Leo's belongings into Matt's place on one trip. Matt left the room and returned with two bottles of cold *Rolling Rock*.

"Cheers, Leo! Welcome, home, man!"

They clinked the shining green bottles, took long sips, then sat down on the sofa.

"Oh, uh, I almost forgot, Leo. I've got a couple of tickets for the Peter, Paul and Mary concert at the Academy of Music tonight. Are you available?"

"I love them, Matt. I have a few of their albums. That would be really groovy!"

"Okay, we're all set, then."

Leo and Matt finished their beers and hurried down the three flights of stairs to the front door, then jumped down the four marble steps out front. They walked up 16th Street to Green, turned right onto 17th to the garage in the middle of the block, where Matt stored his Porsche. Matt got out his key, unlocked the door and removed the canvas cover.

"C'mon, Leo. Let's take this baby for a ride!"

"I can't believe it. It's a *Targa*!"

"Yeah, dad was real kind to me." Matt had already gotten in and had the key in the ignition. "Let's go, man!"

Leo opened the door and hopped in. "Matt, what incredible black leather upholstery. This is terrific!"

Leo had barely finished the sentence when the Porsche was out in the middle of 17th Street. Matt revved up the engine. Driving up to the corner, he turned left and headed for Spring Garden Street. Matt, usually a careful driver, quickly exceeded the speed limit as they zoomed up the parkway. They were off to East River Drive and Fairmount Park. It was a sweltering, mid-June afternoon. Matt's long blonde hair was blowing in every direction as the convertible speeded past the art museum and entered the park.

"Matt, you look so damned cool behind that wheel. I just want to grab you right now!"

Matt took his right hand off the steering wheel and reached over to Leo's thigh. "Oh, man, would I love to take you over to those trees along the river and smother you!"

"*Do* it, Matt!" Leo laughed, alive again after more than a year of anguish and misery.

Matt found a quiet parking area just beyond the old Boat House Row, pulling into a space under the magnificent oak trees along the Schuylkill River. Rowers from the local universities were gliding by in their sculls.

"This is far out, Matt. I love this area. We used to be bused into the city from the seminary over the expressway on the west side of the river. I could get a glimpse of this part of the park."

"Yeah, and I'll bet you really stretched that old Roman collar of yours to get a look at those rowers!"

"I can't say that I tried to ignore them."

Matt turned off the ignition. He looked at Leo. "I want all of our time together to be like this, Leo. You have no idea how much you mean to me."

"Let me try to show you, Matt." Leo leaned closer, put his hands around Matt's head, running his fingers through his thick blonde hair. He pulled Matt toward him, and kissed him.

They sat looking at the placid flow of the river. Matt put his right arm around Leo's shoulder and squeezed it.

"So, Leo, I hope you don't mind my asking, but what made you change your mind about becoming a priest? I know it wasn't just that you met me and, uh, well, uh … " he squeezed Leo again. "I mean, what was it that changed your outlook? That was a humungous decision to have to make. Did anyone give you guidance about what to do, or how to consider your options?"

"Wow, Matt! Those are really heavy questions. Where do I begin? Well, I think I started doubting my decision when my mother died. I was so terribly broken by her sudden passing. I just couldn't focus on my goal, or anything else for that matter. The prayers and meditation gave me no comfort at all. I just kept thinking about my little sister—how awfully tough it was going to be for her; and my dad having to work every day, then come home to take on the responsibilities of a mother, too. It was all so tragic. I loved my mother more than anything else on earth. Suddenly, she was gone! When I started studying philosophy and logic it started a whole new way of thinking for me. There were ideas that I had never pursued before. The clincher was having those private sessions with the brightest professor on our faculty and discovering that he, too, had no real answers to the questions I was asking, like, What is this all *about*? Where are we going? What's the *purpose* of this life? What does it all *mean*? All I ever got was the *lumen gloriae*. We are all destined for the 'Light of Glory'—whatever the hell that is! You know, nobody in our study group back there believed in this God-the-Father-sitting-on-his-throne-judging-the-people-of-the-world thing. Ask them about the presence of evil in the world, and they mock you, asking, 'Who can know the will of God?' How could I live a life like that with all those doubts and denials, and still preach it to others? How much sense would that make?"

Leo studied Matt's face for his reaction. There was none, just a steady seriousness that Leo had never seen before.

"On another point, Matt, I had no sex of any kind after I entered the seminary. I was so enthusiastic about my goal that, even with the normally overpowering sex drive I've always had, I was rarely tempted—and never gave in. When I met you that day at the old hotel and felt your loving embrace, I think it unleashed a torrent of emotions I had been suppressing for years. It was like a whole new kind of life I experienced that day; I didn't want it to end. Oh, sure, I fought it like hell at first. My confessors, more than once, read me the riot act. But, the day after you and I spent that wonderful evening together, I told a priest all about it in confession. You know what he said, Matt? He asked, 'Do you *love* this man?' Matt, I was totally floored by that question. It changed the way I had been thinking, Matt. That night when I was trying to fall asleep, I thought about those words again. That's when I realized it was time to change my life's goal. I knew when I thought about you and how warm, kind and passionate you are, I knew that, yes, I really *do* love you, Matt. I had come to realize that I could not possibly live a life that prohibited me from having sex with another person. It's all so unnatural. That's how we got here today. Despite all the roadblocks, miscommunications and errors, we are here together. Right now that's all that matters to me in the whole world .... Sorry to babble on like this!"

"Whew, Leo! I, I, uh ... That is one of the most amazing stories I've ever heard. I'm so, so *goddamned* lucky you are with me, man. You're just the most incredible person that—"

"Matt, I love you!"

"I love you, Leo!"

Traffic on East River Drive was building steadily as the afternoon had turned to dusk.

"Hey, we'd better get back. We have that Peter, Paul and Mary concert tonight, and dinner before the show. Leo, I'm so glad that we had this time to talk. It's meant so much to me."

"Me, too, Matt. We have so much more to learn about each other."

Matt backed up his car, then eased his way into the heavy traffic. He drove around the art museum, down to 17th Street to the garage. They walked back to the apartment. Matt was wearing his white Nehru shirt to the concert. They grabbed the Broad Street subway to the Walnut-Locust station. When they emerged they walked up Chestnut Street to The Pub, a popular steak house. Leo was excited. He had eaten dinner there a few times when in town on his "Thursday Apostolate" days. He was thinking about his mom as he and Matt entered the restaurant—about all of those wonderful times they had at the Marble Bar. Sitting across the table from Matt, he realized he had found his soul mate for life. After dinner they walked the short distance to the Academy of Music. Peter, Paul and Mary were in rare form. Their opening song, "Puff the Magic Dragon," engaged the audience in a sing-along that set the tone for the evening. As they were leaving the Academy, they were caught up in the enthusiasm of the sellout crowd.

Matt was ecstatic. "Leo will you *ever* forget the sight of Mary Travers, center stage, as the spotlight focused on her, bringing her gradually out of the dark? And then her first words—sung as only she can project." Matt sang softly: "And when I die, and when I'm dead, dead and gone, there'll be one child born, and a world to carry on." Leo stared at Matt intensely. He was detached somehow, as if he were seeing Matt in a dream.

They got back home around midnight and went straight to bed. At about four o'clock, they were awakened by the telephone ringing in the living room.

"Ohhh! Uhh! I'll, I'll, uh, get it," Matt moaned. He got out of bed and hustled his naked body to the phone. "Whaaat? *How*? No, *no*! Just *wait* a minute here; just a *minute* now. I'm his son, Matt. Where have you—? What? No! I'm going to leave right now. Yeah, I know what time it is! I'll be there in about three hours. Yeah, uh-huh, bye. Thank, thank you."

Leo was standing there as he hung up the phone.

"What is it, Matt?"

"Leo, my *father*—he's dead. He died about an hour ago from what they said was some kind of heart attack. He's *dead*, Leo!"

Matt began sobbing convulsively. It was the first time Leo had seen him lose control of himself. He embraced Matt, feeling his tears streaming down his chest, just the way Matt had comforted him on that first day they met.

"Leo, I'm gonna have to leave. I've got to drive up to Newton Memorial Hospital right away. They're keeping his body there until I get up there. I need to see him as soon as possible. I'm sorry, man. I just, we were having such a—"

"I'm going with you, Matt. I won't let you drive up there at this time in the morning by yourself. I want to be with you."

"Leo, you have classes tomorrow. You can't just—"

"Oh yeah, I can! Let's get dressed, Matt."

Leo offered to drive, but the adrenaline was pumping through Matt. He had to get to his father. Matt insisted that he drive the full two and a half hours to Newton himself. They arrived near daybreak. A nurse guided them to a holding area in the basement of the hospital where his father's body had been moved. After they entered the room, and Matt identified himself, the nurse slowly pulled back the white sheet that was covering his father's face. Matt stared at his father's ashen, expressionless face, then placed his right hand on his father's forehead.

"Dad, I am so sorry," he sobbed. "I've been a terrible son to you. You've always given me everything I ever wanted. I never told you how much I really love you. I'll never forget how you took care of me when mom died. You were always there for me. I never told you how much that meant to me." He kissed his father's forehead, pausing above the face, for one last, unspoken good-bye. He moved away from the gurney and turned to Leo.

"Leo, you're all I have in this whole world now."

The funeral at Saint Joseph's church was a community event. The mayor and town council attended. The State Attorney General was there. The bishop celebrated the Solemn Requiem High Mass. Hundreds of Matt's father's friends, neighbors and clients turned out for the service. The Knights of Columbus formed an honor guard as the casket was carried into the church.

Once again, the dreadful cries of the *Dies Irae* echoed in Leo's head.

Leo stayed with Matt for the entire week after the funeral. At his request Leo accompanied Matt to see his father's law partner, Mr. Preston, whom his father had named the executor of the estate. Leo knew how painful the reading of the Last Will and Testament was going to be for Matt—how uncomfortable he would be with the entire scene. It was the first time Matt would be back in that office since his father died. It was a Saturday morning, the office was closed. Mr. Preston greeted them as they entered. Oddly, the attorney was wearing a white linen suit over a snow-white dress shirt unbuttoned at the neck.

"I just want to tell you again how awfully sorry I am about your dad's passing," Mr. Preston said. "He was such a good friend for so many years, and a wonderful, brilliant partner. I'll miss him terribly, and I know that you will feel his loss more than anyone."

"Thanks, Mr. Preston. You know, dad always spoke very highly of you. I appreciate all the help you gave when he had to, uh, when he went through that bitter divorce. I don't think he ever recovered from it, but you surely did make the court proceedings as easy as possible for him."

"Matt, thanks. I did all I could to help calm him, but it was traumatic for him. Now, Matt, I need to go over these papers with you so you can start making some decisions for yourself. You are the sole survivor and heir to your father's entire estate. Here is the document that specifies the terms of his Will. You are to inherit his home at Swartswood Lake and all of his physical property. Your father has bank assets and a stock portfolio that total nearly one-and-a-half-million dollars. In addition, he has a life insurance policy that pays you one million dollars as his sole beneficiary. Matt, son, I know you'll need help with all this, so I would be more than happy to recommend a few financial planners to help you with these assets."

"Thank you, Mr. Preston. I really appreciate your help with this. I, uh, had no idea that my father had so much … such an incredible amount of money. I just can't—"

"Your father was a very wise investor, Matt. He studied the market carefully over the years, and I must say, he was very helpful to me as well. He won a number of high-profile cases up here, you know, and was a very successful and prestigious attorney. Most of all, he was really a wonderful friend. I will truly miss him."

They left the office after signing papers and transferring assets.

"Leo, I have two-and-a-half-*fucking*-million dollars! What am I going to do?"

"Matt, you don't have to do anything. Listen to a few financial experts, like Mr. Preston said, and try to get some ideas. Then you can—"

"No! You know *what*, man, I know *exactly* what I want to do, Leo. And you are part of my plan! I'm going to buy old man Freeling's hotel, and—"

"Hold on, Matt. Wait a second!"

"No! Listen, Leo. That's the place where you and I met. We would never, ever have gotten together if that hotel had not been there. The last time I visited my father, he told me about the growing need for first-class resorts for family get-away times, and where corporate executives and their staffs and potential clients can go for retreats, sales meetings, conferences—stuff like that. He said they want to get out of their offices, out of the cities and go to places like this to train and do business. We can do this together. You have experience with the restaurant and hotel business, and I know this hotel like that back of my hand. We're gonna create a premium first-class resort that will draw the top money people from the east coast. They're extending Interstate 80 near this area, and the lake is being expanded. It will be an unbelievable force for change around here. New York City is only about sixty miles from the place. I know I can do it with your help, Leo. Whaddaya say, man?"

"Matt, you know I told you before. I'll *never* leave you again. If, uh, if that's what you want to do, I'll work with you on it. I just want to be with you."

"Okay, we're both enrolled at Temple for the summer. I'm going to drop out next week. I'm sick and tired of it anyway."

" So am I."

"What about your father?"

"I'll speak with him. I'm sure there'll be no problem after I explain the whole thing to him."

"All right, Leo. Let's go up to Culver Lake tomorrow. We'll meet with the real estate company up there to check things out. Let's get this *fucking ball* rolling!"

As Leo looked at Matt, his vision began to blur; he couldn't focus. Suddenly Matt was fading. Leo could no longer see him clearly; Matt's voice grew weaker … silent.

"Matt? Matt! … *Maaaaatt!*"

CHAPTER 13

As he had done dutifully, almost religiously, countless times over the past ten months, he stepped out of the elevator, turned left and walked slowly, increasingly hopelessly, along the shiny beige marble floor of the long white corridor to room 729. Donna was walking next to him, occasionally stopping to say hello to the nurses. He opened the door carefully. Dr. Wentz was standing at the foot of the bed, studying a report.

"How is he doing today, Doctor?"

Dr. Wentz was a short, heavy, balding man about fifty years old. "Oh, good evening, Mr. Weber. Sorry I didn't hear you come in." The doctor turned around and greeted him in the deep, abdominal ones to which Mr. Weber had become accustomed to hearing. "Well, all his vital signs have continued to be stable, and we've seen some progress toward consciousness. He continues to breathe normally, and appears to be resting comfortably."

"Doctor, do you think he will he ever wake up?"

"Look, Mr. Weber, Leo suffered a severe trauma to his head. He was very fortunate to have jumped—maybe to have been thrown out of that truck—before it crashed and caught fire, but cases like this have persisted far longer than Leo's. There is no telling for certain when—or, I'm sorry to have to say, *if*— he will regain full consciousness, or what his brain function will be like. We think that Leo is in what we call a 'minimally conscious' state. At times he appears to be smiling, and other times he seems to be engaged in long conversations with someone. We've just conducted another complete neurological assessment that indicates he may be improving. His symmetry looks normal. The latest EEG has shown no abnormality in his brain's electrical activity. There appears to be no damage to his brain stem—a *very* significant finding, Mr. Weber. We have observed increased fiber densities and corticocortical sprouting. You see, these kinds of studies are very much untested and are essentially pioneering efforts, but there appear to be promising signs that Leo may emerge from this minimally conscious state. We're giving him the best physical therapy and nutrition that is available anywhere, and he has, fortunately, not suffered from any infections. His body is responding to the physical exercises very well. He's been moving his arms and legs voluntarily in response to stimuli that we have continued to introduce. The therapists have been able to clean his teeth regularly and managed his hygiene effectively. We have also observed sexual arousal on at least two occasions. Another hopeful sign, Mr. Weber, is that his awareness of sound and touch has been increasing."

After Leo had been transferred to the Good Samaritan Rehabilitation Hospital, the neurologist suggested that a few of Leo's favorite phonograph records could be brought to his room.

"Some theories suggest that hearing one's favorite music may help with the recovery process," she had advised.

Donna brought Leo's Beatles and Peter, Paul and Mary albums and played them on his record player, which was set up on a table next to him in his hospital room. She played them often, sometimes for hours, when she visited him. She knew they were his favorites. She heard the music coming from his bedroom so many times over the years—having so much fun listening to him when he used to sing along with them at home.

"Dad, see how *happy* Leo looks today. He has a smile on his face. He *must* be happy."

"I don't know if it's really a change, honey" her father cautioned, "You know your brother has looked pretty much like that ever since they rescued him from those woods nearly ten months ago."

"No, dad, he just looks *different* today!"

Dr. Wentz smiled as he patted Donna on the shoulder.

"Your brother *does* appear to be happy, Donna. At least he seems more comfortable."

As Leo's father looked on, his thoughts flashed back to that horrible late afternoon in the previous summer when he received the frantic call at work.

"Mr. Weber, this is Irv Davis at the Lehigh Restaurant Supply Company. Mr. Weber, I'm afraid I have some bad news. You see, Leo was completing his deliveries in New Jersey today, and he was driving out of the Boy Scout summer camp, up a steep hill when he somehow lost control of the truck he was driving. They think he may have been thrown out of the truck before it crashed into some tree trunks and burned. They found Leo along the side of the steep hill that leads out of the camp. He was unconscious. They've taken him to Newton Memorial Hospital, Mr. Weber. I'm so awfully sorry to have to tell you this over the phone."

"My God, Irv. Is he going to be all right?"

"They don't know, Mr. Weber. One of the Scouts saw the truck careening down the steep hill and shouted to warn everyone. It appears that some low-lying tree stumps stopped it but ripped out the gas line, which caused the truck to explode into flames. They searched for him in the fire, but one of the boys said he had seen a white figure ejected from the truck before it sped down the hill. The boys combed the hillside and found Leo lying in the woods, about twenty-five feet from the road. As far as I know, there were no life-threatening injuries. The hospital informed me he had sustained a fractured wrist and suffered severe head trauma."

Matt Stephenson was spending the summer in Fort Lauderdale, so he missed the small story at the bottom of the front page of the *New Jersey Herald Times* the next morning:

DRIVER SEVERELY INJURED IN TRUCK CRASH

A delivery route salesman was critically injured yesterday afternoon when he lost control of the truck that he was driving and was thrown from the vehicle at a local Boy Scout camp. The truck crashed and was destroyed by fire. The driver was taken to Newton Memorial Hospital, where he is listed in critical condition. No other people were reported injured.

Leo's father remembered calling his friend Ralph. They grabbed a New Jersey road map, filled the gas tank at the service station on Tilghman Street, and drove directly to Newton. Donna's Aunt Sheryl stayed with her at home. When they arrived at the hospital about an hour and a half later, Leo was still being held in the emergency room. Later that evening, Dr. Flanders, the resident physician, explained to Mr. Weber that, although Leo was still unconscious, he was breathing normally.

"Your son appears to have suffered a severe trauma to his head after being ejected from the truck he was driving. We've ordered an MRI scan to rule out any serious brain damage."

Leo's father had never been close nor spent any significant time with his son. Now, when it was so terribly important to tell Leo how much he loved him—Leo could not hear him, and might never. Fortunately, the results indicated no brain damage, so in the following week Leo was transported to the Good Samaritan Home and Rehabilitation Center, in Allentown, for continued treatment.

Dr. Wentz placed the chart back on the end of the bed and cleared his throat, startling Leo's father out of his gruesome reminiscing as he spoke.

"I'll be here for a while longer, Mr. Weber. If you need me for anything, just tell the nurse and she will contact me. Take it easy, Mr. Weber. Try to get some sleep tonight. Good night, Donna."

Donna and her father sat beside Leo's bed, repeatedly looking at his face, then looking around the sterile room. They talked about school and tomorrow night's dinner—small talk to pass the time while they waited for something, any kind of sign from Leo.

"Well, I guess we should be going soon. You have to get up for school tomorrow morning. I'll be right back, Donna." Her father left for the men's room.

Donna was on Leo's right side. His hands were crossed restfully on his chest. The ever-present intravenous needle was taped to his left hand. She reached for his right hand and held it, squeezing it. She missed him so much. She looked at her brother's still, peaceful face. The wide smile and taunting laugh she enjoyed for as long as she could remember were silenced; his face was almost totally obscured by the bulky oxygen mask.

Suddenly, Leo's eyes opened widely. He blinked several times. Donna snapped back in her seat. "*Leo!*" she exclaimed, just as her father was returning to the partially lit room. He ran to Leo's bedside; Leo's face was contorted as he stared blankly ahead. His father dashed out of the room to find Dr. Wentz.

"Matt, Maaatt, ... Maaaaatt," Leo continued to groan, swinging his head from side to side, sweat pouring down his forehead.

"Leo, what do you want? What is it, Leo?"

"Where ..., where's Matt?" I have to ... meet ... we're going ... Cul—" Leo's eyes closed as quickly as they had opened. He collapsed back upon the pillow, raising his left hand to his forehead. He was murmuring again: "Maaaa … I can't see … you … I … "

Dr. Wentz rushed into the room with his assistant and two nurses.

Leo continued to call out deliriously, "Maaatt!"

"What is he saying, Doctor?" Leo's father was standing with Donna next to Leo, across from the doctor, trying desperately to figure out what Leo wanted.

"I, I'm sorry, Mr. Weber, I just can't understand it. I think he's asking for someone. It sounds like *Matt* or *Mack*. Does he have any relatives or friends with either of those names—or something similar?"

"Doctor, I think he's been asking for someone named *Matt* since he woke up!" Donna shouted. "I think he was saying he had to meet him somewhere."

"I can't think of any of Leo's friends named *Matt*," his father said. "Can you, Donna?"

She couldn't. And Leo was silent again, his face and chest soaked with perspiration, his body limp.

"Is he going to be all right, Doctor?"

"Mr. Weber, we have just witnessed one of nature's mysteries. Your son is back from what appears to have been a prolonged minimally conscious state. He is speaking. This is an outstanding development."

"Can we stay awhile? He looks so lonely," Donna whispered.

"Sure, Donna. The nurses will be in soon to freshen him up, and make him more comfortable; so you can stay until they've finished, and say goodnight to Leo. He will need to rest tonight. Tomorrow will be a big day for him—and for all of you, I'm sure. Fortunately, Mr. Weber, we have one of the finest comprehensive rehabilitation programs in place here that will work with Leo over the coming weeks and months."

The next morning, Dr. Wentz entered the room with a nurse and a physical therapist. Leo had awakened early and seemed dazed. They helped Leo out of bed, into a wheelchair for transport to the examination room. The therapist was elated to notice Leo's ability to move his legs and arms as she helped Leo onto an examination table. When the tests had been completed, she assisted Leo back into his chair.

"Ummm, this feels … so, uh, so … straaange, nurse," Leo said softly as he squinted under the bright lights, trying to focus on her face. "I haven't been out of bed for, for … how long, did you say? Was it like … ten months or something?"

"Just a little less than that, Leo, but you're progressing very well right now. I'm so pleased and happy to see you able to move your limbs so easily. This is not a common ability for persons who have experienced what you've been through. I'm going to have one of my staff work with you every day to help strengthen your muscles and get you back on your feet as soon as possible. It will be difficult at first, Leo, but I think you'll make excellent progress if you follow the routine the therapist establishes for you."

Leo's father was reading the newspaper before going to work the following Monday, when the name at the top of the obituary page jumped out at him: *Jonathan Davis.*

Irv's son had finally lost his long and painful battle with colon cancer. Leo's dad was not a socially outgoing person. He sent the Davis family a sympathy card with a note expressing his heartfelt grief for them over their terrible loss. All he could think about was his own son, lying there helpless at the rehabilitation center. A few days later Irv telephoned him to thank him for his expression of condolence.

"Mr. Weber, this is Irv Davis. I just want to, uh, let you know that my wife, Faith, and I are very grateful for your sympathy note. We truly appreciate it. We know how much, uh, all that you're going through at this time, and we pray that Leo will soon be up and around after this long ordeal he's been suffering."

"Thanks Mr. Davis. Leo spoke very highly of Jonathan on so many occasions. They were such good friends. It's just terrible, and my heart goes out to you."

"I appreciate that, Mr. Weber. I know how much they enjoyed each other's company. I also want to let you know that I've sold the restaurant supply company. I just don't have the strength or the desire to keep it going. I always hoped that my ... uh, that Jonathan ..." There was a long pause. "Sorry. Well, anyway, we've put our house up for sale here in Allentown. We're moving to our home in Miami Beach to retire. I wanted to let you know, in case, uh, well, if Leo should ask about us in the future. We'd love to hear from Leo if, uh, when he recovers, and we hope he may be able to visit us sometime." He gave Mr.Weber his address and telephone number in Florida.

"I can surely understand what you're going through, and I hope that you and your wife will have a comfortable retirement down there, Mr. Davis. Maybe you can drop us a line every now and then, and stay in touch. I know that my son would like that."

"Yes. I certainly will do that. We will be praying for Leo and thinking about him. Good-bye, Mr. Weber."

Three weeks later, following a painful, grueling regimen of exercise that daily drained all of the energy out of him, Leo was transferred to a semi-private room. His remarkable recovery continued steadily over the next four months. He continued his physical therapy sessions four times each week at the Good Samaritan Rehab Center, and gradually progressed from the use of a wheelchair to a walker. Then, he could manage short walks along the corridor assisted by the therapists. Six weeks later, Leo was walking unassisted. Soon he was back home and walking around the neighborhood to visit his relatives and friends. Leo responded well to the exercises with the speech therapist. The doctor told Leo it appeared that he had suffered no permanent neurological damage. In the first week of February, Leo's father began taking him out driving to help him get reacquainted with the activity he enjoyed so much. A month later, Leo was able to drive his old Plymouth around the block by himself. One Saturday morning, Leo's father returned home from shopping.

"I have a surprise outside for you, son. I hope you like it."

Leo rushed to the front window. "Oh my *God*! I can't believe this," he shouted. A bright red *Mustang* was parked in front of the house. Memories of Matt flooded his consciousness as he gazed at the spotless red car.

"Son, are you okay? Is it a good choice? Do you *like* it?"

Not responding, Leo slumped into his favorite chair, his eyes still fixed on the miracle outside the window. "Dad, I, I just can't *believe* it. I mean, uh, where ... where did you *find* this car?"

"One of the guys at the shop saw it when it was brought in a few weeks ago. It had been on the lot at our other dealership in the west end of town. I think one of the college kids traded it in. It eventually wound up on our used car lot. Well, what do you think? Do you like it, son?"

"Dad it's nothing less than a miracle. I *love* it!"

"Great, let's take it out for a spin before lunch."

"I can't wait to sit inside that *Mustang*, dad!" His father had no idea what emotional turmoil had taken over Leo's mind. After more than two years he would be reunited in some way with Matt at last. Leo tried to imagine that, maybe, just maybe, it was indeed Matt's car. But he concluded that it had to be simply remarkable coincidence. In either case, he had established a new link to the person he loved so deeply. The feelings he experienced on that snowy January morning seemed to be radiating magically now from the red vehicle in front of his home.

"Okay! Here are the keys!"

Leo grabbed the keys and rushed out the front door, his heart was pounding.

Leo was already seated behind the steering wheel when his father opened the passenger-side door. Leo squeezed the wheel with all of his strength. *Matt, I wish to God you were here!* He didn't want his father to see the tears he had begun to shed.

"For Pete's sake, son! I had no idea you'd like this car so much. I'm, so glad I found it for you."

"Dad, you have no idea how much this means to me. Thank you so much!"

Leo started the engine, pumped the clutch and moved the transmission into Drive. In a moment they were speeding toward Washington Street.

"Take it easy, son. I know you're all worked up about this, but be careful. You haven't driven a car in such a long time."

Leo drove all the way up to Seventh St., turned left onto Tilghman, then left again back to his home. He parked the car and got out, looking it over.

"Dad, this is a'64 *Mustang 289*, eight-cylinder model. It's one from the original batch!"

"Yeah, that's right! How do you know so much about it?"

"Uh, a good friend of mine once had one like this," he said.

They went back into the house for lunch. That afternoon Leo could hardly wait until he was back in that *Mustang*. It was like returning to a previous life.

Afterwards, Leo was back behind the wheel again, having assured his father that he'd "be careful." He sat in the driver's seat for nearly five minutes, trying to imagine—hoping and praying—it was really Matt's car, that his hands were gripping the steering wheel that once had been in Matt's very hands, his back pressed against the very seat that so often cradled Matt's awesome torso. He started the car and headed directly for the Lehigh Restaurant Supply Company. He swerved the car off Linden St. toward the company, his mind flooded by the memories of the time he had walked up that street ten years ago to start his first job. He remembered the anxiety he had felt when reporting to work that first day. He smiled nostalgically as he guided his *Mustang* toward the red-brick building on the right side of the street. As Leo pulled up in the front of the supply company, he was jolted by the sight before him. The large windows of the office that had once imprisoned him revealed a completely empty room inside. The garage door to the warehouse was blocked by a barbwire fence. The "Lehigh Restaurant Supply Company" signs were gone. The building was vacant. Leo paused to catch his breath.

He panicked at the sudden realization that the place where he had spent so much of his young life had been shut down, and the people with whom he spent such a large part of his young life had totally vanished. He had been separated once again from those he loved so much. He drove back home agitated and deeply distressed. When he arrived home Leo's father was getting ready to go out to meet Ralph and some of his other friends for an early evening of bowling.

"Dad, you won't believe this. I just drove past the old restaurant supply company. It's, it's *closed*, dad! They are out of *business*! I just, just can't *believe* it!" Leo was losing control

"Son, I didn't want to tell you until I felt that you'd be stronger. Irv Davis called me when you were, um, when you were in the hospital. He and Faith decided to retire, and they moved to their place in Florida a couple of years ago, and—"

"You *knew*? But, dad, what about Jonathan? He *hates* Florida. Did he go with them.

"Well, uh, well, that's, uh, the other thing I need to tell you, son. See, uh ... Jonathan, well ... you know how sick he had been all those years. They finally discovered he had colon cancer and there wasn't much they could do at that point. Son, I'm really sorry, I wanted to tell you this at a better time, but, uh, you see, Jonathan, uh, he passed away nearly a year ago. I'm sorry, son. I *know* how much you liked him."

Leo couldn't control his anger. He sobbed loudly, covering his face with his hands as he rushed to his bedroom, collapsing face down on the bed. His father cancelled his bowling afternoon, fearing that Leo was experiencing a potentially dangerous relapse. Leo fell asleep on his bed, fully clothed, not waking until the next morning. He was mentally and physically drained when he awoke. He walked feebly downstairs to the kitchen, where his father was brewing a pot of coffee.

"G'morning, dad. Dad, I, um, look, I'm sorry I took off on you like that yesterday. I, when you told me about Jonathan, I just couldn't deal with it, especially right after seeing the old supply company had shut down. It was all just too much! I still can't *believ*e it, dad."

"You know, I'm really sorry I didn't tell you before, but I just couldn't find the right time to talk with you about it. I know what a shock it must be for you now, especially after all you've been through and I—"

"Dad, you don't *ever* have to apologize. I can hardly imagine all you've had to do over the past year while I was, uh, you know, when I was sick."

"Irv Davis gave me his telephone number and address a couple of months ago. He asked that you contact him when you recover. He thinks very highly of you, son."

"That's great, dad. I'll give him a call right after breakfast."

"How about a cup of coffee before you get ready for church?

"Dad, I won't be going to Mass today. It's just that, well, I'm not really up for it today. You know, we haven't talked about it yet, but what's happening with the, uh, seminary. I mean, I've been away for a full academic year and—"

"Yeah, that's another thing we haven't had time to talk about. I called the rectory and told Father Joe about your accident. He notified the seminary. After I sent them a copy of your diagnosis and prognosis, they agreed to authorize a leave of absence for you. So, all we need to do is contact them when you're ready, and they'll have a physician give you a full medical examination before you will be able to return."

"Well, let's hold off on that for a while until I get myself together—there's so much that's so vague and mysterious right now."

His previous year in the seminary—the summer delivery job—the old hotel—Culver Lake—Temple—Matt's red Porsche. Did he really see a Peter, Paul and Mary concert? Did Matt's father actually die? Was he with Matt at the funeral? Did Matt really buy the old hotel? Did any of it ever *happen?* Struggling to figure out what was real, and what he had only imagined, continued to confuse him.

There was no mystery about his religion, though. He had stopped going to Mass and other services. No more praying the rosary and meditating. Only the leather-bound *Saint Joseph's Missal* with its gold-leafed pages retained any vestige of his religious experience. The dried-out leaf he had taken from the seminary lawn on his first visit remained inside, enclosed in the plastic sleeve. The *Missal* itself had become a sacred object to him, a sacrament that nourished him, continuing to connect him somehow with his mother's love. He kept it locked in his desk drawer next to the pale-blue envelope containing the letter he received from "Matthew Stephenson" after they met that first summer. He removed these every day, holding them in his hands, solemnly kissing them in a quasi-religious gesture bonding him desperately to the love they represented.

"Whenever you're ready will be fine," his father said, dissolving Leo's reverie.

"Oh, uh, yeah, sure, of course, dad."

His father handed him the coffee mug. Leo sipped the dark, hot energy-awakening liquid. His mind was still wandering. The letter Matt had written in his desperate attempt to find him never had the remotest chance of reaching him. The restaurant supply company had already closed by then. The futile note probably lay on the dusty floor under the mail slot of the abandoned office. Yet somehow Matt had communicated the message to him, but … *how*? Was there ever really a letter?

"Are you all right, son?"

"Yes! Sure. I'm okay, dad. I'm just trying to make some sense out all that's been going on during the last year."

Leo ate a couple of buttered rolls his father had baked in the oven. Then he went back upstairs to shower and get dressed. He needed to sort things out. There were so many strange thoughts and mysterious conversations he remembered. But, were they real? They *couldn't* have been real. Had the images and sounds of the hospital and rehab center where he had been confined all those months conjured up those scenes in his imagination, Leo wondered as he showered. He needed to think more carefully about what had happened. Since regaining his consciousness, he thought about Matt Stephenson constantly. *What is Matt doing now? Does Matt still think of me the way I think of him? Will I ever see Matt again?*

Donna came home from church as Leo was going back downstairs.

"You look so pretty, honey. How was church today?"

"Oh, it was all right, but I missed walking down there with you. Everyone was asking about you, especially the nuns. I told them you're okay now; they said they were praying for you."

"That was nice."

His little sister was growing up. He marveled at the fact she was already twelve years old. Her bright-blue eyes continued to sparkle, thrilling Leo the way they always had. As challenging as her young life had been, she was growing up to be a confidant, charming young lady.

"Let's go to the movies this afternoon, Donna."

"Oh, okay. Can we go see *To Sir, with Love?*"

"Sure, hon."

Before leaving for the movies, Leo decided to call Irv Davis. He dialed the number. Leo barely recognized the weak, sad "Hello" that greeted him after what must have been seven or eight rings.

"Irv? Irv, hi! This is Leo Weber. I—"

"Oh my *God*, Leo! I can't believe it. How are you, my boy? I've been worried about you since that horrible thing happened to you last year. I think about you often. Faith and I have wondered how you were recovering. It's so good to hear your voice, Leo."

"Irv, look, I, my dad, uh, I just want to tell you how very, very sorry I am about Jonathan." He fought back tears as he continued. "He was so, my God, so young, Irv. I just feel terrible about it. How are you and Faith dealing with all this?"

"Well, it's not the same anymore, of course. It never will be again. I never thought I'd live to see my only son—He suffered so much with that damned cancer. He never had a chance, Leo, never had the opportunity to grow up and become the leader I know he could've been. It's just, ... I never stop thinking about him, Leo. He's—"

"Irv, I can't imagine the grief you must face every day without him. I'm awfully sorry about all of it, Irv."

"Ah, Leo, I remember how you and Jonathan used to kid around at the old company!—how you both loved listening to those Sinatra albums. Remember when Jonathan actually selected his fraternity based on hearing Sinatra's voice blaring from the window of one of the houses? God, how I miss—"

"Irv, those were wonderful times we had. I miss him—and I miss the old place, too."

"Leo, I just couldn't *do* it anymore. Without him, without a future ... there was no point in continuing. I got a terrific offer from our competitor over in Bethlehem. I took it—so here we are in Miami Beach."

"Well, Irv, I hope everything goes well for you and Faith down there. Maybe one day I'll have the opportunity to visit you."

"Oh, my boy, it would be great to see you again. Come down; stay with us for a while. We'd love it. Please take care of yourself, Leo. Listen to your doctors."

"Will do, Irv. Take care!"

After he and Donna returned from the movies, Leo sat reading the Sunday newspapers in his favorite chair. He was thinking about Irv, Jonathan, Culver Lake, Matt.

The next day, a chilly Monday morning—March 11, as he would later remember—after his dad had gone to work and Leo had returned from walking Donna to school, he lingered outside by his red *Mustang.* He stared restlessly at it, unable to enter the house.

"I can't wait any longer. I've just *got* to go there!" he said, loud enough to be surprised at seeing a passerby turn in his direction. "I've got to go back."

For some strange reason, since his accident, Leo discovered that he frequently talked aloud to himself—loud enough for others to hear that he really was awake and alive. He went inside, put on his pea jacket, then jotted a note to his father.

Dad, I'm going into town and then later I'll be going over to Tony's place to spend some time with him and try to catch up. Please don't hold dinner for me. See you later tonight. Love, Leo.

"That should cover me," he said.

But Leo had no intention of going to see Tony. He was being drawn back—once again—to that one magical place in his mind that was *always* real, that had never faded. He was going back to North Jersey—to Culver Lake. He had to see what was happening up there. He needed to be there *now*. He needed to be there *today*!

Leo stopped at the Atlantic gas station on Tilghman Street, filled the gas tank, then drove over to Sixth St. to the Seventh St. Pike, and, several minutes later, onto Route 22 East. He was tracking his old delivery route for the restaurant supply company. In about an hour he was speeding up Route 206 North—back to a past that now seemed a hundred years behind him. A thousand memories bombarded his mind as he passed by his former delivery stops. He slowed down as he approached the area where the Boy Scout camp was located, then stopped at the top of the steep hill that led to the entrance, looking down to ... *So that's where they said it all happened!* Leo had no recollection of the disastrous accident that had nearly taken his life. He shrugged it off. Culver Lake was only a few miles away.

As Leo turned off the road to the old hotel, chills ran through his whole body. His face flushed with anxiety; he felt light-headed; he was perspiring. The blustery wind that had been icy cold that morning had gotten more fierce. He drove his bright red car toward the driveway of the hotel. On his many trips there during the hot summer months, he had looked forward to seeing the lush green foliage of oak, beech, pine and sugar-maple trees swaying against a bright blue sky, surrounding the hotel and coloring the steep hills behind it. Today, however, he saw only thousands of stark black branches blowing menacingly in the cold air, cutting to pieces the dark gray clouds above. He looked straight ahead, then saw what turned out to be the façade of the building—entirely covered with scaffolding. Workers were replacing windows and installing a new roof in what appeared to be a total renovation of the old hotel. He drove his car toward the building to the swimming pool; a heavy black canvas now covered it completely. When he drove by the pool and approached the hotel, he was instantly disoriented by what he saw parked in front of the portico: a red Porsche *Targa.*

Impossible! Something had gone terribly wrong with him. He had made a drastic mistake coming back here. In his therapy sessions he had been warned about potential episodes of hallucinations and memory loss. He should've listened. Still, he knew he had seen that car before. "But it can't be!"

CHAPTER 14

Leo sat paralyzed in his red *Mustang*, mentally obliterated by the scene before him. He wasn't sure how long he had lingered there. A horn blowing behind him awakened him to the fact he was blocking the driveway. He drove his *Mustang* into the parking space next to the *Targa* and just sat there trying to catch his breath. It was the same kind of Porsche he imagined when he—

When he felt strong enough, he managed to get out of the car, then turned to look at the hotel entrance.

I can't go back home now. I have to go in there. I need to know what's happening.

Leo walked haltingly over to the steps leading to the enclosed porch. He turned the weather-worn, wooden door knob, pushed the door open, and stepped inside. Every kind of buzzing, scraping, hammering, sawing noise assaulted his senses. Leo cupped his ears as he looked around and carefully navigated his way through the construction site the lobby had become. Then he heard voices; someone was approaching the door from the adjacent room. Leo cautiously walked toward it as it swung open. Standing directly in front of him was Matthew Stephenson.

"Leo! Wha—? How did—?"

The person before him flickered, then faded away, leaving Leo in darkness. A minute later, Leo was coming to on the old dark-red leather sofa in the hotel manager's office, his head cradled in Matt's lap. Leo opened his eyes and looked up at him. Matt was crying, his tears dripping softly onto Leo's face, the cause of his eyes opening seconds before.

"Leo! Are you all *right*, man?"

Leo sat up with Matt's assistance. He saw that Matt was wearing a dark-blue crewneck, neatly fitted over the top of his light-blue, soft *Lee* denims. His tan *Dingo* cowboy boots made him look about two inches taller. Leo let his head fall back against the sofa. He gazed up at Matt, wondering, hoping, that what he was seeing before him *this* time was, in fact, real.

"Leo, is something wrong? You look confused. You're so thin and pale. Are you *okay*, man?"

"Matt, you, uh, you're not going to believe what I have to tell you. You're gonna think that I've lost my freakin' mind. I don't know what time it is now, but it's going to take me a long time to explain how I got here today, and all that's happened to me over the past year. I only hope you'll believe me—that you won't be turned off by what I have to tell you."

"Whoa, buddy! Before you begin, um, let's get out of this damned construction site. I'm living at my father's house now over at Swartswood Lake. I have a lot to tell you, too, man. Let's go over there to relax. I'll light a nice, cozy fire in the living room; we can have a bite to eat and drink—just like old times." He punctuated his offer with a loud laugh as he ran his hand through Leo's short-cropped hair.

"Still no Beatles haircut for you, huh, man?"

"Matt, I will follow you wherever you want me to go. I'll never lose you again, or I'll just die!"

Matt put his arm around Leo, gripping his left shoulder as they walked out the front door. They turned left toward the parking lot, where Leo had parked his red *Mustang*. Matt stopped abruptly.

"Oh, holy Jesus *Christ*! That cannot be your car, Leo. It just *can't* be!"

"That's *another* thing that I—"

"No! Uh-uh! I just can't fucking believe this, Leo. Why? Where in *hell* did you get this car?"

Matt eased Leo onto the bench in front of the lobby, then ran down the steps and over to the car. He opened the door, looked inside, removed the keys from the ignition and hurried to the back of the car, quickly opening the trunk. He looked inside.

"Christ, Leo! This isn't *possible*!"

"What *is* it Matt?" Leo yelled, rising from the bench.

"Leo, babe, this is *my* car!" Matt had lifted up the gray rug that covered the spare tire inside the trunk. "Here are the initials and date that I carved on the floor of the trunk the day that my, uh, my … father gave it to me! Leo, what's going on?"

"Matt, I, Matt, look, my father bought me this car after I finished rehab and got my driver's license back. As soon as I saw it, I couldn't believe it, and I—"

"Rehab?"

"Can we talk about this when we get to your dad's place, Matt? It's getting kind of cold out here." He was in fact shivering.

Matt looked over at Leo from the red *Mustang*, staring at him, wondering what was happening, trying to make some sense out of what he was witnessing. He closed the trunk gingerly, gazing at it for about a minute afterwards.

"Yeah, we can go to my dad's place. *Sure!* I'm sorry. You know where Swartswood Lake is, Leo?"

"Yes, of course. I've driven over there many times."

"Okay. Follow me there. Are you feeling well enough to drive? I can get one of the guys to drive your car over there if—"

"No, uh-uh! No, Matt. I'm fine now."

"All right, Leo. We'll drive down Route 521. The house is only ten minutes from here. Turn right off Route 521 at the west shore entrance. Just look for a big stone house with huge windows on the front. It's about halfway around the road to the lake on Pine Crest Path, on a steep hill on the right side of the road overlooking the lake—it's the only large house there."

Leo followed Matt down the driveway of the hotel, down Route 521 toward Swartswood Lake. Leo remembered the route very well. He first traveled to the lake with Rick, the foreman from the restaurant supply company, to visit a potential customer. He always enjoyed driving along the winding road; he loved the pristine beauty of the area. As he steered his *Mustang* along the familiar road, Leo noticed the huge stone building set back from the lake, and saw Matt entering the wide driveway. *My God, what an incredible home! I should've known!*

The huge door to the three-car garage opened at the command of Matt's remote, revealing the back of a bright-white *Rover P6 2200 TC* on the far right side. Matt directed Leo to park beside him in the garage. Once out of their cars, Leo walked toward Matt, who was reaching out to embrace the image he had been longing to rediscover for what seemed like an eternity.

"Let me warm you up, Leo. It's getting so goddamned cold out here; the wind is blowing off the lake. *Mmmmm!* God! I've missed you so much, man!"

What would Matt think when I tell him about all of the incredible things that have happened to me over the past year? Leo wondered as they embraced. *Will he accept me as he's always done before? Will he be frightened off when he hears about the traumatic experiences I've suffered since he last saw me?*

Matt was now easing him away. "Okay, let's get inside!"

The garage was connected to the main house by an enclosed breezeway leading up a flight of stairs to the laundry room and down a hallway to the kitchen. Matt unlocked the kitchen door; they stepped inside.

"Wow, Matt! This is a commercial kitchen like I've seen so many times in restaurants. Who does all the cooking around here?"

"Yeah, uh, my dad used to bring chefs in for his parties and special dinners. He planned the house to accommodate his lifestyle."

"Matt, I'm really sorry about your dad. I know he passed away, and—"

"*What?* Wait, Leo. How is that *possible?* We haven't spoken to each other in more than two years. You live in Allentown. You don't even know his name. How could you know that my father died?"

Leo placed his right arm around Matt's shoulders. They walked through the hallway to an extremely large living room, the ceiling soaring some twenty-five feet above the floor. Three huge picture windows framing the front of the house allowed one to enjoy a majestic view of the lake shimmering a short distance away. Opposite the front windows, a huge walk-in fireplace set into a massive fieldstone wall dominated the room. Two plush, matching royal-blue sofas flanked a six-foot-square glass coffee table in the center of the room. An ivory white shag carpet decorated the pristine oak floor. Matt crouched to light the logs in the fireplace with the kindling he had plucked from the basket nearby.

"So, how did you *know*, Leo? That's so far *out*, man!"

"When I returned to Culver Lake during that summer after the old hotel closed, I was in a severely agitated state of mind. I mean, the horrible twists of fate when we failed to communicate—and, uh, stupidity on my part—that it just seemed to have doomed us. I knew the hotel had been shut down, but I, you know, I, uh, just had to *go* there. It was like the only possible way I felt I could somehow be with you. You probably think I'm totally nuts."

"No! No, man! I dig it. I've felt like that myself—so desperately alone and separated."

"Yeah, right, that's how I felt. So, I just had to go back to the hotel and drive around that swimming pool, over to the storage room." He paused before continuing, just as Matt had successfully lit the logs and was turning toward Leo. "It seemed like the only way I could be with you. Can you understand that, Matt?"

"Sure, Leo. I get it."

"Well, it didn't help at *all*! In fact, I became physically ill. Then I drove out of there in a state of panic to finish my deliveries for the day at the Boy Scout camp."

"You know, we've been put through so much shit by the fates, man! There's no justice in this fucking world!"

"Yeah, and then I set myself up for the worst catastrophe of my life, Matt. I was probably still disoriented. When I was leaving the camp, they say I lost control of the truck—and was thrown into the woods—just before the truck crashed and burst into flames."

"*Truck* crash! Jesus, Leo, how the hell did—"

"I was probably so emotionally distraught I hadn't been concentrating. The doctors think I'm lucky to be alive. I know I am now, Matt, because I've found you again. They're not sure what exactly happened to me. You know, they just don't have any exact idea what happens to someone when they lose total consciousness. They told me they believe I was in a so-called "minimally conscious" state for almost ten months. I was admitted to the rehabilitation center, but they admit they really didn't—still don't—have a precise diagnosis. It seems that medical technology hasn't yet caught up fully with the mysterious workings of the human brain."

"Ten months, Leo! My God! You mean you were *unconscious* all that time? Then, how could you know that—"

"Well that's the strangest part about what I have to tell you, Matt. Look, I know you're going to freak out, but I can only tell you what I think was happening to me when I was in that suspended condition."

"Suspended? You mean you were really not aware of what was happening around you?"

"Well, sometimes it just seemed like there were white figures standing around me; I think I even heard music playing occasionally, but I just couldn't get it in any kind of focus. It was like something was at times in reach, but I just couldn't grab onto anything."

"Far out, Leo! Jesus Christ! You are the most amazing person I have ever met in my life, man!"

"Well, it gets even stranger, Matt. Now, just hold on. Please try to understand what I'm about to say."

Matt had joined Leo on the sofa, at once baffled and intrigued by what he was hearing.

"It seemed like I was with you during that time. It was like we were doing things together. I even imagined that you and I had gone to a Peter, Paul and Mary concert when we were attending Temple University together, and—"

"Now, wait a minute, man. Just hold on *right* there. Holy ... You're right! This is getting *way* too spooky. I actually *did* go to Temple last summer and, you're not going to believe this, I *did* go to a Peter, Paul and Mary concert—at the Academy of Music. Jesus Christ, Leo, what the *hell* is going on?"

"Matt, I don't *know*. I just, it was like, it seemed like I was *there*. I just can't explain it."

"Whew! I really need a drink now! Let me get some wine from the kitchen."

Leo trailed Matt into the kitchen, unable to let go of his thoughts.

"Matt, I don't want you to think that I'm nuts or something. It's just that, I had these feelings and thoughts for ... well, I don't know how long. One of the therapists told me that nobody really knows what a person is going through when they are in one of these "altered states of consciousness," as I remember them calling it. Nobody's done any major study about long-term conditions like the one I experienced."

Matt selected a bottle of St. Estephe from the wine cabinet, displaying it before Leo for his approval.

"Whaddaya think, buddy?"

"Where did you get—"

"Man, I bought two cases of these babies in Newton last fall to kind of stock up for the long, cold, lonely winter season. Every time I buy this wine, I think of your story about the Grand Knight of the Knights of Columbus at the Village Inn; it always brings a smile to my face. Then, I picture *your* smiling face telling me all about that evening."

They returned to the living room, sat on the sofa on the right-hand side of the fireplace and slipped off their shoes. They leaned against the huge arms of the sofa facing each other. Their feet were touching. They leaned forward; clinked the *Baccarat* crystal wine goblets together and kissed. The warmth from the blazing fireplace was filling the room.

"Leo, I don't want to interrupt, but now I gotta tell *you* something."

Leo looked at Matt nervously. Had all of what he just told him been too much? The shocked look on his face drew a fragment of laughter from Matt.

"No, no. Hold on, man. It's nothing that'll change anything, but it's something I have to tell you."

Leo was relieved; he took a sip of the rich Bordeaux, and settled back.

"Leo, remember that night when you were telling me about your mother? You told me how terribly broken you became when she passed away. You said the separation from her was so painful that you just had to find a way to communicate with her. Remember you told me how you used to talk to her almost every night before you went to sleep, or whenever you were alone in a quiet place? It was kind of like you were telling her what you were doing, how everything was going. You said it was, uh, a way for you to, uh, to keep her in your thoughts."

"Matt, I can't believe you remember that. It was more than two years ago!"

"Yeah, I know. But when we lost contact after that horrible series of foiled attempts, I thought I'd never see you again. I remembered what you said about your mom—how you continued to try to stay in touch with her after she was gone. So that is exactly what *I* did, Leo. Every night, lying in my bed in the dark before going to sleep, I thought of you. When I sent that letter to you at the restaurant supply company trying to reach you, I wrote each word directly to you. Each night I closed my eyes, concentrated deeply, and spoke to you, telling you what I had done that day or what I was thinking about. It was the only way that I could have you with me. And it *did* help me keep you close to me, at least in my thoughts."

Leo's eyes were filling up as Matt continued to speak.

"You know, now *you're* going to think *this* is weird, but when I took that course in parapsychology last year, they talked about ESP. I thought it was all a load of bullshit then, because it just seemed like so much Houdini and abracadabra, and all that extra-sensory crap. But now, I don't know what to think, man. Somehow, my thinking about you and talking to you on those lonely evenings before I went to sleep seems to have been transmitted to you somehow. I mean, I don't want to weird you out or anything, but doesn't it seem strange that you knew what I was doing, man? You knew that I had a red Porsche and that my father died—and, oh yeah, that Peter, Paul and Mary thing!—all of this while you were supposed to have been in some state of—what was it? *altered consciousness?*"

"It was more than that, Matt. Everything was so detailed. Like, your car; I could see that *Targa,* the color and all, and your dad's Law Office. I saw the two of us sitting in one of those offices talking to, uh, Mr. Preston; he was wearing a white suit and all! How could I have even known his name? Then, to hear the details of your father's will—"

"Well, the Preston name is no mystery, Leo. You probably saw it on the door of the law office. He was my dad's partner in the firm. The sign did list his name, but a white suit? Leo, Mr. Preston would never wear a white suit if he lived to be a hundred years old. He's what I call an 'old county conservative'—and sure dresses like one. And what's this about a will?"

Matt got up from the sofa. He kept speaking as he walked toward the kitchen.

"Look, Leo, it's getting toward dinner time. I have a couple of steaks in the fridge. How about I cook them up and make a nice healthy salad for us? Would that be okay?"

"It couldn't be better, Matt. While you're taking care of that, would you mind if I called my dad to tell him I won't be home tonight? I know that he's still worried about me. I don't want him to get upset or anything."

"Go right ahead. The phone's over there on the table next to the breakfront."

Leo was nervous as he dialed. Would his dad think it was it too soon for him to have ventured out the way he had?

"Hi, dad."

"For Pete's sake, son! Where have you— ... Are you okay?"

Leo told his father how he just wanted to get out for a change—how great it felt to be finally able to do something on his own after such a long time being dependent on everyone, "especially you, dad."

Leo could tell that his father was concerned. But as Leo spoke he sensed that his father seemed pleased that he was in such a happy frame of mind. His father agreed it would be better to stay over, rather than drive home at night.

"Just take it easy. Make sure you get a good night's sleep. You know your physical therapist recommended you go slow as you recover over the next six months or so."

"Right, dad. I, uh, I'll certainly do that. Say goodnight to Donna for me."

"Okay. Take it easy. See you tomorrow."

Leo hung up the phone. His dad had been so helpful to him since Leo regained consciousness and was going through physical therapy and regular neurological evaluations. He and his father had never been so close before in his life. Leo winced a bit, feeling some guilt about lying about being with Tony, but he would soon have to explain the entire story to his father, and just let things happen from there.

"How did it go, man?" Matt yelled from the kitchen.

"Okay. He's worried, I can tell, but he'll be all right." Leo could hear the pans rattling in the kitchen. He went in to help.

"I can make the salad, Matt."

"No, you, uh, well, okay. The fridge is all yours!"

Leo sliced a couple of tomatoes, a carrot and a red onion, mixed them with the fresh green Boston lettuce, and sprinkled it with red wine vinegar and olive oil.

The aroma of the broiling T-bone steaks topped with mushrooms—Leo's favorite—set his stomach growling.

"Ta da! Dinner is served, sir!" Matt plopped the huge steaks on Currier and Ives dinner plates, placing them on the kitchen table in front of Leo.

"Nice salad, too! Thanks! Bon appetite, Leo!"

"To us, Matt!"

They clinked their wine glasses again, looking at each other across the table.

"Leo, babe, can you believe it's been more than two years since we sat together like this?"

Leo was silent. Everything that had happened during their separation no longer had any meaning. They were back together.

After dinner they headed back to the sofa, the warm fireplace still aglow. Evening was settling over the glowing lake out front. They gazed out the window as the last traces of sunlight rapidly vanished from the sky.

"I can't tell you how many times I've sat here alone watching that miraculous scene, Leo. It's all so much more magnificent with you next to me."

"I wouldn't want to be anywhere else in this world."

"Say, uh, Leo, you mentioned my father's will before we sat down for dinner. What do you remember about it?"

"Well, it was kind of outlandish, Matt. I mean, Mr. Preston recited the details—I think it was some crazy figure like a million dollars, or something like that … "

"Christ, this is *too much*, man!"

"Sorry, Matt, I—"

"No, no, Leo. The value of my dad's estate was over two-and-a-half-million dollars, including his life insurance policy. I've also inherited this house, his new *Rover* and all kinds of stuff he collected. Mr. Preston will buy out the law firm, so I'll be receiving the proceeds from that as well. You have some incredible *goddamned amazing* mental power, buddy!"

"I just can't freakin' understand it!"

They sat sipping the deep red vintage.

"So, Matt. May I ask what you were doing over there at the old hotel today? I was so zonked out when I saw that Porsche, I kind of lost track of the whole scene. Then you appeared in that doorway—I was out of it."

"Hold on to that sofa, buddy! Listen, man, I bought the whole fucking *place* last month. When I found out I had so much money and all, the first thing I thought about was the old hotel. I've always loved that place, man. And, just the way you said you had to go up there when it was closed, that's exactly how I felt. It was the only link to you I still had—I wanted to keep it. So, I called Mr. Preston and the realtor over in Newton and just *bought* it! Old Mr. Freeling was damned happy I was getting the place, too. He knows how much I love it there and how well I had taken care of it for him. The place had been for sale for more than a year; it was killing him to see it going to hell."

"You mean you're going to run a hotel?"

"No, Leo. I mean, *we* are going to run a hotel, buddy!"

"Wha ... wai ... wait a second. How—"

"Leo, I want you to be my full partner in all of this. I have grand plans for that old hotel. I'm going to make it one of the most sought-after luxury resorts in the northeast. I've been researching the industry; I've learned a hell of a lot over the past few months. But none of this will happen without you. If you say 'no,' I'll just sell the place; we can go wherever the fuck you want to go. I just want us to be together."

"Matt, I, this is so ... it's such a lot to think about. I've always enjoyed the hospitality industry. You know, I worked in it for many years, even before I entered the seminary. It could be a fascinating career. I—"

"Those are beautiful words to hear from you, man. Look, it's getting late; we should get some sleep. Besides, I've wanted to be naked next to you since the moment I saw you in that doorway this afternoon."

Matt led Leo upstairs and around the landing overlooking the living room. They entered the master bedroom. Only a small street lamp could now be seen in the darkness outside the glass windows.

"The master bathroom's in here." Matt opened the door. "It's a double sink arrangement, Leo. So we can even be together when we're shaving." Matt laughed.

"What a beautiful home!"

"Leo, look, I want you to live here with me. I want to be with you from now on. You've been through such hell over the past couple of years. I know all of this is probably a lot for you to handle right now, but I hope you'll say 'yes'—that you'll be with me."

"All of what's happened—what you've been talking about—has me in a mental tailspin. You know, it all still seems so crazy right now, but how could I possibly say anything else but 'yes'? You know all we've been through, trying to find each other for so long—now, as strange as all of it's been, we're finally together. I need to—"

"And that's how we're going to stay."

They sat on the end of the bed, looking out at the nearly dark horizon. Leo talked about how he needed to convince his father he would be able to handle a hotel management position, knowing his dad would be quite concerned about his stamina. He told Matt that going to work for him would be the best possible therapy he could ever hope for.

"What? *Work* for ... No! Oh no, Leo! You don't *understand*. You won't be coming to work for me. I'm sorry—I wasn't clear. You'll be my full partner. I'll have Mr. Preston prepare all the necessary legal documents to put my plan in motion, and—"

"Wait, Matt. What do you mean?"

"Everything I own—everything we'll be creating together—all of it, will be held jointly. You and I will live and work, enjoying our lives together. You're the only person in the world I truly love; the only one who means *anything* to me."

They pulled back the blanket and crawled into bed next to each other—naked and aroused. Leo turned and straddled Matt's muscular thighs, guiding Matt's solid, pulsing erection inside him. Their lips met, their tongues glided together as they embraced. Matt groaned and pumped, releasing himself deep inside Leo. They rolled onto their sides, still locked in their sacred bond of love, savoring their ecstasy.

The next morning at breakfast they tried to comprehend all that had happened. They looked at each other and laughed about the strange day before, and the excitement of the unimaginable future that lay ahead.

Matt asked Leo to ride up to the hotel with him before going home so he could go over the plans he had developed for the renovations. They showered and dressed and dashed out to the garage. It was another cold March day. The early morning mist was rising from the icy lake outside. Matt drove along Route 521 toward Culver Lake.

"Say, Matt, I forgot to ask. Did you ever do any shows besides the one at the Night Owl?"

"Wha...What are you *talking* about, man?"

"You know that night when—"

"Wait, wait, is this one of those—"

"Matt, are you saying that when I saw you in that stunning white Nehru shirt—"

"Whoa! A Nehru? That sounds really cool! I think I might like one of—"

"So, when I thought I found you at last on the Temple campus; when I saw that sign advertising you performing the Beatles ... it was all—in my head?"

"Hey, man, don't worry about it. We're *here* now. Forget all that stuff."

"Matt, my head is as misty as that lake over there. One of these days I'm going to sort out all of this stuff—figure out what really happened, and what I was imagining. It's just so damned unbelievably strange to deal with all of this. You know, when I saw you in Philly you were wearing white. Irv Davis was wearing a white shirt with no tie. Mr. Preston was wearing a white suit and white shirt ... maybe I was seeing those white-clad figures in my hospital room. Maybe they were the nurses and doctors and—"

"Leo, babe, *listen* to me; you don't have to deal with *anything* right now except the ever-loving, living fact that I'm next to you—right *here*—that's as real as anything gets in this whole, fucked-up, crazy world. Nothing else matters, man."

Leo stopped talking.

They proceeded off Route 206, down the road into the driveway of the magical place that had changed their lives. Matt parked his *Targa* in front of the office.

"Whew! It's colder than a witch's tit up here today. I think we're going to get snow! Look, Leo, I don't want to keep you up here too long, but let me show you around the old place. Over there"— he gestured toward the pool area— "we're removing the old swimming pool so we can install a beautifully landscaped parking area with modern lighting. We're building a new Olympic-size pool behind the building. Let's take a look at it." They walked around the side of the building where Leo had gotten so ill. "It's going to be an enclosed pool with skylights that open up in the summer. So, we can have year-round swimming. Imagine it, Leo! People will be out here swimming while it's snowing overhead. Is that groovy, or what?"

"This all sounds fantastic. It's going to be an incredible place."

"But wait until you see what we're going to do inside," Matt continued. "The whole roof has been replaced; all of the window installations will be completed this week. The contractors will have the entire spring to complete the work on the interior space. When you come back up here I want to take you over to Lake Mohawk to meet our interior designer, Riley Warner. He's the best around—just don't tell *him* I said that. And wait 'til you see the multilevel home he built into a hillside over there." Matt fanned his arm over the spacious area in front of them. "This lobby is going to be gutted entirely. We're going to have a state-of-the-art reception area for guests. No standing in line for check-ins, you know? Small tables with swivel chairs will be provided for that. Our hosts and hostesses will make it a pleasure for guests to check into this place. The main dining room will be located beyond the lobby so its windows will face the pool area and the forest just beyond. It will be transformed into a nightclub in the evening. I'm working with an agency in New York to book a small band here for the entire summer; we'll present variety shows all year in there. There'll be a smaller restaurant at the pool, and one on the mezzanine for breakfast and lunch. The old recreation building has been transformed into a state-of-the-art conference center with all of the electronic connections for overhead projectors and stuff like that. It will seat up to five hundred people and be conveniently connected to the restaurant. Now, let's take a walk upstairs. Are you all right, man? Is this too much for you right now? You've been so damned quiet."

"No, No. Let's keep going. This is far out. I'm so proud of you—the way you've taken on this amazing project. You jumped all the way in!"

"You're the inspiration for all this, man. It would never happen if I hadn't met you here."

Matt led Leo upstairs.

"These rooms are all being reconfigured into suites. Each will have a sitting room and a personal bar. Steam baths will be included with the showers in every bathroom. We'll have a physical trainer on our staff, with a fully-equipped gym. We'll be reducing the number of rooms to about one hundred and fifty, but they will be the most luxurious suites in this part of the country."

"I can hardly wait to get back here."

"So don't wait at all. When do you think you can move up here, Leo?"

"I need to prepare my dad and sister for this, Matt. How about a week? I think that'll be enough time."

"Terrific!"

Matt drove Leo back to the house for a quick lunch.

"I can't tell you how much I look forward to creating this project with you by my side, man. It's going to be the thrill of my life! Oh, I have a big surprise for you. I've decided on the name for the place. Are you ready? *Green Rock Resort!* What do you think, Leo?"

"How, um, what gave you the idea?"

"Think back to that January evening we spent together in my apartment in Allentown. Remember, as soon as we got inside, I hustled my ass to the kitchen and popped open two bottles of *Rolling Rock*, man! Those bright green bottles! Our first passionate night together! I turned a million ideas around in my head, then, all of a sudden the green bottles, the *Rolling Rock*—it just hit me—*Green Rock Resort*!"

"I *love* it, Matt. It's perfect!"

"I knew you'd dig it, man!"

It was already after one o'clock, so Leo got up to leave. "I have a lot to think about on that long drive. I've got to ease my dad into this sudden change."

Matt threw his arms around Leo and kissed him. "It's going to be an awfully long week without you up here. I can't wait to see you again."

"Matt, after all this time—all that's happened to us—it's a whole new world for us now. In a million years I could never have dreamed all of this.""Please be careful driving back down there, Leo, and, whatever you do, please stay away from that *goddamned* Boy Scout camp!"

They laughed loudly, and kissed again. Leo headed out the door to his *Mustang,* Matt following him.

"I still can't believe you own that old baby. This is blowing my mind!"

"Every time I wrap my hands around that steering wheel it's like I'm holding on to you, Matt."

Leo got into the car and backed out onto West Shore Road, Matt, as so many times before, going through his usual antics of departure. Leo drove over to Route 521 on his way to the old familiar Route 206, heading south. He knew he had to reassure his father about his ability to take on the new job. Worst of all, he had to say good-bye to Donna. That would be the most difficult thing he could imagine.

After returning home around three-thirty, Leo began to prepare dinner. He was cooking chili, using his father's favorite recipe. When Donna got home from school, she saw Leo, ran into the kitchen.

"Leo, Leo, I missed you last night!"

"Missed you, honey. It's so good to be home. I'm going to surprise dad with his own chili recipe. I hope he'll like it."

"Dad'll be happy he won't have to cook tonight. I love chili, too, Leo!"

"I know, honey. How was school today?"

"They took us over to church to practice the hymns for Lent and Easter, so we didn't have to stay in school all day. That was fun!"

"Yeah, Donna, I remember those days when we had to go over to church to rehearse. It seems like yesterday, hon." Leo thought about the Lenten services he used to love so much—the sacred aura that had once enthralled him. Leo's father got home around five-thirty.

"Mmmm! It sure smells good in here!"

"Hope you like the chili, dad. I used your recipe."

"Thanks, son. How was your visit with Tony? Is he still living with that young girl?"

"Um. Well, uh, Tony split up with her. I guess we could all see it coming, you know. She's so very young for him. Anyway, I had a great time last night. I talked to one of the guys who used to work at an old hotel that was on my summer delivery route. He knows Tony from the restaurant supply company. Tony made a few deliveries up there occasionally on his old route."

"I'm glad you're able to make new friends. You've been through so much on your own. I think it helps for you to have some close buddies you can depend on."

"Yeah, and—" Leo stopped himself. He needed to talk with his dad about the new plans he was making, but he just couldn't do it yet. He had to explain it all carefully if he was going to gain his support.

When Donna and Leo entered the living room after finishing up in the kitchen, their dad was sitting in his recliner, watching *The Huntley-Brinkley Report*. Leo had been so burdened, thinking about how to approach his dad, that he had been silent throughout dinner.

"Dad, Donna, I've decided not to return to the seminary," Leo announced, interrupting the news show with his own breaking story.

His father turned down the volume on Chet and David.

"It's no longer the life I want to live," Leo continued. "I've thought about it so often over the past few months. It's just not for me anymore." He glanced at his father's face—no reaction. "I've received a job offer from Matt Stephenson. He's the fella I told you about last night. Anyway, he wants me to be the assistant manager at the hotel he is opening up in north Jersey. That's the place located near the Boy Scout camp where I, uh, where the accident happened. It would, uh, it … see, I would have to move up there in order to get that job. Dad, remember way back when I mentioned a few times about my interest in becoming an innkeeper before I went into the seminary? The foreman, Rick, at the restaurant supply company told me that he could place me in a management training program with the Holiday Inn chain that I could have started after graduation from high school. Well, I've always liked working around the hotel industry. I think this would be a great opportunity for me that I'd really enjoy. It's less than two hours away, so I wouldn't be very far from home. I could—"

"Leo, you're not going to move away again, are you?" Donna broke in. "I miss you so much when you're not home with us, Leo. Please don't go away again."

Leo held her hand. "I have to get a job and start a new career. Someday, when you grow up, you'll have to do the same thing. But I'll never be far away from you, honey. I'll only be a couple of hours from home. We'll be together often—I promise."

His father leaned forward in his recliner and turned toward Leo. "You know, I thought you were losing interest in the seminary when you stopped going to Mass in the morning—even on Sunday. And you haven't called Father Joe, nor spoken with Thomas and Patrick since you were discharged from the rehab hospital. So I'm not surprised about your decision. But do you think you're up to the strain of being an assistant manager of a hotel?" His father's voice grew more serious. "You know how much you've been through over the past few years and all. Is it going to be too much for you to handle? I mean, you've been going through your rehabilitation program now for nearly eight months. What about your need for continued observation and rehab?"

"Well, uh, thanks to you and the wonderful care I've received at the Good Samaritan, I'm feeling very well right now. I've been reading a lot about the type of issues my accident created; my physical ability seems to be getting stronger each day. Remember, I managed people in the past at the old, uh, restaurant supply company. I learned so much from Irv Davis there."

"Sure, sure. But you realize that when you're running a hotel, there are lots of demands on you for long hours each day. It can be very stressful. I'd hate to see you suffer any setbacks because of all of that." His dad was growing more concerned.

"Dad, you're right about the stress. It's not an easy job. I think, though, it's time for me to move ahead with my life—start a career. I've lost so much time being in the hospital. I just have to do something meaningful with someone, uh, with something that I can be part of and contribute to. Matt is aware of my circumstances and has assured me that I'll have a competent staff to assist me."

"That's good to know. He must be a real friend to offer you such an important job. When does he want you to begin?"

"Dad, the hotel is undergoing a complete renovation and expansion. They've nearly completed the exterior of the building and are about to begin the interior construction. Matt would like me to be there throughout the completion of the interior design to kind of learn about the place from the very beginning. So—"

"You mean, he wants you to start *right away?*"

"Yes! He'd like me to be there on site at the beginning of next week when he plans to meet with the interior designer and contractors."

"This is all so sudden, so fast, but, well, you're an adult; you've got to make this kind of decision. I'm, uh, I'm just hoping you don't jeopardize your health, or hurt yourself. If you think you can do the work, and I know you'd like that kind of thing, then it's your decision to make. If for some reason it doesn't work out, you can always come home. You *know* that."

"Dad, you've never, ever failed to be there for me. When I needed you most, you were always right there. I can't tell you how much your support means to me now—"

"So, where will you be living?"

Caught off guard by the question he had failed to anticipate, Leo stammered at first, then recovered: "Matt's father passed away last year, so he inherited this humongous house out on Swartswood Lake. He has a lot of room there, so he's invited me to share the place with him for now. Once the resort opens up, there'll be a manager's suite for my use."

"That sounds terrific! You sure have been lucky to find something that you like, and someone who's so generous and considerate. I gotta tell you, son, you always seem to bounce back from just about anything that happens to you. It's amazing to see. You sure deserve this after all you've been through over the past couple of years."

"With all that's happened, I know how lucky I've been."

Leo thought about his mother—all the times he had spoken to her, trying to stay close to her after she died—those lonely evenings when he asked for her help before going to sleep. *She has never left me. She's always been here with me, too.*

The physical therapist at the Good Samaritan referred him to a therapist at a clinic in Sussex County, New Jersey, where Leo could receive all the services he would require as he continued his recovery. By the following Monday, Leo had packed the few items he owned in his suitcase. A cardboard box contained his papers and files, a few books he had kept from his seminary days, and—most important of all—the *Saint Joseph's Missal*, and that blue envelope with Matt's letter. He had an early breakfast with his father. They talked briefly about the cold weather and their hopes for an early spring. Finally, it was time for his dad to leave for work. He got up from the table and shook Leo's hand.

"Well, good luck up there. Take care of yourself. Don't forget to stay in touch with the rehab clinic up there so they can keep an eye on things."

"Dad, I can't ever thank you enough for everything you've done for me. You've been there for me all my life. I've been so lucky to have you."

Leo's father grasped Leo's arm as they shook hands. "Take it easy, son. I know you'll do well. You always have."

When Donna woke up, Leo had already made her favorite breakfast—hot farina topped with butter and milk, and toast with raspberry jam. They chatted. Donna wanted to know how to get to Leo's new home. Leo talked about the long, wide highways and winding roads. He repeated how close he would be and how much he looked forward to her visiting him at his new home. "Just like you used to come to see me at that old seminary, but more often."

He kissed Donna before she left for school.

"Bye, Leo."

"Good-bye, Donna. I'll see you soon, hon."

At ten o'clock in the morning Leo called Matt.

"Are you ready for me up there?"

"Is everything okay with your dad and all? How did they take the news?"

"Terrific, Matt! We are good to go!"

Leo hadn't been so upbeat about his future since the day he left home for the seminary nearly six years before. His life was about to change dramatically—again. He picked up his suitcase and brought it downstairs, placing it next to the box containing his books and papers. Then he stopped before his mother's portrait on the living room wall. Closing his eyes, he whispered: "*God*, mom! I still miss you so much. I'll never forget you—all your love for me, all our good times together. Help me with this new life I'm about to begin. I only wish you could be here with me to experience all that will be happening."

He loaded the suitcase and box into his car, and drove away.

The drive to Swartswood Lake traced Leo's old delivery route. So many memories! He thought about his first ride up there with Rick—all the old tales. How helpful Irv had been through the years. How terribly his good friend's life had turned out. Irv would certainly be surprised when he learned about Leo's new career. As he drove up Route 206, he glanced periodically at his old delivery stops, smiling. When he passed the entrance to the summer Boy Scout camp, his mind was blank. How could he have forgotten what happened down there? They told him in therapy that sometimes the event that causes trauma is forgotten or blocked out by people who've gone through the kind of horror that had nearly taken Leo's life. How strange it all seemed—like a lifetime ago.

When he approached the driveway to Matt's home, Leo was flabbergasted by the sight of a huge banner—at least twelve feet long—draped across the garage, proclaiming in bright blue letters on a white background: *WELCOME HOME, LEO!*

Leo had barely opened the car door when Matt appeared next to him, holding two flutes of champagne, extending on to Leo.

"Cheers, Leo!"

"I love you, Matt!"

"And I love *you*, Leo!"

Matt had prepared a feast.

"Now, don't expect this kind of lunch *every* day, buddy. We've got a lot of work to do, you know."

As they worked their way through the consommé, salad Nicoise, petite filet mignon sandwiches, chocolate hazelnut tarts and coffee, the two new partners discussed the hectic schedule that lay before them.

Matt talked about their upcoming trip to Riley's place in Lake Mohawk. He had been working feverishly to complete his interior designs and furniture orders for the guest rooms, lobby, conference room and restaurants. Matt laughed when he told Leo how he had been cracking the whip over him for the past few weeks. He told Leo how important his input would be. Since Leo had gone into so many of the great hotels and resorts in New Jersey and Pennsylvania on his former job, he would be enormously helpful in the whole crazy process. He cautioned Leo that while Riley was a great designer, he tended to get a bit carried away with his creativity. Matt would need Leo's gentle touch and aesthetic sense to help rein in the flamboyant Riley.

"I'm looking forward to meeting him and seeing what he's been working on for us."

"Leo, you just said the word I've been waiting for desperately. For the first time while talking about this great project, you've said 'us.' I can't tell you how incredibly happy that makes me, man!"

First thing in the morning they drove across the county to Lake Mohawk. Riley's home was located near the top of a high hill overlooking the popular lake. Matt drove his Porsche into the driveway, blasting the horn as he approached the garage door. Leo was inspired by Matt's spirit and dynamism. He was energized by Matt. He needed to be by his side. The wide door opened. Standing in the middle of the garage, lighted by a bright fixture overhead, was Riley Warner. Riley was about twenty-seven years old. He was about six feet tall, with a muscular build. His long blonde hair touched the top of his shoulders and was cut in front so that it fell just above his eyebrows. His dark-brown eyes reflected the headlights of Matt's car. His form-fitting, forest-green T-shirt was tucked into a pair of the tightest white *Levis* imaginable. They touched the top of his Indian moccasins. Matt brought the car to a jolting halt about a foot in front of Riley, causing Leo to brace himself against the dashboard—as much in horror as in defense. Riley jumped back, throwing his hands up in mock surrender.

"Thanks for the eye-opener, Matt!" He turned to Leo. "You must be the famous St. Leo I've been hearing about *constantly* for the past couple of years. Welcome! I'm Riley Warner."

"Hi, Riley!" Leo shook his hand. Riley grabbed Leo's arm playfully. "It's a real pleasure to meet *you*. Riley. It's great to be able to put a face on you at last. Matt's been raving about your talent and skill."

"Hold on a second, Leo!" Matt said. "Don't go on too much about that talent stuff. His fees are already higher than anyone else around here."

"Come on in guys. I have a pitcher of Bloody Marys waiting for us inside."

They entered the house from the garage through a narrow hallway that led to the kitchen. It was located on the top floor of a four-story house built into the side of the hill.

"This is a beautiful home, Riley."

"Thanks, Leo. I designed it a few years ago when I found this great parcel of land. I love it up here any time of the year. It's just so gorgeous!"

"And this guy has the wildest parties you've ever seen," Matt joked. "Wait 'til you meet all his New York buddies, Leo! Far out! You're gonna totally freak out!"

Riley led them down the hall into an office, where a dozen white-leather swivel chairs surrounded a six-foot-square glass conference table in the center of the room. A mammoth, white Scandinavian-style chandelier cast a bright light over the table. A ten-foot-square window looked out over the lake, the view encompassing the entire valley below.

"Please have a seat, guys, while I get the drawings."

Matt and Leo sipped the Bloody Marys as Riley began laying out the sketches and plans.

"Guys, I've chosen hunter green for the theme color that will run through the entire resort. Matt, when you told me that the name of the place will be Green Rock Resort, it just seemed like a natural. Combined with the oak wood that we've selected for much of the interior, the hunter green will convey a warm but very rich feeling to the guests. And the—"

"Hold on a minute, buddy. Leo, what's your impression of the color scheme? Do you like it?"

"Matt, I think this green color is ideal. It will bring the splendid tree canopy that surrounds the building right into the rooms. In the winter, it'll brighten up the place. I think it sounds great!"

"You've found one hell of a smart guy here, Matt. Such great *taste*!"

"Okay! All right! What about the restaurant?"

"This will quickly become known as one of the most beautiful restaurants and night clubs in New Jersey. No—in the entire Northeastern United States! Believe me, Matt. I've created an ambience here that will have your guests feeling like they're dining in a tropical forest. I want to bring in two dozen large palm trees to line the restaurant; maybe along three rows across the dining room floor, and—"

"Whoa, man. Now, how's *that* gonna work?" Matt took another gulp of his Bloody Mary. "I mean, uh, palm trees need lots of light and—"

"Hey, buddy. Remember the *skylights*? We are installing those huge skylights over the restaurant. Think of it. People will be dining under a glass rooftop where they can watch the snow melting during the winter while they dine cozily among dozens of large palm trees. This will really space them out, man!"

"Incredible!" Leo muttered. "This is spectacular, Riley!"

"Okay. So, let's get this goddamned thing started, guys! Time's running out!"

"Wait, wait," Matt said. "We still have the cocktail lounge left to finish. It has that beautiful white marble floor and—"

"Matt," Leo interjected, somewhat timidly, "how about calling it 'The Marble Bar'? My mother and I used to go to a great place over in Pennsylvania that has a marble floor very similar to the one in the old hotel. They furnished the lounge with mahogany fixtures, you know, the bar, tables, booths and all. Then they hung brass chandeliers over the tables and a couple over the bar. It's been the most popular spot in town for decades."

"Leo, I like the contrast it would bring to the place. It would be a kind of gentlemen's lounge with a decidedly masculine ambience." Riley was looking directly at Leo, and gave him an enthusiastic wink. Leo blushed at the sudden attention.

"Leo, you shall have your Marble Bar!" Matt proclaimed.

They laughed as they finished their drinks.

"Let's all get together first thing tomorrow morning at the hotel and get the ball rolling on this right away," Matt said, getting up from his chair. "Leo, babe, I'm so glad you're here. You've already helped us more than you can imagine. Let's get going, man. We have a hell of a lot of work to do. Riley, we are all set. Just order everything and we'll go over the whole thing again, in the morning."

"See you guys tomorrow." Riley winked at Leo. "So great to meet you at last, Leo!"

"Oh, uh, yeah, same here, Riley. It's a real pleasure." Leo could not help staring at his gorgeous new friend.

Matt and Leo jumped into the car. Matt honked the horn as he patched out of the driveway.

"Leo, I thought we'd get a bite to eat for lunch over in Newton. I've made an appointment with Mr. Preston this afternoon, at three o'clock, to go over the final documents and execute them."

"You are *amazing*, Matt. You never stop!"

Matt laughed as he sped back across the county to Newton. Mr. Preston was prepared for the meeting when they arrived in his office after lunch.

"Gentlemen! Please have a seat in the conference room. I'll have the documents brought in immediately."

"Thanks for all your work on this Mr. Preston. I appreciate the quick turnaround."

Mr. Preston's assistant lined the table with numerous documents and papers. The notary public stood by.

"You realize, Matt, that after these documents are filed, Mr. Weber will be joint owner of all your assets?"

"Yes. That's exactly the way I want this all to happen." He nodded at Leo. Leo returned the gesture.

"Fine. These are all the papers we're going to need to finalize the arrangement. I'll explain each one and ask you both to sign each document where indicated." Mr. Preston was now working in full gear.

Within forty-five minutes, all of the required forms and statements had been signed, executed and notarized.

The attorney wished both of them every success with their new venture. He told them he understood they were really doing quite a job up there at Mr. Freeling's old hotel. A lot of his clients had already been talking about it—the whole county was buzzing about all the work that's being done up at the old hotel.

"It's great to see that place coming back to life."

"Thanks, Mr. Preston. I truly appreciate your kind wishes. We look forward to having you join us for our grand opening celebration this summer."

"It will be a splendid thing to see. Thank you, Matt."

"Thanks again." Matt shook Mr. Preston's hand. Leo followed.

Leo glanced at the Notary Public assistant as he passed by her desk. He suddenly realized she was the young receptionist he had met on that miserable afternoon nearly two years before when he was frantically searching for Matt. *I wonder if she recognizes me? What an amazing turn of events!*

When they got back home, Leo was exhausted. The meeting with the incredibly handsome and talented Riley; going over all the details for the interior design of the hotel; then having lunch in town followed by the long conference and document-signing at the attorney's office—he was mentally and physically drained of energy.

"Leo, babe. You look like you're ready to pass out. Are you all right, man?"

"Yeah! I'm okay, Matt. It's just ... I've been thinking, it's been such an unbelievable day. I mean, so much has happened today. It's unreal. My head is spinning."

"Well, you rest up, man. We've got a big week ahead of us. Riley will have most of the materials delivered to the hotel in a couple of weeks. I'm not sure when those fucking palm trees will be arriving, but we're hoping to have the entire place up and running by the Fourth of July—and we'll open it up with a bang! So we have three full months to finish it all. I absolutely love your idea about the Marble Bar, man."

Matt left the living room. Leo could hear a cork pop in the kitchen. He just threw his head back and smiled. Matt returned with two sparking glasses of champagne.

"To us, Leo!"

"To us, Matt!"

They sat close together on the sofa, gazing at the icy blue lake outside. Leo's new life had begun.

"Tomorrow I want to begin interviewing chefs for our restaurant. Do you have any ideas for a name, Leo?"

"How about 'The Palm Court'?"

"I love it! I'm trying to get the chef from the yacht club up here to come over to our place. He has great experience. I understand he used to work at the Waldorf-Astoria in New York, you know. So, he'd be terrific for us."

"You know, Matt, I believe I know him. That club was one of my stops when I worked for the restaurant supply company." Leo's face turned grim and he paused.

"What's wrong, man?"

"Well, I just got so many memories sticking in my mind about that old place where I used to work. Irv was so kind to me. His son died at such an early age. I just feel so sad for all of them." Leo seemed distant for a few seconds, then he continued. "Anyway, Rudy was a well-respected chef down there. Everyone used to rave about his talent. And, you know what? He used to give me free gourmet burgers for lunch when I stopped there. He always said he felt sorry for me because I was so skinny."

"You *see*, Leo! Your experience in this field is already paying off for us. Man, I just *knew* you would be a great fit!"

"Matt, he's going to be pretty damned surprised to see me in the office. I'm probably just as skinny as I was then. Maybe he'll feel sorry for us and take a lower salary."

"Leo, he's a chef—you know *that* will never happen."

They laughed. Matt got up, pulling Leo with him. They embraced and kissed. "Hey, let's go over to Verona Farms for dinner, babe. I just feel like celebrating tonight," Matt said as soon as their lips parted.

During the next few weeks they interviewed scores of prospective employees for all facets of the resort's activities. It was grueling, boring work, but they had been fortunate to receive hundreds of applications, many with excellent experience. Spring weather arrived early, enabling the contractors to begin installing the pool. Riley was making daily trips to the hotel to supervise the installation of the materials and furniture that he had ordered. The parking lot had been completed. The lush landscaping and modern lighting were installed. By the second week in June the old hotel at Culver Lake had been miraculously transformed into the Green Rock Resort. Matt and Leo were busy overseeing and reviewing the invitations and responses for the grand opening to be held on July 3—"With fireworks and all." Matt insisted.

"Leo, Mr. Preston gave me the name of a terrific press agent. He'll be reaching out as far as New York City to bring the press here for our opening. This is our time, man!"

His diligent work with the physical therapist at the Sussex County office had gone very well for Leo. He had gained about five pounds, most of it muscle. He felt fully capable of working the long days necessary to get the resort ready for the opening. He rarely thought of the lost time in that other state of mind that claimed such a crucial part of his life.

"You're not going to believe this, man. The bishop has responded to our invitation for the grand opening. He's coming, Leo! He's going to give the invocation at dinner. Can you believe it?"

"Matt, that should be exciting. Maybe we can get him to bless the pool." Leo laughed.

"Leo, have you no *respect?*"

"Just kidding, Matt."

They laughed, realizing that it was all about to happen. After all the planning and hard work, Matt's dream was about to come true and Leo would be right there next to him, making his joy complete.

The guest list had ballooned to more than two hundred friends, dignitaries and prospective clients. Most of them indicated they would be attending the opening night gala. Matt and Leo completed their final review of the staff and facilities. The Palm Court restaurant was stunning. Palm trees added an exotic touch to the candle-lit dining room, and the crisp, white table linen under brass candelabra looked elegant. The kitchen bustled as cooks were scrambling under the rapid-fire orders of Chef Rudy. The white marble floor of the lounge, more glossy than it had ever been, was reflecting the light of the crystal chandeliers above. Tables replete with hors d'oeuvres were positioned at each corner, and bartenders stood by on both sides of the Olympic-size pool ready to serve any kind of beverage the guests might request. The local fire department was standing by, behind the lodge, for the surprise pyrotechnics that were certain to stun the unsuspecting guests. Leo made sure that dinners were provided for the firemen before they took up their positions.

"Leo, did you know that Mr. Preston belongs to the Knights of Columbus? He's arranged for the Grand Knight to be here. I thought you would enjoy meeting him, since you are used to such elite company at dinner."

"If he is anything like the one that I met, I'm sure it'll be a fun evening for everyone."

As they stood in the center of the restaurant, they saw Riley Warner walking briskly toward them, his arms raised high in the air.

"*Okay*, guys! All *right*! How about those *goddamned* palm trees? Was I right? Are they far *out*, or what?"

"I gotta hand it to you, man, you always seem to come up with the touch that just takes everything one step beyond." Matt reached out to hug him.

"Whoa, wait a second! Don't wrinkle my tux, man."

"Sorry, I wasn't thinking!" Matt laughed.

"Riley, congratulations on this outstanding design! You're really going to put us on the map with all this," Leo said. Riley had gotten a new hairstyle for the event. His long blonde hair was trimmed and combed back. "Groovy new haircut, Riley. It looks great."

"I'll be on the prowl tonight, buddy. There'll be a lot of potential clients here, so I've got to look my personal and professional best."

"Well, it looks like you've caught someone's eye already, man!" Matt joked as Leo blushed.

"C'mon, Matt. I mean Riley looks so *terrific*."

"Just kidding, buddy, but you'd better keep your hands off him!"

They were laughing heartily when Riley spotted his first potential client and dashed off.

"Leo, let's go upstairs and get dressed up. Now we've got to compete with that Steve McQueen over there." He grabbed Leo around his waist as they rushed up the main stairway to the manager's suite.

Valets were busily parking cars for the arriving guests. The modern lighting with its brown metal standards and square floodlights handsomely highlighted the pine trees and juniper shrubs that lined the newly landscaped parking lot; the buzz in the crowd as the guests emerged from their cars was growing louder by the minute.

"Listen to that down there," Leo almost shouted. "This place is driving them nuts already!"

"Wait until they get inside, man. It'll blow their minds!"

Reporters were checking in at the press table set up in the lobby and were receiving their identification badges. Working with their publicist, Leo had arranged for every newspaper in the state to receive invitations. Media in New York City and in nearby Pennsylvania communities had also been invited. Matt and Leo appeared at the hotel entrance just before the dignitaries began arriving. The state senator and assemblyman, representatives from the governor's office of economic development, all the county freeholders and mayors were escorted by models clad in low-cut evening gowns, from the valet parking area into the resort. Riley had hired them through a New York agency. The bishop's arrival created a stir in the crowd. He was dressed in a black suit with a white Roman collar. His black starched shirt highlighted the gold cross that was suspended from a thin woven chain around his neck. Matt motioned toward the cleric.

"There he is Leo, standing next to the knight. How far out can this be?"

"Matt, we've done it. I've been walking around to get a sense of their impressions down there—this crowd is spaced out about the place."

"Yeah, and wait 'til they get a load of Riley's fuckin' Palm trees."

Guests were escorted through the lobby to the pool area, where bartenders wearing tuxedos were pouring drinks, as waitresses in two-piece, emerald green bikinis were serving a variety of delicacies to the dazzled crowd. At seven-thirty in the evening, a bugle call emulating the start of the Kentucky Derby summoned the guests to the dining room for the beginning of the program. To maximize the impact of the news coverage, Leo had arranged for the media personnel to be seated at tables that had been designated for government officials and potential business clients.

Fifteen minutes later, Matt rose from his seat to address the crowd.

"Good evening, friends. I'm Matt Stephenson. Together with my partner, Leo Weber, I want to welcome you to our fabulous Green Rock Resort. A special welcome to our state senator and assemblyman and to the representatives from the governor's office of economic development, to our county freeholders, mayors, to His Excellency, and to all of our good friends and associates. Tonight you have been invited here to celebrate the rebirth of one of New Jersey's grandest old hotels." Enthusiastic applause interrupted him. "It was my great fortune to have worked here in the past for Mr. Joshua Freeling." The applause intensified. "I'm happy to tell you that Mr. Freeling is with us tonight." Matt pointed to the table where Mr. Freeling was seated in a wheelchair, next to Leo. A standing ovation ensued for the popular old innkeeper, who was continuing his slow recovery from a stroke two years earlier. "Ladies and gentlemen, Mr. Freeling is one of the most generous and dedicated persons I've ever met; it is my honor to be rededicating this wonderful venue that he himself had first revived more than two decades ago." Another burst of applause followed. "And now, my friends," Matt continued, "I want to introduce to you the General Manager of Green Rock Resort, my partner, Leo Weber. Please stand up, Leo." The crowd applauded vigorously, some hooting their approval. Leo had met many if not most of them by telephone or written correspondence over the previous few months during his supervision of the invitation process.

"Folks, without Leo Weber, I can tell you truthfully that the rebirth of this great resort could *never* have occurred. Thank you, Leo, for your inspiration and hard work to help make all of this possible." The crowd rose and rewarded Matt and Leo with a full minute of appreciative applause, during which chills ran through Leo's entire body. Matt insisted that Leo join him at the podium. They thrust their fists high in the air like two boxing champs, then pointed to Mr. Freeling for a round of similar recognition. He was in tears. The crowd roared. When calm returned to the Palm Court, Matt handed Leo the microphone.

"Good evening, everybody, and welcome. It is my distinct honor to introduce to you His Excellency, John Brensinger, Bishop of the Paterson Catholic Diocese, who will deliver the invocation."

The crowd rose.

"Almighty God," the bishop began, … "

I'm a former seminarian with no religious beliefs, Leo found himself thinking, as the bishop's tone and gaze rose heavenward in tandem *and here I've just introduced a bishop who's praying for the success of our new resort.*

A chamber music group from New York City provided elegant background music for the dinner guests. Chef Rudy had created a menu that included Caesar Salad, colossal shrimp cocktail, Steak Diane, hearts of palm, and Potatoes Anna. A Viennese table of assorted pastries served with sparkling champagne topped off the magnificent dinner. Before it ended, Matt held his glass high in the air and toasted. "To the chef!" A loud, cheering response greeted him.

"Ladies and gentleman, on this evening before the Fourth of July, please stand and join me in celebrating our freedom," Matt requested.

The crowd rose as the orchestra began playing the national anthem. As the final notes ended, the first thunderous explosion of fireworks startled the unsuspecting crowd. Then, bursts of rockets and waves of sparkling colors shimmered over the guests through the skylights as they gasped, partially in relief, partially in excitement at the spectacle playing out above their heads. The pyrotechnics lasted nearly fifteen minutes, the finishing thrill to a festive evening.

At the conclusion, Matt bid the guests farewell.

"Thank you all for coming here tonight to celebrate the grand opening of Green Rock Resort," Matt shouted. "As you depart tonight, each of you will receive a memento of this great occasion, along with brochures describing the world class service that we are offering here." Matt and Leo had ordered pewter medallions, three inches in diameter, engraved with an image of the Green Rock Resort for the guests. Each memento was neatly arranged in a hunter green, felt-covered box. "Please come back soon and bring your friends."

A last rally of applause brought the magnificent event to a close. Matt and Leo mingled with the crowd, thanking them for attending, welcoming them to return. Leo chatted with the bishop, telling him about his admiration for Pope John. Matt reminisced about his father with the senator. Matt and Leo posed for photographs in the Palm Court restaurant.

It was well past midnight when the last of the guests had departed. Matt and Leo were standing on the veranda overlooking the empty parking lot. Leo pointed to where the old swimming pool had been located.

"That's where we first met."

Matt turned to Leo. They embraced. It had been a long, improbably turbulent journey. Doubts, failed communications, a tragic accident—all had separated them. They were together now at last.

CHAPTER 15

On Monday evening, following the grand opening of Green Rock Resort, Matt and Leo hosted a small private party to celebrate the success of the spectacular event, and to thank those who had made it all happen. Chef Rudy, Riley Warner, Attorney Howard Preston and his wife, Marie; and Joshua Freeling and his wife, Lisa, joined Matt and Leo at the popular Verona Farms Restaurant. The festive dinner included Clams Casino, Chateaubriand, St. Estephe, chocolate soufflé and Dom Perignon. Leo sat directly across the table from Riley, who captivated the group—especially Leo—with his animated conversation about his work on the design of the resort.

One week later, Riley disappeared. Matt and Leo learned from Mr. Preston that Riley had put his home up for sale and left the area without leaving any forwarding address or any other information. Neither Matt nor Leo had any inkling of any plans he may have had. There was no explanation for his mysterious disappearance. Matt and Leo were stunned. Matt had known Riley most of his life. They had grown up together, were classmates in high school, and played on the baseball team.

"Leo, this is the strangest goddamned thing I've ever seen. I just can't figure it out. I know Riley uses a couple of drugs—he calls 'creativity-enhancement vitamins', but I'm not sure what the hell they are, man."

"Matt, he was so much fun at the party last week; it just seems crazy that he'd take leave with no notice."

"I just hope he's all right. I worry about that guy! But I know Riley. When he's ready to talk about it, I'm sure we'll be the first to hear from him."

The response from the public over the next few weeks astounded Matt and Leo. Reservations from corporate groups began pouring in from all over New Jersey, New York and Pennsylvania. The *Times* food critic raved about Chef Rudy's splendid dinner. The *Press* and *Ledger* wrote enthusiastically about the magnificent renaissance of the fabled old hotel. Green Rock Resort had booked all of its 150 rooms for the entire summer and for the week after Labor Day. Organizations and businesses had already begun scheduling conferences for the fall. Matt and Leo were working long days to keep up with the avalanche of reservations, transportation, conference schedules and other details over the next three weeks.

July was nearly over. As they were sitting in the kitchen of the Palm Court restaurant, having a quick lunch on one of their hectic days, Matt was looking at Leo closely. He thought that Leo appeared tired; he had lost more than a little weight since the opening of the resort.

"How are you feeling, Leo? We've been so busy this month that I forgot to ask how those therapy sessions going, man? Have you been able to keep your scheduled appointments with all this activity going on?"

"Matt, I feel very strong right now. In fact, I haven't felt so energetic since I was a student in the seminary Anyway, I, uh, I have something I need to talk with you about."

"Whoa, that sounds kind of suspicious, man!" Matt stared at Leo nervously.

"No, c'mon. Listen, my birthday is July 31. I've always celebrated it at home—with my family, a birthday cake and all. I was wondering, I mean, I, uh, I would love to take you home with me for the day so you can meet my family. I've told them so much about you, and I think it would be great for all of you to meet at last."

"You gotta be kidding me, Leo. My birthday is July 29. I can't believe it. We're practically twins, man. Well, sure, *hell* yeah, I'd love to meet them at last."

"It's just about an hour and a half from here. The 31st is on a Monday. We could go down there for the day and get back that same night."

"Wait, Leo. I got a better idea. We can cruise down there the night before and stay at the Holiday Inn. It's just a few minutes from the Village Inn. You remember we talked about going over there some time for dinner about, oh, I don't know, maybe about a *century* ago."

"Yeah, Matt. You bet, I remember. I know the place well. It's the largest Holiday Inn in Pennsylvania. I think it has more than three hundred rooms, and an Olympic-size swimming pool. I know the owner's son. I used to make occasional deliveries to the place for the restaurant supply company."

"Far out, man! You devil! You're just full of surprises! We can have dinner at the Village Inn on Sunday night. It's just down the road, and then we can visit your folks on Monday and celebrate again before we get back here to the old grindstone."

"Matt, are you sure it will be all right for us to be away right now?"

"Leo, it will be our first birthday celebration together. It'll be the beginning of the week, when things are a bit slower, so there'll be no problem. Lillian has a great handle on the place already. Let's do it, man!"

"Matt, you've been so generous to me since I got here. I just don't know how I can return your generosity and all."

"Oh, uh, I'll think of something, buddy."

"Hi, dad."

"Hello there. How are things going up there?"

"Dad, we had a fantastic response to our grand opening. We're flooded with reservations for the summer and fall months already. Dad, I was thinking about my upcoming birthday, and I'd like to celebrate it at home like I've always done. I've told Matt Stephenson a lot about you and Donna and Ellen, and I invited him to join us. He said he'd love to meet all of you and help celebrate my birthday. Oddly enough, his birthday is July 29."

"Sure! That's fine. The more, the merrier."

"Great, dad! We should be there around three o'clock on Monday afternoon. We'll be heading back to Sussex County right after dinner."

"Oh, uh, what would you like me to cook for your birthday?"

"How about a nice meatloaf?"

"Okay. I'll, uh, wait. No! Look, son, you've been working very hard up there for the past few months, and your boss has been so generous. It's been a pleasant summer around here, and I'll be on vacation next week. We could have a late afternoon cook-out. I could throw some of your favorite T-Bone steaks on the grill. A salad with parmesan dressing, your favorite, and a baked potato should do it. Then the birthday cake! That way you could get an early start back to Sussex County. Whaddaya think?"

"Dad, that would be terrific!"

"Great! That's what we'll do!"

Matt insisted on driving his Porsche to Allentown.

Wait 'til dad sees this car pull up to the house, Leo thought, *He's not gonna believe it.*

They checked into the Holiday Inn in mid-afternoon. After they freshened up and dressed for dinner, they had cocktails at the bar located off the lobby.

"Well, it's not the Green Rock Resort, buddy," Matt was standing up against the worn cushioned bar surveying the layout of the lounge, "but I guess it'll have to do."

"There's nothing anywhere in the world like Green Rock Resort, Matt, and there never will be!"

They finished their gin and tonics and drove over to the Village Inn. When Matt and Leo entered the old restaurant, Leo was transported back to that magical night six years before, when the Grand Knight of the Knights of Columbus had treated him and Thomas and Patrick to that marvelous evening. Leo stared at the beautiful dining room with its handsome dark-green linen table cloths, white napkins and glowing candles housed in sparkling glass chimneys on the tables. It hadn't changed in any way since the last time he had been there. He was day-dreaming now about a different time, a totally different feeling—about a night in 1961, when he had been so eager to begin his studies for the priesthood.

How incredibly odd it is to return to a place that holds so many memories. It's like a time warp where the past and present strangely coexist—each permanently changed by its exposure to the other. It would be impossible to think about that magical evening back then, ever again, without the image of Matt's smiling face tonight. Who was it that once warned that we should never try to relive the past, because the flames will have become ashes? That's not always true. The flames are burning more brightly now because they're rekindled by Matt's presence.

Matt studied his face as Leo looked around the restaurant, still dazed somewhat by the past events seeping into his memory.

"So, where are you drifting off to this time, buddy?" Leo heard him say.

"Oh, uh, sorry, Matt. I was just thinking about that evening with the Grand Knight."

"Leo, I'll never forget that fantastic story. I've told that tale about you and the Grand Knight to so many people. They all get a hell of a kick out of it."

A hostess in a turquoise dress greeted them at the desk.

"Good evening, gentlemen. Do you have a—"

"Stephenson," Matt announced.

"Certainly, sir. Right this way, please."

They were soon seated in a booth surrounded by knotty pine wood, along the far wall of the room. They could see the entire main dining room stretched out more than a hundred and fifty feet before them, all the action in the busy restaurant in full view.

"This is really groovy, Leo. I'm so glad we came here tonight. We finally did it!"

"Matt, yeah, I can hardly believe it. This is like time travel!"

"Gentlemen," a friendly waitress said. "How are you tonight?"

"Much better since we got *here*, m'am," Matt replied. "And we'll be much, much better as soon as you bring us a bottle of St. Estephe.

"Right away, sir. Here are your menus, gentlemen."

Leo could see she was smitten by Matt's provocative style.

"Matt, it's like you've rewritten the scene for this place, turning it into a Broadway production. You're so beautiful! I'm so damned lucky to be here with you."

"Hey, I'm the lucky one. You have deep connections in this establishment."

The wine was poured. They toasted their birthdays, then began devouring the Clams Casino. King-cut prime rib with home-made popovers followed. They concluded their feast with the inn's famous carrot cake.

"Marvelous." Matt declared. "Wait until I tell Rudy about these popovers. He's gonna have to put them on our menu."

Back at the Holiday Inn they changed their clothing, put on swimming trunks and sat together sipping Anisette at a small table next to the pool.

"Happy Birthday, Leo! I hope we'll always be together for this celebration."

"And to you, Matt. You've made it the happiest I've ever had."

The trip to Leo's home on the following afternoon created a lot of anxiety within him. He hoped that his family would like Matt, and that he would become part of it, but he soon discovered he had no need to worry. Donna and Alan, Jr. loved Matt's kidding around. Leo's father closely examined Matt's Porsche, and he was ecstatic when Matt gave him the keys to take it for a ride.

In the kitchen, Ellen whispered to Leo, "Your friend, Matt, is a real knock-out!"

Leo was enjoying the best birthday celebration since his mom passed away. They all sat on the back porch as Leo's dad grilled the steaks. Leo poured the drinks. Matt talked about the resort, and how incredibly lucky he was to have Leo as his manager.

"Look, folks, I want to have all of you up to Green Rock for a few days. You can relax up there, and we can all get better acquainted. What do you think, Mr. Weber?"

"Matt, that would be terrific. My friend Ralph and I used to go fishing up there near Swartswood a long time ago. I'd love to get back up there."

"Done! Leo will make all the arrangements." Matt glanced at Leo. "Okay, man?"

"Whatever you say, boss!"

When they were leaving, Leo and Matt walked through the living room. Matt paused in front of the portrait of Leo's mother. Leo stood close to Matt just a few feet away from his favorite chair in the corner. He was thinking about the times when he and his family enjoyed watching their favorite television shows; when he would read John

F. Kennedy's books and the Sunday newspaper; when his family and friends gave him that wonderful farewell party; when he searched the Bible for comfort after his mother died, and found none; and when, on that cold, lonely night just two and a half years before, he had decided to contact Matt for the first time, knowing deep inside what would happen.

"Your mother was a very attractive woman," Matt said.

"I only wish you could have met her, Matt."

"Somehow, I think I really *have*.

They turned toward each other in front of the portrait. It was a precious moment in time that joined all three of them together.

Donna and Alan, Jr. came rushing into the living room from the back yard. Leo's father and Ellen followed.

"It was a real pleasure meeting all of you at last. Thanks, Mr. Weber, for the wonderful birthday dinner."

"Good to meet you at last, Matt." They shook hands.

Leo turned to his dad. "Thanks so much for making it such a great birthday party, dad. I look forward to all of you visiting us up at the resort soon."

As Leo and Matt raced along in the red Porsche over the roads Leo had travelled so often in his old delivery truck, Leo rested his head against the back of his seat and closed his eyes.

The circle had been completed. Matt was now part of Leo's family.

"Matt, there's nothing I can say to you except that I'm so very lucky that you appeared when my life was miserable and empty," Leo said when they returned home. "Happy Birthday!"

"Leo, man! This is the most spectacular birthday I've ever had."

They undressed and fell into bed, embracing.

Twilight was falling on the lake outside. The deep pink clouds hovered over the dark blue sky, reflecting in the water. Matt's naked body was pressed against Leo's bare back, and his right arm embracing Leo's chest; his face nestled against the back of Leo's neck. Leo could feel Matt deep inside him.

"Matt, your love has ended the painful cycle of separation that plagued me for so long. I'll always love you, Matt."

Matt raised his head and looked directly into Leo's eyes, his body nestling closer to Leo. "I love you, Leo. Nothing can separate us now."

Green Rock Resort became one of the most successful and talked-about new resorts in the northeastern United States during its first year of operation. Matt and Leo celebrated their first anniversary together by presiding over the groundbreaking ceremony for the construction of their Arnold Palmer-style golf course behind the hotel, on land they had purchased earlier that year. Leo brought with him a golf club from the set that Irv Davis had given him. As Matt addressed the gathered guests, Leo took a plastic envelope from his coat pocket, carefully removing from it the elm leaf that it preserved from his first visit to the seminary. He crumbled the desiccated leaf in his right hand, scattering its dusty remains upon the fertile ground below.

After the ceremony Matt and Leo led their guests to the new Marble Bar for a champagne brunch. Putting his arm around Matt as they reached the entrance, Leo glanced toward his right and winked at his mother in the framed photograph on the wall, an enlargement of the original Polaroid of Leo and her laughing in their favorite booth at the old Marble Bar. *Is it this,* he wondered, *the mysterious power of boundless love that gives meaning to our ultimately unfathomable existence?*

"Hey, Leo," a voice interrupted, "where're you off to now, man?"

Made in the USA
San Bernardino, CA
05 September 2013